Freedom's Ransom

Prafulla Roy was born in 1934 in a village in Dhaka district, now in Bangladesh. He started writing at the age of nineteen. The Partition of India in 1947 provided one of the major themes in his writing, the other being rural poverty, and most of his writings in this area emanate out of Roy's experience of life in the economically backward state of Bihar. His work has influenced filmmakers, particularly such major artists as Buddhadeb Dasgupta, Tapan Sinha, Biplab Ray Chaudhary and Sandeep Ray. Many of the films based on Roy's stories have been made in languages other than Bengali, and several of his writings have now been translated into other Indian languages.

Dr John W. Hood is an Australian writer who has spent most of his life studying Indian culture, now divides his time between Melbourne and Kolkata. His translations from the Bengali include Niharranjan Ray's classic, *History of the Bengali People*, poems of Buddhadeb Dasgupta (*Love and Other Forms of Death*), and novels and short stories by Prafulla Roy, including the volumes of stories *Set at Odds: Stories of the Partition and Beyond* and *In the Shadow of the Sun*, as well as Buddhadeb Guha's *Fanfare for a Tiger* and *The Bounty of the Goddess.* He has also written extensively on serious Indian cinema. His work includes books on Mrinal Sen, Buddhadeb Dasgupta and Satyajit Ray, as well as *The Essential Mystery: Major Filmmakers of Indian Art Cinema.*

OTHER INDIAINK TITLES:

Anjana Basu	*Black Tongue*
A.N.D. Haksar	*Madhav & Kama: A Love Story from Ancient India*
Boman Desai	*Servant, Master, Mistress*
C.P. Surendran	*An Iron Harvest*
Chitra Banerjee Divakaruni	*The Mirror of Fire and Dreaming*
Chitra Banerjee Divakaruni	*The Conch Bearer*
I. Allan Sealy	*The Everest Hotel*
I. Allan Sealy	*Trotternama*
Indrajit Hazra	*The Garden of Earthly Delights*
Jaspreet Singh	*17 Tomatoes: Tales from Kashmir*
Jawahara Saidullah	*The Burden of Foreknowledge*
Kalpana Swaminathan	*The Page 3 Murders*
Kalpana Swaminathan	*The Gardener's Song*
Kamalini Sengupta	*The Top of the Raintree*
Madhavan Kutty	*The Village Before Time*
Pankaj Mishra	*The Romantics*
Paro Anand	*I'm Not Butter Chicken*
Paro Anand	*Wingless*
Paro Anand	*No Guns at My Son's Funeral*
Ramchandra Gandhi	*Muniya's Light: A Narrative of Truth and Myth*
Ranjit Lal	*The Life &Times of Altu-Faltu*
Ranjit Lal	*The Small Tigers of Shergarh*
Rashme Sehgal	*Hacks and Headlines*
Raza Mir & Ali Husain Mir	*Anthems of Resistance: A Celebration of Progressive Urdu Poetry*
Selina Sen	*A Mirror Greens in Spring*
Shandana Minhas	*Tunnel Vision*
Sharmistha Mohanty	*New Life*
Shree Ghatage	*Brahma's Dream*
Susan Visvanathan	*Something Barely Remembered*
Susan Visvanathan	*The Visiting Moon*
Susan Visvanathan	*The Seine at Noon*
Tanushree Podder	*Boots Belts Berets*
Tom Alter	*The Longest Race*

FORTHCOMING TITLES:

Ranjit Lal	*Simians of the South Block and Yumyum Piglets*
Paro Anand	*Weed*
Sanjay Bahadur	*The Sound of Water*

Freedom's Ransom

Prafulla Roy

Translated from Bengali by

John W. Hood

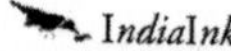 *India*Ink

All characters and events in this book are fictitious and any resemblance to real characters, living or dead is purely coincidental.

This edition published in 2008
*India*Ink
An imprint of
Roli Books Pvt. Ltd.
M-75, G.K. II Market
New Delhi 110 048
Phones: ++91 (011) 2921 2271, 2921 2782
2921 0886, Fax: ++91 (011) 2921 7185
E-mail: roli@vsnl.com; Website: rolibooks.com
Also at
Bangalore, Chennai, Jaipur, Kolkata, Mumbai & Varanasi

Cover design: Supriya Saran
Layout design: Narendra Shahi

ISBN: 978-81-86939-40-6

Typeset by Agaramond Roli Books Pvt. Ltd. and
printed at Perfect Point, Delhi

Translator's Introduction

PRAFULLA ROY WROTE HIS FIRST SHORT STORY IN 1954 AND IN THE HALF century or so since has become one of the most prolific and foremost writers of fiction in Bengal, his work being not only popular but also critically acclaimed. His writing has been very much a response to his own experience of contemporary history and, unsurprisingly, the Second World War, the Bengal Famine and communal tension and conflict have had a profound effect on him. However, it is true to say that the best of his writing emanates from his direct experience of the Partition in 1947, and from his touring on foot over so much of the country, especially throughout the 1950s and '60s. His writing about the lives of the masses, especially the underclass, has a note of authority and a sense of immediacy about it that bear the obvious stamp of direct experience.

India is a vast and diverse country and is, of course, so many different things to different people. The India of tourists, the India of businessmen, the India of NGOs, the India of historians and archaeologists, the India of religious wisdom – to suggest a few – are not one and the same, even though they may overlap to varying degrees. However, underneath all these partial Indias lies the vast substratum of village India in which, as Gandhi said, the heart of India beats. Here too, of course, there is great diversity, but there are also many common basic features, the most obvious being poverty and deprivation, illiteracy, and the exploitation of the weak by the strong. It is this India and its constant struggle to survive that is at the core of Prafulla Roy's interest. Although much of his writing about rural India, including *Freedom's Ransom*, is set in the states of Bihar and Jharkhand, it readily commands a more universal empathy.

Here lies one of the reasons for the importance of a translation of Prafulla Roy's work. It is all too easy to have perceptions of India based on reports of the fabulous wealth of its industrialists, its disputations with its nuclear neighbour Pakistan, the glittering world of Bollywood, or the fortunes or otherwise of the Indian cricket team. With a vision clouded by such perceptions it is also very easy to neglect the truth of Gandhi's dictum concerning the heart of India and so commit to intellectual abandonment some eighty per cent of the second most populous country in the world. The writings of Prafulla Roy about the rural underclass are a cogent reminder of the reality of this vast section of humanity.

A translation of Prafulla Roy, however, is important also for a wider appreciation of Roy's own humanity, a quality that is inextricably coupled with his excellence as a writer. Roy is primarily a realist, recognising reality for what it is and seeing no point in noble dreaming or romanticised wishful thinking. This is not to say, however, that he accepts the *status quo* or, worse, submits to fatalism or defeat. Rather, he presents the human condition as he sees it in actuality, portraying it naked and unadorned, simply for what it is; he does not react on behalf of the reader or try to prompt what the reader's reactions ought to be. His one bias is the natural one of adopting a viewpoint from which to write, and usually Roy chooses to see life through the eyes of the humble people – who are generally oppressed and exploited – rather than through the eyes of the strong and established – who are generally upper-caste, wealthy and powerful and the usual perpetrators of oppression and exploitation.

His humanity, therefore, emanates out of a profound sense of compassion for people who have been traditionally mistreated. It is obvious that distinctions of caste mean nothing to him in determining simple human qualities such as honesty, decency, courage, and extending a hand to the needy. However, it is not only the poor and downtrodden that Roy endows with these virtues, nor does he endeavour to lionise his subjects or make heroes out of the unworthy. Moreover, he is quite candid in exposing the petty cruelties and perfidies that the deprived so often perpetrate against one another. In *Freedom's Ransom* we have the case of the malice of Dharma's mother towards the old widow Shaukhi, in which it is clear that lack of charity is not so much the product of meanness as of the terrible constraints of extreme poverty.

Finally, in asserting the importance of a translation of Prafulla Roy's work, his value as a creator of social documentary cannot be underestimated. His novels and short stories present a graphic depiction of the complexities of life in rural India and are rich in details of day-to-day living, social customs, festivals, work and leisure, and the economic plight of the poor and the various challenges that make life a struggle for them; there are even some valuable perceptions of the workings of the Indian electoral system. Roy also reveals an incisive perception of the relationships between people of various levels of society as well as an insightful understanding of the psychology governing relationships within the same social stratum. As well as their obvious literary value, his writings present a rich and vibrant account of rural India and its people.

The most notable feature of Indian rural society is its social diversity, which is very largely a product of the caste system, a social structure which has traditionally divided society into countless discrete kinship groups defined largely by occupation. More significantly castes are arranged in a hierarchy imbued with a moral dimension: the highest castes, such as the brahmans and kayasthas, are reckoned to be 'better' people, more valuable to society and more deserving of respect and privilege, while the lowest castes are relatively less worthy, their value to society lies only in the physical labour that they perform for their livelihood, and they warrant no respect or privilege at all. Lower than the lowest are the untouchables, for whom contempt, callous mistreatment and unmitigated exploitation are the customary lot.

It is ironic, then, that whenever there is an election in constitutionally democratic India, this vast mass of underclass people should temporarily cease to be contemptible as they become potential votes for aspirants to power; the normally oppressed and despised are now valued, courted, feted, even loved – at least for the duration of the election campaign. It is indeed a great paradox of modern India that a social system determined by caste can survive in a democratic state. It is at election time, however, that the secret ballot allows for the suspension of entrenched inequality for the sake of the passing charade of the voice of universal adult suffrage. Those untouchables not yet old enough to have become cynical must find this a source of amazement, as do the dosads in *Freedom's Ransom*, when the wealthy and the powerful need their votes. But what does democracy promise for them? The spokespersons of democracy are the electoral candidates and they promise nothing less than the rule of heaven on earth, the abolition of every source of unhappiness and the pocketing of the stars from the sky.

Freedom's Ransom is set among a dosad community during an election campaign for the state legislature. The dosads are untouchables, and the occupation of those in the novel is agricultural labouring. These dosads, moreover, are victims of the abusive system of bonded labour, making them virtually slaves in a modern, free and democratic country.

Bonded labour, like child labour, is among the abuses of modern India that the law seems unable to completely eliminate. It is a system of employment in which people work for their mere subsistence; they are paid basic rations, minimal clothing, and almost no wages. One is made liable to this condition through debt, incurred by oneself or inherited, and until the debt has been fully settled the bonded labourer may not leave his master's service. There are terrible consequences should he try, as is evidenced in the novel by the treatment of the determined maverick, Gana. Given the cancerous application of compound interest and the fact that the debtor is usually illiterate, innumerate, utterly unaware of his own rights and gullible to any persuasion concerning his obligations, a simple debt of a hundred rupees becomes one of several thousand and is most unlikely to be paid off in the borrower's lifetime. Hence, the debt is inherited by his heirs, and while they labour for mere rations to service the debt, the interest goes on spiralling.

Marriage is a major cause of debt and a source of prosperity for moneylenders. As Tiumal pleads to Ganeri, marriage is a sacred duty, for a man is enjoined by God himself to marry; it would be a sin, therefore, to remain single. The alleged sacredness of the most basic of all social contracts might well be granted were it not for the excessive expense that marriage in India entails, even among the very, very poor. Such traditional necessities as bride-price and dowry, the bestowal of gifts and the provision of entertainment, all integral elements in the overall social obligation that a marriage entails, serve to make the union of two souls a very costly affair. However, one's inability to afford it cannot obviate the obligation; but then, not having the means is really immaterial: what, after all, are landlords for if not to act as kindly money-lenders at times of such joy and religious obligation?

There are two major narrative strands in the novel, more or less complementing the social structure of the world depicted in it. On one level, set amid the poverty of the dosad community, is the story of Dharma and his quest for freedom from bondage; on the other level, set amid excessive opulence, is the story of the great landowner Raghunath Singh's bid for election to the state legislature. For most of the time these two settings – the thraldom of the untouchables and the luxury of the great landowners – would coexist without actually coming into contact with one another. Prior to the election campaign Raghunath Singh had never set foot inside the dosads' colony, while needless to say most of the dosads had never been seen inside the impenetrable walls surrounding the vast mansion of Raghunath Singh. They would toil from sunrise to sunset cultivating his land, but would never get any closer to him than his soil. However, with the coming of the election they cease to be mere exploited labour and become valued as potential votes. Not only are the untouchables summoned to the lawn at the front of Raghunath Singh's mansion to be served sweets by him in person, but the great master actually visits the dosads' colony on two occasions in order to further distribute his largesse. Nevertheless, the reality of the dosads' condition lies in the time away from elections, when they are of no value to Raghunath Singh other than as a virtually unconditional source of labour, while they in turn are totally dependent on him for their paltry sustenance. On one occasion Dharma is reminded that should he die, it would not mean anything, while the loss of one of the great master's bullocks would be reckoned at five hundred or even a thousand rupees. There is no cynicism in the suggestion that the munificence of a political candidate is but temporary and offered only in his own interests.

These two fundamental narrative strands reveal the two extremes of rural society: the very rich and powerful on the one hand, and the utterly destitute and impotent on the other. The luxurious mansions of Raghunath and Mishirlal are described in detail, along with the opulent lifestyles of wealthy landowners such as they. To the palatial homes of the rich there is a stark and often depressing contrast in the presentation of the dingy shanties of the untouchables and the constant struggle for survival that illiterate, undernourished and scantily-clad people must endure. The novel is set at the end of the third quarter of the twentieth century when, at least according to law, the traditional zamindari system had been abolished and the extent of landholdings had been limited, yet the power that such men hold over thousands of human souls, evident throughout the novel, is reminiscent of serfdom in Tsarist Russia. In fact, so many established landlord families found easy ways of getting around the law, continuing to hold vast tracts of land in their own names and in those of aliases, so securing their wealth and power.

There is, of course, no indication of simmering revolution amongst these appallingly deprived people. Their abjectness is age-old and exists in direct relation to the power held over them by the opulent few. To walk for miles each day in order to dig in the dried-up river bed for the day's necessary water is only one of the constant hardships that they stoically endure. There are occasional alleviations, as seen, for example, in Raghunath Singh's ordering of the cleaning of an old well and the digging of a new one, as well as in less lasting joys such as the distribution of sweets or the declaration of three days' holiday. However, this kind of generosity is compromised by its electoral motivation and eclipsed by the naked political expediency of setting fire to several villages, endangering life and limb and destroying whatever humble things the poorest of poor people might possess, in order that an excessively wealthy man in quest of political power might demonstrate his munificence in distributing charity to those whom he himself has made victims, so furthering his claim for their votes.

The untouchable poor in *Freedom's Ransom* have no control at all over their own lives. They live in extreme poverty and servility, they may be beaten at the whim of the master, and for some petty misdemeanour they may be deprived of rations by one of his toadying factotums. They have no choice but to endure. Indeed, the abasement of these dosads is almost total. Centuries of contempt poured upon them by their so-called betters has made them acquiescent in their servility, while their illiteracy and innumeracy and their complete lack of education have kept their imagination stunted, their vision limited and their minds unquestioning and uncritical. Yet they are also cowed by fear. When the brawl with the herdsmen breaks out in the jungle, their natural inclination is to shrink back in terror, the effect, it is suggested, of an innate timidity bred in them over the ages. But the sources of fear are also more immediate. There is always the threat of their rations being cut for some petty misdemeanour or other, and there is also the threat of worse chastisement as illustrated so sickeningly in the brutal punishment of Gana. The great master, through his henchmen, is also omniscient, due largely to a simple network of spies, at the base of which is Naorangi, the untouchable mistress of Raghunath Singh's brahman manager, Himgirinandan. (Roy does not forego the opportunity to expose the absurd hypocrisy in orthodox notions of pollution by touch, making quite clear that when it comes to the urging of the loins, the upper castes are no less animal than the lower ones, and social discretion is quite blithely put aside for the satisfaction of their carnal needs.) Anything that may be done, said, or even mooted in the dosad colony will be sure to reach Himgirinandan by way of Naorangi, his faithful slut whom the dosads loathe, and fear even more.

In focussing on the society of the lower orders, especially the underclass, Roy does not paint a picture of unalleviated misery and deprivation. He is careful to show that there is a life, albeit one of some hardship, in which a man may be his own master, in which people may live lives with choice and autonomy. The dairy village, for example, is a constant source of inspiration and hope for Dharma and something to aspire to in struggling to pay off his debt and attain his freedom from bondage. There are also those dosads in his own neighbourhood, albeit untouchable and poor, who are not bonded and do have some power over their own lives. On a similar level of destitution are the tribal people who are employed each year as seasonal labour. Indications are given of the hardships of their lives and the temptations to submit to labour recruiters to take them to faraway places reportedly flowing with milk and honey; horribly poor as these people may be, they too are free, and Dharma spares more than a passing thought of envy for them. Especially he admires Gana, who dared to thumb his nose at feudal authority and break free and, despite brutal punishment, broke free again. Naturally, corporal punishment is a caution to Dharma, and so too is the notion of distance. This man who cannot write his name or count much beyond thirty has an extraordinarily narrow concept of the world, and distance beyond the near and known is also a deterrent to the notion of running away like Gana or sneaking off with the tribals and their recruiters. And yet he remains always determined, even through his final disappointment, to break free from thraldom and its abject poverty and utter humiliation.

Perhaps the greatest scourge of the untouchables is their own ignorance. Unlettered, innumerate and cowed by generations of submissiveness, they are hardly even aware of the injustice of their plight. Even as far as their so-called contracts are concerned, their position is precarious. In many if not most cases the signing of a loan contract would have amounted to nothing more than the impression of a thumbprint on a blank sheet of paper; whatever might be written above the 'signature' later could not be read by an illiterate dosad, and his innumeracy would make it impossible for him to have any meaningful idea of the balance of his loan repayments. Fighting a gargantuan uphill battle is the schoolmaster known affectionately to all as Master-ji, another brahman but one with a sufficiently modern outlook to have no prejudices regarding caste and touch. He is an idealistic and selfless teacher who tries so desperately to cultivate a little knowledge in the minds of the dosads and their children, but to over-worked and underfed parents children are also an indispensable source of labour at most times of the year and have no time for such a luxury as learning. It is sadly ironic that the free offer of education cannot be accepted.

Much of the credibility of the narrative evolves readily from the meticulously depicted atmosphere, in this case one that is dominated by the intense and relentless heat of the last month of the Indian summer. The dried-up river bed, the hard, cracked earth, the dry and dusty wind and the constant raising of red dust off the road are frequent reminders of the essential backdrop to the back-breaking labour that the dosads are obliged to perform as well as to the migratory movements of landless tribals desperate to find work and food at any cost. In all, Roy does not indulge in words, but writes with the effect of a first-rate film director, selecting and arranging his material with the utmost care and precision and presenting it with exceptional economy. Nothing is overdone; nothing is allowed to diffuse the narrative. Characters and their relationships with one another are developed by what the characters are given to do and to say, rather than what the author might say about them, while the concentration of time and place enhances the intensity of the treatment.

On a number of occasions Roy gives particular focus to the backward, labour-intensive economy in which these bonded labourers toil and scrape out an existence, and he does this by frequent reference to the mechanised cultivation of Mishirlal's land, where the tractor has replaced the archaic system of human labour. Raghunath Singh, a conservative in every way, is also an economic traditionalist and is happy to persist with bonded labour – cheaper as it is than machines. The depiction of labour is a significant feature of the novel, as it is yet another persuasive condemnation of persistent, pre-modern backwardness and the perpetuation of feudalism.

Prafulla Roy is a humanist, and despite his claims to be completely detached from political interest, *Freedom's Ransom* is, indeed, a political novel in that it is a polity so open to corruption that ultimately is shown to be responsible for the injustice and cruelty that pervade its pages. This inhumanity is not attributable here to personal perversity but rather is seen to be institutionalised, and its entrenchment in the Indian political reality would seem almost inviolable given that the most secure seats of corruption are at the head of the body politic. The nexus of wealth, power and corruption is a tightly tied one and is effectively self-perpetuating – those who have the power to legislate against all forms of injustice and inequity are also very often those who stand to profit from such abuses. A rich and powerful man like Raghunath Singh will think nothing of setting people's humble homes ablaze if it is likely to prosper his campaign strategy, despite the flagrant criminality of the act. No untouchable would ever have the nerve to bring charges against him, and even if anyone did, what police officer would file those charges? The appalling fact is that many, many Raghunath Singhs get themselves elected to government – men who, like the great master, are guilty of assault, arson, rape, and the lesser moral blemishes of perfidy, bullying, and mendacity. As long as democracy can be exploited to bring about election victories for wealthy thugs – and who, after all, can presume to question the 'will' of the people? – the system itself is found to be working against its own ideals and highest values. There are the acts and cries of protest, but these are as drops in the ocean. The nexus of corruption is too strong to allow for untouchables' cries for justice to be heard. At the core the system would seem to be rotten, and making this clear is the basic purpose, the political dimension, of *Freedom's Ransom.*

Given its humanity, its political and social significance and the profound interest of its story, *Freedom's Ransom* stands as one of the great novels of contemporary Indian literature.

1

As on any other afternoon in the month of Jyaistha the entire sky was now tinged with the colour of molten brass. The sun had started to decline in the west and evening would fall in about an hour and a half, but the sun's rays were still as sharp as a knife and their heat was spread about by the hot wind that gusted all over the place like the darting here and there of a mad horse.

Lying beneath the boundless sky was the farming land of Chhotanagpur and a place called Garudiya. Here, wherever one looked, as far as one could see, were countless grain fields of various sizes and shapes – rectangular, triangular, hexagonal – which, like so many kinds of geometrical figures, had been drawn on the face of the earth for hundreds of years.

On one side of the fields was a highway, along which the buses ran in one direction to Ranchi and in the other to Patna. In the rains of the previous year this road had been broken up by the flooding of the southern Koel river. Contractors had built up the road with earth but it still had not been sealed with pitch, and as a result of the constant come and go of buses, trucks, cycle rickshaws and bullock carts the great road was always thick with dust obscuring the view. On the other side of the highway the bed of the narrow Koel, dried up in the heat of Jyaistha, resembled desert sands. A long way off, where the sky bends towards the earth, was the small Chhotanagpur Range, on either side of which unshapely *sisam* trees, an occasional tall palmyra tree and the jungles of bush and undergrowth stood motionless, being scorched by the sun.

In Garudiya taluk, between the highway and the Chhotanagpur Range, there was but one proprietor of all the land, the Rajput kshatriya, Raghunath Singh. On the other side of the highway, beyond the river Koel, all the agricultural land belonged to Mishirlal of the Bijuri taluk.

All the land of the villages of Garudiya was now under the plough. The earth had become cracked while burning in the sun throughout the whole of the months of Chaitra and Vaishakh, and in two and a half months not a drop of rain had fallen. Indeed, rain was still a remote idea here, as eight or ten taluks, accommodating some three or four hundred thousand villagers, had not yet seen even a faint scrap of cloud. And so the earth had turned to hard clods.

Dharma was driving a bullock-drawn plough through one of Raghunath Singh's hexagonal fields. He was not working alone, the land around him was being ploughed by a number of others like Dhaotal, Ramnagin, Dhorailal and Budheri. Some strong and able-bodied women had come out into the fields with them and were plucking *koda* weeds from the earth that had been overturned by the plough or gathering up the dried roots of the previous year's harvest and putting them to one side.

In this taluk of the Rajput Raghunath Singh, Dharma was a bonded agricultural labourer. He was not the only one, for those who tilled the soil to his right and left, in front of him and behind, were all bonded labourers too.

Dharma was about twenty-three. His body was the colour of burnt copper. He had a square jaw, broad muscular shoulders, and an immense chest that was as hard as a rock. His arms hung down to his knees, he had thick flat fingers, and the palms of his hands were huge. His long and clustered hair hung down to his shoulders and his face bore wisps of a sparse beard and moustache. He wore a sleeveless red singlet and striped short pants – clothes that were clammy with sweat and dirt. A silver-plated tiger claw hung from a black cord around his neck.

Dharma's strong left hand held the blade of the plough as far as possible under the soil while he drove the pair of bullocks with smacks to the back with a stick, all the time crying, 'U-r-r-r, u-r-r-r, u-r-r-r - - ' In the intensity of the Jyaistha heat the eyes of the bullocks bulged, yet the beasts went on pulling the plough for the life of them. Sometimes sparks would fly up from the rocky earth as it was struck by the plough. There was no respite for man or beast.

Raghunath Singh had gone to Patna some seven days back. In the markets and villages of the taluk people were saying that he was going to be a Member of the Legislative Assembly, an MLA – or 'emlay', as they pronounced it – and in connection with that he had some urgent business in Patna.

Dharma and the others had heard that he would come back after finalising the matter of his becoming a member of the Assembly, and some tribal workers – Oraons, Santals – and outcaste labourers from Palamau would be brought in to provide labour for the tilling. They were piecework farm-labourers and were brought every year for the cultivation season to work right through it. Once their tilling was finished, they would be dismissed, to come again at harvest time to stock Raghunath Singh's granaries with paddy, wheat, millet, rabi and various kinds of pulses. However, as long as Raghunath Singh was away in Patna and the tribals and other landless labourers were yet to arrive, Dharma and the others and their plough-drawing beasts would have no rest, for Raghunath Singh had given orders that during this time at least half the cultivation had to be completed as the seed had to be planted as soon as the rain started to fall in the following month of Asharh.

Dharma looked towards the other side of the Koel as he ploughed, his eyes squinting in the harsh sunlight, the perspiration pouring from all over his body and a few drops of sweat hanging over his eyes. He wiped his eyes with the back of his hand as he went on looking. Mishirlal's taluk too was being tilled, but not by a bullock-drawn plough but a 'mishin' or 'machine' plough. Under the shimmering sky the sound of the tractor's engine was borne over the vast fields by the fiery dry wind.

On Raghunath Singh's land cultivation still was carried out in much the same way as it had been since time immemorial, by beast-drawn plough. Time had stood still here for a thousand years, yet the new age had come to Mishirlal's land on the other side of the Koel. There the old-fashioned plough made by a blacksmith and drawn by a bullock was no longer used, and for some years now the cultivation had been done by 'mishin'. Dharma was thinking, if only Raghunath Singh would get a 'mishin'-plough like Mishirlal-ji's! But it did not seem as though he ever would. Work on his land remained extremely hard for all creatures – men and beasts.

From the neighbouring field the robust, middle-aged Ganeri was crying out as usual, 'No rain! Not even a cloud! The sunshine's like fire and the earth's baked rock-hard. It's unbearable!'

From another field Dhaotal too was calling out, 'How can we ever survive this month of unending heat – ' while another was saying, 'If this kind of fire keeps burning from the sky, no one will survive, no one at all. We'll all die.' And from all around everyone started calling out, 'Yes! Now God is our only hope. Oh, Lord Ram, be gracious – '

The men said these kinds of things everyday as they drove their ploughs through the scorched earth under the burning summer sky. They were now anxiously awaiting the coming of the month of *Asharh*, when water-laden black clouds would cover the sky and the hot earth and the fiery winds would be soothed and cooled.

Dharma was listening to the snatches of talk of the men around him, but he said nothing. Indeed, he never said anything. His father, his grandfather, his grandfather's father – three or four generations –

had cultivated Raghunath Singh's land every year. And it was not only them, but generations of such men as those around him – Budheri, Ganeri, Dhaotal – had all been ploughing Raghunath Singh's land. Whether or not the sun burned in the sky like fire, they had to till that land. They had no choice but to split it and break it and turn it over and about, year after year, for the sake of Raghunath Singh's harvest. There was no point in futile resentment. Their hardship had accrued to them over a long time.

Dharma was not alone in his field. With him was Kushi, a girl from his neighbourhood. For some years when Dharma worked in the fields Kushi would run along behind his plough, not only in the tilling season but also during sowing, weeding, harvesting and the bringing of the harvest into Raghunath Singh's granaries – in every task the whole year through Kushi was like Dharma's shadow. Now in the month of Jyaistha she would clear away the withered roots and weeds from the clods raised by the blade of Dharma's plough.

Kushi was about nineteen, with a body the colour of polished brass. She had a round mouth with fleshy lips, sparkling white teeth, simple and innocent eyes, and a mass of thick and bushy, tangled hair. Her taut, strong body was like a healthy sapling. She was wearing a short, coloured sari of coarse cloth, which clung to her body with sweat, and a short yellow blouse. She wore a brass bangle on her wrist and a silver nose-ring with an imitation stone.

No matter how long the hot day seemed, it was not endless. Although the sun moved slowly, it would eventually sink in the western sky, which by now was turning as red as fresh blood, and much of the heat had now gone out of it. Overhead a flock of wild parrots called as they drifted on the wind towards the dry bed of the Koel, and for a long time their squawks could be heard in the distance.

Just before sunset, Dharma and the others would leave the fields with their ploughs. As they were doing so today, they suddenly heard the sharp voice of Kushi, 'Hey, look, look!' She pointed towards the highway as she spoke.

Dharma looked, shielding his eyes with his hand from the setting sun. Those who had been tilling the soil around him also heard Kushi. Shielding their eyes they too looked straight at where she was pointing.

There was no longer a procession of horse-drawn carts on the road; only a few cycle rickshaws and bullock carts slowly ambled along. Nevertheless, a cloud of red dust hung overhead. It was not an unusual sight, but one that often met the eye. So what was there to see in it? Impatient, Dharma expressed his annoyance, 'What is there to see in cycle rickshaws and bullock carts?'

Coming towards him Kushi said, 'No, no, look there!'

Two black spots could be seen far off in the distance on the highway running through the vast fields, hurrying in their direction. Kushi's bright nineteen-year-old eyes were as keen as those of a hawk. Before anyone could ask, Kushi said, 'I think it's the master's car. It's definitely Munshi-ji in front – '

Kushi was right. As they watched, the two black spots came closer and there appeared an old fashioned motor car with big wheels and the hood open, as well as a worthless, rickety old bicycle. Clearly visible now in the back seat of the car was the large form and smiling face of the middle-aged master, Raghunath Singh, a garland of jasmine and roses around his neck. Crammed in on either side of him as well as in the front seat were a few of his close friends.

Riding the bicycle a few yards in front of the car was Raghunath's personal assistant and munshi, Ajibchand. With one hand he grasped the handlebar and with the other he held a megaphone to his mouth and called out continually, but from such a distance it could not be discerned what he was saying.

The munshi was about sixty. He looked like a piece of chewed-up, juiceless sugar-cane. His hands and feet were knobbly, and he had a sharp, thin mouth, a clipped moustache and deep sunken eyes. A pair of round, nickel-framed bifocal spectacles sat on his long, hooked nose. He wore a shirt tucked into his dhoti, a grey coat and a round cotton cap. A pocket-watch was pinned inside his shirt pocket. He looked like a cunning jackal. Munshi Ajibchand was known by the people of Garudiya and eight or ten neighbouring taluks as Raghunath Singh's bootlicking lap-dog whose only work was to sit constantly at his master's feet, whimper and wag his tail, and to harass for good reason or none everyone in the world. Fear of him kept all the people in Garudiya on their toes.

Dharma and the others had not known that the master would return from Patna today. However, it was certain that the munshi would have known. When the labourers were tilling the land, none of them had any idea that the munshi had slipped away to fetch the master from the Garudiya railway station, which was beside the highway about two and a half miles to the west.

The car and the bicycle had now come close and the munshi's words could be heard clearly. The veins in his throat protruded like coir ropes as he cried out, 'Get out of the way – the great master is here, maalik is here! Get out of the way! Move aside!'

In a flurry of panic the rickshaws and bullock and buffalo carts all made way and cleared the road. The rickshaw wallahs and the oxen cart drivers and all who were walking along the highway bowed deferentially to Raghunath Singh, saying, '*Namaste*, sir' or '*Namaste*, great Master.'

The munshi's voice gradually became louder. 'Move aside now! Get out of the way! Our great master, the MLA, is here. Move aside, rickshaw wallah! Get out of the way, bullock driver! Move, you pedestrians!' And as he shouted, his tiny eyes threatened to bulge right out of their sockets.

Dharma and the others were standing under the eternal sky in the middle of the half-ploughed field watching the scene, looking like part of some prehistoric picture. A few moments later the munshi's bicycle and the maalik's car disappeared around a bend to the east, kicking up a storm of dust. The labourers remained silent for quite a while after that, until Budheri suddenly spoke up from the neighbouring field, 'What, has the great master become an emlay, then?'

Everyone else in the surrounding fields started talking. 'Has he? Really?'

'Oh, no, no – ' the middle-aged Ganeri called out. 'The master is not an emlay yet.'

Everyone looked at Ganeri. 'How do you know, Uncle?'

Ganeri had had considerable experience of life and the world, having lived in it for fifty or sixty years. His old eyes had seen so much over such a long time, and his old ears had heard so much, too. Anything he had to say was regarded with great respect by the bonded labourers of this region.

Ganeri said, 'It's not so easy to become an emlay. Doesn't there have to be an election first? There was an election five years ago, wasn't there? Didn't you all put a stamp on the voting paper and drop it in the box?'

They all remembered.

Budheri asked, 'Then why was Munshi-ji calling the great master an emlay?'

Ganeri replied, 'That bugger's just a dog, running around day and night with his tongue hanging out to lick the master's boots. The bastard calls him an emlay just to make him happy. May his face be spat on three times – ' and each time he spat on the ground, his face contorted with hatred.

Although everyone else was talking, Dharma kept quiet. He understood what they were all saying. One could not be an 'emlay' without being elected. Dharma had known this since his childhood.

The last election here was five years ago when he was still young, so he had not put a stamp on a printed paper and put it in the box. Now, of course, he was of voting age. But those who were much older and had survived a long time in the world should know that one could not become an 'emlay' without an election. Although they had put their stamps on the printed papers time and again, they could also forget the procedures for becoming an 'emlay'. Yet at this moment he was not really concerned about votes, 'emlays', their master or anything of the kind. It was something else that was making him restless.

On the other side of the highway, a little way along the Koel, there was a jungle of *sabui* grass where, on summer afternoons, flocks of *bageri* birds would come. These days Dharma and Kushi set ten or twelve bird-traps there every day. The contractors working on the bridge or the highway were exceptionally fond of *bageri* flesh. They had a lot of cash in hand and they paid good money – three rupees fifty paise for three dozen.

Dharma was much in need of money, and all the time his mind had been preoccupied with thinking about how many birds had been caught in the bamboo traps he had set yesterday evening. Suddenly he goaded the others, saying, 'The sun's gone down. It's time to go back. Why hang around here in the fields?'

Everyone else was becoming impatient, saying, 'Yes, yes. It's time to go back – '

Every morning Dharma and the others came to the fields from Raghunath Singh's farm compound with ploughs and bullocks, and just before sunset they would go to their own homes after returning the animals and the implements. So a little later, a procession of ploughs and bullocks could be seen moving towards the main road. When they came up onto the highway, Dharma told Kushi, 'You go to the traps. I'll come after putting the bullock and the plough back in the compound.'

'Come quickly,' said Kushi.

'All right.'

'Don't stay there long.'

'No.'

Kushi waited no longer. She went down from the highway and started to run along the bed of the Koel. As far as could be seen in the faint light of the declining day there was no one apart from that copper-coloured girl on the golden sands of the dried up river bed, running, running and running.

Behind her could be seen the Bijuri taluk's tractors returning home, their work too having finished. On this side the tired beasts and their accompanying men were kicking up dust as they trudged at the end of the long day along the highway towards Raghunath Singh's farm compound.

2

A LITTLE WAY ALONG FROM WHERE THE HIGHWAY TOOK A BEND TO the right there was a dirt road with so much dust that one's ankles could sink in it. This road led off to the left from the highway to Raghunath Singh's farm compound. Standing there was a row of twenty-five or thirty tall, broad buildings, with ten-inch brick walls and corrugated tin roofs, which throughout the year were full of various kinds of grain and seed. Once the previous year's paddy, wheat, maize, millet, sesame seed, linseed, mustard seed and various kinds of pulses had been taken away to be sold, the granaries would be filled with the new season's harvest.

The area of five or six acres in front of the buildings was kept very clean, for there the grain was dried, winnowed and sorted before being stored in the granaries. On one side of this spick and span area were many tin-roofed sheds in which Raghunath Singh's hundred or so plough-pulling bullocks and cart-drawing buffalo were kept. Some twenty or twenty-five men were needed to look after so many beasts, doing all sorts of work such as feeding the animals, washing them and, if necessary, fetching the vet from the town ten miles away to give them medicine or an injection. For all this they got from Raghunath Singh their food ration and a few stitches of clothing to last them throughout the year, nothing else. Like Dharma and the others, they had been subjected through generations to bonded labour.

The ploughs and carts were kept in tall sheds near the cattle, and near the granaries there were the many small mud huts for the piecework labourers who would work on the land for about three months each year, but as yet they had not arrived and the huts were still empty.

As Dharma and the others returned to the granaries they saw, as on every other day, Himgirinandan Jha sitting on a thick cushion on the veranda of the very first building. He was responsible for the whole of Raghunath Singh's farm compound and this veranda was his office, although to enhance his status he called it, in English, 'the control room'. He would sit here from six in the morning until night, supervising the peasants' work, distributing ploughs and bullocks at cultivating time, measuring out their rations each evening, apportioning their share of seed at sowing time, taking charge of the harvest and directing which granary each kind of grain was to be stored in – indeed, everything came under the watchful eye of Himgirinandan. Like all other men he had but one pair of eyes, but in effect he had about a thousand eyes, all but two of them unseen, and there was no way any workman could throw dust in those eyes and hoodwink him.

At that moment Himgiri was sitting on his cushion behind a wooden desk, slowly, continually tapping his foot, something which had been a long-time habit of his. The man was in his early fifties and quite corpulent. He had a broad nose, and although the eyes under his thick brows might seem to be drowsy, no one in the world had eyes as keen and penetrating. His hair was greying and was cut close to his scalp, at the back of which was a long tuft with a flower attached. He wore a thick, borderless dhoti and kurta. On his forehead was inscribed in sandal-paste in Devnagari letters, 'Hail, Ram! Hail Krishna!' He was a Maithili brahman, and his skin was very delicate and smooth. The men of Garudiya taluk would say, 'Butter oozes from his body.' They would also say, 'This Jha fellow's a wolf. The great master has so many tame animals, as well as a wolf and a jackal. The wolf is Himgirinandan Jha, the jackal is the munshi, Ajibchand.'

As he went on tapping his foot, Himgiri watched Dharma and the rest. He said, 'The sun's not fully set yet and you've finished your work! You bastards are a pack of cheats.' The man's voice pierced the ears, for it was as sharp as it was high-pitched. It was amazing that such a voice should come out of a fat, heavy, oily body like his.

No one said anything. Year in and year out they had been called cheats after tilling the soil from morning to evening under the burning sky of the month of Jyaistha, but no one was brave enough to raise an eyebrow in protest at Himgirinandan.

'If you bring the ploughs and bullocks back tomorrow before the sunset, as you have done today,' he continued, 'your rations will be cut. D'you hear me?'

They all inclined their heads to indicate that they had.

'All right, the ploughs and bullocks you worked with today - ' As he spoke he took a bulbous bottle of milk from under the desk and held it to his mouth; all that could be heard then was the glug-glug-glug of his drinking.

Dharma and the others all knew that under the desk were arrayed some ten or twelve bottles of milk, pure buffalo's milk. Every now and then from morning to night, just like a cat, Himgiri would drink some of it. Pouring bottles of fatty milk down his throat must have been what made his skin so soft and shiny.

Himgiri finished the bottle, took out a paan from a brass box and stuffed it in his mouth. He took paan as often as he drank milk. While Himgiri was chewing it, Dharma and the others put the bullocks and buffalo in the shed opposite and placed their ploughs in the shed beside it. The other men were waiting inside the sheds to take the cattle and the implements. If there was the slightest doubt that anything was amiss, they would call to let Himgiri know.

Dharma did not hang about. Kushi would be waiting in the *sabui* grass jungle, so he went straight to the sheds with his pair of bullocks and his plough. In the shed in front of him the middle-aged, exceptionally lanky Ramdhaniya, looking like a lightning-struck palmyra tree, was watching with his tiny round eyes. The twisted, protruding veins of his hands and feet were like cords. Dharma had taken his plough and bullocks from him in the morning. As Dharma approached him, he said, 'Hey, bring your bullocks and - '

Ramdhaniya took the plough and stood it on one side of the shed. Then he took a careful look at the pair of bullocks. Having examined one of the beasts from head to foot, he called a young fellow to give it its nightly fodder. Then, inspecting the other one, he suddenly noticed a long mark on its nose. Immediately he asked in his cracked and phlegmy voice, 'How did this happen to the bullock's nose, then?'

Dharma did not know how the bullock got a scratch on its nose. Very likely when pulling the plough it was cut by some thorn bush or was struck by a tough root. However, in the morning he had been given an unharmed beast in the best of health, and in the evening Ramdhaniya would not so easily take back one that had been hurt. Like the rest of them, he was an untouchable bonded labourer who was given food in place of wages, but in the service of Raghunath Singh over generations his nature had become different from theirs. He would guard all Raghunath Singh's estate, animate and inanimate, with his life. That was his nature. The age-old characteristic of servility ran through his blood.

So right now Ramdhaniya was going to start shouting about the scratch on the bullock's nose and then Himgirinandan would come to see what all the fuss was about. Thinking of the likely effects of that, Dharma started to sweat profusely. In a trembling, fearful voice he said, 'I had no idea, Ramdhaniya, brother –'

However, due to the unbounded mercy of Lord Ram the man did

not start shouting this time. He merely said, 'You must be much more careful, Dharma! Just remember that this animal is a lot more valuable than you are. If you died, it wouldn't mean a thing. But if this bullock died, then the maalik would lose five hundred, or even a thousand rupees.'

Dharma nodded – he would remember. Then mentally he touched his head ten times to the feet of Lord Ram for rescuing him from danger and waited no longer in getting away from Ramdhaniya. One of the young fellows took the bullock and led him away to his nightly gruel of chopped hay mixed with oil-cake and molasses.

After this all the other bullocks and ploughs were taken in, and just as Dharma and the others were all about to leave Himgiri called them. 'Listen - ' As he came towards them, his sleepy eyes had completely changed; now ablaze they turned from Ganeri, Budheri and Dharma to the women. After looking at them for a few moments, he frowned and said, 'I can see one of you is missing. Where is she?'

'Who?' asked Ganeri.

'Kushi.'

Before Ganeri could respond, Dharma said, 'Kushi's not here. She left straight from the fields.'

In his sharp, high-pitched voice Himgiri cried out, 'Rubbish! The girl didn't go to work. I didn't send a watchman today and the work was unsatisfactory. How do you expect rations without a full day's work?'

On other days, from morning to sunset, Himgiri would send a man some ten times to the fields. Sometimes even he would go himself. This was to see whether or not the work was being done properly; sometimes he wanted to check if anyone was being negligent. Today, however, Himgiri had not bothered to send anyone.

Dharma said, 'No, sir. She was with me. She worked the whole day.'

'You're lying. It's all rubbish. They say that you're rather sweet on that girl, so you're just trying to make excuses for her. I'm cutting her a day's rations.'

'No, my lord, don't do that. Ask anybody if she came or not – hey, Uncle Ganeri, Uncle Budheri, Dhoraiya, Etwari, Shanichari, tell him all of you, tell him please - ' Dharma turned to each one of them, pleading. Kushi had worked the whole day under the scorching sun, and now, on a false pretext, this Maithili brahman wanted to deprive her of her rations. Dharma was not going to allow that.

Ganeri and the others spoke up, saying things like, 'Yes, my lord, Kushi spent the whole day in the fields. She was there today, in god's name she was.'

'All right,' said Himgiri, 'I'll forget about today. But just one thing – from tomorrow everyone must come here first thing in the morning, and you all must come here again after the day's work is finished. D'you hear me?' In other words Himgiri wanted to check that everyone was actually present. They all inclined their heads in agreement.

There was a brief pause. As he looked at them all, Himgiri's glance fell on Shanichari. He went on chewing his paan noisily as though chewing his cud. Looking at Shanichari, who was five or six months pregnant, he started to frown. In her modesty Shanichari could not look up, but cowered, facing the ground with her shoulders hunched.

After looking at Shanichari for quite some time Himgiri raised his voice slightly and said, 'You filthy bitch! Didn't you have a kid just a couple of years back?'

Shanichari did not answer. She remained standing with downcast eyes, her entire body suffused with all the diffidence in the world.

Suddenly Himgiri burst out tauntingly, 'Are you so modest that you can't say anything? Just say yes or no – come on, speak up!'

Terrified, Shanichari looked up for a moment then lowered her eyes again. 'Yes, lord,' she said.

'Now this is a real disgrace. Can't you sleep without pressing your tits against the chest of your man, then?'

Shanichari said nothing.

Himgiri delivered an obscene tirade, then said, 'You'll go on giving birth every year and using your kid as an excuse to get out of two months' work. Well that's not going to happen. No work, no rations. D'you hear me?'

'D'you hear me' was a characteristic expression of Himgiri. Shanichari and the others would just nod or shrug their shoulders to indicate that they had heard.

A few young married women – Sombari, Gangni, Kundri – were standing close together. Now Himgiri narrowed his eyes and looked at them, and said in his high-pitched voice, 'And what are you young chooks up to?'

No one answered.

Himgiri continued, 'Just remember this. You shouldn't spend so much time enjoying your men. If every year you hatch eggs like chooks and get off work, I'll give every one of you a kick up the arse. D'you hear me?' And so saying he took out his bottle of milk once again, took a few noisy gulps, and wiped his mouth. Then, still chewing his paan, he went on, 'Now get this into your heads. You can hatch one egg in ten years, and after two kids it's full stop. That's a gormin order. D'you hear me?' He mixed his speech with the occasional mispronounced English word, like 'government'.

They all silently nodded their heads.

Himgiri spat out some paan juice through his teeth and went on, 'Like a pack of bitches on heat! Given the slightest chance you'll let your bellies swell up!'

A girl called Kundri, with tangled, rough, reddish hair, a bosom like a pair of hillocks, a slender waist, and thighs like the trunks of deodar trees, was very spirited and quite a daredevil. She had little fear of anyone, including brahmans and other high-caste people, and munshis. She would say nothing to them directly, but what she said behind her hand made the others tremble with fear. Indeed, she had a terribly loose tongue and her speech was quite unrestrained. She put her mouth to Sombari's ear and whispered, 'What's the old wolf saying! When a lively and well-endowed girl sleeps with a man who whispers sweet words in her ear as he presses his chest against her, will she give a thought for this old brahman?'

Sombari recoiled slightly and quickly looked all around. Then she said, 'That's shameful!'

Kundri went on, 'Do you feel shame when a man goes on kneading your flesh like dough? I'm shameful? Oh, ha, ha, ha!'

'Be quiet. Someone will hear – '

'Let them. Hatch one egg in ten years! More often and the brahman'll give you a kick up the arse. Oh, ha, ha, ha! A kick up the arse from that old wolf! Let me spit three times in his face - ' And she spat three times at the ground.

Sombari was frightened. In a panic she said, 'Be quiet, Kundri, be quiet.'

Himgiri's seemingly drowsy eyes were indeed the eyes of a vulture and his ears the ears of a dog. He looked at Kundri and Sombari, frowned, and demanded, 'What are you two talking about? What's going on?'

Kundri had no control over her tongue, and if she had said anything, the consequences might have been bad. Therefore, Sombari was startled into quickly saying, 'Nothing, lord, nothing.'

Himgiri kept looking at her for some moments through his keen, suspicious eyes. However, he asked no more questions, but simply said, 'That Kundri is a very mischievous woman.'

Evening had fallen, the sun having sunk a little while back, and the opaque twilight now hung over everything. By now Dharma had become quite anxious and said, 'Lord brahman, can you let us go home now?' Kushi would have been waiting for him a long time now in the jungle, and he was becoming quite anxious on her account.

Moreover, today was not their ration day. The food they got as payment for working on Raghunath Singh's fields was not paid daily but every second day. Yesterday they had been given two days' rations. After another full day's work in the fields tomorrow they would again get food. Their rations were measured out in the tall, locked shed on the other side of the wide shed in which the ploughs were kept.

As nothing more remained to be said, Himgiri ordered them, 'Go, then.' But just as they all turned and started to move away, he remembered something and called out anxiously, 'Oh, listen, listen!'

They all turned.

'Before going home you have to report to the maalik's house.'

Dharma and the others had no direct connection with the great master, Raghunath Singh, nor would they ever have had the courage to venture so high; all their business was carried out with Himgirinandan. They could not imagine why they suddenly had to go to his house, nor could they remember Raghunath Singh's ever having called them to his own home. And not only them, but they had never heard of Raghunath Singh's father or grandfather calling their fathers or grandfathers to the house. They were both afraid and curious.

Himgiri explained that the great master was going to become an 'emlay', and so he wanted to say a few things to his own people. Having returned from Patna he had sent word to Himgiri that he should send to his house all those who worked his land year after year as soon as they returned from the fields. Himgiri further made known that the great master himself wanted to speak with the bonded labourers, and for them this was the good fortune of fourteen generations. How exceedingly lucky they were! Hurrying them along, he said, 'Go on, then, off you go!'

Dharma's restiveness increased. Going to the great master's house would mean that more time would be wasted. And there was no way of not going, for he did not have on his shoulders such a strong head that he could refuse. Inevitably he nodded and went with all the others to the mansion of Raghunath Singh.

3

IT WAS NEARLY A QUARTER OF A MILE FROM THE FARM compound to the huge home of the great master. The two-storey, colonnaded, old-style home had been built by Raghunath Singh's grandfather, Meghraj Singh. All told there were about a hundred or a hundred and fifty large rooms. Some of the notched doors were eight feet high by about six feet wide, and each door was set with an ornate doorknob in the form of a big brass rose. The windows had panes of coloured glass, and, inside, the walls and ceilings were adorned with finial work. In each room there was a chandelier, before which there had been candelabra. At his own expense Raghunath Singh had brought electricity lines on timber poles from the sub-district town ten miles away.

A few rooms joined together on the first floor served as a small museum. Raghunath Singh's father, Banraj Singh, had been a man with an immense taste for luxury and had decorated the rooms with various curios collected at home and abroad. He had had a great weakness for hunting, too, and three of the rooms had been filled with the hides of deer and tigers, the heads of cheetahs, the skins of pythons, the tusks of elephants, and so on. Meghraj-ji had had a fondness for singers and musicians. He had brought from various parts of India *dhrupad*, *khayal* and *gazal* singers and players of the sitar, sarod and *esraj*, and had even cultivated the art himself with an exceptionally well-practised hand and voice. Two rooms filled with sitars, sarods, harmoniums, tablas and percussion instruments perpetuated the memory of his music, although there was no longer anyone in this house capable of appreciating it. There must have been thousands of mementos of former generations. From time to time the two rooms would be opened and servants would dust the instruments.

There was a huge compound in front of the great house, on one side of which were the stables where Raghunath Singh kept a dozen or so of the finest horses and a brightly shining carriage. Chained to thick posts were several elephants, and sometimes, if his friends wished, Raghunath Singh would take them on elephant back to hunt cheetah, deer or birds in the jungles of Chhotanagpur.

However, Raghunath Singh did not have a great interest in cars. So many kinds of gleaming, new model cars were now coming out and would have caught his eye from time to time whenever he went to Patna or Calcutta. Had he wanted to, he could have bought three or four such cars, but he was quite happy with his old-model vehicle with the big wheels and the canvas hood. In fact, he had a leaning towards the more aristocratic style of a bygone era.

Before the passing of the Hindu Code Bill, Raghunath Singh had settled two marriages. Of course, the Hindu Code Bill prevailed in India beyond the bounds of Raghunath Singh's Garudiya taluk, but this place was his own exclusive little India, and very few of whatever laws and regulations were passed by the Indian Parliament were able to reach here, two and a half thousand kilometres away from Delhi, and so Raghunath made whatever laws and regulations he liked, keeping the old feudal system almost completely intact. Had he wanted to marry a dozen times, who was there to stop him?

One of his wives had come from a Rajput kshatriya family like his own, the other from a kayastha home and had been a nurse in the hospital in the sub-district town. Having seen her just once in the street Raghunath Singh fell in love with her. One night he sent a man to bring her from the nurses' quarters, her face covered by a veil. However, Raghunath Singh's name would be written in his family's history in letters of gold for the reason that he had not exploited all that the nurse had to offer and then cast her away, but that he had called a Maithili priest that very night and had married her according to traditional Vedic rites.

His first wife created quite a commotion over this. After all, the history of the girls of Rajput kshatriya families had been a very spirited one over the preceding few centuries. Nevertheless, Raghunath Singh was the son of a manly man; it was also said that he was the son of a lion. He had put a stop to the commotion within two days. However, the Rajput girl and the Kayastha girl never got on well together. As far as possible, neither wanted to see the face of the other. Raghunath Singh kept two women caged in the one house, yet although they had stayed in mutual proximity for thirty or more years, the two co-wives had never had anything to say to one another. Between them there was an enmity, a war that would last until death. Although the two continued in this way, it did not bother Raghunath Singh at all, for he did not have the slightest concern about whatever they might do.

The two wives each produced seven children. Indeed, it was testimony to Raghunath Singh's utter impartiality that he endowed both women with equal progeny. Moreover, he was exceptionally judicious, spending one fortnight a month with one wife and the other fortnight with the other.

The Kayastha woman and the Rajput woman did not look at one another, did not speak to one another, and maintained their territory marked off by an unseen boundary. However, the enmity of the mothers did not prevail among the fourteen step-brothers and sisters, who crossed that boundary, coming and going as they pleased.

The ambience of this house was suffused with the old feudalism.

***

When Dharma and the others reached the mansion of Raghunath Singh, they saw that something like one of the autumn festivals had seemed to have begun right now in the month of Jyaistha. Many floodlights were burning in the compound at the front, lights that were so bright that one could pick up a needle dropped on the ground.

In the middle of the compound Raghunath Singh was sitting on a huge throne-like sofa. His body carried a lot of excess fat. He had a big face as round as a wheel, huge shoulders, a mass of hair parted on one side, a long, straight nose, and small eyes under thick eyebrows. He was quite clean-shaven, except for a thin, waxed moustache. He was wearing tight-fitting pajamas and a finely spun kurta, under which a broad, gold amulet could be seen on his arm. On his feet he wore a pair of embroidered slippers. He wore a thin gold chain, which at that moment was covered by the garland of many flowers that hung around the neck of the great master. His brow, head and cheeks, as well as his clothing, were smeared here and there with *gulal*, the festive red powder.

He was surrounded by many of the citizens of Garudiya taluk. The sub-district town's prominent lawyer, Girdharlal, was there, as well as the Bengali doctor, Shyamaldulal Sen, the headmaster, Badribishal Chaube, and many more of that ilk. They were all close associates and bosom friends of Raghunath Singh. Everyone in the region, from the agricultural labourers in the villages to the clerks in the government office in the sub-district town knew that the headmaster-ji and lawyer-ji and doctor-ji were all obedient dogs licking at the feet of Raghunath Singh. Indeed, the great master cultivated various kinds of dogs in various ways. There was dog number one, dog number two, dog number three, as not-so-good men from all around were numbered among Raghunath Singh's friends. Whoever licked the great master's feet well was numbered towards the top, while those who licked less well were numbered towards the bottom.

Raghunath Singh's friends sat around him, talking together and saying, 'What great news that Singh-ji is to be an MLA.'

'This is a really happy day.'

'It's the truly good fortune of all the six or seven hundred thousand people of Bijuri and Garudiya.'

'It is by the grace of Lord Ram that Singh-ji has agreed to become an MLA.'

Such was the talk that went on all around, yet Raghunath Singh remained completely silent. With a look of satisfaction and a contrived smile of courtesy he was enjoying the adulation of his faithful dogs.

The number one lapdog, the munshi Ajibchand, had his head and clothing smeared with red *gulal* and was bustling about with a huge basket of sweets hanging from his shoulder, straining the veins in his throat as he called out, 'Our master is becoming an emlay. Thanks be to Lord Ram! Take some, Doctor Saheb, take some, Lawyer Saheb, take some, Headmaster Saheb – take some sweets. Our master is becoming an emlay! Brother Ramnausera, brother Chhedilal-ji, brother Madhukar-ji, take some sweets!'

Ajibchand seemed almost in a frenzy. That day Raghunath Singh had received in the state capital, Patna, his ticket for becoming an MLA, and that was the occasion for the smearing of red *gulal* and the distribution of sweets. In the great master's mansion there were at least thirty or forty servants, and they could have gone about distributing sweets from baskets hung over their menial shoulders, but Ajibchand was loath to surrender that responsibility to anyone.

Just then Dharma and the others were standing about a hundred yards from where all the festivities were going on. None of them was brave enough to come any closer. Standing beside Dharma was

Kundri, who whispered to him, 'What's this? Holi in the month of Jyaistha! All that *gulal*!'

Dharma explained to her that it was not Holi, but that the great master had finalised his candidacy for the election and so the festivities.

'Why has he called us here?' asked Budheri.

'Who knows?'

Night was falling and Kushi would still be waiting among the *sabui* grass. As well as that, Dharma had another reason for anxiety and concern. After dark on the other side of the Koel there were wildcats. The wildcat was a big, dangerous animal, as ferocious as it was fearsome. A human being cornered by one would be quite helpless; it could even overpower a tiger. Dharma started to become very anxious, but despite this he was obliged to stay. Who could say when he would be able to take his leave from the great master's residence?

After a little while Raghunath Singh caught sight of the bonded labourers. After looking at them for a few moments, he beckoned them with a wave of his hand and said affectionately, 'My goodness, why are you all standing so far away?'

No one amongst all of Dharma's fourteen generations of forebears could have thought that Raghunath Singh could ever speak in this way. Staring at him dumbfounded they could only manage, 'Master, sir.'

'Come over here.'

It was extremely odd to hear the gentle voice of a master who from time immemorial had had their backs scarred with his shoe, whose armed force of domestic bully boys had beaten them with lathis and set fire to their shanties. Not consciously, but as though in a trance, they approached him.

Looking at them all Raghunath Singh said, 'How are you, then, Budheri? And you, Dhorailal? And you, Kundri? And

Ramnehal?' He inquired of each of them in turn. He knew all their names, and not only their names but the names of their family members and where they lived – he remembered it all.

'Yes, well,' answered Budheri and all the others, taking a deep breath.

'And your children?'

'By your grace, sir, they are well.'

'Now, Ganeri, last year your wife's stomach couldn't take any water?'

'Yes, master. She went to the hospital.'

'How is she now?'

'She is better. Much better, sir.'

'And how are things with you, Gidhni?'

The young girl called Gidhni, a widow, lowered her eyes and said, 'My lord, I am going to work in your fields.'

Raghunath Singh said, 'You have that job for life. You are a young woman with no parents, no husband. You should look for a young man to marry in your own caste. I will pay for your wedding.'

Munshi Ajibchand interrupted his distribution of sweets to bawl, 'Oh! Oh! What a big heart our maalik has! He wants to pay the whole bill for the wedding of the poor, childless widow. Now that our maalik will become an emlay, the kingdom of Lord Ram will return!' And so he went on with his distribution of sweets.

Not just Gidhni, but the whole party was utterly astounded. What had Raghunath Singh said? Had they heard him right? It was as though the world had suddenly turned upside down! It seemed that Raghunath Singh could read the minds of these people. Even more gently he said, 'You see, I am your own kinsman, I stand by all of you. You live near me, you work in my fields. If I don't stand by you through good times and bad, then who will?'

The bonded labourers could only be totally dumbfounded at what Raghunath Singh was saying. He was their own kinsman – could they have ever imagined such a thing even in their dreams? The kingdom of Lord Ram that the munshi Ajibchand had invoked just a moment ago had truly come! Oh, Lord Ram, such is your mercy!

Again Raghunath Singh said, 'Now, Gidhni, choose yourself a good boy. Next month we will have the election, and after that I will have you married.'

Flushed with embarrassment Gidhni looked down, pinching her nails. She had no father, no mother – no one. Still in the fullness of her youth, she had a great need for a partner, and now she could dream of marrying again. As she listened to Raghunath Singh's words, a flood of emotion welled up inside her. She started to sense a wild storm in her heart.

Now Raghunath Singh looked at Dharma. 'How are things with you, Dharma?'

Dharma made it known that he passed his days by the grace of the great master.

'Are your mother and father well?'

'Yes, master'

Looking here and there Raghunath Singh said, 'I can't see Kushi anywhere. The lass is usually beside you all the time, like your shadow.'

'She went home straight after finishing her work.'

Raghunath Singh understood well the relationship between Dharma and Kushi. He had men to keep him informed. He said, 'How much longer are the two of you going to gad about? It's time you got married.'

Like Gidhni, Dharma just looked down in embarrassment.

Raghunath said nothing more but turned around and called to Ajibchand, 'Munshi, give them some sweets.'

'Yes, maalik. I'm coming right away,' Ajibchand called from the other side.

And no sooner than one could blink, Ajibchand was bringing a servant with a huge basket of sweets slung over his shoulder. Although he had distributed sweets to everyone else with his own hands, he would have the servant do it for the untouchable labourers. The high-caste Ajibchand could hardly send the next fourteen of his own generations to hell this evening due to the touch of these bonded untouchables. However, just when Ajibchand had come close, something amazing happened. Raghunath Singh said, 'Bring the sweets basket to me. I will distribute them with my own hands.'

What! The great lord and master would distribute with his own hands sweets to untouchables such as they! Oh God, heaven had come down to earth! It did not seem at all untrue that Raghunath Singh, now to become an 'emlay', was bringing about the kingdom of Lord Ram, as they had all been saying. Of course, Dharma and the others had no clear idea of just what the kingdom of Lord Ram was. They just had some idea that, if the kingdom of Lord Ram were established, they would no longer have so much trouble and sorrow and that they might live in happiness, more or less.

Raghunath Singh had begun distributing sweets with his own hands, giving everyone two *laddus* that had been fried in pure ghee of buffalo milk. Those who had elderly relatives at home, or children, were given a share for them too.

Munshi Ajibchand did not know what to do. Wringing his hands and contorting his body, he said in a voice choked with emotion, 'The great master is giving sweets with his own hands to untouchables! The kingdom of Lord Ram has, indeed, come! Oh, it has surely come!'

In the distribution of sweets Dharma's turn at last came. Raghunath Singh said, 'Take these. Four for your mother and father, and two for you. Six altogether.'

Dharma took the six sweets and remembered Kushi, just as Raghunath Singh asked, 'What sort of a young man are you?'

Flabbergasted, Dharma asked, 'Sir?'

'My goodness, are there sweets only for you? What about taking some for your bride-to-be?'

Dharma was quite overwhelmed by the master's display of thoughtfulness. He had not forgotten Kushi. Dharma had resolved to give Kushi one of his sweets. He would not take from his parents' share, for when they had heard from all the others in the neighbourhood that the great master had given two for everybody, they would raise a real uproar when they saw that they had but two between them. The great master was lord, a god – because he had not forgotten Kushi, Dharma felt that he had been in his service throughout his last fourteen births.

Again Raghunath Singh said, 'Here, take two for Kushi, and four for her parents.' So saying, he joked, 'And listen, don't you go eating your girl's share.'

Gratefully Dharma said, 'No, master.'

Having distributed the sweets, Raghunath Singh said to them, 'You can go home now. You've toiled in the fields the whole day. I won't keep you any longer. Go home and rest.'

They all bowed their heads to their great master in respectful *namaskar*, and went. When they had all left Raghunath Singh's mansion and come out onto the road, they saw many people coming towards them. They all looked familiar, people from various villages in Garudiya taluk. Among them were some people from the market in the small sub-district town ten miles away. As they drew near, one or two of them called out excitedly, 'Hey, has the maalik become an emlay, then?'

Ganeri said, 'No. There has to be a vote first.'

'We heard that the great master is distributing sweets to everyone from all the villages.'

'Who told you that?'

'The man sent by the munshi told us. Is it true?'

It was clear that, on the pretext of Raghunath Singh's candidacy, the munshi Ajibchand had sent men into the villages and the sub-district town inviting people to partake of sweets. Ganeri inclined his head and said, 'Yes, it's true.'

Their eyes lit up as they asked, 'What sort of sweets?'

'*Laddus.*'

'How many each?'

'Two.'

They did not wait any longer, but excitedly ran off towards Raghunath Singh's grand mansion, wanting to get there before the *laddus* ran out.

4

DHARMA AND THE OTHER LABOURERS HAD SOON REACHED THE POINT where the highway passes through Mishirlal's Bijuri taluk and runs alongside the Koel. 'You go back to the village,' Dharma said to the others. 'I'll be along later.' He leaped straight down to the dry river bed and ran off.

It was the time of the full moon, and on this evening the round moon like a silver goblet was rising in the sky, spreading its light like molten silver. Nowhere was there even a speck of cloud in the sparkling clear summer sky dotted by stars like golden flowers and covering the whole creation. The dried up river bed lay bathed in the light of the eternal moon, the white sands glistening as far as the eye could see. On both sides of the Koel the vast and bare fields looking like man-made geometrical sketches, the untidy underbrush and the one or two gangling trees all seemed at that moment to be amazingly enchanting.

Running over the sands, Dharma now reached the jungle of dense *sabui* grass. On one side of it Kushi, an axe in hand, was standing alone, silently, from time to time standing up on her toes to look over the Koel towards the highway. She looked extremely anxious. Beside her, lying on the sand, were many *bageri* birds bound with a cord, and next to them were twenty or so rectangular bamboo traps, from which Kushi had taken the birds and arranged them as they now were.

Seeing Dharma she said, 'You said you'd come straight here after putting the bullock and the plough away.'

Out of breath, Dharma said, 'What could I do? I had to go to the great master's house.'

'But I've been waiting and waiting here for you,' said Kushi. 'I've been here all alone. I've been really scared.'

'Have any wildcats come out?' Dharma asked.

'No.'

'I was really worried. You were alone, and what trouble you'd've been in if the wildcats had come out.' Saying this, Dharma sighed heavily, a sigh of great relief.

'There were no wildcats,' said Kushi, 'but there were plenty of peacocks. Flocks of them.' And she pointed with her finger.

Dharma noticed a flock of peacocks, their tails spread, running about on the glimmering sands of the Koel a little distance away. By the light of the moon they had come out of the jungle on the other side of the river bed. Dharma now had an urge to fell one or two of them with a stone, but then he remembered that the government had prohibited the killing of peacocks and he repressed his impulse.

Kushi thought for a moment and asked, 'Why did you go to the great master's house?'

'He was giving out sweets. Oh, take these.' Giving Kushi her and her parents' share of *laddus* Dharma said, 'They're not just for you. Give some to your mother and father.'

As she took the sweets Kushi wanted to know why the great master was suddenly giving out sweets. Had the matter of his daughter's marriage been finalised then?

While explaining the reason for the distribution of sweets, Dharma's glance fell on the birds tied with a cord. He almost cried out in joy, 'Oh, so many birds!' and he knelt down on the sand and started to count, 'One, two, three, four – oh, my goodness – two dozen birds!' Dharma could count up to three dozen correctly, but after that he got confused. Kushi could not count as far.

'We'll get a good price, won't we?' she asked, looking at Dharma's face.

'Yes.' Dharma nodded. Then he set the traps anew. Every day, once the work in the fields was finished, he would come here, take out the birds from the traps and set them again. Now, having laid out the traps, he went to a certain place in the jungle and dug in the sand for a heavy old tin box, and took it out. It was almost full of coins and notes. Dharma gave the box to Kushi, then took up the birds in one hand and hung the packet of sweets from the other. 'Let's go,' he said.

Dharma and Kushi would go from this place every day with the trapped birds and the money box, and now, bathed in the heavenly moonlight, they trudged across the sands of the Koel and went on up to the highway.

To the right the highway ran towards Mishirlal's Bijuri taluk and, to the left, towards Raghunath Singh's farm compound, his home, and the nearby village and market of Garudiya. When Dharma and Kushi came up onto the highway, they turned to the left and went straight to Garudiya market where the contractors from Patna had put up. They had been staying here for nearly twelve months of each of the past few years. New roads were being made in this region, the old roads were being repaired, and a bridge was being built, and the men had come here on all this 'gormin' contract business.

The highway was quite deserted except for only one or two bullock carts creaking their way along to the railway station. The lanterns hanging under the distant carts looked like glow-worms. Suddenly a truck or a dilapidated private bus would rumble by the edge of the fields on either side. Then everything would be silent and still once again.

After they had walked for a little while, they saw the flickering lights of countless small kerosene and hurricane lamps in village after village amongst the fields, and they heard the indistinct voices of people coming from them. Then, having crossed many fields and passed many villages, Dharma and Kushi at last came to Garudiya market.

With electricity and rows of shops and stalls, it was a busy market. Most of the buildings were brick and of one or two storeys. There was also a police outpost, a small hotel, a school and a dispensary. Not far from the market there was the medium grade 'gormin' rest house where the contractors stayed. The place was familiar to Dharma and Kushi, who had been coming there almost every day over the past two and a half years.

There was a big grassy area in front of the rest house, and on these evenings the contractors would sit about there on cane chairs playing cards under the light of an electric bulb hanging from a bamboo post. When they saw Dharma and Kushi the contractors stopped their game and several pairs of eyes lit up immediately when they noticed the *bageri* birds. Their voices mingled as they exclaimed, 'So many birds!' Certainly Dharma and Kushi had not brought as many birds before.

'Yes, saheb,' said Dharma.

The middle-aged, burly looking contractor sitting to Dharma's right, Ayodhyaprasad, was the actual boss of this contracting firm. After coming here for so long, Dharma and Kushi knew him well. The man was a great consumer of liquor and meat, especially that of the *bageri* bird. Something like six or seven hundred *bageri* birds would find their way into his stomach every two or three years, so at this rate, Dharma had no doubt, it would not be long before the *bageri* birds of Chhotanagpur would become extinct, but he did not worry himself unduly about it. What did it matter to him if the birds survived or not? For him it was just a matter of money, and for making money he needed free trade. If he and Kushi and their families were to gain their freedom from Raghunath Singh, a total of two thousand rupees would be required. Over two or three years they had been saving that money.

Ayodhyaprasad said, 'This is very good.' And he almost snatched the tied birds from Dharma's hand and started to appraise them by pressing their stomachs, which were very fleshy. Continuing to press them he again said, 'Very good,' though this time he was referring to the birds.

Dharma stood there with his hopes high. Seeing such happiness on Ayodhyaprasad's face, he felt that he would be paid well today. Ayodhyaprasad took a bag from his pocket and shook some notes and coins from it.

How much money was in the contractor's bag? Two thousand, maybe? Dharma tried to imagine. Certainly there was enough to buy the freedom of Kushi's family and his. If he had that money right now, he would run and throw it at the feet of Raghunath Singh's munshi. Then there would be – oh! – what a wonderful life of freedom!

As he peeled off the cost of the *bageri* birds from his wad of notes, Ayodhyaprasad said, 'Why have you come so late today? We've been sitting drinking for some time. But what is booze without fried *bageri*?'

On other days Dharma and Kushi always came just before evening. Today they had indeed come late. Dharma told him, 'The great master was giving out sweets. Because of that.'

'Why was he giving out sweets?' asked Ayodhyaprasad. 'Is his daughter getting married?'

'No, contractor saheb. The great master is becoming an emlay. Because of that.'

Ayodhyaprasad shifted on his cane chair. Suddenly he seemed rather excited. Looking at his companions he said, 'Singh-ji is becoming an MLA. We'll have to meet him tomorrow morning before the other contractors do. For the sake of our work we have to maintain good relations, don't we?'

The others all said at once, 'Yes, yes, of course.'

One of them said, 'We need such powerful men to get all the contracts around here without any trouble.'

Dharma could not actually understand anything they were saying. He just kept his eyes on the money bag.

Ayodhyaprasad then turned back to Dharma. 'This is great news. Raghunath Singh-ji is going to be an MLA. Excellent news!' And he took from the bag three ten-rupee notes and tossed them to Dharma. 'I've given you extra today for the good news. Buy a sari for your bride,' he said, looking at Kushi.

Incredulous, Dharma picked the notes up off the ground. Thirty rupees for some two-dozen birds! Before this he had never got more than three or three and a half rupees. Bowing their heads many times Dharma and Kushi said, '*Namaste*, contractor saheb, *namaste* - '

Dharma was not able to tell how much of the thirty rupees was for the *bageri* birds and how much for the news of Raghunath Singh's becoming an MLA. And then there appeared before his eyes the picture of peacocks spreading their tails on the dry river bed. So many times the contractor had asked them to bring peacock, for peacock flesh was a real delicacy. He had dangled the bait before their noses, telling them that he would pay generously if they caught a peacock and brought it to him. He had paid thirty rupees for two-dozen *bageri* birds – what would he pay if Dharma brought a peacock! But the government had outlawed the killing of peacocks, so what could Dharma do? He sighed deeply.

Ayodhyaprasad said, 'Go now, and hurry back tomorrow with more *bageri* birds.'

'Yes, sir.' And Dharma and Kushi left.

5

EVERY DAY AFTER THEY HAD TAKEN THE *BAGERI* BIRDS TO THE contractors, Dharma and Kushi would go straight to the schoolmaster's house. The contractors had taken two rooms in the 'gormin' rest house, which was on one side of the Garudiya market; on the other side the 'gormin' had opened the school where Master-ji taught. The school was part of the programme of the Social Welfare Department, the purpose of which was the provision of education in a number of regions to the lowest, most deprived levels of society. This kind of government enterprise was intended to give some education to poor, illiterate village people so that they might have their eyes opened to what was best for them. But people like Dharma could not understand so many big words.

Soon Dharma and Kushi were at the other end of the market in front of the new school building with its tiled roof. The schoolmaster, Badribishal Pande, lived on his own in a small, tiled house beside the school. There he cooked for himself, as his frail and ailing wife lived with their children in her family home in Motihari. Whether one went from here to Motihari by train or by bus, two or three changes were necessary, and it took a long time.

As was his habit, the schoolmaster was sitting in a cheap cloth-covered rocking chair on the veranda of his house, reading a book under a light which hung from a slat in the ceiling above. On one side of the yard beneath the veranda was a small flower and vegetable garden, which he had cultivated himself.

From the yard Dharma called, 'Master-ji!'

Master-ji looked around. 'Come up here,' he said affectionately.

Dharma and Kushi came up onto the veranda and sat timidly in a corner.

Master-ji was in his early fifties with a thin, rather weak body and greying hair. He had a longish face with cheeks that usually had two or three days' stuble on them; behind his thick glasses he had tender eyes. He was wearing a pair of shabby, loose-fitting pajamas and a kurta of cheap cloth.

Dharma and Kushi knew, from occasional experience, that inside this slight and frail schoolmaster there was a strong and imposing man. They had first met Master-ji three or four years before when everyone was at the opening of the new 'gormin' school. Master-ji had come to take responsibility for it, along with another couple of teachers. The other teachers were still there, living with their wives and children in a rented house on the other side of Garudiya market.

Since coming here, Master-ji would wander from village to village, combing the fields in quest of pupils. He would take their hands and say, 'Get a little education, learn to write some of the alphabets. Your eyes will be opened to great benefits. Worldly men cheat you, but if you have some learning, no one will be able to cheat you.'

Hearing the schoolmaster's words, everyone in the villages from the old to the young would flash their teeth, smiling, and say, 'What are you saying, Master-ji? You will make edda-cated people of us? You'll turn us into judges and magistrates and lawyers and police inspectors? Oh, Lord Ram! What a joke! Oh, Lord Ram!'

But the schoolmaster was dogged in his persistence and would not be put off by anything. Undaunted, and with unlimited patience and forbearance, he would mount his creaking old bicycle day after day and go out to recruit students for his school.

All his hard work and fine intentions did not go unrewarded, for he did gather a few labourers, peasants and other working people from various villages in Chhotanagpur. Most of these, indeed, had more than half of their lives already behind them. After labouring with bullock and plough all day in the fields, the letters of the first primer would pose to them a bewildering, intricate challenge, yet without learning them they could not enter the world of the educated. At night they would fall off to sleep reciting the alphabet.

Those of advanced age would come one day and then disappear for the next seven. The younger ones were hardly regular in attendance, either. However, Master-ji was able at least to draw to school all the young children of these rustic labourers' and peasants' homes around noon each day, yet even that did not last long, for as soon as they were needed in the fields with their parents they no longer went near the school.

Although he was able to gather quite a few pupils, the schoolmaster was not able to draw Dharma and Kushi to his lessons. They had made it clear that after a day of bone-crushing work in the fields or granaries of Raghunath Singh, they then had to try to make some money, as all they got for all their work for the great master w ere their daily rations, a few drops of kerosene and, to last them the whole year, two short pieces of cheap, coarse cloth and a couple of shirts. Thus, their prime need was for money to secure their freedom, and that was something they had to work for, no matter what.

This matter of freedom warrants a little explanation. Dharma and Kushi's families had been bonded labourers of the great master Raghunath Singh and his forebears for several generations. Both Dharma and Kushi's fathers, grandfathers and great-grandfathers had driven the plough on the land of Raghunath Singh's father, his grandfather, his great-grandfather and his great-great-grandfather in exchange for nothing more than rations. So many years ago one of

Dharma's ancestors probably took a loan, for which he signed with a thumb print, from one of Raghunath Singh's ancestors; the interest then grew astronomically and committed successive generations to bonded labour in service of the debt.

The old landlord system had been abolished by now, and no longer was anyone able to be the proprietor of excessive amounts of land. It could not be said that Dharma and his like did not hear people talk about this in the markets, but it was a matter they were not able to comprehend clearly. However, a few years earlier, the munshi Ajibchand had called them to put two thumb prints on a 'gormin' stamped paper, telling them, 'From now on you are all proprietors of the land and granaries. Our maalik has graciously put the land in your names. So you will no longer have to work on the land of other masters. However . . . '

The elderly leaders of Dharma's neighbourhood, brimming over with joy, asked, 'What, Munshi-ji?'

'It is not quite as simple as that. You will have to pay a small price for it. You will work in his fields as before, and one day you will get your land.'

Then one year went and another year came, then another year came and went, yet they were far from being landed proprietors and were unable to win their freedom. Gradually Dharma and the others came to realise that they had incurred a huge debt in the great master's nominal transference into their names of most of his land. The placing of two thumb prints on a piece of paper was nominally for 'land', and that land was security for false loans. If Dharma and his kind could pay a huge sum of money, then they would get their land. But where would they get so much money? And so the dream of becoming landowners had long ago been dispelled. Moreover, how could they leave Raghunath Singh's employ? Firstly, Raghunath Singh had his obedient, paid strong-arm men, who would break the bones of anyone who dared to run away. Secondly, a long time ago their ancestors had borrowed a lot of money from Raghunath Singh's ancestors, and who could say what the exact interest now stood at? They could not take one step from the place without that money being repaid, and they could pay back the debts incurred by their forebears only by working for mere rations day after day, month after month, year after year.

However, Dharma and Kushi had no desire at all to continue this life of a servile beast. Since childhood they had grown up together like a pair of strong trees, just to labour on someone else's land. Once they had come to understand that the natural course of things would be for neither of them to leave the other, they started to dream of the life they longed for, believing tnat if they got the chance they could turn away from their debased life of slavery and set up home somewhere else.

One day Dharma had gone apprehensively to Ajibchand and asked, 'Munshi-ji, can I ask you something?'

Scraping a feather around inside his ear, Ajibchand said, 'Go ahead.'

'Munshi-ji, how much is the debt owing to the great master by my ancestors and Kushi's ancestors?'

Ajibchand wriggled and sat up straight. His deeply sunken eyes in his face like a mole's were utterly fixed and still. He pursed his narrow lips even tighter, and said, 'Many rupees. Are you going to pay it back, then?'

Dharma could not look into the eyes of the munshi. His head bowed, and making a long scratch in the earth with his big toe, he said, 'No. I just want to know how much.'

'Then I'll tell you. A lot of rupees. A thousand.'

Dharma had no concept of how much one thousand rupees actually was. He merely echoed the words, 'A thousand.'

Smiling superciliously, Ajibchand said sarcastically, 'Yes, Your Highness.'

'And how much for Kushi's?'

'A thousand rupees for them, too.'

That meant that the price for the freedom of his family and Kushi's would be two thousand rupees, yet Dharma was undaunted. From that day he and Kushi had been roaming the grasslands and jungles beside the southern Koel in order to raise the price of their freedom. Sometimes they went to the *sabui* grass jungle to set traps to catch *bageri* birds, sometimes they hunted pigs in the forest, and sometimes they would kill and skin a snake or deer. There were many customers for bird's and pig's flesh and for the hide of snake or deer. Whatever there is in the natural world – animal or vegetable – has a price and a demand in the human world. There were people who would pay them for anything they caught or killed. Small coins and large notes all went towards the cost of their freedom, which they would attain, if necessary, at the cost of the lives of all the birds and beasts of Chhotanagpur.

Dharma and Kushi went to the school every day, but not to become educated. Never before had they met such an honest, unselfish man as the schoolmaster.

Master-ji said, 'I've been waiting here for you for a while. Why are you so late?'

Dharma gave a brief explanation.

'Good heavens! Someone like Raghunath Singh will become an MLA? Oh, dear.'

'That's why he was giving out sweets,' said Dharma.

'Oh.'

'Now will you count our money for us?' Dharma took the moneybox from Kushi and gave it to Master-ji.

'What's the great hurry?' asked the schoolmaster. 'Hey, Kushi. Go inside and bring out what is beside the enamel bowl.'

Kushi went into Master-ji's bedroom and brought from beside the aluminium bowl two ripe custard-apples and two cucumbers.

Master-ji said, 'I kept them for you. Eat up.'

'But what about you?'

'I have already eaten.'

Nearly every day one or another of the schoolmaster's pupils would fondly give him something from their trees or plants, but he did not like taking such things from poor people. He would staunchly refuse, he would be angry, but the day labourers, the bonded labourers and the landless peasant labourers of Garudiya and Bijuri would still bring whatever was in season for their master-ji. If he did not accept, they would feel greatly offended, and so in spite of himself he took what they offered.

Dharma and Kushi divided up the custard-apples and cucumbers and began to eat. Today they had been lucky – they had been given sweets, they had got a lot of money from the contractor for the *bageri* birds, and now from the schoolmaster they had got some delicious, fresh custard-apples and cucumbers. Today had indeed been a good day. If only every day were the same!

They talked as they ate. The schoolmaster gleaned from them such snippets of news as how much of Raghunath Singh's thousands of acres had been cultivated and how all of Dharma and Kushi's neighbours were. The topic of Raghunath Singh's becoming an 'emlay' came up, and Master-ji set about asking who was at the house when the sweets were distributed and who did what, and heard, with a frown, all about the smearing of the *gulal*, Raghunath Singh's giving of sweets with his own hand to Dharma and the others and his sweet talk to them about being their own man. Then he burst into laughter and said, rocking in his chair, 'So it was a vote feast!'

Dharma and Kushi just looked at the schoolmaster, unable to understand quite what he meant.

Master-ji went on, 'Raghunath Singh gave you sweets from his own hand, as well as a lot of sweet talk. You are very lucky!'

'Yes.' Both Dharma and Kushi nodded. They were still

overwhelmed by the great master's magnanimity and kind words to them.

'How long do you think this good fortune will last, then?' The schoolmaster's voice seemed to have taken on a touch of irony, though Dharma and Kushi did not realise that.

There was a pause, then Master-ji spoke again. 'Will you have some tea?'

They did not always get fruit when they came to the schoolmaster's house, but they did get tea, for which they had a great liking. It tasted just as it smelled. Master-ji made it himself, with plenty of milk and sugar, like no one else in all of Garudiya and Bijuri taluks. Dharma and Kushi never went away without a glass. However, they were too diffident ever to mention tea, though Master-ji always guessed what was on their minds.

Dharma and Kushi smiled coyly and inclined their heads. Certainly they would have some tea.

Master-ji said to Kushi, 'Go and bring everything out here.'

By 'everything' he meant the kerosene stove, the tea caddy and the sugar tin, the milk pot, the kettle, the enamel 'gelasses', and whatever else was part of the process. Kushi hurried inside and brought everything out.

Master-ji lit the stove and put the tea on. He said to Kushi, 'I'll give you a little job.'

Kushi knew what the job was. Master-ji was a single man and cooked and served his food himself, but in this regard he was terribly careless. If he had no rice, dal, potatoes or other vegetables, he would have just a couple of chapatis. There were usually green chillies and ghee kept in the house, and when there were not, he would nibble some puffed rice or eat a paste of chick-pea flour and water. However, Kushi and Dharma had been coming for some time, and when they were here Master-ji would get Kushi to wash the rice and things and put them all on the stove; if they stayed long enough, he would have the rice cooked by her. At first Kushi, as an untouchable, was very unwilling to cook for a brahman, but Master-ji was unyielding. He did not worry himself over issues to do with caste and had no concern for proscriptions concerning touch. Although he held to some minor traditional beliefs, he recognised the dignity of all people. At one time he had had to gently rebuke Kushi and insist on her serving him food. However, none of that happened any more, for as soon as Master-ji uttered his request Kushi would set about with the rice, dal and vegetables. The way in which one serves food to a deity was how Kushi served Master-ji, with meticulous devotion.

Master-ji said, 'When you have finished your tea, you can put the rice on.'

Kushi did not wait but got up straightaway to attend to the rice and the vegetables. Soon she had washed the rice, the dal and potatoes and put them in a small pot that gleamed like silver. In the meantime she made the tea.

Master-ji poured the tea into glasses and Kushi put the rice pot on the space that had been left on the stove.

Master-ji finished his tea and, after pouring some more for Dharma and Kushi, had another glass himself. The remaining tea was quickly finished, so Dharma and Kushi did not gulp what they had but sipped it slowly, letting the taste linger in their mouths as long as possible.

As they drank, Dharma said, 'Master-ji, now will you count our money? Today we got thirty rupees from the contractor. Now what does it all add up to?' He pushed the big money box across to him.

The schoolmaster reached out and took the box, saying, 'How many times have I told you both to get a little learning? Then you wouldn't have to get someone else to count your money for you.'

'No, no, Master-ji, not yet. Before that we must pay back the great master. After that we can get some learning.' Every day the schoolmaster said the same thing and Dharma gave the same reply.

The schoolmaster took the lid off the box, tipped the notes and coins out onto the veranda, and immediately started counting. There was a total of two hundred and ten rupees and seventeen paisa.

The schoolmaster knew that Dharma and Kushi had been saving this money for two or two and a half years; he also knew that it was the price for some hundreds of Chhotanagpur's *bageri* birds and the lives of a few dozen snakes, some pigs and some deer, and that with their savings that came with the death of so many birds and beasts they intended to buy their own life of freedom.

Dharma asked, 'How much is two hundred and ten rupees and seventeen paisa? A lot, huh?'

The schoolmaster smiled. He said nothing, but went back to sipping his tea.

'How much more is needed to get to the total of two thousand?' Dharma asked.

How could the schoolmaster make them understand that it would take them a lifetime of toil, privation and saving to repay the debt to Raghunath Singh? He had no desire to disappoint two optimistic, innocent and simple young people who dreamed of a life of freedom. He could only say, 'Keep saving. One day you'll have it all paid off.'

'It's getting very late,' Dharma said. 'We'd better be going.'

'Yes, you had.'

'We'll come again tomorrow,' Dharma said, as he said every day.

'Yes, of course,' said the schoolmaster as Dharma and Kushi got up.

When they left the schoolmaster's house they never went back to their village by way of the highway. Amid the fields a little to the north of Garudiya market some villages lay scattered here and there, and Dharma and Kushi would wend their way through them, taking a very circuitous route back to the *sabui* grass jungle by the dried up river bed where they would bury the money box once more in the sand; then, after setting the bird traps, they would return to their own homes.

The north of the Garudiya market was not busy. There were only a few rows of stalls, set about in a disorderly manner. At this hour all the shops were shut, but for the country liquor shop which was crowded and noisy. As the dark of evening fell, boozers from however many villages there were within three or four miles would come and gather here, and the number would grow as the night wore on. Most of the customers were tribals or men of various untouchable castes. But booze recognises no caste, so even a few brahmans and kayasthas would steal here under cover of darkness.

Once they had left the schoolmaster's house, Dharma and Kushi went on past the grog shop where the crowd of tipplers caught their eyes. They had drunk their fill of booze and were making quite a commotion. Dharma and Kushi lengthened their strides along the narrow path by the grog shop and hurried past at the speed of a storm. But as they passed the shop, they noticed with surprise Ramlachhman among the gathering of drinkers there. Just as Ajibchand was a bootlicking lapdog of Raghunath Singh, Ramlachhman was a bootlicking lapdog of the supervisor of the farm compound, Himgirinandan. He looked like a crane with his bent back and hooked nose and his long, thin arms and legs; he had round eyes and a high forehead, sparse hair, and sandal-paste markings on his forehead and ear-lobes. He wore a knee-length dhoti and a kurta, and slippers of untanned leather.

The fellow had a weakness for women. Just as a cat will salivate at the smell of fish, so Ramlachhman, should he see a sweet, lively young woman, would immediately want to pounce upon her.

'St Satan at his worship!' exclaimed Kushi. The people of Garudiya, especially those of the dosad community, called Ramlachhman 'St Satan', sarcastically referring to his hypocrisy.

For two and a half years, winter and summer, Dharma and Kushi had returned home along the path by the grog shop, but never before had they seen Ramlachhman there. 'The rat also drinks booze! Let's hurry up and get away from here,' Dharma said, quickening his step as he spoke. It was quite likely that had he seen Kushi, St Satan would have come running from the grog shop. In a flash the two of them crossed the track in front of the liquor den.

6

BEYOND THE LIQUOR SHOP THERE WERE THREE OR FOUR tin-roofed houses and six or seven dilapidated mud huts before the start of the boundless fields of Chhotanagpur. Now in the month of Jyaistha not a seedling of paddy or wheat was to be seen anywhere, and the fields stood absolutely bare and desolate.

The moon, like a silver goblet, had risen directly overhead and the ancient earth was bathed in moonlight like molten silver. These undulating fields had been a part of Chhotanagpur from its very beginning, but at this moment there was a wonderful, unfamiliar enchantment about them as a cool, pleasant breeze was gusting from the north to the south and from the east to the west. Who now could have imagined the fieriness of the fields in daytime? A flock of foreign parrots drifted on the breeze overhead. How mild and gentle the world bathed in moonlight now was!

Once they had passed the Garudiya market, Dharma and Kushi came onto the fields and, after a little while, they reached the dairy folk's village. It was a lovely village; everywhere there were spick-and-span tin or mud huts, and in front of each was a spacious 'courtyard' in which there was a small flower garden. Here there was not a house where there were not ten or twenty cows or buffalo, and day and night throughout the year there was a lingering smell in the air in this dairying village, the wonderful smell of ghee made from buffalo milk. In some house or another, ghee would be made every day to be packed in tins and taken to the big cities like Ranchi, Daltanganj, Dhanbad, Patna and Calcutta.

In the houses there was the red flickering of burning oil lamps, and everywhere flashes of pictures of family life met the eyes of Dharma and Kushi. On a veranda here or there a loving wife would be sitting, serving food on enamel plates to her husband and children. Other women would be sitting beside the oven making chapatis, each with her husband sitting beside her rolling out the balls of dough. Somewhere a man would be sitting beside his darling woman, enjoying her light-hearted company after a long and hard day's work.

Somewhere else there would be a musical gathering, with all the men, women and children of a family playing small tom-toms and large cymbals and singing songs of the Holi festival –

In Holi's revelry Ayodhya's folk rejoice!
Lord Ram holds a golden water sprinkler,
and Lakshmanji has a bag of red perfumed powder.
In Holi's revelry Ayodhya's folk rejoice!
Holi has come!
Come out and play!

Holi had been celebrated, however, in the month of Chaitra some two and a half months back, yet it would seem that in this village of Chhotanagpur the days of the colourful festival did not want to pass by. Indeed, Holi was inclined to linger on not only in this dairying village but in Dharma and Kushi's village as well.

The young couple's eyes gleamed with envy at seeing these happy, independent people, free from worry. Since their early youth they had been dreaming longingly of such a life, but so far it had remained just a dream. Each day they took a little more time as they went through the dairy village, filling their eyes with all these pictures of domestic love and devotion.

The village was called Chaukad, and everyone there knew Kushi and Dharma. Almost all of them had come to think fondly of this young couple of the landless, untouchable dosad community. Of course, while these higher-caste dairy people kept their distance to protect themselves from their touch, they did not hold back their affection. When the two walked through Chaukad every day, the villagers would call out to them, as indeed they did today.

'Hey, Kushiya! Hey, Dhamma! Come and sit down.'

Although everyone asked them to sit down, they did not invite them inside. They would have to sit outside on the edge of the 'courtyard'.

Dharma replied, 'No, brother, it's getting very late.'

'Oh, come and sit for a while.'

'No, brother. Please excuse us today. Tomorrow we will sit with you.'

Someone said, 'What about some tea? Paan?'

Their answer was the same. It had got very late, and they could not delay any longer. They did not even have a longing for tea.

Playfully someone said, 'You've been gadding about with your dark-skinned sweetheart for three or four years now. What about getting married?'

Every night after having their money counted by the schoolmaster Dharma and Kushi, coming back through Chaukad village, would have to hear talk of marriage from at least ten or twenty people, and today, like any other day, Dharma kept his head down in embarrassment, guessing that Kushi was blushing beside him. In a shaky, indistinct voice Dharma said, 'By the grace of Lord Ram, we'll definitely get married.'

After they had gone through the middle of Chaukad, the wife of Bhikhun Gowar called out, 'Aren't you a man? You've been strutting around with your young chicken for three or four years now and you still haven't fixed the wedding. Why don't you hurry up and put sindoor in her hair and get her into bed?' And she hitched up her dress and swayed her backside, snapping her fingers as she repeated some ribald verse. The middle-aged woman's hair was greying as though streaked with flour, and rolls of fat had accumulated on her body. There was no obscenity she could not utter as she flashed her teeth that had been drilled and filled with silver. Moreover, she was the most insufferably bitchy and incorrigibly quarrelsome woman in the whole village. Whoever in Chaukad did not quake at the sound of her harsh voice was yet to be born, and so Dharma's heart dried up whenever he saw this wife of Bhikhun Gowar. In a choking voice he said something to Kushi and they lengthened their stride and hurried on.

***

No sooner had Dharma and Kushi got to the south of the village than they heard a couple of excited voices calling, 'Hey, Dhamma! Hey, Kushiya!'

They turned around and saw a fair woman and her dark-skinned husband sitting in a corner of their yard beside some ovens, heating ghee in huge iron pans, filling the air with its wonderful aroma. Catching their eyes the woman and her husband waved and called out, 'Come over here!'

The man's name was Mahadeo, but because his body was the colour of coal, he was known round about as the Dark Milkman. His wife's name was Bijri, and her complexion was exactly the opposite to her husband's, gleaming white like that of a European woman; hence she was known as the Fair Milkwoman.

Although they did not enter the homes of the other dairy folk, Dharma and Kushi were quite comfortable about going into Mahadeo and Bijri's house. However, here there was no one who, like the schoolmaster, did not defer to caste and would invite them in and even have them sit on the bed, so the two untouchables were kept at some distance. Mahadeo and Bijri, though, like the other dairy people, made them welcome, but they let them sit on the veranda, close enough for chatting, laughing and joking. In Mahadeo and Bijri's tone of voice there was a genuine affection, and their invitation could not be ignored.

The house covered quite a large area. On both the east and west boundaries there were hedges of thorny *putus* bush, and on the north side was the house, consisting of three adjacent buildings with wooden walls and tiled roofs. There was a spacious yard in front, and the view to the south was completely open.

Dharma and Kushi left the village road and went into Mahadeo and Bijri's yard where they sat down a little way away from them. The untouchable labourers needed no warning, for since birth they had observed the traditional prescripts and kept their distance from people of higher castes.

Bijri said, 'Have you been to have Master-ji count your money?'

Dharma nodded. 'Yes,' he said.

Bijri and Mahadeo were among the very few people whom Dharma and Kushi had told about their savings; they trusted them and regarded them 'as their own'. And Bijri and Mahadeo also thought of Dharma and Kushi as their own, too. Both couples had good reason for this.

Bijri was about thirty, Mahadeo nearer forty, and they had been married for fifteen or sixteen years without any children. Two years of marriage went by, five years, ten years, twelve years passed, but Bijri and Mahadeo were unable to produce a child. The people of Chaukad would not look them in the face, especially Bijri, for an infertile woman was as unwanted as barren land; it was a curse to look upon her, a curse to fall under her shadow. In fact, Bijri and Mahadeo had been more or less ostracised in Chaukad village. As far as was possible no one spoke with them, and the Dark Milkman had even been virtually excommunicated from his caste. That had been around the time when he and Bijri first met Dharma and Kushi, when they had just started to come and go through Chaukad village on their way from the Garudiya market. Dharma and Kushi would chat for quite a while as the glum and rejected Bijri and Mahadeo sat quietly to one side. Kushi had explained the cause of their dejection to an old aunt, from whom she brought all sorts of roots and things for Bijri to eat. The aunt knew quite a bit of occult medicine and many incantations, and whether it was on account of her treatment or some other cause, Bijri at last had a baby. Her social standing immediately was enhanced and Mahadeo was restored to his caste. For this reason they bore untold gratitude to Kushi and Dharma.

Now Mahadeo said, 'How much more money do you need to break free from your Rajput Singh?'

'Master-ji says we need a great deal more,' answered Dharma.

'Hurry up and get it,' said Bijri. Then she turned and said to Kushi, 'Do you know what we're going to give for your wedding?'

At the mention of marriage, Kushi just sat there and said nothing, her head bowed.

Bijri went on, 'We'll give you lots of clothes, a silver comb, silver necklace, earrings, fine quality cloth, a pair of shoes ...'

The ghee was cooking away on the fire beside her and gradually thickening. Kushi and Dharma had not noticed earlier that rice was simmering on a wood stove beside the one on which the ghee was being prepared. A little beyond the stoves so many *saphediya* and Queen of the Night flowers were blooming, and their perfume, the aroma of the steaming rice, the smell of the thickening ghee, and the talk of marriage and expensive presents coming from the Fair Milkwoman all together seemed like a wondrous dream to Kushi.

While Bijri was talking there came the sound of the baby crying from inside the house. Apparently they had lulled the child to sleep before sitting down to prepare the ghee, and now, at the sound of his crying, Bijri ran into the house. A little later she returned, cajoling the baby she held clasped to her breast. 'Don't cry my little one, don't cry, don't cry!'

The child's crying at being suddenly woken up did not stop, so Bijri had no choice but to sit back, undo her blouse and suckle him, while continually saying, 'Oh, my gold and silver, my little diamond, my ruby. I'll bring you a memsahib from Calcutta for your wife. Don't cry, now, don't cry!'

Smiling, Mahadeo said, 'Listen, Dharma, Kushi. Listen to the grand daydreams of the Fair Milkwoman. She'll bring him a memsahib from Calcutta for his wife. Ha! Ha! Ha!'

Bijri turned around and said, 'I will indeed. I'll certainly bring him one.'

After taking his milk the child was now satisfied and quiet. Bijri fondled her one-and-a-half or two-year-old boy, who was like a lump of butter, tweaking his nose, kissing him, and saying, 'Oh, Kitten, my little kitten - '

Feigning a look of sadness Mahadeo said to Dharma and Kushi, 'Just look. See how she treasures him, making herself no more than a kitten's mother.' And he looked towards his wife and said, 'Hey, Fair Memsahib, what about doting a little on me?'

Bijri took a stick of firewood and reached over to give her husband a gentle smack on the back. 'Be quiet,' she said, 'you disgraceful Dark Milkman.' She called her husband Dark Milkman only in great affection.

The wife, her husband and their child – what a lovely, happy family they made. Kushi's eyes flashed and sparkled, spreading their silver glow. She glanced sidelong at Dharma out of the corner of her eye, and noticed that he too was looking at her. A slight smile played on both their faces.

After a few moments Dharma said, 'It's become very late. We've got a long way to go. We'd better leave now.'

'No, no,' said Bijri. 'You must eat before you go.' Like the schoolmaster, they too did not want to let their visitors go without having eaten. Dharma and Kushi made their objections on account of the lateness of the hour, but Bijri and Mahadeo brushed them away, and eventually they sat down to eat.

Bijri was an exceptionally efficient woman who seemed to work with ten hands. She set the baby in Mahadeo's lap, took the pan of ghee from the stove and put it inside the house. Taking the big pot of rice off the other stove she cut some banana leaves from the garden, set some before Kushi and Dharma and, a little distance away, for herself and Mahadeo.

It was a simple meal of steaming hot rice, boiled sweet potatoes, a drizzling of fresh ghee, dal and mint chutney. As they ate and talked about this and that, suddenly something occurred to Mahadeo. He said, 'Oh, Dharma, I heard that Raghunath-ji was distributing sweets at his mansion today.'

'Yes,' said Dharma. 'Who told you?'

'Ramlachhman-ji came this evening, just as it was getting dark. He said to go to Raghunath-ji's residence, where the best of *laddus* would surely be given out. But we had an order for twenty seers of ghee, so we couldn't go. But why was he giving out *laddus*? There's no festival yet.'

'The great master's going to be an emlay. He brought the ticket for becoming an emlay from Patna.'

'Is that so?'

'Yes.'

After dinner Dharma and Kushi cleared away their own scraps, threw some water over where they had been eating, and took their leave. As they were leaving Bijri reminded Dharma once again to hurry up and arrange for the mark of marriage to go on Kushi's forehead.

They passed through Chaukad and came to another village, and another after that, passing through one village after another as they crossed the fields of Chhotanagpur. They all presented the same picture, one of domestic loveliness bonded by that kind of love and affection, joy and playfulness, common to people who lived free and happy lives under the eternal sky. And as they passed through all these villages, the young untouchable bonded labourer and his young untouchable bonded woman felt an intense yearning in their hearts, thinking that when they got their freedom from the hand of the great master, Raghunath Singh, they too would be able to set up such a home and family.

After a little while they reached the highway again. The road was now completely deserted. The sky with the countless stars looked like it was embroidered with silver, while here and there among the trees and bushes masses of fireflies glimmered as they fluttered on the breeze.

Dharma and Kushi walked on side by side in the soft, dreamy light of the moon. Then Dharma put his arm around Kushi's shoulder and drew her to him, and as they walked close together he said, 'Dairy people, brahman people, kayastha people, they all have such happy homes.'

'Yes.' The word rose up from inside Kushi's breast. They had left Chaukad village quite some time back, yet Bijri's words still seemed to ring in Kushi's ears. Bijri had often been at Dharma 'to arrange for the vermilion', and now she had given cause to hope for valuable wedding presents – silver necklace, silver earrings and combs, clothes.

Softly Dharma said, 'We'll make a home just like theirs.'

'Yes,' Kushi said, seriously.

Every night, having come through all the villages amid the fields and up onto the highway, they had this conversation, resolving to realise their dreams of home and family.

A little later Kushi said very quietly, 'We must hurry and pay back our debt to the great master.'

'Yes,' said Dharma, 'we must.'

'I don't like us living apart any more.'

'Oh, my dusky sweetheart!' and as he spoke he suddenly surrendered to the urge to throw his arms around Kushi and hold her close. Like a strong vine Kushi's arms gradually reached up to Dharma's neck, enclosing him and bringing his mouth down onto hers. Then, under the free and boundless sky in the moonlit fields in the cruel world of men, a bondman and a bondwoman stood for quite some time, like a sculpture.

Then they loosened their arms and let them fall from one another. Gently Dharma said, 'Let's go.'

A little later, having buried their box in the sand of the *sabui* grass jungle, they returned to the untouchables' colony.

7

On one side of the jungle of *sabui* grass beside the dry bed of the Koel, there was a hard, stony and uncultivable tract known locally as 'the wasteland', stretching as far as one could see. It was so hard and strewn with rocks that nothing would grow there apart from dry, yellow grass and weeds, a few date palms, and one or two varieties of ugly, twisted trees.

This tract fell within the personal domain of Raghunath Singh. To one side of it a large number of suffocatingly small mud shanties stood pushed up against one another. The mud was flaking off the walls of most of them, and although the small holes in the walls may have been called windows, they had neither bars nor shutters. Sheets of beaten tin or pieces of cheap timber served as doors, which were so small that one had to crouch in order to get through them. Not even light nor air could easily enter, and many of the huts were like those of primitive man in the earliest of times. This was the colony of Dharma and the others of the dosad community where, notwithstanding all the empty space in the world, each inhabitant enjoyed a dwelling area of no more than seven or eight square feet. The colony must have been one of the world's most densely populated.

A long time ago, maybe fifty or sixty years, even a hundred or a hundred and fifty, Raghunath Singh's forebears established this colony for Dharma's forebears, where untouchable bonded labourers and their families, imbued with all the contempt of the world, set up home far away from the market-villages and the big towns.

Dharma and Kushi could see from the distance that the dosad colony had not yet gone to sleep, as kerosene lamps were still flickering in the shanties. Then, all of a sudden, they heard the sounds of a loud commotion as though some fearsome altercation had broken out. In the dosad colony violent brawls could erupt over anything, trifling or extraordinary or for no reason at all, and when they did, the trafficking of abuse and obscenity would cause the hawks and crows to take to flight for at least ten miles.

As Dharma and Kushi came close to the neighbourhood, they caught sight of their parents, four elderly people, standing outside their doors on the dirt road. Seeing Dharma and Kushi, the elderly people started beating their breasts and wailing, immediately prompting the question, 'What's the matter? Why're you making all this noise?'

Their parents were getting quite old. Their skin was a mesh of wrinkles, they had lost most of their teeth, and their hair was like jute fibre. The two old men were wearing just a few grimy rags around their waists, and the women were wearing not much more, barely covering their breasts and their legs down to the knees.

They spoke so quickly through their wailing that their words could hardly be understood. Kushi and Dharma cried out, 'Stop making such a fuss! Just tell us what's happened!'

Along with their crying, which did not stop even for a moment, they delivered a rebuke. Spinning their words out as they went on weeping, the four old people demanded, 'Where are our sweets? The great master was giving them out.'

Apparently the news of the sweets distribution had by now reached the dosad colony. Those who had gone along with Dharma to the great master's mansion had already come back and talked about it.

It had been two years since Kushi's and Dharma's parents had worked in Raghunath Singh's fields. Once they had got old, they no longer had the strength for toil, and being unable to work made it pointless for the master to maintain them with rations or clothing. However, for as long as they could remember the four old people had got their rations in return for their work on Raghunath Singh's land, which they did in order to pay off the debts of their forebears. They had had no idea of when their youth or their middle age had come and gone. Year after year they had fertilised with their own blood and sweat the harsh, hard soil of Chhotanagpur and reaped the harvest for Raghunath Singh. But now they were old, they were simply cast aside.

However, the great master, Raghunath Singh, was magnanimous. Although they had been rejected for agricultural labour, he had not forgotten them. He had remembered to count out *laddus* – fine *laddus* made from pure ghee – and send some to each of them. The four old people had not been able to go to him themselves and receive the sweets from his own hand, yet he would not deny them their share.

Most of the people of the dosad colony, worn out from toiling in the fields for the whole day, would come home as soon as evening had fallen, bolt down some food, and sleep like the dead until they woke again before dawn, but today lamps were burning throughout the whole neighbourhood and Dharma's and Kushi's parents were standing outside their shanty on the road, all because their master, Raghunath Singh, had distributed *laddus*. In the lives of these people, getting sweets from the hand of Raghunath Singh was a genuine cause for celebration, a matter for great excitement. Even at this hour of night, that excitement had let no one go to sleep.

'Who told you that the great master had given out sweets?' Dharma asked.

'Everyone!' they cried out. 'Two *laddus* each. We went to the gathering at the great master's house. Munshi-ji told us to get them from you, as he had given them to you himself.'

Dharma and Kushi stood gaping for a moment. They had not imagined that these old people could go running off all that way for sweets.

Then the parents started crying out again, 'Where are our sweets then? Where are they?'

Dharma told them there was no reason to be upset for they had the sweets with them, but it did not seem that the elderly people were greatly reassured, for they kept on crying out, 'Give us our *laddus* now! Give us them now!'

'All right, old ones, you will get your *laddus*, don't be so impatient. But first go inside, and then you'll get them.'

'Do we have to die first? Why shouldn't we be impatient for our share of the *laddus*!'

As they went inside a loud hubbub started to be heard from many other shanties, undoubtedly disputations over the sharing of sweets.

***

Dharma and Kushi lived with their parents in two adjacent huts near the road just at the entrance to the dosad colony. Their huts were so close together that even words spoken quietly in one could be heard quite clearly in the other.

When they got inside they struck a match and lit their lamps, and then Dharma and Kushi satisfied their parents with the sweets due to them, bringing smiles to their faces. For a few moments they turned the costly *laddus* over in their hands, looking at them by the light of the lamp with avid and sparkling eyes, and then they started to eat them. When they had finished, they said to Dharma and Kushi, 'Now you must eat.' But this time they were talking about the evening meal.

Dharma and Kushi explained that they had been to Chaukad

village and eaten at the house of the Fair Milkwoman and the Black Milkman, so they would not eat any more now. This was nothing new, as once or twice a week the two of them would come home from Chaukad village having already had their evening meal. Nevertheless, their parents protested that today something very special had been cooked and they would be quite upset if their children did not eat it.

In their neighbouring huts Dharma and Kushi asked, 'What have you cooked?' and learned that it was rice, a curry of *suthani* yams and meat.

At the sound of the word 'meat' in Kushi's place, her eyes lit up, as did Dharma's in his. 'What kind of meat?' each of them asked.

'Wild pigeon.'

'Where did you get it?'

'In the forest, where we went to dig for *suthani*. It had been wounded, probably by some animal or a hawk, and could no longer fly. So we brought it home.'

Although they had been cast off by Raghunath Singh, the elderly parents still got hungry and thirsty, but they did not get a skerrick for their stomachs from the great master. But how could they survive if they did not eat? Whatever was left over from the rations Dharma and Kushi got from the master's granaries was hardly enough to keep their parents going, and so they had to provide somehow for themselves.

Dharma's parents got on exceptionally well with Kushi's parents, never experiencing cause for a quarrel. Many of the people in the dosad colony envied them for their amity. And come what may, they had to go three miles every day to the jungle beside the Koel in search of food. There they found such things as roots and tubers and sweet potatoes, and edible leaves and vines, and very occasionally a rabbit or some kind of bird, like the wild pigeon they had got today. Whenever they got some kind of meat, their shanties took on something of a festive air.

Dharma and Kushi had quite satisfied themselves at Bijri and

Mahadeo's house, but could they not manage three or four mouthfuls of rice with meat? Indeed they could, but ultimately they did not. They both told their mothers to put their share of the meat, the rice and the curry away and they would eat it all next morning before going to work in the fields. 'Put some water with the rice to keep it moist,' they said. It was indeed unusual for two people's meals to be saved like this, and that was a most remarkable thing for a dosad family.

All the shanties in the dosad colony looked much the same. Some of them would have cheap enamel plates, earthenware vessels, a handful of simple, grubby clothes, and some ragged pillows, hessian bed covers and grey, dust-laden blankets nibbled by mice. In a few shanties a charpoy of woven coconut fibre on a bamboo frame might be found. Dharma and Kushi's places were much the same, except that there was no charpoy in Kushi's place whereas there was one in Dharma's, on which he would sleep at night with a torn and flattened pillow. This was the one luxury of his life.

It was now very late, but although the dosad colony was dozing, it was not fully asleep. From the distance came the gentle sound of Nathwa's wife's singing her baby to sleep:

Sleep now, my darling child.
You have roamed the whole town through.
Come, Sleep, come.
My darling now is lying down.
My darling wants to sleep,
having roamed throughout the town.
Oh, give him milk to drink.
Come, Sleep, come.

From the shanties of Mungeri, Bhirgulal and Gulabi came the indistinct sound of conversation. However, what could be heard most clearly was the sound of Ganjuram's mother's continual weeping.

Dharma was lying flat on his back on the coir charpoy. He turned slightly onto his side and saw in the dim darkness his mother and father lying against the wall but not yet sleeping. 'Why is Ganju's mother crying?'

'Ganju ate her *laddus*,' Dharma's mother replied.

That was typical of Ganju. He was extraordinarily selfish. Dharma knew that Ganju's mother's wailing would go on for the rest of the night. He said, 'He's a rotten pig.'

After a little while Dharma's mother and father fell asleep with a strange sound like a sigh, but even after an entire day of back-breaking work sleep would not come to Dharma. He knew that only ten feet away in another room Kushi's parents would be in a deep sleep, and that their daughter would be wide awake.

As on any other night Dharma just lay there, thoughts of the contractors and the dairy folk – especially Bijri and Mahadeo – going around in his mind and of how they all nagged him daily about making a wife of his dark-skinned girl, Kushi, and their telling them what wedding presents they would give them.

Dharma also wondered when their bonded life with Raghunath Singh would come to an end, when they would be free after paying off the debt incurred by their forebears. Without freedom there could be no question of marriage. Dharma heaved a long, deep sigh. Maybe in another room, only ten feet away, a bonded dosad girl, her eyes wide open, was having the same thoughts.

Dharma's musing lapsed into sleep, and so ended another day in their lives.

8

THE LIVES OF THE UNTOUCHABLE BONDED LABOURERS WERE quite uneventful. After a gap of five or six years, something greatly significant had occurred only yesterday. Indeed, none of the dosads had ever heard of anything as sensational as the great master, Raghunath Singh, distributing with his own hand sweets made of the purest ghee to untouchable labourers like themselves. Indeed, those people of the colony who were very old – sixty, seventy, approaching a hundred, even – could remember nothing like it, nor had they ever heard of such a thing from their parents or grandparents. And so the matter of Raghunath Singh's distribution of sweets would keep the dosads in excitement for a good few months, and they would come to talk about it time and time again.

Except for the occasional incident, the lives of the untouchable labourers were as dull and motionless as the meagre stream of a river amongst the sandbanks in summer. Since this country had become independent, so many successive five-year plans had elapsed, and so many elections had come and gone with campaigners rending the heavens with their resounding slogans and exhortations. In the last ten or twenty years the number of trucks, buses and motor cars on the Patna-Ranchi highway had increased twenty times. The cities had changed, with so much grandeur and so many magnificent new houses, an ever-flowing stream of gleaming new cars – both local and foreign – and so much expensive clothing and expensive food. And yet the condition of the untouchable labourers of Garudiya taluk remained no different from what it had been before Independence. The lives of these people were the other side of the coin of independent India's immense brilliance, untold comfort and great abundance. Not a glimmer of the splendour of independent India had fallen on their neighbourhoods; they continued to pass their lives in exactly the same way as their forefathers had twenty, fifty, one hundred years ago, with no advancement in their way of life at all. For them, today was always the same as yesterday, yesterday was the same as the day before, and the day before was the same as the day before that. Difficult to distinguish one day from another, all their days were but one and the same.

***

As on any other day, the dosad colony was awake while it was still dark. For the dosads, no sooner would one day end than another would seem to begin. While everyone else would be awake for quite some time after sunset, the dosads would be asleep, and in the dark before the dawn when everyone else was still in bed, these bonded labourers would be wide awake, for as soon as the sun rose they would have to assemble before Himgirinandan at the farm compound of the great master. In what little time there was left they would have to prepare their meals.

Stoves were being lit in all the shanties to heat the leftover rice. Having had this for their breakfast, some of them would make a midday meal of maize or chick-pea flour with some raw chilli, salt and a little tamarind chutney, which they would take to the fields. Others would do the exact opposite, having maize or chick-pea flour at dawn and leftover rice at noon, with maybe some vegetable or other.

In Dharma's place the cooking was being done in a corner of the veranda, where his mother had lit the stove and had put the rice on.

His father was sitting a little way away, coughing continually his old, phlegmy cough. Dharma was sitting on one side, leaning against a worm-eaten bamboo post, by now having had his 'bath'. Raghunath Singh's father or grandfather had once dug a well for the convenience of his bonded labourers. With the accumulation of sand its water had become greatly reduced, and a few times it had been almost blocked up altogether. Raghunath Singh had had it cleared out three or four times, the last time being a good ten years back, but now the sand had built up anew leaving only a trickle at the bottom of the well. This meagre blackish water was quite insufficient for the whole colony in this hot weather. Dharma had drawn a little water before the others had woken up and poured it over his head. Of course, he could have walked two miles to the dried-up bed of the Koel and dug for some water from the sand and brought it back to wash himself, but had he gone all that way he could not have been at the farm compound by sunrise.

The shortage of water in this month of Jyaistha was a cause of great difficulty here and would continue if the well were not cleared of sand. However, no one was brave enough to go and speak to the great master. For some years they had been going to Himgirinandan with repeated requests and pleas for clearing away the sand, but they all went in one ear and out the other.

While Dharma was sitting on the veranda looking into the distance, a crowd had gathered at the well and a loud and abusive clamour was being raised over the sharing of the water. This was a daily occurrence in the dosad colony every summer, and their days would always begin with a commotion of shouting and quarrelling.

Dharma's eyes wandered from the well to rest on Kushi's place, where her mother too had put leftover rice on the stove and Kushi was running a cheap plastic comb through her dried and tangled hair. Once she had her comb in her hand, Kushi had no consciousness of time. Combing her hair was her one real indulgence, but the girl did not seem to understand that those whose every minute belongs to the great master cannot waste time on their hair.

It was getting brighter in the east and Dharma called out to her, 'Hurry up and finish doing your hair. The sun'll be up in no time.'

Kushi turned to him and said impatiently, 'All right, I'm coming,' and vigorously ran the comb through her thick hair.

In all the shanties the poor quality rice was now frothing and bubbling and its sour smell was floating on the breeze throughout the neighbourhood. It was only the very old rice that was rationed to the dosads from the great master's granaries.

As he sat on the veranda, Dharma saw Mangilal taking out his two monkeys and his goat, as he did every day. Mangilal and his three animals were all dressed in the same way, with shirts made of a patchwork of pieces of coloured cloth. Mangilal also wore patched pajamas and a turban made from the excess of the same material.

Mangilal had no family – no wife, no children – and had only himself in all the world. He too was a dosad, like Dharma and his family, but was not one of Raghunath Singh's bonded labourers. His father had been a one-generation bondsman, and at the time that he took a loan from Raghunath Singh it was written in the document of loan that as long as he was bodily able he would be given food in return for labour; however, neither his sons nor his wife would have to inherit that obligation. Thus Mangilal was an independent man and a very fortunate one at that. His trade took him to the marketplaces of Garudiya, Bijuri and even further afield, putting on his animal act with his two monkeys and the goat. By and large, the money he earned from this was enough to feed him and his animals. Dharma secretly envied the independent Mangilal.

Mangilal was singing to himself.

Dance, little monkey, dance!
You're so lovely and bubbly

and wibbly wubbly,
swinging your hips
and swishing your tail
as you dance,
my darling little monkey!

It was a song for the monkeys' dance, and he had been unconsciously singing that one song for twenty or twenty-five years.

Dharma called to him, 'Hey, Uncle Mangi!'

Mangilal stopped his singing and turned around. 'What is it?'

'Where are you going today?'

'Not too far. I'll go to Chaukad.'

'When will you come back?' Dharma asked him.

There was no necessity for any of these questions. Moreover, there was really nothing in common in the ways of life of the two men. Dharma was a servile bonded labourer, Mangilal was a free man. Dharma envied and respected all the free men of the world, and so Mangilal was, to him, a particularly important man – both respectable and enviable – and so he felt important, too, talking with him.

'I'll come back once it gets dark,' Mangilal replied.

'Where will you go tomorrow?'

'If I don't feel well I won't be going anywhere – tomorrow, or the day after, or the day after that or the day after that.'

Mangilal might not leave the dosad colony for the next four days and he would not have to give anyone an explanation nor would Himgiri send his man to drag him by the scruff of the neck and order his rations to be cut. With a profound sigh Dharma said, 'You're all right, Uncle Mangi. You're really lucky. You don't have to be chained to your work like us.'

Mangilal had heard this kind of talk from Dharma many

times. He did not stay any longer, but went on his way with his animals.

Mangilal had not gone very far when along came Phaguram. Like Mangilal, Phaguram too was an independent man whose father had been a one-generation bondsman in whose document of loan it had been written that no one born to him would have to inherit bonded labour. However, Raghunath Singh – a most magnanimous man – would not drive anyone from the dosad colony, even though he may have obtained his freedom, or become physically disabled, but would let him stay as long as he wanted to.

At one time Phaguram used to sing in rustic folk musical theatre – a *nautanki* troupe – but then he became weak with age. He developed a chest complaint singing night after night in Muzafarpur, Purnia and Bhagalpur districts and became very sick. Now he did not have the strength to stay awake at night, nor could he find the breath to keep himself going for four or five hours at a stretch. As a result, he had to leave the troupe. Despite his frailty and shortness of breath, however, Phaguram still had a fine singing voice, as sweet and enchanting as that of a young man. Those who heard him sing said that his voice was magical. Some called him 'the Nightingale of Garudiya'.

For the last three or four years, since leaving the troupe, Phaguram had earned some money by singing solo. Everyday at dawn he would go along the highway to the railway station. Outside the station, under a luxuriant, shady pipal tree, he would sit and sing, accompanying himself on a battered old harmonium. Nowadays the number of train travellers had increased greatly, and Phaguram would earn well the whole day.

'Are you off now?' asked Dharma.

'Yes.' Phaguram nodded.

There were a few other independent men like Mangilal and Phaguram in the dosad colony, supporting themselves by various means. For example, Birkhu dug for the contractors, Mungeri carried goods for bus travellers, and Lakhiya chopped wood in the timber yard at Garudiya market. They all went off to their work, one after the other. Dharma's shanty was very close to the main road, so the people of the dosad colony had to come and go past it. Dharma would sit on his veranda and watch them all go by.

After a few of them had passed, along came the old woman, Shaukhi, tapping with her twisted stick. In the meantime, Dharma's mother had taken the rice off the stove. Dharma had noticed before that as soon as his mother took the rice off, Shaukhi would immediately turn up – not a moment before, not a moment after. The old woman had an amazingly keen sense of time.

It was hard to tell if Shaukhi was seventy or eighty or even near a hundred. She needed her stick to support her stooped back. Her skin sagged in wrinkles, her hair was like pellets of hemp, and there was not a remnant of a tooth in her gums. Her eyes were lifeless and had cataracts like thin films of milk, making her sight very dim.

Shaukhi's name had long been removed from the extensive list of bonded labourers that Raghunath Singh kept in his safe, yet once when she was strong, she used to do back-breaking work on the great master's land. Shaukhi now had no one in the world, although there had been a son, Ganesh – or Gana – who also had been a bonded labourer of Raghunath Singh; however, in the depths of the night some years back he ran away from Garudiya. Raghunath Singh's lapdog, Himgirinandan, kicked up no end of a fuss about it, for any boss would have been slighted if a bondsman had run away like that. In his opinion there was not enough control over the other bonded labourers. Although the whole dosad colony was turned over from time to time, there was never any trace of Gana.

Since Gana had run away, Shaukhi's circumstances had got worse, though her stomach still wanted to be satisfied. Now she was a beggar, and would get up at daybreak to wander around so many of the villages of Garudiya taluk seeking alms. However, no one gave her rice, though some gave maize and some gave cash, maybe two or three paisa. She had great trouble chewing the grains of maize with her toothless gums, and so in hope of a little rice the old woman would appear at Dharma's shanty at dawn each day, seeming to sense that Dharma felt some compassion for her. However, Dharma's mother would get quite angry whenever she saw Shaukhi in the early morning. They were such a terribly poor family, whose three stomachs had somehow or other to get by on the rations of one man. How could they manage if they had to share their daily rice with her?

Today, as on other days, Dharma's mother shouted venomously, 'You old beggar, go and eat your head in shame! You jackal! Every day you have no qualms about going from one house to another, gobbling rice. Clear off! Get out!'

Shaukhi was impervious to all this abuse. She just smiled her toothless smile and lurched up onto the veranda with her stick and her begging-bowl and sat down.

Dharma's mother became heated. 'Who asked you to sit here? Clear off right now!' And she tried to shoo the old woman away as one does a dog or a cat or a crow.

Shaukhi did not answer, but looked piteously at Dharma.

Dharma said to his mother, 'Give her a little. She's not just anybody.'

Dharma's mother raised her voice a little louder. 'Who is she to us? What are we to do? Everyday she comes here. Is there no one else in the neighbourhood? Let her go somewhere else.'

'How much longer can she survive!' Dharma said. 'Go on, give her just a little rice.'

His mother went on grumbling: this old woman would not die so easily, she would go on like a jackal for another twenty or twenty-five years sucking the marrow from their bones. Of course she was angry, but she could not ignore the words of her son, their one and only breadwinner. She put a little of the starchy liquor in which the rice had been cooked along with some salt on a *shal* leaf and pushed it towards Shaukhi. Her mouth watering, Shaukhi very carefully drew the now fermenting gruel to herself, and as she ate, her purblind eyes lit up.

Dharma said, 'You're only giving the old woman rice water? What about the meat you cooked last night?'

Dharma had scarcely got the words out when his mother screamed, 'There's none left, you devil! And if you've got any more to say I'll set the old hag's face on fire!'

She had shown quite enough magnanimity in giving Shaukhi a share of the rice water, and Dharma did not have the temerity to insist on her giving some meat as well. His mother asked him, 'What are you going to eat out in the fields – flattened rice or leftover rice?'

As he had eaten the night before at Bijri and Mahadeo's house, his mother had saved his share of the rice in a little water. Dharma thought for a moment, then said that he would eat the leftover rice now. He would take the flattened rice and the meat to the fields to have as his midday meal.

Dharma's mother put the leftover rice kept from the night before onto a battered, cheap enamel plate along with some of the previous night's vegetables and served her son, then her husband and herself. Having put something in their stomachs first thing in the morning, they would then have to go out in search of food.

They ate in silence. With a look of profound satisfaction on her face as she ate the foul-smelling, rancid rice water, Shaukhi said, 'I won't be troubling you for many days more, Dharma's ma.'

Dharma's mother did not answer. She just frowned at Shaukhi in intense anger and disgust.

Again Shaukhi said, 'I'm leaving Garudiya.'

Startled, Dharma asked, 'Really?'

His mother cried out from the other side of the veranda, 'The old woman's going to leave this place! Then who'll suck the marrow from our bones? Huh! What a load of rubbish.'

Shaukhi's mouth was full of rice water. Somehow she swallowed it and, waving her hand impatiently, said, 'No, no, Dharma's ma. It's absolutely true. I'm leaving.'

'When, you old vulture?'

'In three or four days. Yesterday I went to beg at the station. I met Gana there.'

Again Dharma was startled. 'Gana!'

Slowly Shaukhi waggled her head on her skinny neck and said, 'Yes. Gana.'

Dharma's father, Shiulal, was a man of few words who said little and listened a lot. However, even he became excited. 'Your eyes are no good any more,' he said. 'Were you able to recognise him for certain?'

'Yes, yes, of course. He spoke with me. A mother might be blind, but she'll still recognise her own son, Dharma's baba.'

Just as Dharma was about to say something, he caught sight of Naorangi standing surreptitiously on the road in front of their veranda. It was anyone's guess how long she had been there. Just the sight of her sent a shiver down Dharma's spine.

Naorangi was a middle-aged woman who, like Dharma, belonged to the dosad caste. Despite her age she was still lithe and robust of body, her eyes flashed like lightning, and her glamorous dressiness was just as dazzling. She was wearing a very showy, embroidered Gazipuri sari in rich colours and her eyes showed a thin remnant of collyrium. A silver, net-like comb was inserted in her now dishevelled bun. She wore a broad, silver necklace, and on her breast hung a locket in the shape of a fish; there were rings on her toes and she wore a nose stud.

Naorangi had no one in all the world. Three times she had been married within her caste, but each had ended within three or four months. Having been married three times, it was not in her fate to be married again, yet for that Naorangi was not at all regretful.

She had been only fifteen or sixteen when she was first wed, and her parents were still living. Although she was married, she had caught the eye of Raghunath Singh, who straightaway sent his expensive silver-studded palanquin with its eight bearers for this girl who looked like a flower. And so her days were spent in her husband's shanty in the dosad colony, and her nights belonged to Raghunath Singh in his pleasure chamber. No one would demur in the slightest at the great master's extending his favours to an untouchable girl. Just like all the land and the trees, the birds and the animals, the rivers and the canals of Garudiya, the untouchable bonded labourers were also his personal domain and he could enjoy whoever took his fancy.

Naorangi married again when her first marriage had broken up, and her third marriage was celebrated three years later. Of course, the great master would not have objected to a third or even a fourteenth marriage. In the daytime she would be subject to her husband, but when night fell, she would ascend her silver-embellished palanquin.

After about ten years of this, however, Raghunath Singh's interest waned. As the crane is able to select the best fish, so he took for himself another woman, having no more enthusiasm for a now older, much handled, well used Naorangi. Since her parents had died, Naorangi had had to live apart from her third husband, but that offered no great bother for her, for after Raghunath Singh had cast her aside, she was kept by Himgirinandan, who was able to offer her substantial compensation.

For the brahman Himgiri, keeping a woman who had been another's mistress, especially one enjoyed by a less eminent, Rajput kashatriya was something not very respectable. However, no matter that the master's caste might be somewhat lower, it was not very likely that Himgiri's own caste would be violated by enjoying the master's leftovers. Himgiri was quite gratified, by and large, and so too was

Naorangi. Indeed, in Garudiya, Himgiri was the most powerful man after Raghunath Singh, and although his prestige was somewhat less, this affair did not cast any shadow of scandal over his face. He continued to hold undiminished power over the dosad colony, and no one would dare scruple at his keeping a mistress.

Each evening Naorangi would get dressed up like a charming peahen and sit and wait. In her time with Raghunath Singh a silver-embellished palanquin used to come for her, but under the patronage of Himgirinandan she would go and come in a buffalo cart.

Being the mistress of the great master or the high-caste brahman was not viewed as scandalous among the dosads, for such had been the custom for generations. The beautiful young women of bonded labourers had always been an object of enjoyment for their masters, and no one worried themselves greatly about this. Indeed, there was even a kind of social status attached to being connected with influential men, and such women still enjoyed some deference from people of their own community – except that the opposite was the case with Naorangi. Everyone of the dosad community both hated and feared her, and they would mentally spit at the mention of her name. Of course, they kept their feelings secret, for who would want to make trouble for himself by revealing them!

The reason for all this fear and hostility concerning Naorangi emanated from the fact that she would take to Himgiri details of all the petty incidents of the dosad colony – who was doing what, who was thinking what. In fact, it was from Naorangi that Himgiri first heard that Gana had run away. The management of Raghunath Singh's vast estate and its countless bonded labourers was not an easy job, and it was at present gradually getting more difficult. Although they continued to bend their backs cultivating the land as they had done for so many years, one still had to be very watchful, as things were now changing – from time to time disturbing stories would come from Bhojpur or Purnia about people in the city inciting unrest among bonded peasants.

Therefore Himgiri needed to be forewarned about his bonded labourers, and such information was provided to him by Naorangi. For that reason no one wanted to say anything in front of her, as far as was possible.

Shaukhi, with her dim and hazy eyes, had not seen Naorangi. She just went on as before, 'Gana's got a good job. He earns a hundred rupees. In three or four days he'll come and take me away.'

How could anyone have warned Shaukhi of the danger of saying all of this in front of Naorangi? She would not have been able to see any meaningful facial gesture, and Dharma, unable to do anything, was becoming afraid. Even his mother, who had daggers in her eyes for Shaukhi, was now terribly worried for her and secretly called upon the gods by whose grace Gana might be freed from danger.

Naorangi did not wait around. With her precious piece of news she went off towards her own shanty near the well.

When Naorangi had gone some distance, Dharma's mother muttered in emphatic annoyance, 'You silly old bitch. That she-devil was standing there and you went on talking about Gana. You want to kill your own son!'

'What she-devil?' Shaukhi looked up.

'Who's the she-devil in this neighbourhood? There's only one – that Naorangi.'

'Did Naorangi hear about Gana?' Shaukhi's face paled in fear.

'Yes, you blind old woman. Are you killing your son with your own hands?'

At that Shaukhi slapped herself on the head and whimpered, 'What have I done! I've put Gana's life in danger! O, Lord Ram!' And the sound of her sobbing drifted off through the dosad colony on the early morning breeze.

9

AFTER HE HAD EATEN, DHARMA SET OUT WITH HIS TIN BOX containing his midday meal of leftover rice and meat, chilli and salt. He also took three cloth bags and a big bottle, for today was the day when he would get his ration of rice, maize, salt and so on, as well as kerosene for the lamp at night. Kushi would go with him, and she too had brought bags for her rations.

All the bonded dosads set out in a group – Dharma and Kushi, and Ganeri, Budheri, Kundri, Shanichari. A number of rejects also accompanied them – old people who, like Dharma's and Kushi's parents, had been deleted from Raghunath Singh's register as being weak and too old and no longer useful. Most of these discarded people would walk the three miles to the jungle beside the Koel each day in search of food. They would all take big earthenware pots; as there was no potable water in the dosad colony, they would have to dig for it in the sands of the river bed after they had gathered whatever food they could find. Some of them would then walk another two miles to the Maithili brahmans' village or to the Garudiya market where they would go around from house to house or shop to shop looking for any kind of work, such as roof repairing, carrying goods, house cleaning and the like, while others would go to graze Raghunath Singh's two or three hundred milch cows and goats.

'Be careful when you go into the jungle,' Dharma told his parents.

The old man and woman both nodded their heads.

'And don't linger there.'

'No.'

'Be sure to be back in the village before dark. Once it's dark, the bears'll be out to crush your bones.'

'Yes, we know.'

Dharma would give his parents these warnings every day when he set out for the fields.

Setting out with everyone else, the elderly Shaukhi sobbed inconsolably. 'What have I done? I've brought death upon my own son. Oh, Lord Ram! Oh, Lord Krishna! Save my Gana, save him, save him . . .' she cried.

Her crying filled Dharma with sadness. Gently he said to her, 'Don't cry, don't cry.'

But Shaukhi did not stop crying.

It suddenly occurred to Dharma to ask, 'Where's Gana working now, do you know?'

Shaukhi shook her head emphatically. 'No. I didn't ask.'

Dharma thought, only if he knew Gana's whereabouts, he could go to him at night after work and warn him. Disappointed, he said, 'This is a real mess. Now we can only depend on God's mercy.'

They had now reached the fork in the road between the dosad colony and the highway: one way led on to the main road, and the other led diagonally to the stony land and beyond, towards the southern Koel.

***

The elderly and other castoffs of the dosads went on from here, as they did every day, to the sandy bed of the river; others went across the fields to the distant market and villages; and Dharma and his companions walked on up to the highway and then to Raghunath Singh's farm compound. Shaukhi went with them, but along the way she went down into the fields on the other side of the highway, the sound of her whimpering drifting away on the breeze. Today she would cross the fields to the Maithilis' village.

By now the buses were starting to run along the highway between Ranchi and Patna, and cycle rickshaws, buffalo carts and the long-distance trucks were also starting out. Once the sun had come up, the highway would be bustling and noisy. It would not be long before it did emerge, as it was now becoming light in the east. From the back of the group the middle-aged Ganeri urged, 'It'll be daylight soon. We must hurry.' And so they all quickened their pace.

When they got to the farm compound, they saw that Himgirinandan was already there and sitting in his 'control room'. The Maithili brahman would have spent the night with Naorangi and, right at the crack of dawn, would have completed his bath, adorned his forehead with sandal paste, and come and sat in his own special place at the compound. He never wavered from this routine. Dharma and the others simply could not imagine getting to the compound and not seeing Himgiri sitting in his 'control room'.

Himgiri did not immediately address the dosads. With his eyes shut, swaying from side to side and gently clapping to mark the rhythm, he sang softly a verse from the *Ramcharitmanas*:

Earth and water, fire, sky and air -
In all of these consists
this worthless human body.

And so, having cultivated the body with Naorangi all night, at daybreak Himgiri would softly bewail its mortality and its worthlessness.

The rations were available from a long asbestos shed behind the 'control room', where Dharma and the others left their sacks, boxes and bottles with Ramdhaniya. They would not get their food rations until the evening, after their day's work, for it would be a great nuisance to carry their sacks and things with them to the fields. They took their ploughs and bullocks from Ramdhaniya and set out.

By the time they had reached the farm compound, the sun had come up. Far off in the east, beyond the dairy village and the Garudiya market, it looked like a bright red ball of fire. When the dosads left their neighbourhood before dawn, the breeze was quite cool, but now it was starting to get warmer and, as the sun got higher, it would get more and more fiery.

As they approached the fields, a bus coming from Ranchi pulled up on the side of the road under the big pipal tree that served as a bus stand. Whether the bus came from Ranchi or Patna, it would stop here for a few minutes for passengers, and then be off on its way again. Under the pipal tree three shops with old and cracked tin roofs had been set up: one sold paan and bidis, another sold tea and biscuits, the third sold chick-pea flour, salt and chillies. A barber had set a couple of bricks in place on which he attended throughout the day to the rustic men's hair and beards.

A few people got down from the bus and one of them called out as the bonded labourers approached, 'Hey Dharma! Dharma, ho!'

Dharma stopped suddenly. The man who was calling was now standing in front of him. He was Tirke.

Tirke was in his early forties, a tribal Christian from Ranchi, a short and healthy looking man with glistening, copper-coloured skin, small eyes, thick dark lips, and hair that stuck up. He was wearing khaki shorts and a white short-sleeve shirt, canvas shoes and, around his neck, a silver cross on a black cord. He worked as a waiter at a big hotel in Ranchi. In his boyhood days he had been close to the missionaries and now, with important foreigners continually coming to the big hotel, he was all the time prattling away in English.

Tirke often came from Ranchi to Garudiya to see Dharma. This was because of the strange fancies of the foreigners who bought the claws, teeth, horns, feathers and the like of the beasts and birds of this country and had charged Tirke with the responsibility of providing such things for them – or maybe Tirke was continually soliciting orders from them. But after his long hours of duty in the hotel, how could he manage to procure so many animal relics? Therefore, he had to maintain contact with men like Dharma. The foreigners usually paid generously for their souvenirs of animals and birds. Tirke kept half the payment and gave the other half to Dharma; if there was not much profit, what would be the point in taking all the trouble for it?

Already Dharma had earned good money providing the foreigners with animal skins through Tirke, and his arrival now would mean a little more money. Dharma was very excited as he greeted him. 'Hey, dada, it's you! What are you doing here so early in the morning?'

Tirke told him that he had taken the four o'clock morning bus from Ranchi.

'So what's the news?' Dharma asked.

'Something really big,' Tirke replied.

'Am I going to get any money?'

'Sure you will. You'll get quite a bit.'

Dharma waited, restlessly, his eyes gleaming. Eagerly he said, 'May you feast on sweets and ghee! But tell me quickly, dada, how much? I have to go to the fields now. I don't have time to stand and talk.'

'Go on,' said Tirke. 'We'll talk as we walk.'

'Right.'

As they walked towards the fields, Tirke said, 'An American has come. We have to get him a pair of young barking deer.'

'How much will he pay?'

'Ten.'

'No, no. That's not enough. I'll have to go to the jungle. I'll lose two or three days in the fields. My rations will be cut. Dada, you'll have to give me more.'

Tirke thought for a moment, and then said, 'All right. I'll get you twenty.'

'But – '

'No buts,' said Tirke. 'That's just your share. Don't talk any more about the money. Now listen. I'll come again the day after tomorrow. Have the pair of barking deer ready. The goods in your hand, the money in mine.'

'No, no, dada. Not the day after tomorrow. God knows how many days I'll have to spend in the jungle looking for barking deer. Give me seven days.'

'No, no. The American doesn't have that much time. I'll come again in three days.'

'No, give me an extra day. Come in four days.'

Tirke frowned and thought for a moment. 'All right,' he said. 'I'll be back in four days. Is it a deal, then?'

Dharma shrugged and said, 'It's a deal.'

Tirke waited no longer but turned and walked back towards the highway.

While he was talking, Dharma had fallen behind with Kushi beside him. She stuck to him like glue all the time. The other workers and their animals had got quite some way ahead by now. Dharma gave a twist to the tails of his bullocks, produced a strange sound in his throat, and called, 'Come on boys, get a move on!'

The bullocks quickened their pace, and so did Dharma and Kushi.

Kushi had said nothing so far. Now she spoke. 'You'll get twenty rupees?'

'Yes,' Dharma nodded slowly.

'That's a lot of money.'

Dharma did not answer her. He could only wonder how much there would be left to pay for their freedom once they got the twenty rupees. He would have to find out from the schoolmaster.

10

THE JYAISTHA MORNING WAS GETTING ON. IT WOULD NOT BE LONG before the sun was directly overhead, now that the shadows of trees and men were quickly becoming shorter. The wind had become dry and hot and was gusting about everywhere.

In the middle of the scorched field Dharma drove his plough in the same way as his forefathers had done, while Kushi ran along behind him, picking out roots and weeds. And on the other side in Bijuri taluk, beside the river bed, tractors drove about as they did on any other day, while on the highway there was no respite in the stream of buses and lorries and cycle rickshaws.

As on any other day this part of Garudiya presented the same picture, that of cultivating the fields. But a little while earlier a number of young men in jeeps, headed along the highway towards Bijuri, were shouting out, 'Vote for – '

'Raghunath Singh!'

Raghunath Singh had returned from Patna with his election endorsement only the day before, and already his men were out starting to canvass votes. From another field Ganeri, experienced and now advancing in years, remarked simply, 'The vote game has started.'

Just before noon Ramlachhman came along on a squeaky, rickety old bicycle. As Ajibchand was Raghunath Singh's bootlicker, so Ramlachhman licked the boots of the general factotum of the great master's farm compound, Himgirinandan. Ramlachhman's job was to supervise the work of the bonded labourers in Raghunath Singh's fields or, put more simply, to see who was cheating on the job, who was sitting around chatting, or who was loafing or not working at full pace, and, perforce, to report all this to Himgiri. There was no one who could throw dust in this jackal's eyes.

Ramlachhman had not gone to the fields the day before, so he would certainly make up for that today. As they went on driving their ploughs, Dharma and the others caught their breath in apprehension. It was not that he was a terrifying man in his speech or conduct, but rather that there was no certainty of when he might run off to Himgiri, the consequences of which could be perilous.

Ramlachhman leaned his bicycle against an unsightly *sisam* tree beside the field, straightened out his long, crane-like legs and sang a song of Ram and Sita – 'Ram and Sita went into exile in the forest – ' as he approached; he sang the same line as he went about the whole day. As Himgiri would always say 'D'you hear me?', Ramlachhman's catchphrase was his refrain, 'Ram and Sita went into exile in the forest.'

Although there were pious lyrics on his lips, Ramlachhman's mind was constantly in the gutter. He kept watchful eyes, certainly, on the toil of the bonded labourers, yet the same eyes revolved hungrily all the time over the robust, young untouchable women. Indeed, not only the untouchable women but any vivacious lass would excite him. He would stand up close to them, all the while singing his refrain. It was because of this that the people of Garudiya and Bijuri called him St Satan. The bonded labourers also spoke of him in this way, as well as calling him 'The Rat', as he was continually reporting them by name to Himgiri. He was so nasty that any trifling lapse on the part of a bonded labourer would immediately be whispered into the ear of Himgiri, and the hapless untouchable would have no comeback.

Seeing Ramlachhman in the distance set everyone on edge. In a suppressed voice Ganeri said, 'Be wary now.'

Others mumbled, 'The Rat is here,' while some of the more impetuous and daring of the young women said, 'Here comes Garudiya's St Satan.'

Singing his same line over and over again Ramlachhman wandered around from this field to that, his dhoti wrapped around his stick-like thighs, and as he walked about, he came upon the elderly Dhanpat's hexagonal field. Dhanpat was one of the oldest of the bonded labourers and had become rather weak and ineffectual. The previous year he had become debilitated with chicken pox, and his body started to let him down. Now as he drove the plough, panting and gasping, it seemed likely that Raghunath Singh would not go on paying him his rations much longer and that he would be rejected very soon.

As soon as he saw Ramlachhman, Dhanpat summoned up all his strength and for the life of him drove the plough into the hard earth. The strenuous effort made the veins in his hands and neck stand out like cords, his dull eyes bulged, and streams of sweat ran down over his shining copper coloured body.

Looking at how much land had been cultivated, Ramlachhman frowned and said, 'What's this, old man? In half a day you've ploughed no more than this?' Indeed, Dhanpat was not able to plough more, but even if he had, Ramlachhman of course would still have said the same thing, as he did to everyone, strolling from field to field.

Dhanpat did not answer but went on pushing the plough, knowing what the consequences would be if his cultivation were not up to standard. He had become very fearful for his own future.

Ramlachhman spoke to him again. 'You bastard of an untouchable ox! "Ram and Sita went into exile in the forest – "' And having sung that line he went straight on, 'You good-for-nothing, lazy, deceitful old owl! So little in half a day! But you still want your rations! You still want to fill your stomach! "Ram and Sita went into exile in the forest - "'

The circumspect Ganeri came from the opposite field, his palms pressed together. As the leader of the dosad colony he would provide strong support to anyone who was in trouble. Now he started to plead on behalf of Dhanpat. 'Dhanpat is not a strong man. He was very sick last year. Don't be angry, revered brahman. It's extremely hot.'

Turning to Ganeri, Ramlachhman snarled, 'Extremely hot! Is the bastard a lump of butter that he'll melt away?' He then sang his one line, followed by, 'If all this land is not ploughed before the rains, all you bastards will have your rations cut right off!'

'It'll be done, my lord, it'll be done, certainly,' said Ganeri. 'Don't be angry.'

'Words won't get the work done!' said Ramlachhman. 'If the fields don't get thoroughly ploughed, you'll all have your ribs crushed.' He then looked over to where Budheri was ploughing. One of Budheri's legs was a little shorter than the other. Ramlachhman shouted out, 'Hey, Budheri, you lame goat, you haven't ploughed half that field!'

With his palms pressed together, Budheri said fearfully, 'I'm going to. Before the rains start, the fields will certainly be ploughed, your honour.'

'We'll see.'

Ramlachhman intimidated not only Dhanpat and Budheri but a few others as well, shouting and bullying. Those he picked on would be in great trouble. He would go straight from the fields to the farm compound and report their names to Himgiri, and, as a result, some of what they had been rationed might be reduced. Himgiri and Ramlachhman would call such a penalty by the English word, a *fine*, and every week someone or other would be fined on account of Ramlachhman's informing.

Ramlachhman treated no one differently, shouting urgently a

each one of the bonded labourers, 'Get on with your work! Put some effort into it! The great master has done so much for you, feeding you and caring for you. You must never be ungrateful to him. How many times have I told you it is a pious thing to do good work for your maalik?'

In the fields the bonded labourers were twisting the tails of their bullocks and crying out, 'Urra - urr – urr - '

Standing in Budheri's field, Ramlachhman cast his vulture's eyes all around while singing his refrain. After a few moments he went into Dharma's field. As usual, Kushi was running along behind Dharma, picking out the weeds and now and then stopping for a moment to stoop and crumble up some clods. Ramlachhman stood on the ridge around the field for a few moments, frowning, inspecting the work of Dharma and Kushi. But try as he might, he could find no fault. Inwardly that made him angry. He thought for a moment, then called, 'Hey, Dharma!'

Dharma looked over his shoulder as he drove his plough. 'What is it, sahib?' he asked

'Didn't I see you and Kushi last night near the liquor shop at the market?'

Dharma was suddenly caught off guard. He gulped and said, 'We were over that way.'

'Was it because you saw me that you rushed off?' Ramlachhman asked.

Dharma thought that the beast must surely have the eyes of a jackal. Their seeing him as they hurried along the road by the liquor shop could not escape his notice! How could anyone ever throw dust in his eyes! He audibly drew in a breath and said, 'No, sir. No. We didn't see you.'

'Bullshit.'

'No, sir. No.'

Ramlachhman did not muddy the waters any more. His stick-like legs brought him toward Kushi and he stood there close to her body. Should she make a move, he would move with her; should she stop, he would stop. This was apprehended by Kushi and by Dharma. After all, it was not in Ramlachhman's nature to look at the girl while standing on the embankment twenty feet away; rather, the crane-like hypocrite would come to the fields and say this or that about the work, then attach himself to the women like glue. Such was his daily routine.

Ramlachhman grinned lewdly and then, having quickly sung his line of song, said, 'What a sexy body, Kushi. You must look after it! What a lusty lass you are! You could be a movie star. Oh, yes!' And he broke into his one-line refrain once more. Ramlachhman had been to see many Hindi movies in the tent that was set up to house the temporary cinema of Garudiya and Bijuri throughout the year, except during the rains. Whatever films should come, he would see them. Along with his Ram-Sita song, filmy talk had come to permeate his speech.

Exuding the stench of his lust, Ramlachhman let his beady eyes wander over Kushi's breasts, her waist and her nether region. Kushi's body recoiled and she breathed with difficulty as she went on picking out the roots and weeds, for her short sari and blouse did not fully cover her ample and vibrant body. She once paused in her work to cover her breast with her hand, and then again in an attempt to cover her bare midriff.

While looking at Kushi, Ramlachhman took a box from his kurta pocket, out of which he took some lime and a tobacco leaf and rubbed them together in the palm of his hand to make a *khaini*. He went to put it into his mouth, but then offered it to Kushi. 'Take it,' he said.

It was not that Kushi did not enjoy a *khaini*, but she had a perfectly good idea of the far-reaching consequences of taking such an offering from Ramlachhman. Giving her *khaini* for looking at her body from a distance would hardly satisfy him. Indeed, whatever she might take from him would have to be repaid tenfold in other ways. With a wave of her hand and a look of discomfort, she said, 'No, sir. No.'

'Go on, take it.' Ramlachhman was insistent.

'No, no.'

'All right, then.' Ramlachhman held the *khaini* between his lower lip and teeth and spat, then said, after singing his one line, 'What a mouth, what eyes, what breasts you have, Kushi! A woman as lovely as you would not be found even in the homes of brahmans, kayasthas and Rajputs.'

Kushi wondered what to do with her body, how to hide it. With a piteous look, she said, 'No, no, sir. Don't talk to me like this.'

Ramlachhman was going to say something else just as Dharma, who had not said a word, suddenly turned the bullocks and the plough around, looking over his shoulder. He said, 'Revered brahman, may I say something?'

'What?'

'If Kushi can't tidy the field, our work won't be complete before the rains. Now, by your grace – ' As he spoke, Dharma looked into Ramlachhman's face. The guileful hypocrite had to be prevented from harassing Kushi from behind, and the only way of restraining the sly devil was on the pretext of work. An intense anger welled up inside Dharma just looking at Ramlachhman's lewd gestures. He really wanted to run home and fetch an axe and deliver a blow to the rat's neck. He knew only too well why this bastard son of the devil was positioning himself close behind Kushi, yet he realised at the same time that a blow with an axe would do no good but would only endanger his and Kushi's lives. Instead he had to repel him by some stratagem.

For a while Ramlachhman fixed his beady eyes on Dharma. He sprayed some *khaini* juice from his mouth as he said haltingly, 'This girl is to be your bride, isn't she?' And without waiting for an answer, he took up his one line of song and went through the four fields to the right and over to Gidhni.

Gidhni was tidying up the soil in the field being ploughed by Madholal. Seeing Ramlachhman she stood without a hint of fear and frowned as she called, 'Come, come, good brahman, my lovely bridegroom!' This dosad girl's tongue lacked restraint, and it was not in her nature to exempt anyone from it, least of all Ramlachhman, for whom she had no fear at all. After all, as he had no self-respect, who would have any respect for him?

Ramlachhman bared his uneven, blackened teeth and cackled like a jackal. Smiling, he said, 'You're a bitch of a woman.'

'Then why do you rub your body up against mine everyday, good brahman?' Gidhni replied.

Ramlachhman did not answer but broke into another burst of cackling, a laugh that was tinged with filth.

'What brings you to me?' asked Gidhni. 'What do you want?'

Ramlachhman smiled and winked. 'Don't you know why a young man runs around after a young woman?'

Gidhni took a quick glimpse of the middle-aged jackal, then said, 'You, a young fellow?'

'Then what? An old man? I'm not even thirty, even though half my hair went grey in last summer's extreme heat.'

'Will you do something, good brahman?'

'What?'

'Will you marry me?'

On other days Gidhni would contend with Ramlachhman in crude, dirty banter, but today it went beyond the limit. A girl of an untouchable dosad family mentioning marriage to Ramlachhman would be seen as very foolhardy. No matter how nasty and unsavoury a character St Satan might be, he was a brahman nevertheless – a member of the supreme caste. Who could say how Gidhni mustered such courage, such audacity? It seemed as though the whole of Garudiya taluk had been struck by a thunderbolt.

A sudden stop had been put to Ramlachhman's laughing. He had never heard Gidhni say such a thing. Ramlachhman's face and ears started to burn with anger, and through clenched teeth he said, 'You wicked bitch! You trollop!' And as he spoke his head swung from side to side.

The bonded labourers in the fields around were standing stock-still. Having enjoyed the fun they were smiling, baring their teeth, but as their eyes caught Ramlachhman's, they quickly twisted the tails of their bullocks and started shouting, 'Urr – urr – urra – '

Then Gidhni said to Ramlachhman, 'You want to drink honey without marrying me? I'll leave the door open for you tonight. Be sure to come.'

For generations, powerful upper-caste men like Raghunath Singh or his employees such as Himgiri or Ramlachhman had enjoyed the young women of the homes of their bonded labourers. This was a natural, self-evident fact like sunrise and sunset. However, it was exceptionally distasteful to make banter or fun of it in public. Laughter arose from all around at what Gidhni had said, laughter that sounded just like so many fireworks all going off together, the sound spreading over the empty fields on the hot wind of Jyaistha.

Gesticulating frenziedly and looking this way and that, Ramlachhman kept crying out, 'Who's laughing? Who's laughing, you sons of apes?'

No one answered. Innocently they all bent their backs at the reprimand and went on with their ploughing.

Turning back to Gidhni, Ramlachhman said, 'You shameless slut! You're bad-mannered, foul-mouthed, and you stink!'

'So is that why you come to me, good brahman, to absorb the stink? Who makes you come to the untouchable girls, St Satan?'

Raising his voice to the highest level, Ramlachhman screamed, 'I will crush you, you whore!'

It seemed then that Gidhni had become possessed of a ghoul or some such spirit. She gesticulated contemptuously with both her hands, and then, striking various poses and making various gestures, she said, 'Well go, then, good brahman, go. I've already seen so many of your fine resolutions. Go, go! I spit in your face!' And having said that she spat seven times, not exactly in his face, but on the ground in his direction.

Sending Gidhni's parents and her fourteen succeeding generations to hell on account of her vile abuse, Ramlachhman strode off on his stork-like legs and mounted his bicycle. Then he rode off on the squeaking and rattling cycle along the hard, stony road beside the fields towards the highway.

As soon as Ramlachhman's bicycle had disappeared around the bend in the highway, everyone came out of their fields and surrounded Gidhni. 'Because of you that brahman rat will see to it that all our rations are cut. We'll fairly starve for who knows how long.'

Gidhni tried to console them. 'It's my fault. If rations are cut they'll be mine. Why should yours be cut? Don't worry.'

'We laughed at what the Rat said. That's made that bastard St Satan angry. Is that jackal of a brahman likely to let us off? Don't you know what a terribly dangerous man that one is?'

Waving her hands about, Gidhni said, 'Don't be afraid. I'll put everything right.'

Madholal cried out at the top of his voice, 'You'll put everything right? You'll put everything right? We'll all die! For certain we'll die!' He always said something twice if he wanted to emphasise it or if he got excited.

Gidhni said, 'Oh, no! No! If St Satan has your rations cut, I'll go straight to the great master's house. I'll confess my fault. I'll tell him – if any rations are to be cut, cut mine.'

So far Ganeri had been listening silently to what Gidhni had been saying and the shouting and crying of everyone else. Now, stepping forward a little, he said, 'Don't worry. None of your rations will be cut.' Ganeri spoke slowly, exuding the strength of his character.

'How come?' they all asked at once, taken aback by Ganeri's words.

'There's an election coming, isn't there? The maalik gave us all sweets. No rations will be cut as long as he wants our votes.'

Ganeri was a man of considerable depth who had had vast experience of life and the world. Among the bonded labourers his wisdom on any subject was the greatest, and the truth of what he had to say had been demonstrated many times already. From his experience and understanding he explained that at this election Raghunath Singh would not offend his voters, even though they might be his bonded labourers, untouchables or impoverished beggars.

So, heartened by Ganeri, they all went back to their work, no longer having anything to worry about.

Just before evening, as the sun was starting to set and Raghunath Singh's bonded labourers and his herd of dumb beasts were all returning to the farm compound, they caught sight of the campaign jeep coming back from Bijuri taluk.

'Vote for – '

'Raghunath Singh!'

'Vote for – '

'Raghunath Singh!'

The jeep passed them by and went on out of sight around the bend.

That Ganeri was indeed exceptionally wise and far-sighted was truly felt when they got to the compound. None of them had had one grain of their rations cut.

11

EXTENSIVE PREPARATIONS HAD BEEN GOING ON SINCE MORNING IN the mansion of Raghunath Singh, for in just a little while he would be going to meet Mishirlal. The electoral centre was in Raghunath Singh's domain, as Garudiya taluk had a total of some seventeen or so villages, whereas Bijuri had fifteen or sixteen. Altogether there were about thirty-three villages with more than two hundred thousand voters, almost half of whom were in Bijuri. In order to win the election, consideration had to be given to those voters, for it would be impossible to win without them. Moreover, there would be a few other candidates in this election, and it could be disastrous should any of them get first to Mishirlal to flatter him and gain his support. Therefore, Raghunath Singh had to go to Bijuri without a minute's delay.

The high-caste brahman Mishirlal maintained a direct, personal control over the people of his taluk. His was a tight administration which brooked no dissent; at his word Bijuri's two or three hundred thousand people would sit or stand. Therefore, for Raghunath Singh, a meeting with this man was not just important but absolutely necessary, for Mishirlal would only have to lift his finger for the voters of Bijuri to cast their votes in favour of Raghunath Singh.

Raghunath Singh was by no means indifferent towards Mishirlal – indeed, he bore him a degree of affection and amity. Mishirlal was a high-caste brahman and Raghunath Singh was a Rajput kshatriya, and although they were not directly related, there was no strict caste discrimination either. Mishirlal accepted Raghunath Singh's invitations to his home in Garudiya and Raghunath Singh would go to Bijuri. On festival days or family celebrations such as weddings, they would sit together, eat, chat and enjoy themselves. From a social and economic point of view Raghunath Singh was an influential representative of the same class as that to which Mishirlal belonged. In this outreach of independent India they both upheld the power of the old feudal system, and in this regard they had a close relationship, one that was stronger even than a blood connection.

Whereas it is natural for two men of the same class to enjoy a closeness, there can be inconveniences. Very often the enhancement of the influence and prosperity of the one can give rise to envy in the other. However, even if Raghunath Singh or Mishirlal should ever have felt envious of the other, it would be a very subtle, private matter, never an open one. Externally they showed extreme gentility, courtesy and class.

On the previous night the servants had washed the big old Ford with its huge wheels and retractable hood and made it sparkling clean. Then, early in the morning, another coat of polish was administered after the inspection of the munshi, Ajibchand. Straining his vocal cords, he would shout continually, 'Hey! Polish this part, and clean those tyres!' Then, overwhelmed with emotion, he would say, 'My maalik is going to be an emlay! What great joy!'

A little way away, on the marble-tiled veranda, Raghunath Singh was sprawled on his side on the thick cushions of a lounge chair. He was not wearing expensive shoes or embroidered kurta, but quite cheap ones – a plain white handloom kurta with loose-fitting pajamas and heavy leather sandals. There was no gold chain around his neck, no diamond rings on his fingers. Now he must not stand out among a thousand others, but be seen as a man of the people.

Sitting around Raghunath Singh in eminent array were the great lawyer, Girdharlal, the Bengali doctor, Shyamdulal Sen, and the headmaster, Badribishal Chaube – Raghunath Singh's close friends and lapdogs, who were going with him to Bijuri, and without whom he could not put a foot forward.

On the other side of the veranda was a tin of fresh buffalo ghee, some cashew nut sweets and a huge basket of *laddus*, two baskets of mangoes, a sack of bright, shiny litchis from Muzafarpur, the entire hide of a cheetah and two gleaming white elephant's tusks. All of this was a present from Raghunath Singh to Mishirlal – or, it might be suggested, a subtle bribe.

While consulting the lawyer and the doctor on the matter of ensuring the votes of Bijuri through Mishirlal, Raghunath Singh's eyes were on the Ford. He hurried Ajibchand saying, 'That's clean enough. We can't wait any longer. If this summer sun gets any hotter before we go out, the fiery wind will spring up before we get back.'

Ajibchand looked around and said, 'It's ready, maalik.'

Raghunath Singh came down from the veranda with his followers and, pointing to all the fruit and sweets said, 'Pack all these in the carrier.'

The order was immediately carried out, and a few minutes later the old model Ford started up noisily and they set off.

Left behind, Ajibchand kept on muttering, 'My maalik is going to be an emlay. He will bring about *Ram raj,* he will bring the rule of God to earth.'

In about an hour Raghunath Singh and his cronies reached Mishirlal's mansion in Bijuri.

***

Mishirlal's home was spread over nearly three acres, and the vast compound was surrounded by a high, sturdy wall. There was a huge iron entry gate embellished with copper-work, at which were posted a couple of six-foot-six, rifle-bearing, moustached gatekeepers, wearing khaki uniforms and bandoliers slung over their shoulders.

Mishirlal's house was just like all the houses of the big landowners in this region. On entry one came straight upon a large open space, on one side of which were some five or so shiny Indian and imported cars in an asbestos shed, but unlike Raghunath Singh's place, there were no Waler horses, no tandem carriage, and no elephant. Opposite the car-shed was a smaller one in which a few benches were arranged. This served as a waiting-room for those who had come to see Mishirlal. Mishirlal saw everybody who came, up until eleven in the morning. It was customary for a servant to conduct to Mishirlal each person who sought an audience; as soon as Mishirlal had finished talking with one, the next man would be brought in.

The huge three-storey house was like a medieval fort with its three-foot thick walls and large columns. On top of the house was a Ram-Sita temple, the pinnacle of which could be seen from two miles away. The two gatekeepers recognised Raghunath Singh; they gave him an extremely smart salute and made the way clear for his car.

Inside, under the shed on the left, many people were sitting waiting to see Mishirlal. As well, there were servants all around who, like the gatemen, all recognised Raghunath Singh, as he had come here many times before for family celebrations or festival days. About four servants came running as the Ford drew in on one side. Bowing their heads they said, '*Namaste*, master,' and one of them was quick to open the car door. They all acknowledged Raghunath Singh as a very great man, like their own master, someone like a raja or a maharaja, though from a different taluk.

'Is Mishirlal-ji at home?' asked Raghunath Singh.

'Yes, maalik.'

Raghunath Singh got out of the car. He said to his companions, who were also getting out, 'You wait for a little while. I'll go and greet him first.'

Raghunath Singh was familiar with every brick of this mansion. He knew everything, such as where Mishirlal held his public audiences in the mornings and how he conducted them. And so he went up the great flight of steps onto the immense veranda and, having gone a little way to the right, stood before the door to a spacious room. Inside, a six-inch thick carpet was spread, and expensive sofas were arranged around a centre table, entirely in the Western style. Mishirlal was sitting on a huge sofa with his feet tucked up under him. And, like all wealthy people, he was surrounded by sycophants.

Raghunath Singh noted the contrast between the bright Western interior of Mishirlal's house and its resemblance to a medieval fort on the outside. Though at times Mishirlal had had an urge to pull the house down and put up a modern one in its place, he refrained, for his grandfather had built this house and he still valued old-fashioned sentiment.

Although the medieval was well established in this part of the world, Mishirlal liberally mixed modern styles with the traditional. Having got rid of his elephants and horses and an old model vehicle, he had bought a gleaming new model car and had replaced with tractors the bullock-drawn ploughs of ancient times. (In fact, no one else's land was ploughed by 'mishin' in this region or even within twenty miles of it.) He had sent his sons and daughters to study in Calcutta and London, and although he himself wore traditional dhoti and kurta or punjabi, his children dressed in the Western style. Indeed, Mishirlal's philosophy and way of life were very largely Western.

From where Raghunath Singh was standing he could see Mishirlal out of the corner of his eye, though Mishirlal had not noticed him yet. As he was about to enter, a servant took someone else in through another door. Once inside, the man reached out to touch Mishirlal's feet, but Mishirlal, feigning discomfort about the man's obeisance, held up his hands in assumed embarrassment saying, 'Oh, no, no!'

while at the same time stretching his feet towards the man. Not only Raghunath Singh but everyone of the few hundred thousand who lived within twenty or even fifty miles knew that if one were to offer *pranam* to Mishirlal, he would say 'No, no,' yet straightaway offer his feet to the person's forehead. Indeed, in this region he was known as the Touch-my-Feet Zamindar.

After the man had touched his forehead to Mishirlal's feet, Mishirlal said, 'Sit,' and the man sat very deferentially on a corner of the carpet below, his hands pressed together submissively.

Again Mishirlal spoke, asking, 'What is it you want to say?' But before the man could answer, he caught sight of Raghunath Singh, and in great excitement he got up immediately. 'Ah! What good fortune is mine! Today I have seen everybody, but now a star of the heavens is waiting by my door! Come in, Raghunath-ji, come on in!' And as he spoke he came and took Raghunath Singh by the hand and sat him down on the sofa beside himself. Then, sitting in his own place, he said to the other man, 'You go now. Come again the day after tomorrow.'

The man touched Mishirlal's feet with his forehead once more and left. Mishirlal told the servant who was still standing there that he should send away anyone who wanted to see him as he would see no one else that day.

Raghunath Singh said to Mishirlal, 'If you would kindly permit –'

'What's this about permission! Say whatever you will.'

'Three of my friends have come. They are outside waiting in the car. We have also brought a few things. If your servant could fetch them and bring the things - '

'What an odd thing, to leave your friends waiting!' Mishirlal turned to a servant and said, 'Go and bring Raghunath-ji's friends, and send Phagua.' As the servant hurried outside, Mishirlal turned back to Raghunath and said, 'Am I daydreaming? Is this really Raghunath Singh?'

Raghunath Singh smiled.

In the meantime Mishirlal's bootlickers were bowing their heads this way and that offering *namaste* or *pranam*, for it was only right to offer cordiality to this man of their master's class. If Mishirlal should ever be angry with them, they would have another rock to fall back on. Such was the way with parasites.

Mishirlal went on. 'I am very pleased that you have come, Raghunath-ji.'

'I've caused you some inconvenience by coming suddenly and without informing,' said Raghunath Singh. 'However, there is no way I could not have come. There is a particularly urgent matter.'

Mishirlal interrupted him, saying, 'Tell me about that later. But first I have a request to put to you. Now that you have so kindly come here, you must have lunch with us.'

With hands folded, Raghunath Singh said that Mishirlal would have to forgive him on this occasion, but he would certainly come to eat with him some other day, and Mishirlal pressed the matter no further.

Just then the strong-built servant Phagua came into the room, followed close behind by Raghunath Singh's three lapdogs. Another three servants carried in on their heads and shoulders the various baskets of sweets and other offerings.

Mishirlal was taken aback when he saw all the presents. 'What is all this?' he asked.

It was, according to Raghunath Singh, a trivial matter. When one had an audience with a maharaja, it was customary to bring a present. Mishirlal's face almost betrayed the embarrassment that he was feeling, although inwardly he was quite delighted at being called a maharaja. 'But was this necessary, Raghunath-ji?' he asked.

'As I said, it's nothing – a simple homage to you.' And as he spoke, Raghunath Singh gestured to the two servants to take the fruit and sweets inside the house. In the meantime Girdharlal and the others were bowing their heads offering *namaste* and *pranam* to Mishirlal in the same way in which Mishirlal's lap-dogs had paid their respects to Raghunath Singh, for it was a sacred duty of sycophants to be obsequious and flattering towards people of their master's class. The bootlickers of the world are all the same.

Mishirlal smiled slightly and said a few words, as though extending a great favour to Girdharlal and fourteen generations of his ancestors. He then turned to the servant Phagua and said, 'Inform Ma that Raghunath Singh-ji has come from Garudiya.' By giving this news to 'Ma' – his wife – Mishirlal meant to suggest that due arrangements should be made for his guests.

'Yes, malik,' said Phagua, and he left the room.

Raghunath Singh now wanted to raise the main issue. Because he had come across the scorched fields under the blazing sun and magnified five hundred times the prestige of his equal, even calling him a maharaja, and having very cleverly described as a present what was really a bribe, he was starting to feel a little agitated. He said, 'I have come to you on special business.'

Mishirlal raised his hand to stop him. 'Life is full of business. But first of all tell me, how are things with your family? How are my sisters?' (Mishirlal called Raghunath Singh's two wives his sisters.)

'They're all right,' said Raghunath Singh.

'Are they getting on well together?'

In this region the quarrels of Raghunath Singh's kayastha wife and his Rajput wife were well known – indeed, had become almost legendary – and everyone in Garudiya and Bijuri taluks knew about them. Raghunath Singh said indifferently, 'As long as they live, they won't get on. It can't even be said that they won't fight even after their deaths. But I don't worry about that.'

'And the children?'

'They're well.'

Raghunath Singh also asked politely about Mishirlal's family, and during all this inconsequential talk the servant Phagua brought in silver trays of numerous sweets and expensive summer fruits and set them down in front of everybody. He also brought chilled sherbet – an excellent aromatic mixture of pistachio nuts, yoghurt and ice – in silver-plated goblets. In this month of Jyaistha there is nothing better for cooling the inner man.

Seeing the extent of what was being offered, Raghunath Singh said apprehensively, 'Oh, my goodness, this is ten day's rations for me. Why so much?'

There was a door leading from this room to the private quarters of the house. A curtain was hanging there, and from the other side of it came the gentle and melodic voice of a woman, 'I won't hear of "no". You must not say such a thing.'

It was Mishirlal's wife, Padmavati. Living in such a house as this, she did not go out much, though she was not confined to the women's apartments either. She was a woman of few words and a remarkable and affectionate personality. She managed most wonderfully Mishirlal's extended family and its numerous dependent relations. To come to this house meant to be touched by her care and tenderness.

Raghunath Singh stood up respectfully. Everyone else in the room, except Mishirlal, followed his lead. With his hands pressed together, Raghunath said, '*Namaste*, dear sister. Why do you take the trouble to come down here?'

Padmavati replied, '*Namaste*. You have arrived, so why wouldn't I come down? So where is the trouble?'

'Had you ordered your subject, I would have come to you.'

'My goodness, what are you saying! There is no end to your courtesy. Now sit down like a good boy and eat up. I'll stand here.'

Padmavati's father had been honoured with the title of 'Raja' of Ara district, and her demeanour was totally different from that of others. Raghunath Singh respected the lady greatly. He said,

'I shall surely die if I eat so much, sister.' He drew a sad look on his face.

Perhaps Padmavati pitied him. She said, 'All right, then. Eat what you can.'

Thus obliged to reach out to the silver plates, Raghunath Singh and the others in the room pursued disjointed snippets of conversation as they ate. Padmavati, like Mishirlal before her, made it known that she would be delighted should Raghunath Singh and his companions stay for lunch. Begging forgiveness as he had before, Raghunath Singh again answered that he would come another day and eat with them.

'In that case fix a date and let me know,' said Padmavati. 'And my sisters must kindly come too, then. Agreed?'

'Agreed.'

***

They finished eating and the servants came and cleared away the plates and goblets. Padmavati also moved away from the other side of the curtain.

Then, before Raghunath Singh could open his mouth, Mishirlal began, 'I think I know the urgent business on which you have come. Let me see if I am right.'

Somewhat surprised, Raghunath Singh turned to Mishirlal.

'The election is coming, and you will become an MLA and go to the Assembly in Patna. Isn't this the urgent business on which you have come to me?'

Raghunath Singh's amazement increased markedly in a moment. He said, 'How did you know?'

'Oh, brother, throughout your Garudiya and our Bijuri the news has spread from village to village. Could only I not know? The news of your return from Patna with a ticket for the election and your distribution of sweets to everyone in Garudiya also reached my ears.'

'Then you know everything.'

'But brother – '

'What?'

'Why are you going into politics? Politics is such a grubby business. It has a *stench* about it.' Mishirlal had not been very well educated and had learned much more from experience, though from time to time a few English words crept into his speech. He paused for a moment, and then went on. 'It is only right that those of us who are landowners should keep an eye on the land. If that eye turns to something else, the land suffers and the other business also suffers. Of course, it's up to you whether you take any notice of what I say.'

Extremely humbly Raghunath Singh replied, 'Please do not take offence if I say one thing.'

'Of course not. Why only one? Say twenty!'

'Some of us have to go into politics in the interests of landowners and sit in the Assembly as popular agents. Otherwise you will not be able to keep so much land.'

Mishirlal frowned, 'Why not?'

By way of explanation Raghunath Singh said that, given the strictness of the land reform laws, the old feudal system, along with the practice of paying only rations for the hard work of the bonded labourers, would not last forever. That the practice still survived was, in fact, illegal. The matter had been written about in the newspapers of the big cities and many political parties had come to take notice of it. They all had kicked up quite a fuss over it, and now there could be controversy. Moreover, every year the legislatures of the national and state parliaments were passing land reform laws that were diminishing the power of landowners. If this were allowed to continue, no one would be able to have ten inches more than the bare necessity of land. No matter what, these dangerous land reforms had to be checked, and for that reason it was essential that the landowners' own men should be among those who make the laws. Thus Raghunath Singh wanted to represent the landowners in the legislature at this time.

Mishirlal sat restlessly on his huge sofa, listening. He said, 'You've thought it out very well. I had not considered all of this. We must indeed look to our own interests. For so long we have been used to listening to the gospel of socialism from our leaders. If socialism really comes to India, then we are finished.'

The bootlickers of both Raghunath Singh and Mishirlal, the party of yes-men, all together said, 'Yes, of course! Certainly!' They would agree with whatever came from the mouths of their masters.

Raghunath Singh said, 'This is why I have come to you. I need your help in the election.'

'Tell me, what kind of help can I give?' Mishirlal asked.

Raghunath explained that it was necessary to capture the popular vote in order to go to the lower house of the parliament in Delhi or to the Assembly in Patna, and that in this election almost fifty per cent of the voters in his electorate belonged to Bijuri taluk. If Mishirlal would kindly give them the nod, they would all support Raghunath Singh, and if he could get to the Assembly, he would do everything to look after his and Mishirlal's class interests. It all depended on Mishirlal's good grace.

Mishirlal said, 'As this is indeed a matter of our own class interests, I will do everything necessary to get you to the Assembly.'

Raghunath Singh reached out and took both Mishirlal's hands, saying, 'I cannot thank you enough. I am your trusted servant.'

Mishirlal had no trouble in recognising this as mere flattery of the first order, but he did not object to it. He knew in his heart that his eyes had been opened by Raghunath Singh. Far-sighted as he was he had not given much attention to the land reforms, although he should have, and he ought to have been aware of their dangerous potential. He said, 'Why should you thank me? It is for me to thank you. I could not have imagined all that had you not made me aware of it.'

'In that case, then, I need not worry at all about the Bijuri vote.'

'Absolutely not – this is an illiterate mass. If I say, all the Bijuri voters will line up like goats to put their stamp on your symbol. Do not worry at all.'

So after a few minutes of small talk Raghunath Singh and his three lapdogs took their leave. A little later, as they drove along the highway into Garudiya, Raghunath Singh looked at his land being ploughed by Dharma and the others. None of these illiterate, untouchable bonded labourers could have any idea how their fortunes and future might be determined by the coming election.

12

On account of Tirke and his need to procure a pair of young barking deer, Dharma had thought that the next day he would miss work and go to the jungle. However, that was not to be.

Of course, he had three days, yet after two days he had still not gone into the jungle. He was by no means certain whether or not that would be enough for him to find the young deer, but he would have to try. He decided that at dawn the next day he would go to the jungle with the rejected old people who rummaged around near the bed of the Koel.

However, when the time came, he could not go, for when he returned his plough and bullocks to the farm compound after his work in the field the previous day, he learned that he would have to go with Ramlachhman to the fortnightly market at Chaharh five miles away. Every year in the tilling season landowners needed to select men from among the tribal people – Oraons, Mundas, Santals and Cheros – who would come to the market in the hope of being hired for work. They would toil throughout the season for rations, each getting a little cash and a few kilograms of cheap cereal or maize or low-quality rice. They would come again at harvest time and fill the granaries with grain and complete the planting of the spring rabi crop. This had been the tradition year after year.

So Dharma would have to go with Ramlachhman to the market at Chaharh to select tribal labourers. His job would be to lead them back, for Ramlachhman would return on his bicycle. Each year Ramlachhman would appoint one of the bonded labourers for this task of escorting the tribal workers, and this time it was Dharma's turn.

In his high-pitched voice sounding like a carpenter's drill Himgirinandan had said, 'At daybreak tomorrow, before it gets light, you should be waiting at the bus stand on the highway under the big pipal tree. Ramlachhman will meet you there and take you with him. D'you hear me?'

Going to Chaharh meant that Dharma could not go to the jungle, and there would be no hope of getting the twenty rupees from Tirke if he could not catch the young deer. However, Dharma, like all the bonded labourers, did not have the nerve to say no to Himgiri. He had merely bowed his head and said, 'Yes, my lord.'

Himgiri had then said, 'You won't have to work in the fields tomorrow after coming back from Chaharh. You can have the rest of the day off. Understood?'

In other words Dharma was getting some relief on account of all the trouble taken in his come-and-go on the road, but he could not see how that could compensate for his twenty rupees. Nevertheless, he inclined his head in gratitude and said, 'Yes, my lord.'

'You will get breakfast and your midday meal at Chaharh.'

It was known that those who went each year to Chaharh to fetch tribal workers got breakfast and the midday meal at a shop there. Obviously these benefits were due to the great master, Raghunath Singh. As a rule it was a grand meal with rice; the untouchable bonded labourers could count on the fingers of one hand the number of times in their lives that they had had such a fine feast of meat, dal, fritters, pickles, green chillies and onions. Yet Dharma was not enthused even by the idea of the meal, for the twenty rupees was a far greater matter. But he gave the obligatory smile as he said, 'Yes, my lord.'

So before daybreak the next morning Dharma ate a little leftover rice and set out. Today Kushi would have to work with Ganeri or someone else in the fields, sorting out the weeds and roots and breaking up the big clods of earth.

When Dharma reached the large pipal tree at the bus stand on the highway, there were still millions of stars in the sky. None of the shops here was open yet, except for the tea stall. At this time there was very little traffic on the highway and only the occasional long-distance bus was to be seen on the empty road. The last stage of the night was still listless and dreamy, with the bats on the top of the pipal tree flapping their wings, owls hooting mysteriously and flocks of fireflies darting over the road, through the woods and off into the distant cornfields. And there were thousands of mosquitoes which incessantly nipped at Dharma's skin.

Dharma had to wait there, being eaten by the mosquitoes, for as long as it took Ramlachhman to come. Of course, the teashop opposite was open and the split bamboo benches in front of it were still quite empty, but they would fill up just as soon as the light started to spread from the rising sun. From then until late into the night crowds would gather like swarms of flies. There was no reason why anyone should not sit on the bamboo benches, except that there was no possibility of Dharma's doing so. After all, he was an untouchable bonded labourer and the proprietor of the shop was an upper-caste kayastha who would give Dharma a beating should he sit there.

He had no idea how long he had been waiting when a bus coming from the direction of Patna pulled up under the pipal tree and, after letting out a sound like a deep sigh, started on its way once again. A man had got down from the bus, but in the dark Dharma was unaware of him. He was almost holding his breath waiting for Ramlachhman.

The man came and stood beside Dharma. 'Dharma? Is it you?' he asked.

Dharma suddenly turned to look at him, but did not immediately recognise him. He could not have imagined that anyone would get down from the late night bus from Patna and call his name. His mind was on nothing other than Ramlachhman, and so he took a few moments to get over his surprise. Dharma looked at the man, startled. 'You – you are . . . ?' he mumbled.

The man came closer and laid a hand on Dharma's shoulder, 'Don't you know me? Can't you recognise me, you idiot?'

'No.' Dharma slowly shook his head.

'I'm Gana.'

Dharma was even more amazed. Was this the son of the old woman, Shaukhi, her one and only Ganesh, or Gana? He was wearing trousers, a shirt, shoes, wristwatch, a coloured silk kerchief around his neck, and his hair had been combed. He had an expensive leather suitcase in one hand. To look at him, Dharma could not believe that this stunning fellow wearing such expensive clothes was Gana. He had changed from head to toe. Yet it was only a few years ago that this same Gana had been one with them in ploughing the land of the great master, Raghunath Singh, planting the crops and harvesting the grain. Getting about the fields the whole day his skin became dry and rough, and his hands and feet were cracked having been burned by the sun, drenched by the rain, and shrivelled in the cold. His entire body had borne the stamp of hunger and misfortune.

Since that day a year ago when Gana ran away from the dosad colony, Dharma had secretly admired and envied him. He admired him for having claimed on his own his freedom from the contemptible life of an untouchable bonded labourer, and as long as Dharma himself still passed his days in servile thraldom, he envied him. At that moment in the dark, this independent man seemed a demigod to Dharma. The days when Gana used to drive the plough with him in the fields, when he used to cart the harvest to Raghunath Singh's granaries, all seemed an illusion. Dharma bowed almost spontaneously to Gana. Quietly he asked, using the polite form of 'you', 'Where have you been?'

'Why do you flatter me?' Gana interrupted him. 'Why not call me *tumi*?'

Although Gana was the same age and had been his companion since birth, it had been so long ago that they shared their life of servility in the dosad colony that Dharma did not have the nerve to use the familiar pronoun. After much insistence, of course, he had to agree. He asked, familiarly, 'Where have you been all this time, Gana? Since you left, all of us in the neighbourhood have been wondering.'

Jokingly Gana said, 'You were probably thinking that I was dead.'

'Oh, no, no.'

Gana went on. 'From here I went first to Ranchi, then to Patna, and from Patna to Farbisganj. I wandered around a bit and went to Dhanbad. That's where I am now.'

'What do you do there?' Dharma asked.

'I work in a factory. I get three hundred rupees a month.'

None of Dharma's ancestors in fourteen generations had even seen three hundred rupees all at once, nor did Dharma have any clear conception of the sum. He said, 'That's a lot of money, isn't it?'

Gana gave a serious kind of laugh, but said nothing.

Again Dharma asked, 'What's a factory?'

'Where things are made. All sorts of things are made by machines.'

Dharma barely understood. He then asked, 'Where are you coming from now?'

'From Dhanbad,' Gana replied. 'Will you have some tea? Let's go to the shop.'

Dharma was very fond of tea, but he knew that the upper-caste proprietor would not give a glass of tea to untouchables like them. His enthusiasm waned, and he explained his feelings to Gana.

'Don't worry,' Gana said. 'I have some plastic cups with me.' He opened the leather suitcase and quickly took out two coloured plastic cups, went and bought some tea at the stall, and came back to the pipal tree.

'Do you know why I have come after all this time?' Gana spoke while drinking his tea.

Dharma was drinking his tea carefully. He looked up and asked, 'Why?'

'I'm going to take Ma away. I'll get company quarters. With the money I earn, she shouldn't have to go about begging.'

Dharma suddenly remembered that he had heard this from old Shaukhi a few days before. Immediately he thought of something else and felt terribly fearful. He said, 'Naorangi found out that you are coming. Go there and slip away with your mother while it's still dark. But be very careful.'

Dharma was surprised that he had not thought of Naorangi before, but it had been such a long time since he had seen Gana, who had changed so much. Moreover, any minute now Ramlachhman would appear. That spelt danger for Gana.

'Who is Naorangi?'

'That hip-swinging whore – don't you remember?'

'She used to be kept by Raghunath Singh? Then by Himgiri?'

'Yes. You can bet she's told Himgiri about you. You ran off without settling your debt. Himgiri will kill you if he catches you.'

'It's not as simple as that. We have police in our country. We have laws that have to be obeyed.'

Gana had undoubtedly seen much and learned much this last year travelling around such big towns as Patna, Munger and Dhanbad. Perhaps what he said was right. But Dharma's innate fears and the prejudices of his caste would not go away and his breath caught in his chest. He swilled down the rest of his hot tea and gave the cup back to Gana. 'Take this. I can't get water to wash it. Go. Go away. If they see you, the neighbours'll make a fuss and immediately the news'll get to Himgiri. Go into the colony very quietly. Don't take your mother up onto the highway, but go across the fields. No one'll see you that way.'

'You're worrying too much. I'm meeting you after so long – just a few more words.'

Dharma felt even more admiration for Gana's nerve, but fearfully he said, 'No, no. Ramlachhman will come any minute. If he sees you, there'll be hell to pay.'

'All right. If you say so, I'll go.' He had gone but a few steps when something occurred to him and he turned back. 'The life of untouchables like us in Garudiya is the life of animals,' he said. 'If you don't want to live like a rat or a dog, come with me. I'll get you a job in the factory. You'll do really well.'

Not only his town clothes and appearance, but also his talk had something of a gloss to it. It was indeed true – their life here was that of animals, demeaning and insufferable. Gana was talking of getting out of this dark and suffocating hell, talking of opening the door himself for Dharma to a respectable, independent life. The blood rushed through Dharma's veins and his eyes lit up avidly. With great earnestness he took Gana's hands and said, 'Can you really arrange to get me away from here?'

'Really. Remember my address: Usha Engineering Company, boiler division. It's a huge factory near the Dhanbad railway station. Ask at the gate for the boiler division. Then ask for me.'

Dharma muttered Gana's address over and over again.

Gana waited no longer. Having set a seed of freedom in Dharma's mind he went off along the highway.

***

After Gana had gone out of sight around the distant bend in the highway, Dharma waited a little longer. The darkness was quickly dispelling, and as it become lighter in the east, Ramlachhman came along on his rickety, creaking old bicycle. Without stopping he looked with keen eyes under the pipal tree and called, 'Hey, Dharma, are you ready?'

Dharma replied immediately, 'Yes.'

'Follow me.'

In other words, Dharma was to run behind Ramlachhman's bicycle a good five miles along the highway to Chaharh. There was a carrier seat on the back of the bicycle and, if he had wanted to, he could have sat Dharma on that, but the high-caste Ramlachhman could not find a way around his own potential hell this morning to convey some untouchable bonded labourer.

***

The sun had well risen by the time they reached Chaharh, where the market was held every fortnight. There was no market within thirty or forty miles as big or as busy as this one.

By now buying and selling had got underway under the market's thatched awnings, though many stall-holders were still coming in bullock or buffalo carts from all around and crowds of rustic folk were streaming in on foot.

Ramlachhman went into the middle of the market. Along one side cows were huddled beside rows of trees. Clusters of brilliant red flowers had blossomed on the *karaiya* and *palas* trees in the month of Chaitra, and they were still blooming. In the blend of sun and shadow under the trees on the other side many Munda, Oraon, Chero and Santal people were sitting with their children. Every year at ploughing time the tribal people would sit like this, their bodies intertwined, under the trees beside the Chaharh market, and landowners or their agents would come from all around to select labourers.

For a long time Himgirinandan himself used to go to Chaharh to get labourers, but for the last three or four years Ramlachhman had been going. Now, having ridden his bicycle five miles along the highway, Ramlachhman was out of breath. He leaned his bicycle against a tree and went and sat down some distance from the tribals, keeping himself from their touch, panting with his tongue out, as a calf does. Dharma too sat down under a tree, puffing.

After a quick recovery Ramlachhman got up. 'I'm just going to have some tea and a snack,' he said. 'I'm terribly hungry. You can have something when I get back. In the meantime keep an eye on the bicycle. And have a look for who might be good workers among the tribals. We don't want any weaklings. Understood?'

Dharma nodded, and Ramlachhman went off into the buzzing crowd inside the market, leaving the untouchable bonded labourer sitting under a tree to look at a group of landless tribal labourers. The Jyaistha day was getting on and the sun was becoming terribly hot.

Dharma noticed that no other landowners or their agents had come yet to look for labourers. However, two men were sitting close to the Oraons and Mundas under the *palas* trees opposite. They were not tribal men of the jungle or hills but seemed like townsmen, wearing trousers, smart shirts, and shoes. One of them was gesticulating and saying, 'How much will you get for working on someone else's land? They'll send you away after one or two months. Come with us. Each man will get six or seven rupees wages a day and rations, and after four months you'll get new clothes, shirts even, and saris and blouses for your wives.' He paused, and then went on. 'But we won't send you away after one or two months, because you'll be able to work for the whole year. You needn't worry about filling your stomachs or covering your bodies. That'll all be looked after for you. We guarantee it.'

The eyes of a group of simple, innocent and hungry tribal people, whose permanent companion was hunger and whose bodies were never fully covered, lit up avidly. Maybe they did not really believe what they had heard, for a middle-aged Munda said, 'Bullshit'.

Waving his hands about frantically, one of the men said, 'No, no, it's absolutely true. So many of your community have come to earn good money working for us.'

'Yeah, we heard. We'll get six or seven rupees a day, eh?'

'Definitely.'

'New clothes too?'

'Yes.'

'Where do we have to go with you?'

'Assam, Agartala.'

'So far?'

'No, no, it's quite close. Just a little distance from Hazaribagh.'

The people of this region knew the name of Hazaribagh. The middle-aged Munda thought for a few moments, then asked, 'Do we have to travel by train?'

The two men nodded and said, 'Yes. So then what's the point of waiting here? Come with us. Come on, get up. Let's go to the shop and we'll get tea and biscuits and sweets and samosas. When we get to the station we'll give you a meal with rice. Come on, get up.'

Sitting apart from them, Dharma heard all that they were saying. He had heard of these places once before – probably from the schoolmaster – so he knew that the recruiters were taking these tribals to somewhere far away.

Nevertheless, in spite of the enticement of good food and a future free of worries, the tribals did not get up. The Munda elders counselled the members of their community in their own language, and the older, experienced Santals and Oraons went over and talked with them. They explained that they could not make up their minds whether or not to go to some strange place. However, the idea of the money and the two good meals a day lingered and could not be passed aside easily.

The two recruiters kept urging them. 'What's the matter, then? Hurry up, now. The sun's getting high in the sky.'

There was good reason for their impatience, namely that it would not be at all easy to take the tribals once the agents of the landowners had come. For better or worse, generations of landowners were familiar with this system, and the tribals had a very clear idea of how little they might get from them, yet despite seeing considerable advantage they were wary of going away to a remote and unfamiliar place. There was no response to the urging of the recruiters, and the tribals continued their discussion among themselves.

Ramlachhman now came back, having had his breakfast and tea. He sang his line of song and asked, 'Have you chosen any men?'

While listening to the talk of the recruiters and the tribals, this matter had completely slipped Dharma's mind. He became frightened and the breath caught in his throat. He got up immediately and said, 'I'm sorry sir. I've not chosen anyone yet.'

Whether it was because he had eaten well or for some other reason, Ramlachhman's anger did not rise quite as much as it might have. He said, 'You useless buffalo! You'll be fined – no breakfast, and you'll get only one item for lunch.'

All morning Dharma had been looking forward to a good breakfast. That it had been cancelled made him feel terrible. He had a raging hunger after having run five miles along the highway, yet there was nothing he could do. His stomach would just have to suffer until noontime. Looking miserable Dharma walked over to the tribals. Ramlachhman followed him, keeping a distance of about ten feet.

The two recruiters probably had not realised at first that Ramlachhman and Dharma were agents of some landowner, but now they did. In great haste they got up and went and sat under another tree some way away. All these recruiters were wary of the landowners, who had a lot of trouble finding itinerant peasants. For a very long time the recruiters had been taking these seasonal workers to the tea gardens and brickyards of far-off Assam and Tripura, which made the agents of the landowners very angry, and for some years a number of the recruiters had been getting beaten mercilessly by the agents of the landowners, who would spare nobody if the masters' interests were threatened.

Keeping his distance Ramlachhman asked the tribals, 'Hey, there. Will you come and work in the fields in Garudiya?' The question was just for the sake of it, for he knew that there was nothing they could do other than agricultural work.

Many of the Oraons and Mundas knew Ramlachhman, as he had been coming for a few years to find labourers. Instantly they forgot about the recruiters and said, 'Yes, sir. That's why we're waiting here.'

Although he had not had any direct experience of how the agricultural labourers were selected, Dharma had heard a lot about it from older men in the dosad colony such as Ganeri and Madholal. He approached the tribals and said to one Oraon, 'Stand up.'

The Oraon stood up. Dharma looked him over from head to foot and said, 'Go and stand over there.' He had selected someone.

The Oraon stepped to the right, but Ramlachhman called from behind, 'Hey, idiot, you have chosen after just a glance!' He sang his one line of song, and then said, 'Examine him thoroughly. Feel his hands, feet, back, chest. It's not all that easy to choose workers.'

Dharma had no choice but to obey Ramlachhman's order and feel the man's body.

Ramlachhman went on, 'What sort of man is he? Does he have the strength of a beast?'

At Dharma's word the Oraon could have been turned away just as easily as his twice a day worry for his stomach might come to an end for a month or so. With proof of his physical strength called for, he looked at Dharma with pathetic eyes. Although his mouth said nothing, his eyes begged Dharma not to reject him.

'He does, sir,' said Dharma.

Although he relied on Dharma's word, Ramlachhman nevertheless asked the Oraon, 'Can you drive a bullock-drawn plough twice a day, then?'

'I can, sir.'

'All right. Go over there and sit under the tree.' He looked at Dharma, sang his one line of song, and said, 'Now for some more.'

Dharma did not lay a hand on the women's bodies in the way in which he had examined the men. However, Ramlachhman was extremely keen that the women should be assessed in the same way, and he reproached Dharma, saying, 'Will you get blisters feeling her body? Do they come from some maharaja's family?' His line of song was followed by, 'Grab hold of the bitch's flesh!'

Dharma recoiled. Extremely embarrassed, he said, 'No, no, sir. She's a woman.' Indeed, all Ramlachhman's bluster could not induce Dharma to lay a hand on the body of any woman, and finally he had to give up in impatience.

The selection process reminded Dharma of a cattle market. The way in which animals are assessed by pinching and prodding was the same as the way in which these human beings were appraised and chosen. He did not like it at all.

Soon Ramlachhman and Dharma had gathered to one side a total of forty men and women. As well there were about a dozen or more children with the women. The children were not included in the selected number but were separate from it. Their mothers and fathers would be paid for their labours and given rations, but the children would get nothing. It was the responsibility of parents to provide for their children, which had been the case for years. Nevertheless, Ramlachhman still reminded them, 'But your kids won't be getting anything.'

The tribals nodded their heads. 'We know that, sir.'

'So don't go grouching about it later.'

'No, no.'

Having disclaimed the children, Ramlachhman now counted the

heads of the others and gave some money to each. 'I'll give you one rupee in advance. Now go and eat something. Come back here when you've finished. Understood?'

'Yes, sir.' The tribals were extremely happy to have one rupee in their hands. They all went off to look for a stall where they could buy some barley or maize flour.

It was just then that sounds of shouting came from the other side of the market.

'Vote for – '

'Sukhan Ravidas!'

'Vote for – '

'Sukhan Ravidas!'

All together some thirty or forty people were coming this way, all shouting. In their midst could be seen the smiling face of the medium-built Sukhan Ravidas, a man in his late twenties. He was wearing a shirt and dhoti, both made of rough cloth, and cheap sandals. This son of a tanner was known and respected by many people far beyond Garudiya and Bijuri. Sukhan had been 'schooled', had even studied for a few years at a college in Patna, and spoke English fluently. He was also exceptionally charismatic. He could stand up to brahmans and kayasthas, lawyers, doctors and government officers, and had been beaten up many times for arguing on various issues with high-caste men. Once he had been given such a hiding that he was unconscious for a whole two days afterwards.

Dharma had known Sukhan for a long time. He also lived in Garudiya, in the chamar or tanners' colony, which was near the western corner of the dairy folk's village. Sukhan was an untouchable who did not care at all about brahmans or kayasthas, and Dharma secretly admired him for this. Although he was an untouchable, Sukhan Ravidas was a man nevertheless, a strong man who held his head high.

Ramlachhman, too, noticed Sukhan's election rally. Gradually his brow creased into two furrows and his face reflected his contempt, anger and disdain. 'Well,' he said, 'the son of an untouchable rat is standing in the election! The rat has come to vie with the elephant! The bastard will be trampled flat.' The elephant he was referring to was, of course, Raghunath Singh.

Dharma did not hear most of what Ramlachhman said. He just kept watching Sukhan with eyes full of worship and wonder. As far as he knew, this was the first election in which Sukhan Ravidas was standing. Somewhat distracted, he asked Ramlachhman, 'Will Sukhan Ravidas be up against our maalik in the election?'

Ramlachhman pulled a face baring his fang-like, blackened teeth, and said, 'Oh, yes, you owl. Oh, yes. The son of a rat has grown feathers. He'll die. Definitely he'll be killed. Can you compare this bastard with our maalik?'

Sukhan Ravidas and his supporters passed Dharma and Ramlachhman, moving to the north where they blended in with the bustling crowd. Ramlachhman went on looking after them with intense malice. He turned from Sukhan and his party and said to Dharma, 'When the tribals get back we'll go straight to Garudiya without any delay.'

The middle of the day was wearing on as the sun climbed to its highest point in the sky, and Dharma felt that his stomach was ablaze with raging hunger. Wondering whether or not to mention this, Dharma at last said, 'Sir, my lord, I'm terribly hungry.'

Ramlachhman bawled out his line of song and cried, 'You've been fined, you bastard – no breakfast! Have you forgotten?' But as he spoke he was reminded of how, some days back, the great master had with his own hand distributed *laddus* made from the purest ghee to the dosads. And now with the election coming up it was good sense to offend no one, no matter what his caste might be. These were not mere people, but votes. How many brahmans and kayasthas were there in the country? But there were far more of these poor, untouchable people. To make them angry would mean to turn electors against Raghunath Singh. Of his own volition the great master had distributed sweets to the hungry, half naked, animal-like untouchables and all the rustic people of Garudiya taluk! He was very clever.

The government had produced a machine called the election. Votes were the machine's oil. The more the people voted, the better the machine would run. Be they upper-caste or untouchable, literate or illiterate, everyone had to be well treated and gratified if the election were to be won. After the election they could be brought down and put back in their proper place, under the soles of the great master's shoes.

This had all been at the back of Ramlachhman's mind, and he had been reminded of it while watching Sukhan Ravidas's election rally. It would not be right to offend anyone just now. Hastily he spoke again, 'Forget the fine. Take this. One rupee for breakfast, two rupees for lunch. Hurry up now and eat.'

For Dharma, holding three rupees in his hand was the same as clutching three stars from the sky. His heart thumped with joy and excitement as he ran to the stalls. A little later he came back to the shade of the trees having feasted for the price of two rupees on dal, fried brinjal, vegetable curry, meat and mint pickle and rice. The one rupee for his breakfast would stay in his hand. This was a bonus he would save for his future.

By now the tribals had finished eating and Ramlachhman did not want to wait any longer. Hurrying them along, he said, 'Now your stomachs are satisfied, let's go.'

Everyone was ready. 'Yes, yes,' they all said.

Apart from the forty people that Dharma and Ramlachhman had selected, there were many other tribals still sitting under the trees, while everywhere landowners or their agents, who had all come while

Dharma had gone to eat, were sorting out and selecting from these leftover Oraons and Mundas.

Dharma now left with the tribals, the women having hitched their children to their backs. Up ahead Ramlachhman was heading off towards Garudiya on his rickety, creaking bicycle. Everyone else followed under the blazing hot sun. In the middle of this summer day the heat of the sun was deadly, and there was also a strong wind, which gusted from the north to the south as well as cutting diagonally from the east to the west. The earth was cracking in the heat; there was not a grain anywhere, and one would probably have to dig ten feet in the sand to get a small pot of drinkable water.

A middle-aged Munda, the leader of the group, was walking alongside Dharma. Not long before he had been sitting under the trees while the two recruiters had been trying to cajole them into being taken to the far northeast. They talked about various things as they walked, from which Dharma was able to glean that their village was about thirty or forty miles to the north. They underwent extreme hardship the whole year through, especially in this dry, hot season. The Munda told Dharma that now that the tilling season had come, landowners were selecting only strong and able people to work for them. He was appalled to think of the condition of the remainder – no work, no money, no food. Their only hope was either mahua and roots, or to be taken a long way away to some strange place by men from the towns offering them a full stomach for work.

There was little difference between bonded labourers like Dharma and these landless tribal labourers. Their lifestyles were virtually the same, the only difference between them being that the tribals were, generally, free, while Dharma and his kind were bound through generations by the chains of debt.

Curious, Dharma asked, 'Where are the townsmen taking your people?'

The Munda waved his hand and said, 'No idea.'

'Do those who go away get to eat? Do they get paid?'

'No idea.'

'Why not?'

'None of those who've gone away have ever come back. Last year a hundred men went from Dhamuda village. The year before a hundred and fifty went from three other villages – Golgoli, Pattan and Chauhat. No news of them either.'

'Are they still alivc, thcn?'

'No idea.'

There was silence for a while. A long distance bus rushed by, cutting the wind like some mad animal; cycle rickshaws and bullock and buffalo carts went along their way; and under the freedom of the sky a bonded labourer led a party of landless tribals. Having placed responsibility for these seasonal workers on Dharma's shoulders, Ramlachhman had ridden away out of sight.

After a few miles the two recruiters from the Chaharh market caught up with them. They had probably been following them, and now, seeing that Ramlachhman had gone on out of sight, they approached them. There might have been some trouble had Ramlachhman, a landowner's agent, seen them, and so they had followed them stealthily, waiting for their opportunity.

One of the recruiters came close to Dharma, who was talking with the middle-aged Munda, and asked, 'Where are you going?'

'To Garudiya,' the Munda replied.

'Whose land will you work on?'

'No idea. Ask him,' said the middle-aged Munda indicating Dharma.

The recruiters had seen Dharma a little while ago under the trees beside the Chaharh market, and although Dharma had come with a landowner's agent, they guessed from the look of him and the state of his clothes that he was a small peasant and of some low caste. They were not intimidated by him. They wanted to know whose land in Garudiya the tribals would be set to work on.

Dharma told them, 'Our maalik, Raghunath Singh's.'

The recruiters did not wait around to ask any more questions, but turned and went back towards Chaharh. Dharma had no wish to know why they should come running so far in the scorching summer heat to get such a trifling piece of information and then turn back again, but being totally unconcerned, he asked no questions.

Having had a rest here and there along the way, they at last reached Raghunath Singh's farm compound when evening had fallen, and by then Ganeri, Madholal, Kushi and the others already had handed in their ploughs and bullocks and returned home.

13

HIMGIRINANDAN WOULD NORMALLY WAIT IN HIS 'CONTROL ROOM' for the tribal labourers so that he might make arrangements for their first day's rations and accommodation. However, he was not to be seen there, nor was his bootlicker, Ramlachhman.

There were others there, however, who informed the tribals of all the arrangements that Himgiri had made for them. Maize flour, salt, chillies, kerosene and so on had all been measured out and were distributed to them. There had been no difficulty in arranging accommodation, of course, for behind the long tin sheds of the farm compound there were permanent mud huts for them, and they would be staying there for as long as their work lasted.

It was while they were doling out the tribals' rations that the compound staff told Dharma that Himgiri and Ramlachhman had gone to the dosad colony. Dharma was quite taken aback that Ramlachhman, with his long, stork-like legs, should be there in the midst of his neighbourhood. He had probably gone there on the pretext of some farm business, but his real purpose would have been to walk around drooling over the young girls. However, Himgirinandan had never been seen to go to the dosad colony for any reason whatsoever, even though Naorangi was his mistress. He might take an untouchable woman to his bed in the dark of night, but the high-caste Himgiri would never compromise his brahman status by going into her locality.

'Why have they gone there?' Dharma asked.

'No idea.'

'When did they go?'

'Just now. If you go there, you'll find them.'

Dharma could not imagine what reason Himgiri and Ramlachhman might have had in rushing off at evening to the untouchables' quarter, and a strange shiver of fear ran up his spine. He waited no longer. Even though his arms and legs were exhausted after walking five miles in the blazing sun to Chaharh and another five miles coming back, he forgot this as he ran off to the dosad colony.

Within a quarter of a mile of his neighbourhood the wind carried from the distance a sound like whimpering. Dharma stopped briefly. He felt his heart throbbing. He listened carefully and discerned that the sound was not of whimpering but of weeping. Someone was crying, sometimes loudly, sometimes softly. It was a woman. What could have happened? He took a deep breath and ran across the hard, stony ground.

As he got closer his bones shook with fear. A number of lanterns were burning on the ground and, in their light, he saw Gana lying face down on the ground, naked, his hands and feet bound. His body was lacerated from head to toe and covered with blood, and his cheeks were stained with froth. Apparently he was not quite unconscious yet. His chest rose and fell like a blacksmith's bellows as he took each breath after the other.

Standing on one side of Gana were Himgiri, Ramlachhman and three or four of Raghunath Singh's household thugs. Domestic bully-boys had been fostered by Raghunath's father and grandfather and by generations before them. As one age passed and a new one followed, the old strong-arm men would be replaced by young ones. They were kept for one purpose – to keep wilful and unruly animals, or bonded labourers, in their place. There is nothing they would not stoop to, from setting fire to houses to murder and concealment of the corpse. It was now clear why Himgiri and Ramlachhman had come after nightfall to the dosad colony.

Dharma had been frightened when meeting Gana under the pipal tree on the highway. He had told his boyhood friend to be careful entering the dosad colony, for he knew what a mess Raghunath Singh's men would make of him if he were caught, for the great master would by no means tolerate a man's running away to the town without his debt having been paid. While he was choosing tribal labourers at the Chaharh market and bringing them back to Garudiya, Dharma had forgotten about Gana, his friend who had fled from the bonded labourer's life of a subjugated and servile beast and who now, a year after becoming totally independent, had come back to rescue his mendicant mother. But Dharma had a sudden suspicion. How did Gana get caught? Apart from Naorangi there was no one in the colony who would go and betray him to Himgiri. Seeing that Gana had freed himself from his life of thraldom, the dosads had been very envious of him, but no one would dream of harming him. For a long time after he had run away everyone in the colony used to say to one another, 'None of us could leave this place, but Gana could. He's escaped,' and 'Gana's been smart enough to throw dust in the maalik's eyes and run off. Good for him!'

The entire colony secretly cherished a kind of awe for Gana's achievement, and that being the case, it was clear that only Naorangi could have told Himgiri about him. However, it had still been night when Gana went to the dosad colony and that whore still would have been in Himgiri's bed, although no sooner had the dawn sky started to become light than she would have come back. Dharma wondered and longed to know how Gana had been caught. He would find out later from Kushi.

Gana's mother, the old Shaukhi, was crying incessantly as she ran her hands gently over her son's torn and blood-smeared body, and the tears streamed continually down her sunken cheeks.

On one side of Gana and Shaukhi were Himgiri, Ramlachhman and the thugs, on the other side the dosads, who were appalled at seeing the consequences of one of their number wanting to be free. Noticing Kushi in the middle of the crowd, Dharma sneaked stealthily like a thief to stand beside her.

In the meantime, Himgiri's thin, sharp voice was penetrating the ears like a drill. 'Look! Look at what the son of a rat has come to now! Just you look at the consequences of running off without settling your debts! If any of you plan to run off like this, I'll break your bones. D'you hear me?'

The dosads were so frightened that no sound came from their mouths. Silently they inclined their heads to signal that they had heard.

Had Himgiri wanted, he could have had the thugs drag Gana to the farm compound and flay the flesh from his bones. Instead he had come straight to the dosad colony, called out the bonded labourers and had Gana beaten ruthlessly before their eyes as an example to them, to show these untouchable dogs – all of them – the consequences of wanting to run away from the life of a bonded labourer. Having witnessed such a frightening example, none of them would ever have the nerve even to dream of the illusion of freedom.

***

Scowling, and turning this way and that, Himgiri had watched with a frown the entertainment that had been Gana's beating. It had been a particularly good flogging. Now a bright smile of satisfaction beamed on his face and he suddenly cried out in his shrill, piercing voice, 'Well then, Gana, now call your police! Show us your police! Show us your laws! You son of the devil, only one man is the law in this Garudiya taluk, and he is Raghunath Singh. D'you hear me?'

The half-conscious Gana tried to speak, but it was unintelligible, little more than a slight trembling of his blood-smeared lips. But old Shaukhi, in a confused and twisted voice, said, 'He hears you, sir, he hears you.'

As he stood close to Kushi, Dharma remembered how before daybreak at the mention of Himgiri, Gana had said that it was not easy to break the law as there were police and judges in this country. Apparently he had said this to Himgiri too, and so the great master's bootlicking lapdog was both warning and taunting him.

Himgiri started screaming at Gana again. 'I've done nothing to you today! But if you plan to run away from here again, I'll crush your bones and plant your body in the sand and your police will be able to do nothing about it! D'you hear me?'

As before Shaukhi said, 'Yes, sir. Yes, sir.'

The experienced Ganeri stepped forward slightly and said, 'He won't run away, sir. Gana won't run away.'

'Well said,' Himgiri replied. 'You're their leader. You make the son of a rat understand as well as you can that the consequences of running away from here will not be pleasant. D'you hear me?'

'Yes, my lord.'

Himgirinandan did not wait any longer. He had staged an excellent performance, and now he left with his henchmen. In the meantime Ganeri, Madholal, Nathu and some others took Gana and carried him towards his hut. Still weeping, old Shaukhi followed them. No one else remained there on the hard, stony ground.

As he walked alongside Kushi, Dharma remembered his wish to know how Gana had fallen into the hands of Himgiri. Had he not taken care? Dharma put his mouth close to Kushi's ear and whispered, 'At dawn today when I went to Chaharh, I met Gana under the pipal tree on the highway.'

Kushi was alarmed. 'Did you?'

'Yes,' and Dharma went on to tell all that had transpired between him and Gana. 'How did he get caught?' he asked.

Kushi told him that while it was still dark that morning, Gana had not returned silently and taken old Shaukhi away, but rather had gone from house to house chatting about where he had been in the past year and what he had done, enticing everyone to leave this dog's life. However, everyone had to hurry off to the fields and no one had the time to talk to him any more. Meanwhile, Naorangi had come back from spending the night with Himgiri, to whom she returned as soon as she saw Gana. The dosads had been so excited by Gana that no one noticed her come or go. When everyone had finished their breakfast and had chatted with Gana, they were about to go out when Himgiri arrived at the dosad colony with the household thugs. However, they did not beat Gana then but tied him to a thick tree beside the well and two of the thugs stood guard over him. Gana then started shouting – he would go to the police station and lodge a complaint, and the police would put the lot of them in the lock-up, and so on and so on. As soon as the dosads came back from their work in the fields at evening, Himgiri turned up again. Had he not mentioned going to the police, Himgiri probably would not have had Gana beaten, and he might even have forgiven him. But one had to admit that Gana was an extraordinarily outspoken, insubordinate fellow.

As he listened, Dharma bowed his head in respect for Gana, as he had done so many times before.

14

THE NEXT FEW DAYS PASSED VERY QUICKLY, AND IN THIS TIME DHARMA had no chance to go to the jungle to look for young barking deer. Tirke had said that he would come back from Ranchi two days back. For Dharma it was good that he had not come yet – maybe he had been caught up in some work. Nevertheless, he would come any time now.

Dharma got up while it was still dark, just as on every other day. He had decided that today he would not go and drive the plough but, after having something to eat, he would go out with the field and jungle fossickers. In the jungle on the other side of the Koel he would see if he could find any young barking deer. If he could find one by midday, he would deliver it to Tirke in the afternoon. It was good working with Tirke.

Dharma had not yet told Kushi about not going to the fields. When, after eating and bathing, everyone was leaving the dosad colony, he said to her, 'I'm not going to the fields today.'

'Why not?' Kushi asked.

Dharma was carrying an axe over his shoulder. He put it down and turned to face Kushi, saying, 'You see this? Today I'm going to the jungle.'

Suddenly Kushi remembered, 'To look for deer?'

'Yes. Tirke said he'd come the day before yesterday. He's not come yet. If he comes today, tell him to wait.'

'All right. Don't be too long there.'

'I won't.'

'What'll I say if St Satan asks about you?'

'Tell him I've got fever.' He paused, then went on, 'You go and work with Uncle Ganeri today.'

Kushi nodded. 'All right.'

After going some way across the hard, stony ground outside the dosad colony, Kushi and the others went to the left up onto the highway, and Dharma walked on with the fossickers to the right. His parents, and Kushi's, were in the party, along with the numerous children of the colony. Most of the group were carrying on their heads earthen pots for the drinking water they would dig up from the sands of the Koel.

When Dharma and his group had reached the middle of the river bed, the Jyaistha sun could be seen starting to rise up in the eastern sky, its colour that of a blazing fire and its early morning radiance making the sands of the river bed look like millions of sparkling golden seeds. On either side of the Ranchi-Patna highway the grain fields of Garudiya and Bijuri taluks were starting to shimmer. Overhead, flocks of foreign parrots were drifting on the wind, which was gradually getting hotter, and a few sparrows and pigeons could be seen too. Birds seemed to come from everywhere in summer. The sky was now a deep blue, with white clouds like lumps of cotton wool here and there, their edges sparkling in the sunlight like gold.

Dharma did not notice any of this – the birds, the sky, the clouds. He had to get from the jungle a pair of young barking deer, for which he would be paid twenty rupees in cash, and the money meant a considerable advance towards a life of freedom. As he trudged over the sands, he thought only of how he would find and catch the deer.

They soon came close to the jungle of *sabui* grass where Dharma and Kushi came each day to set their traps for *bageri* birds. Beyond the thickets of *sabui* grass there was sparse jungle and a lot of grassland on both sides of the river bed where the cattle and goats of Bijuri and Garudiya were taken to graze. However, there had not been a scrap of cloud or a drop of rain since the month of Chaitra, and what little grass there had been in the fields in the first week or so of Vaishakh had been finished off by now. Whatever was there had faded a lifeless yellow in the blazing sun, and cows and goats would not even look at it. In fact, these days the herders hardly brought their animals this way at all.

A few of those who had come with Dharma from the dosad colony were young women and their children, who now sat down on the sandbanks of the Koel to dig for water. Once they had filled their water pots, they would go into the jungle to look for fruit and tubers. Most of them, however, had already gone into the jungle with Dharma, and once they had gathered some food, they would then go and dig in the sand for water.

About fifty yards from the *sabui* clumps they came to the start of the jungle. The forest at this point was very sparse, with thickets of various kinds of trees scattered about haphazardly. Now, in this month, there were blossoms that looked like clusters of flames on the branches of the *palas* and *simar* trees, but it was the mahua fruit that was mostly in evidence, and a strong smell of flowers and fruit wafted on the breeze.

Dharma's companions would collect food from this sparse region of the jungle, but he would go another sixty or seventy yards to where the jungle was very dense. If he did not go there, then he would not get any barking deer. However, when they all got to the edge of the jungle, they stopped where the jungle remained silent and still and where the herders no longer came, as the grass had already been eaten by their cows and goats. But today a crowd of energetic people could be seen picking mahua fruit and loading it into large bamboo baskets. Dharma and the others recognised them.

There were a few other wealthy people in Garudiya and Bijuri taluks beside Raghunath Singh and Mishirlal, with whom they bore no real comparison, of course, as they did not have vast holdings like those of Raghunath and Mishirlal whose families had, over generations, acquired almost all the cultivable land of this region. However, the negligible remainder was shared by these lucky few. In addition to land they were in the business of moneylending, they had big warehouses in the markets of Garudiya and Bijuri, they were shop owners, they rented out bullock and buffalo carts, cycle rickshaws and lorries, and did various other things. They also owned herds of cows, buffalo and goats, and the people who were picking mahua fruit were all herders of those wealthy men.

By the start of the month of Vaishakh all such edible things as sweet potatoes and other tubers were finished, and so, with food and water both very hard to come by, the summer months promised great hardship for the people of these parts. Having exhausted the tubers, the cast off people of the dosad colony began gathering mahua fruit, for if no other good food were available, then mahua fruit would do; they would have to survive on it for one or two months, as had been the case for years. However, Dharma and the others had never seen the herders picking the fruit as they were doing now.

Dharma and all the other dosads were standing close together. If all these workers of the wealthy were reaching out for the food of poor and hungry people like themselves, then the dosads were in danger of dying of starvation. They had no idea what to do.

Suddenly they all looked around at the sound of the feet of many people. A hundred and fifty or two hundred tribals – Mundas, Oraons, Santals – were coming across the sand. They were little more than skin and bone, famished looking, with deep sunken eyes and dressed in dirty rags. Most of the women carried babies on their hips, and they were crying after sucking at their mothers' breasts, which were as dry as the desert sands. It seemed that none of them had eaten for two or three days.

The tribals came and stood near Dharma and his group, who looked at these starving, half-naked people for some time. No tribals had ever been seen before in this region of the southern Koel. As though he were the representative of the dosads, Dharma asked, 'Tell me. Where are you from?'

An elderly Oraon came out from the midst of the tribals and, pointing directly to the west, said, 'Over there.'

'We've never seen you here before.'

'No. This is the first time.'

'What brings you here?'

Indicating the concavity of his leathery stomach the Oraon said something which Dharma could not understand, but went on looking at him. The old man spoke again. 'We've got nothing there – no rice, no wheat, no maize, no grain of any kind, not even any tubers – nothing. The leaves in the jungle are also gone. The day before yesterday we heard that we might find something in the jungle here. Maybe some mahua fruit. So we all left the village. If we don't get anything, we'll starve to death.'

Dharma stood there motionless for a little while. He and the other untouchable bonded labourers were also hungry and half-naked, yet theirs did not appear to be such a frightful state of adversity. Of course, he had heard a few stories from the tribal people the day he had gone to the market at Chaharh to fetch seasonal workers. Now he said nothing, but pointed to the jungle where mahua fruit was being picked. After surveying the situation the old Oraon and his companions were terribly despondent. The old man's chest was rising and falling like a blacksmith's bellows, and he sat down on the sand. 'A dead place. We're sure to die of starvation.'

Dharma did not wait any longer. He went and stood a few steps inside the jungle where the mahua fruit was being picked by people who were indeed rich men's herders who got fed well twice a day. In that case, why were they picking the mahua fruit, the food of the poor? Dharma thought about this for quite a long time. He then asked, 'Hey, bhai. Why are you picking the mahua fruit?'

The herders were of quite a different temperament. At first they saw no necessity to answer Dharma's question, but after repeated inquiry one of them said harshly, 'For the cows and goats.'

'Why will you give mahua fruit to the cows and goats?'

'Why do you think? To eat.'

'They'll eat mahua?'

'And why not? Where are we to find grass within ten or twenty miles? It's all shrivelled up. Should the animals starve?'

Dharma wanted to say that it was more urgent for people to survive than for animals, but he refrained. He did not know who were the masters of the mile after mile of this jungle alongside the Koel, but it did seem to him that a solution could be found by falling at the feet of the great master Raghunath Singh. He must be told that in these days of extreme hardship in this dry season the cowherds and goatherds should not be picking the mahua fruit, for that should be reserved as food for the poor and starving. If Raghunath Singh were informed, none of these herders would be entitled to go into the jungle. He believed this about Raghunath for one reason – that day of the distribution of the *laddus*. In the words of the schoolmaster, it was a vote feast. Would the man who loved the untouchables enough to give them sweets with his own hand allow poor folk to starve to death? But who would go and meet him? Dharma thought that he would discuss this matter later with Ganeri and others.

By now there were fourteen baskets full of mahua fruit, which the cowherds and goatherds loaded onto their heads and left.

Dharma knew that there were not many good mahua trees in the jungle just in front of him, but a little further in there were a great many. However, if the mahua fruit were continually being picked for cows and goats, in no time there would be none left at all! Indeed, this was cause for worry, and there could be no further delay. The day was wearing on. Who knew how long it would take to cover the seventy odd yards from here to the depths of the jungle and find some barking deer? Tirke might come from Ranchi, so Dharma would have to come back from the forest in the afternoon.

He called to the dosads behind him, and to the tribals, 'Come here.'

His and Kushi's parents and the tribals slowly approached him. Dharma told them that if they went a little further into the jungle they would find countless mahua trees.

The old Oraon who had seemed so decrepit now got up, greatly revived, a sparkle in his sunken eyes. 'You have saved us,' he said. Then he turned to his companions, waved his hand and said, 'Come on.'

Dharma led them all a little further on to a grove rich with mahua fruit. Then, warning his and Kushi's parents behind him, he said, 'Be careful in the jungle.'

'Yes,' they replied, as Dharma strode over the sandy ground of the forest.

'There are big wildcats.'

'We know.'

'There are tigers.'

'We know.'

'There are snakes.'

'We know.'

'There are bears.'

'We know.'

'There are many dangerous animals.'

'We know.'

The voices of the four old people gradually got fainter and fainter behind him.

15

It was almost noon by the time Dharma reached the heart of the jungle, where it was so dense and the overhead branches and foliage so thick that even the burning Jyaistha sun could not penetrate. Even in this fiery summer the interior of the jungle was very cool and shady, while the gentle breeze made the body feel thoroughly refreshed. The nearby channel of the southern Koel had become a narrow trickle with so much water having dried up in the summer heat, but what little water there was looked as clear as glass. However, the one thing that deterred the dosads from coming here to fetch water was their fear of such wild animals as cheetahs, bears, jackals and the like.

Dharma was well acquainted with this jungle. He knew by heart the names of all the trees and vines and recognised every thicket on sight. There was a great variety of trees here and, wherever one might look, all sorts of different coloured flowers adorned the forest as though it were a queen. Overhead were the brilliant red flowers of the *simar* and *palas* trees, making it look from a distance as though the roof of the forest were on fire, and the smell of the mahua fruit was wafted all about on the breeze.

Having walked so far, Dharma was out of breath. He sat down with his axe over his shoulder under a tall and clustering tree to take a little rest before going off to look for barking deer. Swarms of insects and grasshoppers were flitting all around, and through the gaps among the leaves he could see gliding about some incessantly squawking and chirping foreign parrots, some sparrows and, some way away, a few peacocks.

Dharma noted that the sun had now risen directly overhead, so he could not go on sitting there any longer. With his axe over his shoulder he got up and moved off. A little way on he noticed a snake zigzagging into a thicket. He took a few steps towards the thicket, then stopped suddenly and, in a twinkling, set the axe down and waited, standing stock-still. About ten feet ahead, standing against a thick *saguan* tree, was a big wildcat looking straight at him, its face narrow and its eyes glowing in the jungle shadows, ready to leap on Dharma at any moment. It started snarling, now and then baring its sharp, saw-like teeth.

Dharma was prepared. If the beast sprang, Dharma would summon all his strength to hurl a blow at its neck with his axe. But the wildcat did not spring. It started backing away, then turned suddenly, broke into a run, crossed the dry river bed and disappeared into the jungle on the other side. Dharma took a long, deep breath. Then, with his axe hanging from his hand, he walked on.

Some more time passed and Dharma guessed that the sun had progressed noticeably in the western sky, as the patches of sunlight in the forest had now started to turn a deep yellow. There was not much time left, and he would have to get out of this fearsome jungle somehow or other while it was still day. Straining his eyes, he kept continually looking to his right, to his left, behind and in front. However, it seemed as though the barking deer had conspired not to come out of the depths of the jungle today – and not just the deer but also the porcupines, bears, cheetahs, wolves and wild pigs. There was nothing to be found.

Dharma knew everything about the jungle and its animals and birds, and just then he remembered that the deer were friendly with the monkeys. If the monkeys should see from the treetops a cheetah in the distance, they would shout a warning to the deer with a very strange sounding call. If the deer came close to them, they would spring onto their backs from the branches of the trees, hold on to their antlers and ride them like horses around the jungle.

Dharma could do a precise imitation of the call of the monkeys. He stopped, put his axe down on the ground, cupped his hands around his mouth and whooped continually. Making this noise for a while made him breathless and his jaws ached, yet the barking deer still stayed away. He did not even get sight of any other kind of deer, plain or spotted. He fell into a bad mood and became quite disconsolate. The day had been a total waste.

The sun had declined a little further in the west and the shadows in the jungle were becoming heavier. It would be dark here before evening and he would have to get out before then. Danger lurked throughout the forest. A cheetah or a wolf could leap out from the cover of the foliage without his knowing about it. Tired and glum, Dharma gave up hope of finding any barking deer today, so he would have no chance of getting his twenty rupees. All he could do was head home.

As he approached the more sparse region of the jungle, he suddenly noticed three or four hares moving slowly from one thicket towards another. For as long as Dharma had been coming to this jungle he had never returned empty-handed, and so he decided that today he would not go back empty-handed either. He would kill these harmless creatures. They might not bring him any money, but at least he would feed on meat for a couple of days.

He took the axe from his shoulder in a flash, but just as he started to creep towards the animals, an arrow flew out of the jungle to his left and shot down one of the running hares. The gentle, harmless creature, like soft cotton, shuddered twice and then lay still.

Dharma was stunned. Who could have fired the arrow? No sooner had the question crossed his mind than he saw the remaining hares dart off like a flash of lightning. They had lengthened their stride, but before they had taken many steps another arrow shot down one of them on the run. The remaining hares were now no longer to be seen.

Dharma had never seen such an unfailing aim. Who was this archer who could shoot a running hare? He looked all around and saw a man come out from behind a vast *saguan* tree. He had flaky skin, cracked feet, yellowish eyes, his hair was sticking up and he was wearing dirty rags. His age could have been anywhere between forty and fifty-five. He looked like a Munda, and his body showed all the signs of hunger. Dharma had never seen the man; he was not one of the tribals he had brought into the jungle just before noon. So where had he come from?

The Munda had very likely not hoped to get a second trophy in this jungle. As he walked towards his arrow-pierced, bleeding prize, he noticed Dharma and stopped suddenly. Dharma moved slowly towards the Munda. He had not wanted anyone else to come here, and he furrowed his brow and asked angrily, 'Who are you?'

'Rukhiya Munda,' the man replied.

'I've never seen you.'

'I don't belong to these parts.'

'Where are you from?'

Pointing to the west, Rukhiya said, 'Over there. Ten miles to the west.'

'What did you come here for?' asked Dharma.

Looking at the two hares, Rukhiya said, 'You can see what I came here for.'

'Why did you kill the two hares?'

'Why? For three days my children have been hungry. We've not been able to get a scrap to eat. I went looking for work. There's no work. I went begging. Got nothing. Then I heard from someone that there were animals in this jungle, some edible grains, tubers, fruit. So at first light of day I set out with my bow and arrows.'

The other tribals, who had come in the morning, had come from the south; Rukhiya had come from the west. Perhaps a lot more would come over the next few days. Dharma could imagine many people laying claim to this jungle, people who, for the sake of survival, were coming from all around. For so long Dharma had had this jungle much to himself, but in no time there would be a scramble for a share of it. Despite this, though, Dharma was not hostile towards Rukhiya. On the contrary, he felt some sympathy for this scantily clad, hunger-stricken man. He said to him, 'I too had a mind to kill those two hares. But you shot them before I could.'

Rukhiya considered this, and said, 'All right then. You take one, I'll take the other.'

Dharma was not averse to this arrangement. He said nothing, but nodded his head in agreement.

Rukhiya pulled the sharp arrow heads from the bodies of the dead hares, and a little later the two men, each with a carcase swinging from his hand, moved out of the jungle and onto the burning sandbank of the river bed, which was now long deserted by the rejected people of the dosad colony and the tribal people who had come from the south. Who knew when they had gone with whatever they had gleaned from the jungle?

The sun had sunk further and the western sky now was aglow with a brilliant blood red. However, the temperature was not yet any lower than it had been in the middle of the day. For miles and miles the sand looked like grains of flame, and to walk over it felt as though one's feet were blistering, yet there was some relief in the strong wind.

As they walked along together, Dharma said, 'You must have a great aim to shoot a running hare. I've never seen anyone shoot like that before.'

'I can bring down a bird from the sky,' Rukhiya said.

'Really?' Dharma was amazed.

'Oh, yes. Do you want to see for yourself?'

Dharma did not know what to say, but Rukhiya told him that from now on he would come to this jungle nearly every day, and if Dharma should come too, he would show him how he could shoot a bird flying in the sky.

Dharma said nothing as he walked on over the sand with Rukhiya, but looking up at the sky he suddenly became anxious. All this time he had been preoccupied with the magic of Rukhiya's archery, but who knew whether or not Tirke had come yet? He started to lengthen his stride, as he had to get back to the fields before sunset. Immediately Rukhiya too strode out with him. Then he said, 'Today is the first time I've come to your region.'

'Yes,' Dharma replied, somewhat distracted.

'There are lots of birds and animals in that jungle, aren't there?'

'Yes.'

'Boars?'

'Yes.'

'Deer?'

'Yes.'

'Barking deer?'

'Yes.'

'*Tetar* birds?'

'Those too – '

'By the grace of God, my kids won't have to starve.'

Dharma did not answer.

Rukhiya went on, 'From tomorrow, I'll come to this jungle of yours every day.' Rukhiya had already said this once before. Dharma said nothing, and increased his pace.

Some way on from the clumps of *sabui* grass Rukhiya said, 'I'll go left here.'

'All right,' said Dharma, inclining his head.

'Do you come to the jungle every day?'

'No. Only now and then.'

'I'll see you next time, then.'

Rukhiya Munda, the hare swinging from his hand, crossed the dry river bed and climbed the steep bank to the left. Then, with long strides, he walked directly to the west, the sharp heads of his arrows glinting in the late rays of the sun, and soon he went on out of sight behind some trees and a small hill.

By the time the sun had started to decline towards the horizon, Dharma came up onto the highway where he saw Tirke standing at the bus stand under the pipal tree. Once Tirke saw Dharma he came towards him and, noticing the hare in his hand, he said, 'What's that? I ordered live barking deer kids and what you bring back is a dead hare!'

'The hare's not for you,' Dharma said. He paused, and then asked, 'When did you come from Ranchi?'

'At midday. Now the sun's starting to set. I went to the fields and Kushi told me you'd gone to the jungle. You'd have to come back this way, so I waited here. Naturally I thought that you'd bring the deer. Instead it's a dead hare.'

'I tried really hard, but I couldn't find any deer. So what do I do, then?'

Tirke thought for a moment, and then said, 'The American gentleman is leaving tonight. He'll come back again in a month. Will you be able to get the deer by then?' Then, to reassure Dharma, he took two ten-rupee notes from his shorts pocket and, giving them to him, said, 'Take this. I'm paying you fully in advance.'

No sooner had Tirke finished speaking than the Ranchi bus pulled up. Jumping aboard he said, 'I'm off now. Don't forget the deer.'

'No, no.' Dharma was very happy to have been given a month's grace. He had given up hope of getting the twenty rupees for the deer, and then, quite unexpectedly, he had the money in his hand and his optimism increased tenfold. He would be able to provide the deer on time.

The Ranchi bus set off and Dharma went straight to the east along the highway, stuffing the money into his waistband through the hole for the cord. After walking a little way he noticed the tribal people of that morning, cooking on the lowland beside the highway. Most likely they were boiling the creepers and mahua fruit they had got from the jungle. He also saw among them the old Oraon man. Dharma called out, 'Are you going to stay here, then?'

The old man replied, 'We'll stay as long as there are creepers and mahua fruit.'

Dharma was about to say something when he heard a cry.

'Vote for – '

'Raghunath Singh!'

'Give your vote to – '

'Raghunath Singh!'

The now familiar jeep was sending up dust and heading towards Raghunath Singh's house. The election festival was underway.

After the jeep had disappeared around the bend, Dharma looked at the grain fields beside him. There was no one there, and even the big field was completely empty. After a whole day's work the bonded labourers from the dosad colony had gone back with their ploughs and bullocks.

Dharma did not tarry, but went off along the highway.

16

THE SUN HAD QUITE DISAPPEARED FROM THE SKY NOW AS evening fell.

Without any diversion Dharma headed straight back to the dosad colony. By now the bonded labourers had finished their work, put back their ploughs and bullocks in Raghunath Singh's farm compound and gone home. Now the kerosene lamps were being lit in the houses. Dharma reached his own place and, as he set the hare down on the veranda, his mother's eyes lit up. In her joy she almost cried out, 'You've brought a hare!'

'Yes. I got it in the jungle.' Dharma bent over and went inside the shanty through the little door that was like an opening to a tunnel. He put his axe in its proper place and went back out onto the veranda. He could not see his father, Shiulal, anywhere. This seemed odd, as his mother and father were always together. Whenever they went to fetch food or water, they would go together, and when they had come home his mother would light the stove and sit down to cook, while his father would sit back against one of the bamboo posts. Today was an exception. Dharma asked, 'Where's *baba*?'

This seemed to jolt his mother's memory. She quickly told him that the men of the dosad colony had gathered in front of Ganeri's place. Ganeri had told her to send Dharma there as soon as he got back.

'Why?' asked Dharma.

'I've no idea,' said his mother. 'Just hurry up and go.'

Hearing Dharma's voice Kushi came out of the shanty next door. She too was overjoyed at the sight of the hare, for she would get some of it. After finding out how he came by the hare, Kushi then told him, 'Tirke came.'

'I saw him,' Dharma replied.

'Did you give him the deer?'

'I didn't find any,' said Dharma, coming down from the veranda.

'You went to the jungle in vain, then,' Kushi observed.

'Yes. A waste of a day,' said Dharma as he headed towards Ganeri's house.

From behind, Kushi said, 'St Satan came to the field. He was asking about you.'

'What did you tell him?'

'That you had fever.'

'What did he say?'

'Nothing.'

Dharma quickened his pace and came to Ganeri's place in the middle of the village. There was a large space in front of Ganeri's hut, where all the men of the colony were sitting around in a circle, in the centre of which burned a kerosene lantern. Amongst Raghunath Singh's bonded labourers were also those who had been rejected by him, as well as independent men like Mangilal and Phaguram. On one side of the assembly sat Ganeri, the leader of this dosad society, looking like a rough-hewn statue. The lantern flame was flickering slightly in the breeze, its light playing over the faces of all who were there.

Ganeri saw Dharma first and called, 'Hey, Dharma, come and sit here,' and he indicated the place he was making beside himself.

Dharma asked as he sat down, 'What's the matter? Why have you called me, Uncle Ganeri?'

'There's some urgent business.'

'What?'

Ganeri cleared his throat. Then, looking very serious, he began, 'The drought this year has been particularly harsh. No one has known such a severe drought in twenty or twenty-five years. The sun has cracked the fields and the rivers have dried up and are little more than sand. There's no drinking water, and there's nothing to eat. Those of our colony who don't go to work on the maalik's land have had to get by for two months on mahua fruit from the jungle. But now the goatherds and cowherds of wealthy men are coming and taking that fruit and feeding it to their animals. There are also such herders among those who graze animals for the great master. If they're going to take mahua fruit like this every day, our poor folk won't survive.' Having said all this without a break, Ganeri paused for a moment.

Dharma guessed that the rejects of the dosad colony had told Ganeri about the cowherds and goatherds taking the mahua fruit, and that was the reason for this day's urgent 'mitin'. Thanks to the election, everyone of the region – young and old, men and women, caste and outcaste – knew this word 'mitin', for every few years the 'vote babus' would come and hold 'mitins' here.

Dharma said, 'I saw those herders today with my own eyes taking the mahua fruit. But what is this mitin for?'

Ganeri replied, 'Before you came we decided that we would all go to the maalik.'

'Why?'

'He must put a stop to the taking of mahua fruit for animals. We'll fall at his the feet and say, "Save us, O father and mother of the poor!"'

Nathu spoke up from amongst the crowd. 'Will the maalik listen? He too has many buffalo, cows, goats – '

'He'll listen, Nathu,' answered Ganeri. 'Of course he'll listen. This year the maalik has to listen to our concerns.'

This surprised Dharma. 'Why?' he asked.

'This is election time. Doesn't he need our votes?'

Ganeri was right. Raghunath Singh would certainly want to keep them happy at this election time. He who had distributed with his own hands *laddus* to untouchable bonded labourers like themselves would certainly look kindly on their request for mahua fruit. And if he said so, the other rich men of Garudiya and Bijuri would stop sending their men into the jungle for it. It was because Ganeri had such vision that he was their leader.

Ganeri said, 'We'll go right now with our request. Then the herders will be stopped from going to the jungle as from tomorrow.' No one ever disagreed with Ganeri. Anyhow, mahua fruit had become an issue of life or death for the dosads.

Just as they were all about to get up and go, they heard the voice of Ramlachhman singing his one line of song, then, 'Hey, Phaguram! Are you about?'

Neither Raghunath Singh nor any of his bootlickers had ever had any reason to come looking for Phaguram. His father Bhiguram had been a one-generation bonded labourer, on whose death Phaguram immediately became free. In twenty or thirty years no one had ever come calling him on Raghunath Singh's behalf. It had seemed as though Raghunath Singh and his men had forgotten about this man who was only in name and bearing a member of the dosad community; now, suddenly and at night, the high-caste brahman Ramlachhman had come into the untouchables' quarter to look for him. They were all dumbfounded. Phaguram answered apprehensively, 'Yes, sir,' and stood up. He was afraid, as he did not know whether or not he had unwittingly committed some offence for which he was now being called to answer.

Ramlachhman had by now come upon the gathering. He looked at Phaguram and said, 'You have to come with me, Phagu.'

'Where to, sir?' Phaguram inquired, with bated breath.

'To the maalik's house. He has summoned you.' He sang his line and then said, 'Come on, then. Hurry up.'

Phaguram's knees started to tremble at the mention of the great master, and he clenched his teeth. He tried extraordinarily hard to say something, but the words would not come out.

Now Ganeri slowly got to his feet. He looked frightened as he asked, 'Has Phaguram done anything wrong, sir?'

'No, no,' Ramlachhman replied and sang his one line. 'The Maalik has asked me to bring him, that's all. I know nothing more than that. Come on, then, Phagu, let's go.'

Phaguram had clenched his teeth in fright at the mention of the name of Raghunath Singh, and felt as though his bones were about to turn to jelly. He clasped Ganeri's hand and said fearfully, 'Brother, you must all come with me,' for he did not have the courage to go on his own.

Ganeri said, 'We have to go to him anyhow, about the mahua fruit.' He cast his eyes over the gathering and urged them, 'Come on, get up, all of you.'

'What's this?' asked Ramlachhman. 'Is the whole dosad colony going to accompany Phaguram?'

Ganeri informed him of their earlier decision to go to the great master's residence.

'What's your intention in going to him?' Ramlachhman asked.

'We've urgent business.'

Ramlachhman asked no more questions, but just sang his one line of song. 'We can't wait any longer,' he said, as he set off.

***

It had got quite late by the time the dosads, walking behind Ramlachhman, reached the home of Raghunath Singh. Four or five electric lights illuminated the vast compound of the mansion, lights so strong that one could see well enough to pick up a needle from the ground.

Raghunath Singh was lolling back in his own special easy chair on the stone-tiled veranda. Three of his lapdogs were with him – the doctor, the lawyer, and the munshi Ajibchand. Raghunath Singh was taken aback to see all of a sudden so many of the dosads with Ramlachhman. He looked frowningly at them for some time, then he slowly sat up and said to Ramlachhman, 'I told you to bring Phaguram, and you bring me the whole dosad colony, you stupid idiot.'

In fear Ramlachhman hastily uttered his one line of song and said, 'But I have brought only Phaguram. But they all came too. They have some urgent matter to put to you.'

Raghunath Singh looked at the dosads and asked, 'What is the matter, Ganeri?'

All of the dosads paid their respects to Raghunath Singh by pressing their hands together and touching their heads to the ground. Then Ganeri, as their representative, came forward a little way and, keeping his hands together, put his petition about the mahua fruit.

After listening to it all, Raghunath Singh remained silent. Seemingly distracted he said, 'All right. The herders will not take the mahua fruit.'

The dosads were amazed. Despite their trust in Ganeri they still had entertained some doubts and fears that their petition would not be favourably accepted. But the opposite had been the case. Ganeri was truly a man of the world with a profound understanding of the human heart. What a leader! The whole dosad colony's respect for him suddenly increased tenfold.

Then Ganeri remembered something else. Grasping his opportunity he said, 'Sir, there is one more thing.'

'What?'

'Our well has been blocked with sand for twenty years. We have great trouble getting drinking water. If your lordship could give orders for it to be cleared . . . '

'All right. I will tell Himgiri.'

The tenfold increase in the dosads' respect for Ganeri over the business of the mahua fruit now increased even more! In fact, at election time Raghunath Singh would offend nobody, becoming a wishing-tree for whatever one wanted, and Ganeri had taken advantage of this. All the time he thought only of what would bring advantage and happiness to the dosads.

As soon as Raghunath Singh had finished speaking, the munshi Ajibchand leaped to his feet and concluded the business by crying, 'O, dosads, by the grace of your master you have got your mahua fruit and he has agreed to have your well cleared. The rule of God has come upon us! *Ram raj* is here!'

Raghunath Singh liked to hear this kind of continuous flattery and exaggeration. However, he feigned a look of impatience as he said, 'Come now, Ajibchand. Be quiet, old man.'

Ajibchand had been well trained in where to stop and which of his master's words to let go in one ear and out the other. He raised his voice even louder as he cried, '*Ram raj* has come to us! *Ram raj* has come to us!'

Wanting to completely change the subject Raghunath Singh said, 'We'll have no more of this nonsense.' He then turned to Ganeri and said, 'I have approved of all you have asked for. Now you may go. But Phagua must stay. I have need of him.'

Ganeri pressed his hands together and, bowing, said, 'If your lordship pleases?'

'What?'

'We will wait with Phagua, and return to our quarters with him when his work is done. By your grace, sir . . . '

'All right. You can all go and sit over there. Let only Phagua stay here.' Raghunath Singh gestured Ganeri and the others to the front part of the compound. Phaguram was standing near the veranda, while Ganeri and the others went away and sat down on the grass. Raghunath Singh now looked at him and spoke softly and affectionately. 'I have heard about you from everyone. You were once a member of a *nautanki* troupe?'

Since Ramlachhman had gone to the dosad colony to make known Raghunath Singh's order, Phaguram's knees had not stopped shaking, but Raghunath Singh's gentle tone now provided him with a little reassurance. He answered, 'Yes, sir.'

'Everyone says that you have an exceptionally sweet voice, a magical voice. No one can forget hearing you sing.' Phaguram hung his head at the great master's praise and said nothing. Raghunath Singh continued, 'When you were in the *nautanki* troupe, you were known as the Nightingale of Garudiya, isn't that so?'

Phaguram nodded without looking up. Indistinctly he said, 'Yes, sir. People fondly gave me that name.'

'And you are no longer with the *nautanki* troupe?'

'No, sir. I left it three years ago.'

'Because of some chest ailment?'

'Yes, sir.'

'And now you earn a little money by singing at the station?'

Phaguram was amazed. How could a man as great as Raghunath Singh know so much about one such as he, more worthless than the merest insect? He said, 'Yes, sir.'

There was a brief silence, after which Raghunath Singh said, 'I have heard that you can also compose songs.'

With a look of modesty Phaguram said, 'By your grace, sir, I had to write songs when I was in the troupe.'

'Excellent. Now listen. From tomorrow you are no longer to go to the station to sing and beg.'

Phaguram looked up, his eyes questioning. 'Sir, if I don't beg, what will I eat? I will starve to death, master.'

'You will not starve to death. From now on, responsibility for your stomach will be mine.'

'By your grace, my lord.'

Raghunath Singh thought for a moment, and said, 'There is only one thing that you will have to do.'

Having found out about him now after such a long time, Raghunath Singh was certainly not so magnanimous as to have taken on full responsibility for Phaguram out of mere kindness. Phaguram waited with bated breath for his orders.

Raghunath Singh said, 'The election is coming. Do you know that?'

'I do, sir.' Phaguram inclined his head.

'I am standing in the election for the first time. Apart from me there are five others – Sukhan Ravidas, Pratibha Sahay, Nekiram Sharma, Abu Malek, and a fifth whom I am not concerned about at all. These four cause me to lose sleep. Sukhan Ravidas is an untouchable, a tanner. He will try to draw the votes of the untouchables of Bijuri and Garudiya taluks. Pratibha Sahay is married into a wealthy Patna family who own ten or twelve factories in Jhariya and Ranchi. Pratibha-ji will draw the votes of the kayasthas. Garudiya's Nekiram Sharma will want to have control over the votes of the brahmans. Bijuri's Abu Malek will draw the Muslims' votes. Do you understand all this, Phaguram?'

Phaguram had travelled around quite a lot with the *nautanki* troupe and had had a wide experience of people. If someone yawned he could even tell what he had had for breakfast. He answered, 'I understand, sir.'

'What do you understand?'

'That if the brahman, the kayastha, the Muslim and the untouchable draw the votes, then you can't win the election. You'll have no hope at all.'

Raghunath Singh was pleased. He said appreciatively, 'Then you do understand. You are a very intelligent man. You must work for me.'

'What must I do, master?'

Raghunath Singh then explained that he would provide various pieces of secret scandal about Nekiram Sharma, Pratibha Sahay, Abu Malek and Sukhan Ravidas. From that material Phaguram would compose some witty, entertaining songs and sing them wherever Raghunath Singh's men were campaigning for him or wherever his 'vote mitins' might be. Having explained the whole business Raghunath Singh asked, 'Can you do that, then?'

'I can, by your grace, sir.'

'Then you start tomorrow.'

'As you command. But, great master . . . '

'What?'

'My harmonium is no good at all any more, and does not fit the prestige of the great master. If I go out to sing vote songs with it, people would scoff at me for using it in your election and your honour would be ruined. They would say – '

Raghunath Singh raised his hand to stop Phaguram. He could see that Phaguram was trying to wangle a good harmonium from him on the pretext of the election. Phaguram was an exceptionally clever, crafty fellow. However, on a grand occasion like an election a harmonium was a very negligible thing, and he had indeed arranged for it even before he had sent for Phaguram. 'That's all right. Tomorrow you will have a new harmonium.'

Phaguram almost cried out for joy. 'A new harmonium! A new harmonium by the great master's grace!'

Raghunath Singh just smiled slightly. Sitting right beside him was Badribishal Chaube, who said, 'You'll get your harmonium tomorrow. But we want good songs.'

'Don't worry,' said Phaguram. 'I'll compose such songs that will enchant everyone in Garudiya and Bijuri. If I can't bring down your four opponents, then my name isn't Phaguram.' He looked at Raghunath Singh and went on, 'It's got very late. By your leave, sir, we will now go home.' The other dosads would never have had the nerve to talk about going home straight to the great master's face. They would all have sat there in silence until Raghunath Singh had given the word, but Phaguram was altogether different. He could talk like that as he was an independent man.

'Yes,' said Raghunath Singh, 'you can go now.'

A little later, after they had left the great master's house and were on their way back to the dosad colony, Ganeri said to Phaguram, 'I'm very worried, Phagu.'

Phaguram was bubbling over with joy at getting a new harmonium. He turned to Ganeri and said, 'What are you worried about, Uncle?'

'Pratibha-ji is a wife of a very wealthy family. They've got so much money, and they keep so many strong-arm men. Sukhan is an untouchable like us, and he is respected by the untouchables of the two taluks. There are also many people in the hands of Nekiram and Abu Malek. Think wisely before you make up songs about them and sing them.'

'Don't worry, Uncle. I'll be very careful.'

'And so you should. But I can only go on repeating, you must be very much on your guard.'

'I'll bear your warning in mind, Uncle Ganeri.'

By then everyone had reached the dosad colony.

17

THERE WAS A SPREADING *KARAIYA* TREE AT THE ENTRY TO THE untouchables' quarter, and from the distance Dharma and the others could see a covered bullock cart standing under it – made visible from far away by the lantern that was hanging from underneath it. Of course, it was common knowledge to all that once evening had fallen the bullock cart would be there, for it had been coming there at nightfall for some years. Today, however, it was late.

It was the cart sent by Himgirinandan, and everyone in the dosad colony knew that as soon as the moon had risen after the setting of the sun, Naorangi would make herself ready and, after it had got a little darker, go and get into the cart under the *karaiya* tree and set off towards the farm compound, the cart creaking and grating as it went.

As Naorangi was the mistress of one of the great master's leading bootlickers, none of the dosads had the nerve to say anything to her directly. However, as they all hated her, they reviled her behind her back.

Keeping their distance from the cart, as though avoiding sin, Dharma and the others entered their colony. As they passed by the cart, someone said with restrained hostility, 'That slut of a bitch.'

Budheri said, 'They flogged Gana, thanks to that harlot from hell!'

It was the excessive beating of Gana that underpinned the fear and dread that was evident in the dosad colony when Phaguram had been suddenly sent for by Raghunath Singh, and Budheri's words reminded everyone of it. Ganeri spat and said, 'All on account of that whore.'

The dosads' eyes could be seen blazing in the moonlight. Their intense hatred and malice towards Naorangi was suddenly greatly intensified, though no one said anything else as they went one by one into their neighbourhood, their teeth clenched.

A little while later the whole neighbourhood had finished eating and the kerosene lanterns were no longer burning. After a whole day of back-breaking toil, the dosads had gone now to their beds. Dharma, however, had not gone to bed – altogether he was totally exhausted. Nevertheless, he sat smoking a beedi, leaning against a post on the veranda. He needed to see how Gana was after his ruthless beating by the bully-boys. Gana was his friend from childhood days, and he felt deeply troubled on his account.

Dharma continued to sit and pass the time smoking, however, for one reason. He had been keeping an eye out, but Naorangi had not gone yet. God only knew why the whore was taking so long today. As long as she had not gone, Dharma did not have the nerve to go to Gana's hut, for if Naorangi saw him going to Gana, needless to say she would tell Himgiri about it and his life would be totally finished. He smoked one beedi after the other for as long as Naorangi remained in the dosad colony.

When the beedi in his hand had burned right down, he heard the jingling sound of silver anklets. He turned around and saw Naorangi coming from the other side of the well. Despite the boundless hatred and malice he bore for her in his heart, this comely, middle-aged, kept woman still seemed like a fairy to him in the light of the moon – a demon in disguise.

When she came near, Naorangi suddenly stopped. 'You're not sleeping yet?' she asked.

'No.' Dharma shook his head.

'Why are you still up?'

'I couldn't sleep.'

'Go to bed. It's very late.' She waited no longer. The sweet sound of her jingling anklets could be heard again as she went and got onto the bullock cart.

A few moments later the cart set off, creaking and grating, and Dharma got up straightaway. Having now reached Gana's hut at the far end of the colony so late at night, he was quite taken aback. By the light of a lamp Shaukhi and Gana were bundling their things together – a few enamel bowls and plates, a brass jug, some pots and pans, Shaukhi's few dirty, tattered clothes, and so on.

They were surprised to see Dharma so late at night. Gana said to him, 'Come in.'

'What's going on?' Dharma asked. 'Why are you packing your things?'

'We're leaving.'

'But the great master's men gave you such a beating!'

Fearfully Shaukhi said, 'I've told Gana so many times, they've already beaten you once. If you run off again without paying the debt, they'll kill you.'

Gana got angry. 'It's not as simple as that!' He paused, then said, 'For three generations we've slaved on that Rajput's land. Hasn't that paid off five hundred rupees? They can't exploit me if I'm dead. Never ever.'

Suddenly Dharma felt rather glum. If only he could talk like Gana! But he had a thousand drawbacks. There were his elderly parents, and then there were Kushi and her elderly parents. Of course, Gana had said that he would arrange a job for him at his factory. But Dharma was weak and afraid; he did not have the nerve of Gana. Having taken on responsibility for five people, he trembled at the thought of leaping into an unknown future.

'You mustn't do any more bonded labour, Dharma,' said Gana. 'I told you before and I'm telling you again, I'll get you a job. Kick this bastard Rajput Raghunath and his household arse-lickers in the face and clear off from here.'

This was the sort of thing that free men said. Dharma realised that, now Gana had got a taste of freedom, nothing at all would make him crawl back to the contemptible life of the dosad colony. 'I'll remember what you say, Gana.'

Their packing was finished, and Gana asked, 'You came from over there. Did you see the slut? All this time that bitch has been sitting in her place watching me. Now I don't hear any sound of her.'

Dharma had no trouble understanding who the 'slut' or 'bitch' was, and he now understood why she had gone so late to Himgiri. He said, 'Naorangi has just left in Himgiri's bullock cart.'

'I thought so,' said Gana, 'so I lit the lamp and set about packing ma's utensils and clothes. If I should come across that whore in Dhanbad market . . . ' He said no more, but simply drew his finger across his throat.

Dharma remained silent.

Gana took the heavy things on his shoulder and in his hand and told Shaukhi to carry the small, light bundles. He blew out the lamp and put it in the cloth bag hanging from his shoulder. He said, 'Goodbye, then, Dharma.'

The effects of yesterday's terrible beating had not yet abated. Gana could not walk easily, but somehow managed to get along, dragging one foot after the other. Dharma walked beside him and Shaukhi came behind.

A little later Gana and Shaukhi left Dharma at his shanty and went off along the road outside. Looking over his shoulder, Gana once more said, 'Goodbye, Dharma.'

Dharma inclined his head and said, 'Goodbye.'

Gana took his elderly mother over the stony field bathed in moonlight to a life of freedom, while a bonded labourer remained standing motionless beside his shanty in the dosad colony and feeling a sudden, unbearable discomfort in his heart.

18

WHEN NAORANGI CAME BACK EARLY THE NEXT MORNING, THE FIRST thing she did was to look in on Gana. Finding no sign of him or his mother, she raised a hue and cry alarming the whole dosad colony. A little later the news of Gana's flight had somehow spread to Raghunath Singh's farm compound and straightaway Himgiri, Ramlachhman and their thugs came running, sending all the dosads into a panic.

But where was the man for whom Himgiri and his men had come running in such urgency? Actually, Gana and his mother had fled Raghunath Singh's own little India and were now close to Dhanbad. Gana would not be kept confined in thraldom, and Himgiri and his men would always resent that. Their only consolation was that after catching him they could give him a thorough flogging. However, the same man had to cultivate the land of the great master until his death, so where was the profit in beating him?

The matter of Gana's running away again after having been severely flogged was extremely serious. Of course, the absence of one man hardly caused a problem in the cultivation of the thousands of acres held in the great master's name, or in his various aliases, but if Gana's example should provide some nerve and inspiration to the rest of the untouchables, the consequences could be grave indeed.

Screeching at the top of his high-pitched voice, Himgiri said, 'All right, you sons of buffaloes, tell me how Gana got away from here! How did he have such hide?'

Their voices trembling with fear, the dosads answered, 'We don't know anything, sir – '

'The bastard and his ma can't just disappear with the wind! They had to walk through your neighbourhood. There are so many of you here, and none of you had any inkling? Am I supposed to believe that?'

On behalf of the dosads the prudent Ganeri told him that having worked so hard the whole day they all had returned to their homes and were dead to the world as soon as they had gone to their beds. No one was at all conscious of anything that happened in the world after that. As they were asleep, they had no idea of when Gana and Shaukhi had run away.

Himgiri raised his voice even higher so that it pierced the ears of everyone. 'You're a pack of animals!'

Ganeri, gaping, was about to say something when suddenly Naorangi called out from the other side, 'Hey, Dharma!'

Dharma looked at Naorangi, startled. 'What?'

'Last night you were sitting up late, weren't you?'

Dharma's breath stopped. He could sense what Naorangi was leading to, and although he tried to speak not a word would come out. Her eyes were fixed on him like those of a viper as again she asked sharply, 'Well then, have you lost your tongue?'

With great difficulty Dharma cleared his throat and somehow managed to say weakly, 'After you had got into the bullock cart last night, I didn't stay up any longer. I went inside and went to bed.'

Dharma felt that with this small lie an earthquake had been let loose inside his chest. However, the mention of Naorangi's nightly boarding the cart had an amazing effect, just like a conjuring trick. It was hardly any secret, of course, that this woman of ill-repute went every night to Himgiri. Everyone in Garudiya knew about it, as did the cats and dogs and even the night-prowling jackals. However, that so many should know of the sordid doings of a brahman and his untouchable mistress, even see them with their own eyes, and then hang out their dirty washing in front of them, was just too much – Himgiri's social reputation would be eternally sullied. The man's psychology was indeed peculiar.

Himgiri quickly broke in, 'Just take careful heed of the fact that wherever Gana has gone, he'll never get away. Maybe today, maybe tomorrow, maybe the day after, we'll get a rope around his neck. He's not going to succeed. We'll bury him alive. So if any of you here thinks of going the same way, you can't imagine what fate awaits you. D'you hear me?'

All the dosads inclined their heads to signal that they had heard him.

Then Himgiri pointed to the sky, and said, 'Well, don't you see?'

On any other day, as soon as it was starting to become light, the bonded labourers would be setting off to Raghunath Singh's farm compound. Today, however, with Gana and Shaukhi having run away and Himgiri and his men rushing to the colony, everyone had lost track of the time; meanwhile, the sun had come up on another summer morning. And no sooner had the sun risen than the temperature started to soar.

Ganeri and his people took a look at the sky and understood Himgiri's gesture – they could no longer stand around stupidly but must now go to work. The labourers made a rush to their shacks where they hurriedly bolted down some leftover food, fastened their midday meals to their backs and set off for the farm compound, where they would collect their ploughs and bullocks and hurry off to the fields.

As he approached the compound, Dharma looked at the back of it, where the huts, all joined to one another like pigsties, were now empty. The seasonal Oraon and Munda labourers whom he and

Ramlachhman had brought from the Chaharh market had already gone to work. Since coming here they had gone each day with Dharma and the others to the fields and returned together after their full day's work. Today, noticing that the morning was getting on, they had not waited.

Once they had got to the fields, no one had the time even to breathe before getting down to work with plough and bullock. From all around came the cries, 'Urra, urra, hat, hat – !' mixed with the sounds of the ploughs' striking against the rough, stony ground.

After a long, uninterrupted spell of work, Dharma lifted his head and had a look all around. The tribal peasant labourers were cultivating the land as far as he could see to the left. Up until yesterday afternoon that area had not been ploughed. It was very likely that last night Himgiri had told the seasonal labourers to work on that uncultivated land, and probably he had sent someone with them this morning to familiarise them with it.

The summer sun was gleaming on the sweat-smeared backs of the Oraons and Mundas. Since his childhood Dharma had known that the tribal men of mountain or jungle never stinted in their work. Once they had taken on the responsibility of ploughing and sowing, there was never any need to watch over them or goad them. Let there be storms and floods, let the sun burn everything up, but they would never look askance until the job had been done.

Everywhere on the other side of the highway there was the same familiar picture. As on any other day, the tractor was running over Mishirlal's land beside the dried up Koel, its puttering sound being wafted all about by the hot summer wind. Flocks of foreign parrots were flying overhead and, on the great master's side of the road, sparrows were sitting on the telegraph wires. But today there was something more, something new: there were clouds in the west. They were nothing spectacular, just a few wisps holding their shape as they floated idly about in the western sky.

Shading his eyes with his hand, Dharma watched the movement of the clouds for a moment. As the plough had stopped, Kushi too paused. She came and stood beside Dharma. 'Clouds,' she said.

'Yes.' Dharma nodded slightly.

In the neighbouring field Ganeri too was looking at the clouds. 'The first clouds of the year,' he remarked. 'But the rains will be late.'

'How late, Uncle Ganeri?'

'Certainly another eight or ten days.'

'That long?'

Ganeri explained that this year the coming of the clouds had started only today, and there would be no rain in such small clouds. Heavy clouds, like black boulders, would have to gather in the west, yet still no rain would fall. But all that would not happen in one day. Ganeri went on to say that without rain no one would survive – rivers and streams, men and beasts, mountains and jungles would all burn up.

'Even if the rains are ten days late, there's at least some comfort in having the clouds overhead. We can survive the summer heat,' Dharma said.

Ganeri was about to answer, but just then there came shouting from the highway.

'Vote for – '

'Pratibha-ji!'

'Who will win?'

'Pratibha Sahay! Who else!'

Dharma and the others looked around to the highway in surprise. An open jeep was running towards Bijuri, raising red dust. Ten or twelve young men were standing in it, huddled together and shouting at the tops of their voices. On the front of the jeep was a red cloth bearing the sign of a horse. Something was written underneath it, but the illiterate labourers could not read it. If they could, they would have known that for Pratibha Sahay to win the coming election, they should make their marks beside this sign.

They went on watching as the jeep became a speck in the distance, clouding the sky with red dust.

Ganeri took a deep breath, drawing some of the hot summer air into his lungs. He said, 'So a woman is contesting the election this time.' So far the electoral battles in Garudiya taluk had been fought only by men, and Ganeri seemed surprised to see on this occasion a woman candidate.

'Who is Pratibha-ji, Uncle?'

'You didn't hear the master speak of her the other day?' retorted Ganeri. 'She is married into a very rich family.'

He then went on to relate how Manpatthal village in Bijuri taluk was her father-in-law's home, or rather, it was her father-in-law's home in name only, for no one actually lived there. The dilapidated, old-style home was falling apart and much of it was covered with weeds. The family, however, had factories in Jhariya and in Ranchi, and they might live today in Patna, tomorrow in Calcutta, the day after in Delhi and the day after that in Bombay. It was a family of tremendous wealth.

Dharma listened to all this, gaping. There were not just the two of them now, for many others from the nearby fields, seeing Ganeri and Dharma chatting, had come and stood around them. Ganeri urged them, 'Go back to your work, now. Go on, go!'

And they all returned to their fields.

Some time later, when the sun was shining overhead through the gaps in the thinly scattered clouds, it was time for the midday meal. They all unharnessed their bullocks and sought out the shade of some crooked *sisam* tree, where they sat down. After a few moments rest they unwrapped their cloth bundles, took out rice, vegetables, dal, salt and chillies, and began to eat.

Dharma and Kushi sat down to their meal under a withered palmyra tree. It was an ordinary meal: some flat bread of millet flour, some whole boiled black beans, fried okra, salt, yellow chillies and a little tamarind paste.

As they ate, Kushi suddenly noticed Masterji coming towards them along the highway on his bicycle. It was not an unusual sight, as for some years now the master had been seen riding his bicycle around Garudiya and Bijuri taluks, come rain or shine, trying to gather pupils for his school from six or seven miles around. On some days he took the highway straight to Bijuri. He was not going that way today, however. He got down under the vast pipal tree at the bus stand and then pushed his bicycle the rest of the way across the fields towards Dharma.

Kushi said, 'Master-ji is coming.'

Dharma saw him just then, too. He called out, 'Hey, Master-ji – over here!'

From all over Raghunath Singh's land various voices could be heard. 'Master-ji is coming! Master-ji is coming!'

The schoolmaster was looked upon with great respect by the poor and hungry untouchable people of this region. He was loved, even revered. More than anyone he was thought of as one of their own.

As the schoolmaster approached, from here and there came Ganeri, Budheri, Madholal and others. No one could think of how to treat him or where to seat him, so with great urgency Ganeri shook out his own *gamchha* and spread it on the ground, saying, 'Sit down, Master-ji, sit down.'

The schoolmaster did not sit on the *gamchha*. He leaned his bicycle against the *sisam* tree in front of him and sat down on the dead grass of a ridge. He wiped the sweat from his brow with a corner of his thick homespun dhoti, looked at them all and smiled affectionately, saying, 'What's your news? Are you all well?'

'Yes, by the grace of God,' they all replied together.

'Have you had your lunch?'

'Yes.'

Having inquired of their health and their families, the schoolmaster got to the point. 'What are your intentions? Tell me frankly.'

Ganeri could guess at what the schoolmaster was getting at. With a faint smile, he asked apprehensively, 'Intentions, regarding what?'

'Why aren't you sending your children to school?' Having made the point directly, the schoolmaster then repeated his original question. The times had changed, he argued. Ganeri and the others were what they were, their lives having been wasted by working as bonded labourers on the land of others. But they should arrange to feed their children a little literacy so that their minds might be opened; otherwise they too would end their days driving bullock-drawn ploughs on someone else's land, never being able to realise their just dues.

Ganeri looked sad and helpless. 'What can we do, Master-ji?' he asked. 'You know our situation. How can we send our children to school in summer? For ten years our well has not been cleared. There's not a drop of drinking water in the colony. As soon as the sun rises we send the children to fetch water. If they don't dig for water in the sand of the dried up river, everyone will die of thirst. Let the rains come, and then we will send them to you.'

'Once the rains start you will bring them to the fields to sow the paddy.'

Sadly and slowly Ganeri nodded his head. The schoolmaster was right. For some time he had observed that after the land had been ploughed in the summer and a few drops had started to fall from the sky, the sowing of paddy would get underway. First the seed would be planted on small strips of land, then paddy shoots would be taken. After the shoots had grown to about a hand's length high, they would be taken up by the roots and set at intervals in rows in the big paddy fields. This was a time when a great many people were needed, notwithstanding the tribal seasonal workers, and there were difficulties in coordinating the whole enterprise. Parents were obliged to take their children to the fields to help them, for how else could they manage? Then no sooner had the paddy been sown than the rains would come and fall continually day and night. Soaked by the rains, the roads and paths would be in a terrible condition. And where were there any *pucca* roads in Garudiya and Bijuri taluks? Except for the highway that ran from Patna to Ranchi all the roads were unsealed and, in the rainy season, one walked along them through ankle-deep, sticky mud. No parents would agree to sending their children to school through four or five miles of that.

Of course, in the two months after the rains the peasant labourers would get some relief, for agricultural work was suspended then. The ears of paddy would go on growing longer and the juice within the green stalks would quickly thicken. Then, within just a few days, the colour of acre after acre of grain fields would have changed, and as far as the eye could see there would be nothing but boundless golden paddy.

During the time that the paddy was ripening the bonded labourers would go to Raghunath Singh's farm compound to thresh and sort out all the various pulses, lentils and paddy from the previous year and dry them in the sun. It was only then that they would remember Master-ji's school, and as soon as morning had broken the parents of the dosad colony would wake their children, give them something to eat, and take them to the unsealed road on the other side of the highway. From there they would go straight to Master-ji's school beside the Garudiya market, and after school the master himself would take them back across the highway. He feared that if he did not see the children across the road, along which buses and trucks ran so recklessly day and night, they might get run over.

However, how many days a year could be given to education for those born into a bonded labourer's family? Once the paddy had ripened, Master-ji's school would again be emptied as the children would follow their parents around the fields. And after the paddy had been harvested, was there any end to their work? Again the land had to be cultivated for the sowing of pigeon peas, sesame, linseed, and various lentils. Sugar-cane, maize and millet also had to be planted. Then too the children would accompany their parents to the fields. As soon as the rabi season had finished, the summer would come around again. And so their lives followed the cycle of the seasons. Indeed, where was the time to feed their children's minds a little literacy?

The schoolmaster said, 'When the rains stop, you send your children to study for a few days, then for the rest of the year they don't even see the school. What can they learn in this way?'

Wringing his hands in embarrassment, Ganeri said, 'There's work to be done, so what can we do, Master-ji? If the work were not done, would the great master excuse us?' He gave a profound sigh and said, 'We were purchased as slaves at our birth.'

The schoolmaster was in no way deterred, for he was greatly optimistic about people and life. He said, 'You will have to find the time, Ganeri. Work is no reason for keeping your children downtrodden and ignorant.'

As they spoke the day wore on. The clouds that were sparse just a short time ago had now massed and were being swept by the westerly breeze towards the horizon, while the Jyaistha sun that had been hanging straight overhead was now starting to decline towards the west.

The schoolmaster was about to say something when suddenly there came more shouting from the highway.

'Give your vote to – '

'Nekiram Sharma!'

'Place your stamp – '

'On the sign of the camel!'

Everyone turned and looked towards the highway. A small van was running from Bijuri taluk towards the Garudiya market. A red cloth with a drawing of a camel – evidently Nekiram's symbol in this election – was attached to the front of it. In the back of the van eight or ten young men were continually shouting at the top of their voices for people to vote for Nekiram, until the van disappeared around the bend in a cloud of red dust.

For as long as it was visible, the schoolmaster had watched Nekiram Sharma's campaign vehicle. He turned back to Ganeri and asked, 'Which Nekiram is that? The master of the high school?'

Ganeri replied, 'So I've heard.'

'An arrogant brahman, isn't he? Big on impurity of touch?'

'I heard that too.'

'So he too is standing in the election?'

Ganeri thought for a moment, and said, 'There is also a woman standing.'

Somewhat incredulous, the schoolmaster asked, 'Which woman?'

'One from a very wealthy family, Pratibha Sahay. They've got big businesses, factories. They're very rich.'

The schoolmaster was surprised. 'I see.'

'Pratibha-ji's vote car went off towards Bijuri a little while ago.'

The schoolmaster then said to himself, 'The industrialist Pratibha Sahay, the landowner Raghunath Singh, the orthodox brahman Nekiram Sharma – they're all after votes. It seems this election in Garudiya and Bijuri will be a real festival.'

Ganeri fixed his eyes on the schoolmaster, unable to comprehend the significance of his remark. He asked, 'What did you say, Master-ji?'

'Oh, nothing.' The schoolmaster changed the subject by asking, 'Do you know who else is contesting?'

'Sukhan Ravidas – '

'A brilliant young man. And?'

'I heard that a Muslim man from Bijuri is standing.'

Indistinctly the schoolmaster muttered, 'Hindu-Muslim, casteist, industrialist, landowner – all under the umbrella of democracy. Very good.'

A harsh voice could be heard calling in the distance, 'All right, you dogs and hell kites!' The voice was familiar. Then they all saw Ramlachhman on his rickety bicycle coming over the fields. His mouth never shut, as he kept on shouting, 'I come a little late, and there you are slacking! Clouds have been seen in the sky today. In ten or fifteen days the rains will come. The fields still have not been fully ploughed. So you sons and daughters of the devil, get off your backsides and get back to the fields. Come on, you dogs and hell kites!'

Those who were gathered around the schoolmaster started taking their ploughs and bullocks back to the fields as soon as they caught sight of Ramlachhman. From all around came the sounds, 'Hat, hat, urra hat hat, urra hat hat – '

Even the strong-built dosads were always unsettled in their fear of him, and Ramlachhman took some secret satisfaction at this. Squinting, he watched the labourers as they ploughed for a while. Then he leaned his bicycle against a *palas* tree and said to the schoolmaster, 'So Master-ji, how are things?'

The schoolmaster thoroughly disliked Ramlachhman. 'All right,' he said, disinterestedly.

'How is your school going?'

'Not so well.'

'And what brings you here?'

Master-ji did not answer the question, for he had met Ramlachhman here many times before and had been asked the same question at least fifty times, to which he had always given the same answer. How often could he go on saying the same thing!

Ramlachhman gave an ugly smile baring his crooked, stained and decaying teeth, and said, 'I know. You've come to catch children for your school.'

The hypocrite was quite right. Indeed, everyone in Garudiya and Bijuri knew that the schoolmaster went about on his bicycle from village to village and field to field to try to recruit pupils for his school. Again Master-ji said nothing.

Leaning towards the schoolmaster's face, Ramlachhman asked, 'Any luck?'

Although the schoolmaster was becoming more and more irritated, he did not show it. In a serious tone he simply said, 'No.'

Ramlachhman was extremely pleased to hear that. Baring all his teeth at once he said, 'I've known that for a long while. Schoolmaster, for you this place is a wasteland – education is not cultivated here. Government has wasted its money in opening a school. And you are just wearing yourself out going around here and there in search of pupils. Do something else.'

'What?' The schoolmaster looked at him suspiciously.

'There's no point in a school here. There are better places to set up a school than here. You want customers, otherwise all your labours will be wasted.' Having thought he had made a grand joke, Ramlachhman was bubbling with glee. He went on laughing, sounding as though he were hiccupping.

The schoolmaster was not visibly heartened by this kind of gratuitous advice. He gave a joyless smile and, without a word, took his bicycle from beside the *sisam* tree and started to ride off toward the main road. In his mind his resolve was becoming firm. He would show Ramlachhman the cultivation of education in this wasteland.

After the schoolmaster had gone, St Satan, taking his long, stork-like strides, wandered about from one field to another watching over everyone's work. Then he followed the young women around. First his gaze fell on Shanichari who, as on other days, was sorting out the roots of last year's dead plants in Madholal's field.

Shanichari was six or seven months pregnant. Looking straight at her Ramlachhman's eyes screwed up as he laughed his jerky laugh. 'Well now, Shanichari,' he said. 'What a size your stomach is! How big is that kid inside it?' His laughter was suffused with all the filth of the world.

Shanichari did not know what she could do about her six or seven months' blossoming. She tried to cover herself with her short sari, but it was not wide enough to cover both her stomach and her bosom. Pressing her hands against her stomach she recoiled and stood for a moment in embarrassment and diffidence. If the earth had opened up at that moment, she would gladly have let it swallow her.

Ramlachhman got a lot of fun out of seeing Shanichari cowering in terror. His eyes danced as he asked, 'When are you going to drop it on the ground?'

Shanichari still did not answer, but just stood there looking down.

Just as Ramlachhman was about to speak again, Gidhni called from the opposite field. 'Hey, brahman, come here to me. I'll tell you all about when Shanichari'll drop her kid on the ground.'

Ramlachhman suddenly looked towards Gidhni. She was the one dosad he feared like the god of death. The bitch had a tongue like a knife and nothing could restrain her mouth. Only a few days back this no good woman had left him feeling very discomfited. He stood looking at Gidhni with a look of fear and suspicion.

Waving her hand, Gidhni called out, 'Come, my bridegroom, come! Come to me!'

The hypocrite waited no longer. The bitch had bad intentions. He felt that this day, like the other day, would certainly bring trouble. He was not very close to her, and straightaway he strode off like a stork to where the tribal seasonal workers were ploughing some distance away.

The bonded labourers were relieved. At least today St Satan would not bother them.

***

At evening, after the ploughs and bullocks had been collected at the farm compound, everyone returned to the dosad colony, except for

Dharma and Kushi who went straight to the *sabui* grove. Two days had passed since they had set the traps for *bageri* birds: one had been taken up looking for barking deer, another getting labourers at the Chaharh market. And before that the day on which Gana had been beaten up by Himgiri's thugs had also been lost, and on another day Dharma had been unwell. In all, it had been four days, four days in which he could have earned fifteen or twenty rupees selling *bageri* birds to the contractors. Such a sum would have got them quite a way toward their freedom. Moreover, once the rains came, it would no longer be possible to catch the birds, as flocks of them would then fly away from the region, and that meant that his income would be virtually nil for the wholeof the monsoon season. And now four days' earnings had been lost.

Once the traps had been set, Kushi asked, 'What will we do now?'

'Go home. What else can we do?' he replied.

'We haven't been to see the dairy folk for some time. Shall we go there?'

For Dharma and Kushi the dairy village of Chaukad was a different kind of attraction. The time was always well spent in going there, and the Black Milkman and the Fair Milkwoman were very good people. Dharma now wanted to go to Chaukad with Kushi. After some thought, he said, 'Not today. Tomorrow we'll go to Chaukad, after taking the *bageri* birds to the contractors.'

Kushi said nothing more.

A little while later, when they had gone along the highway and come to the dosad colony, they found themselves quite startled. In the west of the neighbourhood, where the well was, five or six gas lamps were burning, and a large area round about was illuminated. All the dosads had gathered there.

Dharma and Kushi could not see their parents in their shacks. They slowly approached the well, both of them very curious to know why there was so much light there. When they got closer, they saw that the work of clearing the whole well of its sand was going on, along with the digging of a new well beside it, for which countless huge discs of burnt earth were piled up at the side. Some twelve or fourteen men working on excavating the old and the new wells were bathed in sweat.

Dharma found Ganeri among the crowd and asked, 'What's happening, Uncle? Two wells together?'

'Yes.' Ganeri slowly nodded.

'When did the well-diggers come?'

'A little while back. Our maalik himself brought them.'

Dharma's eyes widened and his voice trembled. 'The great master himself!'

'Yes. Oh, yes. He came himself and gave orders to clear out the old well and to dig a new one.'

The matter of clearing out the well had provided great excitement among the residents of the dosad colony, as could be seen in their faces so brightly illuminated by the gas lamps.

Someone or other called out, 'The great master is so good!'

A few others said, 'We're so lucky!'

It was indeed their good fortune. The dust of the great master's feet had fallen in the neighbourhood of untouchables such as they. Dharma tried to think if such an exciting event ever had occurred in all the twenty-four years of his life. For ten years the old well had been blocked up with sand, and so many times they had unsuccessfully entreated Himgirinandan to have it cleared. And yet today the great master had not only arranged for the clearing of the old well but had come in person to give orders for a new one to be dug as well. The dosads had not known such good fortune in fourteen generations!

Dharma whispered into Ganeri's ear, 'Why is the master suddenly having two wells dug?'

Ganeri frowned and said in a suppressed voice, 'You bloody idiot. Didn't you hear everyone saying that he is so good and generous, and it is the good fortune of our father and our father's father and our father's father's father – the good fortune of everyone?'

Ganeri's voice could hardly be heard. Dharma looked at him for a few seconds, then slowly shook his head and said, 'No, no.'

His voice now harsh, Ganeri asked, 'What do you mean, no?'

'That's not the reason.'

Ganeri remained silent for a long time. Then almost putting his mouth inside Dharma's ear, he said, 'Hasn't the election festival started? Just wait and see how many things these vote-seekers will offer now.'

Dharma asked nothing more. He just stood there in silence, watching the digging and clearing of the wells. People all around were both moved and gratified by such a grand example of high-mindedness, and so they prattled on about the magnanimity of the great master. Then the crowd on one side of the well gradually thinned out. Most of the people in the dosad colony had been following the bullock-drawn ploughs on Raghunath Singh's land from sunrise to sunset. Another group had been to the river bed to dig for water or to the jungles to procure tubers or mahua fruit. When they came back and saw Raghunath Singh and the workmen they were altogether speechless and, overwhelmed with excitement, they forgot their hunger and thirst. But now their earlier amazement and excitement had subsided somewhat and each one of them was feeling fraught with the hunger of a wild beast. Consequently, they started to return to their shanties in ones and twos.

Dharma and Kushi fetched their parents from the crowd, saying, 'We're terribly hungry. Let's go home.'

Dharma and Kushi lived to the east of the colony, and together they passed the well and walked on in that direction. A little way along on the right was Phaguram's hut, and from it came the sound of harmonium and singing. The voice was familiar. Phaguram, the Nightingale of Garudiya, was practising his songs.

Dharma suddenly stopped. A few years ago he had had an irrepressible inclination for songs, and whenever he got the opportunity he would come and sit by Phaguram, who taught him many of the *nautanki* songs and trained him to play the battered old harmonium. It had been his fond wish to make Dharma his apprentice. Phaguram was a free man, but could a bondsman like Dharma ever achieve that status? Working to pay for his own freedom after an entire day of backbreaking toil in the fields of the great master, he had long ago lost his inclination for singing, and without practice he soon forgot whatever Phaguram had taught him. But from time to time his ears pricked up when he heard the sound of singing.

Phaguram saw him, though in the dark he could not definitely recognise him. He stopped his song and asked, 'Who's there?'

'I'm Dharma, Uncle Phagu.'

'Why are you standing outside? Come on in.'

Dharma sent Kushi and the others on, and went into Phaguram's hut. As he entered he was amazed to see a bright and expensive glass lantern instead of the red kerosene lamp that burned in every one of the shanties in the dosad colony, and the harmonium he was playing was brand new and gleamed brightly in the light of the lantern. Dharma noticed Phaguram's old harmonium, with its broken reed and the paint peeling off, cast to one side. He also noticed some new clothes hanging on a cord in a corner of the room, and in another corner a pair of smart, raw leather slippers – for three or four years Dharma had always seen Phaguram barefooted. It was also quite a shock to see the new dhoti and shirt, for he always used to wear a patched and stitched, dirty old shirt. Everything had changed so drastically, as if by magic.

Phaguram noticed the amazement on Dharma's face. Smiling proudly, he said, 'See these new clothes, new lantern, new harmonium – the great master gave them all to me. And a hundred rupees. With that I bought the slippers, a metal cooking pot, some hair oil, a new comb and all sorts of things.'

The list of things that Phaguram rattled off was truly the stuff of dreams for bonded labourers like Dharma. Dharma didn't say anything, but went on looking with sparkling eyes at the dhoti, slippers and lantern, and as he looked he was reminded of that day when the great master had talked of giving Phaguram a new harmonium for writing songs for the election. However, Dharma was beset by a kind of envy at Phaguram's getting not only a new harmonium, a new dhoti and shirt, a new lantern, and so on, but a hundred rupees in cash as well.

Phaguram spoke again. 'Everything is by the grace of the great master.' He paused for a moment, then said, 'Who would have thought I would get so much for doing election songs? So much is by the grace of the great master.' Phaguram's voice was choked with gratitude

Dharma thought that had he kept up with his singing training, he too might have had work at this election time. While he felt bad about this, it occurred to him straightaway that there was nothing to be gained from regret. In a dry voice he said, 'Have you written the election songs?'

'Not much, just a little,' Phaguram said. 'Would you like to hear what I've done?'

'Yes, let me hear it.'

Phaguram valued having his former pupil with him. The great master had paid him much respect and given him money and a harmonium for his songs, and he had been told to write new songs and to sing them at election meetings in order to create in the listeners' minds an unfavourable view of Raghunath Singh's rivals. Having entertained gatherings night after night with the *nautanki* troupe, election songs were something quite new to Phaguram. If he could let someone hear an example of what he had written, he could get an idea of whether the people at meetings would like them or not.

With the swiftness of the storm the thin, gnarled and fleshless fingers ran over the keys of the harmonium and Phaguram began to sing.

Hail Raghunath Singh,
foremost among the kshatriyas!
To vote for him
will bring good to all.
Now say, my dear people -
'Raghupati, Raghava, Rajaram.'

Phaguram had such a sweet voice. He stopped singing and asked, 'How do you like it, Dharma?'

Dharma had become engrossed as he listened to it, and all his earlier envy had now dispersed. The great master had done well in valuing such a voice. 'It's good,' Dharma said.

'Will people like it?'

'Of course.'

Phaguram was happy. All the while he went on quietly playing the harmonium.

Dharma said, 'Why did you stop? Sing me the rest of the song, Uncle Phagu.'

Phaguram told him that he had not yet made up the last part of the song, and then suddenly, as though something had just occurred to him, he said impatiently, 'Go home now, Dharma.'

Dharma was quite surprised why Phaguram should tell him to go home after receiving him so warmly and letting him hear his song. Phaguram guessed at what Dharma was thinking, and explained, 'The great master will hold an election mitin at Garudiya market tomorrow, and I have to sing at the opening of it. Now I'll be up all night composing the rest of the song and getting the tune right. If you stay I'll get none of it done. Now don't be cross.'

After that there was no question of being cross. Dharma was known as an exceptionally considerate man. He got up. 'I'll let you hear the song when it's finished,' Phaguram said.

'All right.' Dharma went outside, crossed the veranda and stepped down onto the path.

19

WHEN DHARMA AND THE OTHERS ARRIVED AT THE FARM COMPOUND compound to collect their ploughs and bullocks the next morning, Himgiri told them, 'Today you must quickly finish up your work in the fields. The ploughs and bullocks must be lodged back here well before sunset. From here the munshi will be taking you somewhere. D'you hear me?'

'Yes, sir,' they all replied at once.

Dharma suddenly remembered that yesterday he had gone and set the traps for *bageri* birds in the *sabui* grove. He did not know how long they would have to wait at the farm compound for the munshi Ajibchand, nor did he know how much more time would be taken up by the munshi's taking them somewhere. If it got too late, Dharma would not be able to take the *bageri* birds to the contractors, and he would miss out on the few rupees he had hoped to get.

Apprehensively he asked, 'Sir, where will the munshi-ji take us?'

'You'll see where,' whined Himgirinandan in his high-pitched voice. 'Now the sun's coming up, so get off to the fields.'

Dharma did not have the nerve to ask anything more, though suddenly he was furious. He wanted to shout out, 'No, never!' and that he would not wait for the munshi after having returned his plough and bullock well before sunset. But then the wishes of his heart were not always translated into the words of his mouth, so

Dharma, angry and aggrieved, hung his head, went off to Raghunath Singh's land and began to plough his field.

***

There was no difference between that day and any other day: continual ploughing before noon, a little rest after the midday meal, then back to the field again – altogether the same routine. During this time the great master's campaign vehicle and Nekiram Sharma's horse-drawn cart had gone along the highway towards Bijuri and had come back again, all the time accompanied by the shouting of slogans. Nekiram did not have a jeep, as did the great master and Pratibha Sahay, so he had to have a few young men in a tonga crying for votes for him.

The day before, a few stray clouds had been seen, and today they were a little more substantial, but the sunlight still radiated from the summer sky like molten bell-metal.

***

The afternoon had scarcely begun when St Satan was seen coming on his creaking bicycle. On other days Ramlachhman would lean the cycle against some twisted old tree and go about the fields scrutinising everyone's work, after which he would loiter lustfully around the dosad women. Today, however, he held on to his bicycle and started to call out with terrible impatience, 'Hey, Ganeri! Hey, Dharma! Hey, Madho! Don't do any more work today. Bring your ploughs and bullocks quickly and come with me.'

Ramlachhman urged not only Dharma and his friends to finish their work, but the seasonal tribal labourers as well. Then he took everyone straight to the farm compound.

As they were walking along the main road, Ganeri asked, 'Why have we stopped work before sunset today, sir?'

Baring his teeth, Ramlachhman said, 'It's your day, jackals. The voting festival has come. Now the boots are on the head.'

The matter was still not clear. Ganeri asked, bewildered, 'What's it all about, sir?'

'Never mind. You'll find out when you get there.'

When Dharma's group arrived at the farm compound, they saw that all the dosad colony's elderly, rejected people and the children were sitting there crowded together, and 'many hundreds more' people, having been brought by bullock carts from distant villages in Garudiya taluk, were assembled there too. On the road in front of the farm compound stood a long line of some sixty or seventy more carts.

Dharma and the others were amazed to see so many people and carts. Ganeri, Budheri, Dharma and all those who had come from the fields with Ramlachhman asked their rejected elders, in suppressed voices, 'What is all this? Why are you here?'

The old people told them that Himgiri had sent a man to fetch them.

'Why?'

'Who knows?'

They got the same answer from the people from the other villages, whom men had been sent to fetch. No one knew the reason for bringing so many people here, only that they had been called by the great master, Raghunath Singh, and that was enough to make everyone come one, two, three or more miles by bullock or buffalo cart under the blazing summer sun without asking any questions.

Suddenly Himgirinandan started shouting in his piercing, high-pitched voice at Dharma and his company. 'Hurry up and lodge your ploughs and bullocks and get into the carts!' he said, pointing to the carts in front of them. Within a few moments Himgiri and Ramlachhman were also urging everyone else into the carts, and straightaway the sixty or seventy carts set off in procession, raising the red dust as they went.

Meanwhile, the summer sun had started to set and dusk was falling over Garudiya. Until now the heat was spread by the gusty breeze, but as soon as the sun had set, everywhere gradually cooled down.

The carts came to an empty field on the west side of the Garudiya market, where Dharma and the others were utterly nonplussed to see masses of people sitting throughout the field as far as the eye could see. There must have been ten or fifteen thousand of them. In gaps among the crowd there were bamboo posts supporting electric lights and loudspeakers. Everywhere there was light and more light. At the front there was a big, high platform, draped in red cloth and arranged with many chairs and tables. On one side a white carpet had been spread over a wooden podium. As yet there was no one at all on the stage.

Ganeri was sitting beside Dharma in one of the bullock carts. 'Now I understand,' he said.

Dharma asked, 'What, Uncle Ganeri?'

'The maalik's election mitin is going to be here. That's why he's brought us all.'

'Is that so?'

'Yes.'

In the morning Himgiri had told Dharma and the others to come quickly and without any delay after finishing their work in the fields. And then, right in the heat of noon, he had sent Ramlachhman. At last it was clear why they had been taken from the fields before sunset and brought here in carts.

In a low voice Ganeri said, 'We're all extremely lucky.'

There was something in Ganeri's voice that made Dharma turn to him. 'Why, Uncle?'

'Oh, you stupid jackal, aren't we lucky being brought in carts to this mitin?'

Dharma wanted to say something but could not, for just then the munshi, Ajibchand, the contractor, Ayodhyaprasad, and a few other men seemed to emerge out of nowhere, men whom Dharma and the others had often seen while ploughing their fields coming and going along the highway in the great master's campaign vehicle. Ajibchand was calling to the carts, 'Stop there! Stop!'

The carts were parked near the crowd on one side of the field. Ajibchand, Ayodhyaprasad and all the others were running to the carts and calling out to all the passengers, 'Come this way! Come this way!' In all of this Ayodhyaprasad was the most exuberant. Apparently he was the one in charge of arrangements. Everyone scrambled down from the carts.

Pointing to that part of the field where a few thousand people had earlier taken their places, Ayodhyaprasad was saying, 'Go and sit over there. Don't rush, go quietly! Raghunath Singhji is coming soon. Then the mitin will begin.'

Dharma and the others got down from the carts and, not sure of when the meeting would begin, mingled with the crowd in the field. From chatting with the people who had come earlier, they learned that since daybreak the great master's men had been sending carts to fetch them all. All this was just for a meeting.

A little later the great master Raghunath Singh, driving an expensive tandem, arrived at the rally with his lapdogs; he got down from the tandem and mounted the stage. And what an amazing sight! Following behind the great master's party was Phaguram, carrying around his neck his gleaming new harmonium. He looked completely different now, dressed in his new dhoti, kurta, turban and raw leather slippers. He went and sat down with his brand new harmonium. Evidently the great master had arranged for some songs at this meeting.

The great master and his constant companions occupied the chairs on the stage. Ayodhyaprasad and a few other young men went up with them and in full voice at the microphone started shouting slogans.

'Vote for – '

'Raghunath Singh!'

'Give your vote to – '

'Raghunath Singh!'

'What will we get from our emlay?'

'*Ram raj*! The rule of God!'

'Place your stamp on – '

'The sign of the elephant!'

All this shouting was spread by the loudspeakers and the whole field was buzzing with excitement.

Then the slogans stopped. The mood of the rally had been well established. The great master's close friend, the big lawyer of the district, Girdharlal, gestured to the young men and went and stood at the microphone. 'Brothers and sisters, you all know that Raghunath Singhji is standing for election in the taluks of Garudiya and Bijuri. For us this is a matter of extremely good fortune. With the compassion of God and by the grace of Raghunath-ji, the troubles and worries and needs of everyone in the two taluks will be completely removed. Smiles will burst onto the faces of everyone hereabouts. No one will be hungry and unclothed. Oh yes! But if you want all this, you must remember one thing – he must win the election, and that, brothers and sisters, is in your hands. Since Independence how many elections have you seen? How many people have become MLAs, MPs? But has anything come of it? No. Elections come, elections go. You are exactly where you were before Independence. But seeing your sorrow has brought great distress to Raghunath-ji. So many people appealed to him with hands pressed together, entreating him to stand in the election this time. He will win on the sign of the elephant. And remember, if your maalik wins, *Ram raj* will come to the taluks of Garudiya and Bijuri!'

Having finished, Girdharlal gestured to the young men to start up the slogans again.

'Stamp your vote on the sign of – '

'The elephant!'

'What will the victory of Raghunath bring?'

'*Ram raj*!'

After the second spell of slogan raising, Girdharlal spoke again.

'Brothers and sisters, you have all heard that as well as Raghunath-ji, there are others standing in this election – Pratibha Sahay, Nekiram Sharma, Sukhan Ravidas and Abu Malek. So remember, if you want to be rid of sorrow and hardship and want, you must give your vote to Raghunath-ji. Remember to put your stamp on the elephant symbol on the ballot paper.' Raising his hands to the heavens he cried out, 'Long live – '

The young men had been trained earlier in this, and all together they threw their hands into the air and cried out, 'Raghunath Singh!'

'Long live – '

'Raghunath Singh!'

'Victory to the sign of – '

'The elephant!'

'Victory to the sign of – '

'The elephant!'

Having stirred up the spirits of the meeting, the eminent lawyer Girdharlal said, 'Brothers and sisters, now you will hear from the Raghunath Singhji himself!' And so saying he went and sat on his own designated chair.

Raghunath Singh slowly raised his immense body and went and stood in front of the microphone. His appearance well befitted the symbol of the elephant. Taking hold of the microphone, he said, 'Brothers and sisters, I am not going to say anything just yet. Before I speak, we will have a few songs. You know Phaguram, the Nightingale of Garudiya.'

A few thousand of the audience all together cried out, 'Yes, yes, the trouper – '

'Yes, the trouper. What a sweet voice! Phaguram has composed a few songs. First let us hear them.' He looked towards Phaguram and beckoned with his eyes.

Immediately Phaguram began to play the harmonium. There was a microphone in front of him too.

There was no one like Phaguram the Trouper within fifty miles. More than once he had fallen on bad times and, because of the trouble in his chest, he could no longer sing at *nautanki* performances. However, those who had heard him sing before could never forget him. At this election rally by the Garudiya market, an audience of some thousands sat up attentively.

Phaguram stopped playing and said, 'You have heard from the eminent lawyer that Nekiram Sharma, Pratibha Sahay, Sukhan Ravidas and Abu Malek are standing at this election. I will sing you all a song I have written about them.' With a flourish he began playing the harmonium. Setting his voice to the key, he started to sing as well.

Say, dear people, say
'Raghupati, Raghava, Rajaram.'
Just see how Sharmaji
sinks deep in immorality,
with four hands he will grab
the interest due on loans,
and now he badgers you for votes.
Say, dear people, say
'Raghupati, Raghava, Rajaram.'

The young men standing at the back of the stage clapped along with the rhythm of the song. In the bright electric light the great master's face could be seen contorted in mirth. His companions were also laughing. Evidently they were well pleased with Phaguram's song.

The audience too were greatly amused. Dharma was sitting beside Ganeri, overcome with laughter. 'That's a very good song Uncle Phagu has written. So funny!'

It should be explained here that although Nekiram Sharma taught in a school, he also had a private moneylending business and was a well-known usurer in the region. On every rupee of a loan taken from him there would be two rupees payable each month in interest. There was no telling how many people in Garudiya whose blood he had sucked dry.

Phaguram now began his second song.

The whole world laughs at Pratibha,
The aristocratic kayastha,
When coquettishly she pleads
For votes.
To vote for her would give our land
A petticoat domain,
A raj of barren women.
Tell me, dear people, tell me,
Is such the kingdom of God?

This time the applause was even louder, spreading like a contagion, not so much among the young men on the stage but throughout the audience. In quest of votes in the election the childless Pratibha, from such a wealthy home, had been seen going around three or four villages, glamorously attired. So perceptively had Phaguram stung her in his song.

Along with all the rest of the crowd Dharma was beside himself with laughter as Phaguram now commenced his third song.

Now at this election time
We're all amazed to see
Sukhan Das –
son of a tanner
and scion of thieves -
come forward as a candidate,
for Sukhan Das has become great
by the wondrous grace of the ballot box.
Say, dear people, say,

'Raghupati, Raghava, Rajaram.'

Caste awareness was exceptionally strong here. Even though he was an untouchable landless labourer, Phaguram had written for Raghunath Singh a song about another untouchable. Thousands of hungry and ragged untouchables, born to servility, seasonal workers and landless labourers, could not fully realise the import of this song, for they had little power of understanding. They were enchanted simply by the surface meaning of it, and so they went on laughing, without fully realising its import.

Before taking up his fourth song Phaguram stopped playing the harmonium, moved his face to the microphone and said, 'You know what sort of people Sharma-ji, Pratibha-ji and Sukhan Ravidas are. However, I have just given you a reminder. It would be a disaster if any of them were to win the election and become an emlay. Now listen to this.' And gesturing towards Raghunath Singh he began his song.

Hail, Raghunath Singh,
foremost among the kshatriyas!
To vote for him
will bring good to all.
Say, dear people, say,
'Raghupati, Raghava, Rajaram.'

After the song had finished, the young men once again took up their slogans about stamping the symbol of the elephant so that Raghunath Singh might win the election.

After the slogans Raghunath Singh stood once more before the microphone and began to speak. 'Brothers and sisters, you have heard what Girdharlal-ji has had to say, and you have heard Phaguram's songs. So you can certainly realise what sort of people Pratibha Sahay, Nekiram Sharma and Sukhan Ravidas are. Although Nekiram is a brahman, he is a usurer, and whoever takes a loan from him also ha the life sucked out of him. Sukhan Ravidas is an untouchable, though for that I bear him no malice and would not spit three times at the sound of his name as the high-caste people do. But what does he know? What does he understand? Is being an MLA a simple matter? Can an outcaste ascend the throne of Lord Ram? And what about that Pratibha Sahay? She comes from a wealthy family. She would not go anywhere except by car. She will not wear saris worth as little as a thousand rupees. This wealthy city woman has had a fancy to stand in the election. But what does she know of the sorrows and hardships of the hungry and ragged villagers of India? Before now how many days has she ever spent in a village? Could she tell the difference between paddy and wheat? Has she ever sat in the stall beside the highway and drunk tea with peasants, or answered a call of nature in a ditch beside a field? She has nothing in common with any of you. Let me just say that I alone am one of you – your own man. Since my birth I have been among you in these villages. I have never left you and gone to the city. I know you will not mistake me for the others. That is all I have to say. Brothers and sisters, I humbly bow before you all. Let no one walk home. There are carriages waiting for you. I salute you all! I salute you all!'

Raghunath Singh moved away from the microphone, and the young men started shouting their slogans at the tops of their voices.

'Vote for – '

'Raghunath Singh!'

'Make your mark on – '

'The sign of the elephant!'

Dharma got back on a bullock cart just before midnight, Ganeri sitting beside him. In front and behind there were about another hundred carts. The squeaking of the two hundred wheels of the hundred carts extended as far as the horizon. Indeed, the whole road was busy and noisy. As well as the sound of the wheels there was also animated discussion in each of the carts about the election 'mitin'.

Some nights back there had been a full moon, looking like a huge silver goblet hanging in the middle of the sky. Now it looked like a quarter of a dull, worn coin. On either side of the road were the open grain fields, and in the hazy distance a couple of villages were still and asleep. All around there were swarms of millions of fireflies.

Suddenly Dharma spoke up, 'Uncle!'

Ganeri was sitting with his chin resting between his knees. He looked up and asked, 'What?'

'Uncle Phagu sang really well tonight. His songs were good too. Don't you think so, Uncle Ganeri?'

In a serious voice Ganeri said, 'They were good. But I've been wondering about something else.'

'What?'

'Whether Phagu's life is in danger.'

Dharma now looked worried. Fearfully he asked, 'Why, Uncle?'

Ganeri then went on to tell him that those into whom Phaguram's songs had plunged the knife were rich and important people. They would certainly not be happy to hear these songs. If Phaguram had gone beyond the limit, he might well be in peril.

Suddenly Dharma remembered how, a little while ago at the election rally, when everyone was overcome with laughter listening to Phaguram's songs, Ganeri had sat in glum silence. Moreover, he had also expressed misgivings that day when the great master had called Phaguram and asked him to write songs about Pratibha Sahay and Nekiram Sharma.

In all these election songs there was not only laughter and fun, there also lurked a terrible danger, and Dharma suddenly became anxious thinking about Phaguram's future.

In a little while a few of the carts reached the dosad colony, while the others went out in various directions throughout Garudiya taluk.

20

The excavators sent by Raghunath Singh had cleared the sand from the old well and had also dug a new one, so now there would be no more bother over water in the dosad colony. Previously, one used to have to make do with a trickle of turbid water to pour over one's head, but now, even in the summertime, all could bathe to their hearts' content. No longer did they have to go to the dried up Koel and dig for hours for drinking water – now they could get crystal clear, good-tasting drinking water in their own locality. For this the bonded labourers would be grateful to their master Raghunath Singh for the rest of their lives. But as Ganeri had said time and time before, and would go on saying time and time again, it was all on account of the election. Had the great master not been standing in the election, the new well would not have been part of their fortune nor would the old well even have been cleared of its sand.

Having returned the plough and bullocks to the farm compound after a full day's work in the fields, and then having sold their *bageri* birds to the contractors, it was very late when Dharma and Kushi got back to their colony. At the entrance they suddenly caught sight of a meeting going on in the open space beside the well. There was no one in any of the shanties, for everyone – children and all – had gathered there together. Dharma and Kushi had no idea what was going on; somewhat surprised, they approached the gathering.

A few kerosene lanterns burned here and there, and in their light

Abodhnarayan Pande could be seen sitting on a battered old chair in the middle of the crowd. He was more than sixty, tall and broad, with a round face, small, cunning eyes, a sharp chin and thick dark lips. He wore a thick, stitched dhoti and shirt and heavy, untanned leather shoes; he also wore gold earrings, a red sandal-paste mark on his forehead, and a braid tied in a knot. Abodh-ji was a big businessman of this region. At the Garudiya market and the weekly market at Chaharh he had a number of warehouses with paddy, rice and wheat, sugar, sesame and linseed, and various kinds of pulses. It was said that one of his sons ran a cycle business in Dhanbad and the other had set up a radio, sewing-machine and harmonium factory in Katihar. People also said that Abodhnarayan had an iron chest full of money. So Dharma could not imagine why such a rich man should be here, so late at night, in the neighbourhood of hungry and ragged untouchables.

Abodhnarayan was saying, 'Well, Ganeri, you heard what I said.'

Dharma realised that before he and Kushi arrived, there had been some discussion between Ganeri and Abodh-ji, and he was very curious to know what that discussion had been about.

Ganeri inclined his head and said, 'Yes, I heard, Pande-ji.'

Taking from his pocket a big silver box from which he distributed bunches of tobacco leaves and lime to Budheri and Ganeri, Abodhnarayan said, 'Make some *khainis* for everyone.' Then he started to rub some lime and tobacco in the palm of his left hand.

It was a matter of extreme good fortune to be given lime and tobacco by such an important man as Abodhnarayan. The untouchable bonded labourers earnestly prepared the *khainis*. Only Ganeri's face had a serious look.

Abodhnarayan took his fresh *khaini* with two fingers from the palm of his left hand, placed it in the gap between his lower teeth and lip, and sat silently for a few moments. He spat out some blackish juice and said, 'In seven or eight days Pratibha Sahay will hold an election rally on the field beside the Garudiya market. All of you must come. Raghunath Singh took you all to his meeting in buffalo carts. Do you know how we will take you?'

Apparently the businessman Abodhnarayan Pande had taken on the duty of helping Pratibha Sahay in the election in the same way as the contractor Ayodhyaprasad had takenon his shoulders the responsibility for Raghunath Singh's election rally.

By now the crowd all around had become restive, and they asked, 'How?'

'You will be taken by motor vehicle. Pratibha-ji has twenty vehicles ready for you. Do you understand?' Abodhnarayan smiled, baring his teeth and gums that were as black as the seeds of custard apples. He turned around to see the reaction of the dosads to the temptation of a ride in a motor vehicle.

Apart from a ride in a local bus once or twice, none of these bonded labourers or any of their ancestors had ever ridden in an automobile. Now they were to be taken to an election rally in one. Although they had heard this with their own ears, they could not fully believe such a great stroke of fortune. They sat gaping, dumbfounded, for a few moments before they started calling out, 'By automobile? Really?'

Abodhnarayan smiled. 'Why? Do you think it's a false promise?'

'No, no. We were just asking.'

Just before Abodhnarayan could answer, Dhanpat's old father, Gairunath, called out in his hawk-like voice from a veranda on the western side of the well, 'We're going in a motor car! We're going to a mitin in a motor car!'

Gairunath was close to a hundred. Fifteen or twenty years ago he became paralysed from the waist down, he developed dropsy, and his skin started cracking and exuding tannin. The light in his eyes dimmed and went out, but still the God of Death had not touched him. Maybe this crippled, disabled and rejected old man, who lay on a rope cot on the veranda day and night, was indestructible. His son Dhanpat, his daughter-in-law Lakhiya and his grandsons and granddaughters constantly longed for him to die, for even at his age he had an amazing appetite, being able to digest the entire share of food of a robust young man. As he was bed-ridden and unable to earn even a grain of food for himself, who would be glad to have to go on providing for him? However, Gairunath kept on surviving, amazingly, year after year. Although the light had gone out of his eyes, his hearing was exceptionally acute, and this one hundred-year-old was suddenly beset by an inflexible urge to ride in a motor vehicle.

Gairunath's daughter-in-law Lakhiya was sitting near the old man on the veranda, her long veil drawn, listening to the talk of Abodhnarayan and the others. From behind her veil she cried out stridently, 'The old fox has suddenly got a desire to ride in a motor car. The son of a jackal! I'll put you in a car and take you to your cremation! Just die, die, die!' The woman had venom in her voice and her tongue was as sharp as a knife.

Exercising his familial authority, Dhanpat roared at her, 'Shut up, you old hag, shut up!' How his father was treated in the house was their own business, but a son could not possibly allow his wife to insult his father in front of so many people, especially a man as respectable and important as Abodhnarayan. It was extremely embarrassing.

With the authority of the leader of the dosad colony, Ganeri spat out in a low voice, 'Be quiet, Dhanpat's wife!'

Lakhiya lowered her voice somewhat but went on muttering under her veil.

Gairunath was not worth a penny to his own family. Although he was utterly rejected by his son, daughter-in-law and grandchildren, as far as the election was concerned he was an extremely valuable man. A man meant a vote. Abodhnarayan was not stupid. He quickly spoke up, 'Yes, yes, of course you will go to the mitin in a motor car.' He then turned to the gathering and said, 'Now remember, in seven or eight days I will send the vehicles after sunset. At that time you will all be in the neighbourhood. I will come and let you know the day before the mitin.'

A buzz of suppressed excitement at the idea of going to the election rally by automobile ran through the crowd.

Abodhnarayan said, 'Now think about this. If you vote for Pratibha-ji, it will be to your advantage. Pratibha-ji is a woman from a very fine home, a woman of a very wealthy family. The gormin will do whatever she says. If you can make Pratibha-ji an emlay, Garudiya and Bijuri will be better off. She will set up a hospital here, lots of good roads, schools in the villages, and a factory. You won't have to waste your lives driving a plough on someone else's land, for you'll be able to make a living in the factory.'

None of the bonded labourers said anything. They just looked at Abodhnarayan, then at their leader Ganeri. That a factory would be set up in Garudiya-Bijuri and that they would get jobs there and not have to break their backs ploughing the land of Raghunath Singh was news to them, and very attractive news.

Abodhnarayan also said that he had given them only a few hints. Pratibha Sahay would explain to them at length what other opportunities they would get and what improvements there would be. And not only that, there would also be some gain to whoever went to her election rally.

'What sort of gain?' Ganeri asked.

Abodhnarayan smiled briefly, and then told them that along with the ride in the motor car each of them would get three rupees.

So much money just for going to a meeting! Their eyes lit up with wonder and hope.

Abodhnarayan did not stay much longer. Now that he had planted temptation in the hearts of the hungry and ragged untouchables, he got up. 'It's got very late, and now I must go,' he said, as he pushed on the arms of the chair and raised his huge, fat body.

Just then the old Gairunath called in a confused voice from Dhanpat's veranda, 'We'll get three rupees! We're going to the mitin!'

This time there was no strident rebuff from under Lakhiya's veil. She was wholly agreeable to her father-in-law's going to the rally in a motor vehicle and getting three rupees. The coming election had given her the sense that this one-hundred-year old lame and decrepit man was not a complete millstone around her neck, and that even at his age he could earn a few pennies.

As soon as Abodhnarayan got up, so did Ganeri and all the others and, as a matter of courtesy, they accompanied him as far as the road outside. Abodhnarayan had said that they had all been toiling the whole day and they should not go to any more trouble, and insisted they leave him there.

Even after Abodhnarayan had gone, the excitement still buzzed throughout the dosad colony over the promise of a motor ride and three rupees each. They all looked at Ganeri and said, 'What'll we do now?'

With a serious look, Ganeri replied, 'Think about it.'

'Think of what?' They all had become terribly impatient. 'Pratibha-ji will take us in motor cars, give us three rupees in cash. Who else would give us three rupees? There is nothing else to think about.'

'Of course there is.'

'What?'

Ganeri explained to them that Pratibha Sahay was standing against Raghunath Singh in this election; moreover, they were Raghunath Singh's bonded labourers, they had worked his fields for generations, and they had raised their homes on his land. Would the great master be happy if they went to Pratibha Sahay's election rally for a ride in a motor vehicle and three rupees? Absolutely not. 'Think about what I have said,' he kept telling them.

They were all bewildered. Up to now no one had seen any reason to worry, but from long experience they could see that it was wrong to hope that the great master would be so high-minded as to suffer his own bonded labourers to attend Pratibha Sahay's election rally out of greed for three rupees. 'Then what should we do?' they asked.

Ganeri had no desire to disappoint so many people. He said, 'The mitin is not going to be held for at least seven or eight days. Let's wait and see. Now it's late, so what's the point of staying here and using up kerosene? Let's all go home.'

***

Dharma was again amazed when he returned home – not only he, but also his parents, even Kushi and her parents had gone out to hear what Ayodhyanarayan was saying. After his arrival no one stayed at home, for all the dosads in the quarter went to hear what he had to say at the open space beside the well. And now, here in the dark, leaning against a bamboo post on the veranda and smoking a beedi, was Tirke.

In great excitement Dharma said, 'Tirke! It's you, dada!'

'Yes, it's me,' Tirke laughed.

'How long have you been here?'

'A good hour.'

'Why didn't you call me?'

Tirke explained that he had not wanted to disturb them as long as the gathering about the election was going on.

Tirke had come to Dharma's shanty a few times before. Dharma's parents – and Kushi's – knew him and got on very well with him. They knew that with his help Dharma and Kushi had been able to earn quite a bit extra. Now the four old people could not think of what to do, seeing Tirke there so late at night. Dharma's mother hurried inside and brought out a lantern, which she lit, and then she lit the stove. She brought out some millet flour from inside, added water to it and said while she was kneading it, 'I'm making some *littis* for us to eat tonight.'

Tirke shook his head and said that she was not to go to any trouble for him so late at night. He would come the next day and fill his stomach. But Dharma's mother did not want to hear any of it. Only after a lot of talking did Tirke stop her from making *littis*.

Kushi's mother had made tea and poured some in an enamel mug, which she placed in front of Tirke. She gave some to Dharma and the others too.

Sipping his tea, Dharma asked, 'Where have you come from at this hour?'

'Straight from Ranchi.'

'Anything urgent?'

'Yes. Why else would I come at this hour? I've got some very urgent business with you.'

'Tell me what it is.'

'First let's finish our tea.'

Finishing his tea, Tirke got up abruptly, and said to Dharma, 'Come outside.'

The two of them went up onto the stony field outside the dosad colony. Tirke's bearing and speech seemed today to be rather mysterious to Dharma. He also felt some obscure kind of curiosity. Looking at Tirke's face, indistinct in the dark, he said, 'Tell me now.'

Tirke took a packet of cigarettes from his pocket and lit one. He also gave one to Dharma. Dharma lit it with the burning end of Tirke's cigarette, and waited in eager expectation.

'What about the young barking deer?' Tirke asked.

'I haven't gone back to the jungle,' said Dharma. 'I haven't had the time.' He paused for a moment, then went on, 'You gave me a month's time, though, the other day. By then I'll certainly bring the deer to you.'

Tirke was quiet for a little while, then he said, 'Forget about the barking deer.'

'Why?' Dharma was completely dumbfounded.

Lowering his voice Tirke asked, 'Would you like to earn a lot of money?'

'Who doesn't want to earn a lot of money?' Dharma replied, 'Sure, I do. But from whom?'

'From me.'

Jokingly, Dharma held out his hands and said, 'Give it to me, then.'

'It's no joke,' Tirke said. 'Listen to this. The American gentleman who wanted the young barking deer has come back to Ranchi.'

Dharma looked at Tirke, saying nothing.

Tirke went on, 'He doesn't want the barking deer. He wants to rear cheetahs. He wants a pair of Indian cheetah cubs to take back to his country.'

Dharma said, 'It's a very dangerous business catching live cheetah cubs and taking them from the jungle.'

Tirke then appealed to Dharma's sense of need. 'You'll get many rupees to put toward your repayment of Raghunath Singh, and then become a free man.' Tirke knew well that Dharma was the bondsman of the Rajput kshatriya Raghunath Singh on account of the debts of his father and grandfather.

Dharma was suddenly reminded that to acquire an independent life he needed a lot of money. They had been able to save little more than two hundred rupees from selling *bageri* birds for two or two and a half years. The sum needed was two thousand rupees. Dharma could not do the difficult sum to tell how much he still needed to raise. However, the schoolmaster had told him that there was still a great deal of money to save. The opportunity that Tirke had brought was indeed fortuitous and could not be allowed to slip by.

Dharma asked, 'How much will he pay?'

'Lots.' Encouraging Dharma, Tirke said, 'Don't worry.'

'Okay, lots. But how much?'

'How much do you want?'

Dharma had never named the price for getting young deer or buffalo horn or the like, and he was not sure how much more he needed to make up two thousand. He thought for a few moments, mentally working out the calculation in his own way, and then said, 'Fifteen hundred.'

'Fifteen hundred? One thousand and five hundred! No, no. You're asking for too much, Dharma bhai. Such a high price!'

'I won't do it for a penny less. I could lose my life catching cheetah cubs. Is my life worth less than fifteen hundred rupees?'

For some time Tirke haggled over the price, but he could not move Dharma, who remained adamant, and Tirke had to agree to his fifteen hundred. Of course, there was no loss in that to Tirke. He had told the American that the price for a pair of cheetah cubs was two and a half thousand. His intention had been to give half to Dharma and keep the rest for himself. But now who could say why this innocent, bashful dosad fellow had become so obdurate? Never mind, he was still lucky that one thousand rupees was going into his pocket out of the two and a half thousand. It would not be such a bother to come by bus two or three times to Dharma in Garudiya if so much money were to come from the endeavour. He could not catch the cheetah cubs himself – he certainly did not want even a scratch on his body. Yet he would certainly get the money.

Tirke said, 'All right. You'll get fifteen hundred. When will you make delvry of the two cubs?' By 'delvry' he meant 'delivery'. And in his enterprise with Tirke, Dharma too had learnt three or four English words.

'I'll need some *time*,' he said, using the English word. 'It's no easy thing to snatch the cub from the cheetah's mouth. All you have to do is say the word and you get it. But for me it's not as easy as that.'

Tirke said, 'The American will stay in Ranchi for fifteen days now. He'll then go to Calcutta for two weeks, then return to Ranchi.' He did some mental calculation and then said, 'Will you be able to provide the two cubs within a month?'

Tirke then took out a bunch of notes from his pocket and peeled off a one-hundred-rupee note. As he gave it to Dharma, he said, 'Here's an advance. Get the job done quickly.'

Never before had Tirke given such a big advance all at once. Dharma could sense that he had some interest in the business of the cheetah cubs.

Then Tirke said, 'It's a deal. I'll go now.'

Dharma folded up the one-hundred-rupee note and stuffed it into the seam of the waist of his shorts. He nodded, and said, 'All right.'

Tirke did not wait any longer. He crossed the stony field and went on towards the distant highway.

And Dharma kept thinking that in a few days he would have to go to the jungle in search of cheetah cubs. Preoccupied by this he headed back home.

21

PHAGURAM – THE GARUDIYA NIGHTINGALE – HARDLY HAD THE TIME now to breathe and even less to bathe, eat and sleep. With his new harmonium slung around his neck he would go out from the dosad colony each morning. No one had any idea when he returned at night, for by then the bonded labourers of his locality were all sunk deep in sleep.

Of late Phaguram had been busy all the time. How could he not have been? As the election date got closer, the more the great master visited this village or that in the taluks of Garudiya and Bijuri. Almost every day there was a rally at some marketplace or other, and Phaguram had to be there. Daily he was writing various new songs about Raghunath Singh's adversaries, and singing them at the rallies.

Some time back, when there had been nothing wrong with his chest, Phaguram would stay awake night after night and sing at *nautanki* performances. However, there was a huge difference between the theatre stage and the rally platform. The theatre audience would sit on hay spread about, or on torn sacking, with lanterns flickering overhead, and in the dim light Phaguram would sing his songs while being bitten by mosquitoes or, in the wet season, *ranipokas*. However, the great master's election rallies were quite a different matter. Here the stage would be splendidly adorned with red and blue cloth, and a new carpet would be laid out for Phaguram when he was about to sing. In the electric light or in the dazzling glow of the kerosene lantern that glittered as bright as day, he would sit in front of the microphone and absorb himself in playing his new harmonium and singing his songs. Even though they were election songs, the laughter and applause of thousands of listeners would make Phaguram's heart overflow with joy. Having been rejected by the *nautanki* troupe he had once wondered whether his life had been a waste. He was a singer and an actor. What would his life be without singing and acting? He was so grateful to the great master for giving him a new harmonium and the opportunity to sit on an adorned stage and sing before an audience of a thousand. No, Phaguram was not dead. His belief in himself grew knowing that at his age, in spite of his chest complaint, his voice could still work magic and bring delight to thousands of people. Deep down, he also believed that the power of his songs would bring victory to the great master in this election. He had good reason for his belief, for whenever there was a rally these days, Raghunath Singh's men would go about beforehand in cycle rickshaws or bullock carts announcing that before the speeches the Garudiya Nightingale, Phaguram the Trouper, would sing 'songs of the election'. He was a famous man. Only a few years ago, by virtue of the *nautanki* troupe, everyone within fifty or a hundred miles knew his name, and even since then, though not appearing with the troupe, he was by no means forgotten. In fact, Phaguram believed that it was really he who drew the crowds to Raghunath Singh's election rallies.

On days when there was no rally the great master sent him to various villages and markets. Playing his harmonium, he would draw a crowd and sing them the songs he had composed. This was essential to Raghunath Singh's grand design, for he well knew that to win the election battle this strategy must be constantly employed against his opponents. Both Raghunath Singh's enthusiasm and the constant applause of audiences at election meetings greatly heartened Phaguram, who was now living in a dream. His voice gave expression to new songs that burst forth like a stream from his breast, and now all those songs were on the lips of young and old alike in the villages and markets of Garudiya and Bijuri.

***

When he got up one morning, Phaguram went to the market at Manpatthal, taking the main road from Garudiya to the border of Bijuri. He walked straight on for a couple of miles and then took the unpaved road through the fields which led to the Manpatthal market, a huge marketplace sprawled over a vast area. The summer sun had risen quite high by the time he got there and, as he was out of breath from the strain of walking so far in the hot sun, he sat down to rest on the bamboo bench of a familiar teashop.

The teashop proprietor was very excited to see him. He gave Phaguram a hearty welcome and served him tea made from fresh leaves along with a biscuit and some savouries. He certainly would not hear of payment, saying, 'No, no. It is my good fortune that a great man like you should come and drink tea in my shop.'

Insistent, Phaguram held out the money to him. Thanks to the great master his pocket these days was replete with a ten-rupee or twenty-rupee note and some small change. Nevertheless, in about thirty villages throughout the region he was now the most famous and favoured man. Wherever he went, he was cordially received and well looked after.

Seeing Phaguram, people started to come until gradually quite a crowd had gathered. Surrounding him, they said, 'Well now, Phagu bhai, will you sing for us?'

Phaguram smiled and said, 'Certainly. I have come here to sing to you.'

'Funny songs?'

'You listen and say whether or not they're funny.'

And in such talk the morning wore on. Then Phaguram got up,

his harmonium around his neck, and went and stood under a vast *karaiya* tree in the middle of the Manpatthal market, the crowd from the teashop following behind him while many more people came hurrying from other parts of the market.

Phaguram moved around, dancing, his slender fingers all the while running over the keys of his harmonium. As soon as the audience was ready, he said, 'Listen, brothers. First I'll sing you a song I have written about Sukhan Ravidas.' And he began the song.

Now we are in
the dark age,
the last age of creation,
when Sukhan, the thieving and swindling tanner,
comes soliciting our votes.
Toddy and arrack are his mentors,
while in his home
whores dance
to his endless glory!
Say, dear people,
'Raghupati, Raghava, Rajaram.'

There was no truth at all in the words that Phaguram was singing. Nevertheless, people – rich and poor, landowners and labourers – love to hear slander and gossip about others, and so they rolled in laughter listening to the songs of his comic fancy.

Phaguram finished his song about Sukhan and then took up a song about Abu Malek:

There is uproar in the back streets
as the cry goes out –
Abu Malek is a thief!
So give your vote to Raghunath Singh,
and blow Abu Malek away.

Phaguram went on in this way, singing one song after another about Raghunath Singh's adversaries. By the time he had finished singing, the sun had risen directly overhead.

The people who were crowded about in the Manpatthal market were saying such things to one another as, 'We've heard it all in Phaguram the Trouper's songs! They're all lousy thieves and cheats. Except for only Raghunath Singh. What's the point in voting for thieves and cheats!' This was exactly the desired intention of composing and singing all these humorous songs, and now it was reflected in the reactions of the people.

Phaguram stayed no longer, but pushed through the crowd and mounted a cycle rickshaw. He had decided that, once he had returned to Garudiya, he would go straight to the dosad colony. Since he started singing election songs for the great master, he no longer returned home at midday but would go about to the various marketplaces or villages, enjoying tea and bread, or tea and biscuits, or rice, dal, vegetables and meat at this stall or that. Today, however, he would cook for himself when he got back home. He was no longer young, and his body was exhausted after the constant moving about for so many long days. Today, Phaguram decided that after he had had his lunch, he would sleep right through until evening.

The cycle rickshaw set off, leaving the Manpatthal market behind and took a dirt road in the direction of the highway. They had gone only a little way when a cry came from behind, 'Cycle rickshaw, pull over there! Stop!'

The rickshaw wallah stopped peddling. Startled, Phaguram turned and looked behind him. Some five or six rough-looking thugs wielding brass-studded lathis approached him, raising a storm of shouting.

'What's the matter?' Phaguram asked.

The men were unfamiliar. They had hard, stony faces and fire flashed from their round eyes. One of them said, 'How would you like to die, you son of a rat?'

The look and nature of the men sent Phaguram into a panic. Trying to smile, he said, 'What's the matter, bhai?'

'What's the matter!' Slapping his lathi, the man roared, 'Bloody Garudiya Nightingale! We'll kill you and feed you to the crows!'

'What have I done? Please help me understand.'

'All this time playing the harmonium in the Manpatthal market, what have you been saying about important people? Calling them thieves, swindlers, cunning exploiters – weren't you?'

Now Phaguram was flabbergasted. It was not as though his songs were as holy as Ganges water, for everyone who was standing against Raghunath Singh in the election had been stung by them. It was evident that that was why these rowdy, rough-looking fellows were so angry. Phaguram gulped in fear and smiled feebly. He said, 'They're just songs, bhai.'

'Just songs!'

'Just meant for fun.'

'You come back here again just for fun and we'll cut your throat. Understand?'

'I understand, I understand.'

'On your way, then. But watch your step.'

'Yes, yes, of course I'll be careful.'

The men moved aside and cleared the way. The cycle rickshaw set off once again and was soon coming up onto the highway from the dirt road.

On the way towards Bijuri, through the hot wind and fiery summer sun, Phaguram was preoccupied with trying to get a perspective on the whole affair. Why had these men become so angry at his funny songs? Of course, they contained barbs for all those standing against Raghunath Singh in the election. So were those rough-looking thugs who had just set upon him employed by any of them? Who had incited them? Nekiram Sharma? Abu Malek? Pratibha Sahay? Sukhan Ravidas?

Suddenly Phaguram recalled Ganeri's warning that the great master's rivals were not just any old common folk – they were wealthy and they had strong forces of thugs. It was clear that Ganeri had been right.

Phaguram decided now that he would not go back to the dosad colony and cook, but he would go straight to Raghunath Singh. It was vital that he tell the great master about this. He had become extremely worried.

***

Raghunath Singh was at home. Inside the huge compound three or four tarpaulin tents had been set up for the election campaign. The young men helping him through the election – the ones who shouted at the tops of their voices 'Vote for Raghunath Singh!' in the villages and marketplaces – usually came back there at noon to eat, rest, read the papers or handbills, or check the voters' lists. After all, the election was no simple thing, but rather like a thousand festivals.

The campaign workers were sitting in a line eating and the great master himself was standing in front of them supervising the meal when Phaguram came rushing in. He had come a long way in the blazing sun and his skin seemed scorched, while his face reflected his anxiety and fear.

Raghunath Singh glanced at Phaguram and asked, 'What's the matter? Where have you been?'

Phaguram took a breath, 'Manpatthal market, my lord. I went there to sing election songs.'

'How did it go?'

'Very well, by your grace. But – '

'But what?'

'I have something terrible to tell you.'

Raghunath Singh looked carefully at Phaguram and asked, 'Something terrible? What?'

In one breath Phaguram told him about the thugs and their threats. As he listened, Raghunath Singh's jaw set as hard as iron and his eyes flashed fire. 'Who were these sons of animals?' he demanded. 'What are their names? What village are they from?'

'I don't know, my lord,' Phaguram replied.

'Have you ever seen them before?'

'No, sir.'

Raghunath Singh frowned and thought for a moment. Then he said emphatically, 'Something has to be done about this.' He turned back to the campaign workers and said, 'Maheshwar, Ramratan, Muklal, Vajrangi – you four must go to Manpatthal market right now. From there you will go straight to meet with Mishirlal-ji.'

As Raghunath Singh spoke the four men immediately stopped eating and got up, but Raghunath gestured them to sit down again, saying, 'Finish your meal first. While you are eating listen to what you must do.'

Having told them about the rowdy, rough-looking swine, according to Phaguram's description, Raghunath directed them to go to Manpatthal market to find out about them. If they could be tracked down, well and good, but news or no news they must go straight to Bijuri and meet Mishirlal-ji, for Manpatthal was in his domain. He should be informed that in his own region a campaign worker of Raghunath Singh, Phaguram, had been menaced, and appeal to Mishirlal-ji to put things right.

Hurriedly stuffing their mouths with rice, dal, chapati and vegetables, the four election workers went off in the jeep. The great master asked Phaguram to wait until their return..

Later in the afternoon, when they got back, Raghunath Singh asked, 'Did you find out anything about those bloody animals?'

Shaking their heads, they said, 'No.'

'Did you look carefully around the Manpatthal market?'

'Yes, sir. We asked everyone, but no one could tell us anything.'

Raghunath Singh's brow was creased. Frowning, he said, 'It seems that someone has brought in goons from outside.'

The four election workers stood there in silence.

Again Raghunath Singh asked, 'Did you go to Bijuri?'

'Yes, sir.'

'Did you see Mishirlal-ji?'

'We did, sir.'

'Did you tell him everything?'

'Yes, sir.'

'What did he say?'

'When he'd heard what we had to say, he sent a man to look for the louts. If they're caught, their flesh will be flayed from their bones. He said to tell you that he will keep a careful eye out to see that those swine don't start any more trouble in Bijuri.'

Raghunath Singh was extremely pleased. Not only had Mishirlal given him his word, he was ready to do all he could to help him in this election. Clearly his word had worth.

Relieved, he said to his election workers, 'All right. You go and have a rest now. Tomorrow we have a rally at the fortnightly market at Sajjanpura, don't we?'

'Yes, sir.'

'Is everything ready for the rally?'

'Yes, sir.'

'Go on, then.'

The election workers went into the camp under the tarpaulin awning, and Raghunath Singh turned to Phaguram. 'You can go home now,' he said. 'Remember, you have to go to Sajjanpura tomorrow.' He walked away only a couple of paces when something occurred to him and he turned back. He was surprised to see that Phaguram had not moved but was still standing there looking anxious.

'What's wrong? Aren't you going home? Have you got something to say?'

Apprehensively, Phaguram said, 'Yes, my lord.'

'What is it?'

'I'm very frightened.'

'Why?'

'Those men said they would cut my throat.'

Patting Phaguram gently on the back, Raghunath Singh said, 'There is nothing to fear. I'm here. Go home now.'

Raghunath Singh had been reassuring, but it seemed that Phaguram's mind was not entirely at rest. However, there was no turning back now: if he stopped singing election songs, the great master would be angry, and if the singing continued, his rivals would be angry. He had known Raghunath Singh all his life. Now he had sent for him and treated him well, giving him new clothes, a new harmonium and money. Life and death notwithstanding, Phaguram would have to go on singing for him.

22

THE WORLD OF CONTENTED AND HAPPY PEOPLE WAS INDEED REMOTE from the dosad colony of Garudiya taluk, whose residents led a life of thraldom on account of the debts incurred by their forefathers. Yet strange it is to say that among these wretched folk, who were poorer than the destitute, hungrier than the famished and dressed in mere rags, many signs of simple humanity were apparent. Birth and death had their place here, just as they did in the distant, glittering world of great abundance. A young life, engendered by the age-old desire innate in one's parents and inherited from them, would gradually become a young man or woman who, in keeping with tradition, would one day marry. A virile man would plant the seed of new life in the fertile womb of his young woman, and so there would come into the world new people – or new bonded labourers. Like their fathers and grandfathers, they would cultivate Raghunath Singh's land and fill his granaries with precious golden grain until one day they would be erased from existence. But before that they would bring into the world their own issue of subsequent bonded labourers. And the Raghunath Singhs would never be short of unpaid labour.

Today the betrothal of Shiumal, the eldest son of Tiumal Dosad, would be arranged. He was to marry Radhiya, the youngest daughter of Gaibinath of Tilai village some six miles away, after the coming *Chhat* festival and just before the harvest season. And so Gaibinath, with his two brothers, the father-in-law of one of his sons and a nephew would come before midday, having already had preliminary discussions with Tiumal about the proposed marriage. Radhiya was a beautiful, well-developed girl of fourteen; normally such a comely girl would not be kept at home after fourteen years by the dosads. In fact, the only reason that Radhiya was not already married was Gaibinath. He had settled the girl's bride-price at one hundred and fifty rupees, which for this girl was not so very high at all. No one had ever seen such a girl as Radhiya in any dosad house in fifty surrounding taluks. She was indeed one in a million.

However, no matter how fair a price Radhiya's one hundred and fifty rupees might be in the marriage market, in fifty taluks there was not one dosad who could afford it. Those who came to see the girl would withdraw as soon as they learned the price.

In his quest for a wife for his son, Tiumal was wonderstruck when he saw Radhiya. He promised himself that somehow or other he would bring this girl to his home. But how could he afford her? In his eagerness, and without thinking the whole thing through, he instinctively bowed his head and offered fifty rupees, but Gaibinath remained unmoved on one hundred and fifty. Tiumal had worn his legs out walking from Garudiya to Tilai and back so many times, and after a year's extensive haggling over the issue of bride-price, he at last managed to make Gaibinath budge somewhat. Gaibinath came down little by little and Tiumal went up a bit, and a compromise was reached at one hundred rupees. Yet for a bonded labourer a hundred rupees might just have been ten million.

Everyone who lived in this dosad colony consulted with everyone else, especially with Ganeri. Tiumal had kept Ganeri informed about the business of his son's marriage right from the start of his earnest endeavours. The day that Gaibinath accepted the one hundred rupees Tiumal had returned dancing to the dosad colony, his face covered in a brilliant smile, and said to Ganeri, 'It's settled, Ganeri bhai, the goods have been purchased.'

Ganeri had nodded his head sombrely and said, 'So you have purchased the goods. But where will you get the hundred rupees?'

'From the munshi,' Tiumal had answered, an ingenuous look on his face. He was brimming over with joy at the prospect of bringing the finest of the dosad girls to his house in marriage.

Ganeri was startled. 'You'll take a loan, but how will you pay it back?'

'It'll be all right, Ganeri, bhai. It'll be all right.'

Ganeri had smiled sadly. He knew that to take a loan from the munshi Ajibchand meant putting one's foot in the trap of the great master Raghunath Singh. It was in taking a loan on bended knee for a marriage that the dosads brought about their own ruin. They believed that they would pay back the loan by any means, but the excessive interest would grow and turn into a noose around their necks as they became more and more bound in debt, and there was no way of cutting away the noose in their own lifetimes nor in succeeding generations.

Tiumal was a one-generation bonded peasant, and with him his family's thraldom would end. After that everyone in his family would be able to live in freedom and with dignity, but now he had put his own son's neck in the great master's noose as well.

'You'll get yourself into terrible trouble, Tiumal,' Ganeri had said.

Ignoring what the future might bring if he took out a loan, Tiumal had replied, 'Oh no, no. By the grace of Lord Ram, say what a beautiful daughter-in-law I am bringing. She is one to be looked at in amazement and to be shown to everyone with pride.' For having but seen this beautiful girl, Tiumal was obsessed with bringing her into his home.

However, his wealth of experience helped Ganeri to see well into the future. Appreciating the position in which the obligation to settle this loan would place Tiumal, Ganeri had said in a melancholy voice,

'Break off this betrothal, Tiumal. Don't impose such trouble on your own son.'

Tiumal shuddered. 'No, no, bhai. Don't say such a thing.'

'Oh, you fool, if there is no wedding, then no one dies.'

'It's my duty. Marriage is a divine law. It's like the practice of religion. I must have him married, brother.' Like a philosopher Tiumal then offered some profound words about birth, death and marriage occurring by God's decree, which man did not have the power to disobey. And so the son of Tiumal, bonded labourer of Garudiya taluk, must marry Radhiya, the daughter of Gaibinath Dosad of Tilai village, beckoned by the finger of an unseen god, for this divine law was infallible and inescapable.

Whenever there was a wedding in any home here, it was like a festival to the entire dosad colony. Tiumal and all the others of the colony had gone to meet with Raghunath Singh, and for the settlement of Tiumal's betrothal, they had appealed for half a day's break from their work, but Raghunath had magnanimously given them the whole day off. This made all the dosads overwhelmed with joy, although Ganeri was sceptical. He realised that the election was imminent, and that it would be unwise for Raghunath Singh to offend the voters in any way.

Since long before sunrise women of various ages, in groups and individually, had started to gather and sing marriage songs outside Tiumal's hut.

The marriage party has entered my courtyard.
It is a poor man's yard.
Now the groom's new grandparents
come into my courtyard
with the marriage party.

As one group stopped singing to catch their breath, another would start up.

Oh, my dear friends, cheer the marriage party
with sweet songs.
Put a cap on the head of the father of the groom,
give slippers to the bridegroom's sister.
Grandfather has no good dhoti –
then give a fine dhoti to grandfather,
and a fine sari to the bridegroom's sister.
Give the groom's father a singlet to wear
and a fine blouse to his grandmother.
Oh, my dear friends . . . .

Once the sun had come up, a few of the men of the dosad colony accompanied the singing with their drums. It was like the start of a festival day. And as the sun climbed higher not one of the dosads remained at home, all of them having gathered happily in front of Tiumal's place. Getting a whole day off from their back-breaking toil on account of a betrothal was not a common occurrence in their lives.

The groom's parents, Tiumal and Paheli, were as light as the air in their joy. They had bathed at daybreak, put on fresh, clean clothes scrubbed with the ash of burnt herbs, and gone from this one to that offering tea and sweets.

Tiumal had known everyone in the colony all his life, and he was now around fifty or fifty-five. He had grown up with all those of the same age and had known younger ones since their births. He had worked shoulder to shoulder with all the other bonded labourers of the colony, cultivating the great master's land and harvesting his crops. Sharing unremitting hardship, sorrow and want, and sometimes even engaged in feuds, Tiumal had so long survived in his world, along with the others of this neighbourhood, and he had an intimate knowledge of the lives of all the dosads. But today was something completely different, for today they were all his guests, and he must attend cordially on each of the men, otherwise they would be slighted. In the same way as Tiumal extended his hospitality to each of the men, his wife attended to the women.

Shiumal, the groom was sitting on a veranda some way away. He too had had to bathe after getting up at daybreak, but before bathing he had massaged his head with a great deal of oil, so that his hair was still profuse with it and drops were rolling down over his forehead and behind his ears. He was wearing a clean dhoti dyed yellow and a brand new, very fine, net-woven singlet bought from the fortnightly market at Chaharh, with its stamped trademark still visible. Shiumal smiled shyly, yet he was very proud that all these preparations and the attendance of so many guests were all on account of him.

Shiumal's friends of the dosad colony were sitting around him, enjoying banter and joking with him. Dharma too was among them. To one side of this gathering, sitting with his chin resting on his knees under a spreading *palas* tree, was Ganeri, looking unhappy and solemn. All around there were so many people, so much singing, so much laughter and joking, yet he seemed to be quite detached from it all.

As Tiumal went about serving tea and sweets, he came upon Ganeri. Genially he said, 'Have some, Ganeri bhai. Have some tea.'

The blackish tea was in enamel cups and the sweets were in leaf-wrapped packets. Reaching out to take the cup and the packet of sweets, Ganeri said, 'You're serving tea and sweets to so many people. Where did you get the money?'

Tiumal was embarrassed. Without looking Ganeri in the eye he mumbled, 'Oh, I managed to get it.'

Ganeri had no trouble working out how Tiumal could afford so much. Looking at him intensely he asked, 'For the loan of how many rupees did you give your thumb-print to the munshi?'

Looking down, Tiumal shook his head slowly, saying, 'Not much. Not much at all.'

Ganeri looked quite downcast. Seeing a bleak future for the family of this middle-aged dosad, he said in great disappointment, 'You're being an idiot. You're not celebrating your son's betrothal, you're bringing about his death. This will be the very end of you all.'

On such a festive occasion Ganeri's words were most inauspicious. Without responding to them, Tiumal said, 'Drink your tea, it's getting cold.'

Ganeri did not listen to what Tiumal said. Harshly he asked, 'Tell me, how much did you pay for the noose for your necks?'

'I told you, not much.'

'Not much, all right. But how much?'

His head bowed, Tiumal said, 'Two hundred – '

'You took a loan to entertain your guests! You poor, unfortunate fool!' Getting angry, Ganeri was about to say more, but suddenly the whole dosad colony was almost electrified. All at once people started calling out, 'They've come! They've come!'

Tiumal's future in-laws, wearing finely stitched, bleached clothes and heavy slippers of about two kilograms of raw leather, together with some of their relations and an elderly family priest, could be seen coming along the road near the well. Gaibinath had not said that his wife would be coming, and so her appearance was a very pleasant surprise. Although she was the bride's mother, she still looked like a young woman with her slender waist and taut shape, her elegant hands, arms and face, and her sparkling eyes. She wore a beautiful sari, silver bangles on her wrists, floral ornaments in her ears, a nose-stud set with an artificial gem and, on the middle toe of each foot, a toe ring with tiny bells. She had tattoos on her hands and between her eyes, and she was redolent with the fragrance of aromatic oil. Such a shapely, well-presented woman had never been seen in the homes of the dosads. When he had gone to see his future daughter-in-law, Tiumal had also enjoyed eyeing the girl's mother. What an in-law! The women of the dosads generally had tough hands, teeth like the seeds of custard-apples and blackened by tobacco and *khaini*, no grace or beauty in their faces, and a sound coming from their gaping mouths like the call of a dozen crows. But this wife of Gaibinath! She was like a celestial nymph. Tiumal would decide how many times his son would visit his in-laws' house after the wedding, and it was as certain as the rising of the sun and the moon that the mother-in-law's attraction would draw Tiumal to Tilai village from time to time, too.

Tiumal became extremely excited at seeing Gaibinath and his family. 'They're here,' he said. 'I have to go.' And without waiting for Ganeri to say anything, he ran off.

The marriage songs and the beating of the drums had been going on since daybreak, and the singers and drummers were getting a little tired, but on seeing Tiumal's new kinsfolk their volume increased tenfold. With great cordiality Tiumal and his wife and some of the other dosad women seated Gaibinath and his party on the veranda of their shanty. Other arrangements were hurriedly made to accommodate the family priest: from the new well fresh water was drawn, with which he might wash his hands and feet, and a charpoy was brought for him to sit on. Of course, this kind of brahman who performed various functions for untouchables was, amongst brahmans in general, regarded as degenerate and prevented from having social relations with 'pure', upper-caste brahmans.

Once everyone was seated, tea and sweets were brought. This was the first part of the entertainment. Then, after the exchange of pleasantries, the priest consulted the almanac and settled on the day of the wedding. Gaibinath's daughter would be married to Tiumal's son on the first full-moon night after the *Chhat* festival. Gaibinath and his wife blessed their future son-in-law with five rupee coins and a new, unbleached dhoti.

Brimming over with joy Tiumal called out, 'It's settled! By the grace of Lord Ram the wedding date has been fixed!'

Something else had been going on during all of this. While everyone was preoccupied with the business of the wedding date or with the singing, Dharma and Kushi were continually exchanging glances. There was melancholy in Kushi's eyes, and every time Dharma glanced at her, she was looking at him.

It was already midday by the time the wedding date had been fixed. The sun had risen directly overhead and was starting to decline towards the west. The gathering broke up and one by one the dosads returned to their shanties to eat their midday meals, for there was only tea and water in Tiumal's house – although for his new kinsfolk there was a midday feast of rice, dal, vegetables, meat, yoghurt and sweets. Indeed, Tiumal had arranged quite a spread.

***

Back home, Dharma and his father were filling their mouths with large handfuls of coarse rice mixed with blackish pigeon-pea dal, occasionally biting into some onion or chilli. Opposite them Dharma's mother continually muttered while eating her rice, 'Everyone's children are getting married. Only in our house is there darkness.'

From the tone of her voice it was evident where her talk was leading to. Whenever any of the young people in the dosad colony got married the old woman would start to grumble. Her great hope was for her son to marry Kushi and set up a home. However, Dharma did not answer her but kept his eyes on his food, which he bolted down urgently so that he might soon get away from his mother.

Again the old woman spoke. 'Well then, what is your intention?'

'What do you mean?'

'Are you going to get married, or get around like a wild buffalo for the rest of your life? Boys younger than you are already married.'

As she sat eating on the veranda of the neighbouring hut, Kushi's mother could hear every word of Dharma and his mother. Raising her voice she said, 'Make your boy understand, Dharma's ma, he should fix the marriage now.'

Dharma's mother was saying, 'Don't you know that my throat is raw from talking and talking about this?'

'Have I ever said I won't get married?' Dharma said. 'But – '

'But what?'

'Where's the money? Who's going to pay the cost of the wedding?'

'Why can't you pay for it with the money you've got from the *bageri* birds?' The old woman knew that Dharma and Kushi had saved some money from the sale of the birds as well as from the claws, tusks and hides of wild animals, which Dharma had sold to foreigners through Tirke.

'That money is not for the wedding.'

'Then?'

'It's to settle the debt.' He then went on to explain that when every penny had been paid back to the great master they could be completely independent. Once they had won their freedom from the hateful drudgery of a life of bonded labour, he would then think about marriage.

'That'll take until I die, you swine.'

'Then so be it.'

Kushi's mother called out from the neighbouring veranda, 'Oh, Lord Ram! Just for your son my daughter has to wait to get married. That wretched animal – '

Dharma's mother could speak as she liked to the child of her own womb. She could beat him or cut him, but what right did someone else have to abuse him? She snapped, 'You're insulting my son, you old hyena, you snake! I'll set your face on fire!'

Kushi's mother was not one to shirk and she sprang into the fight, furiously flinging her arms and legs about, shouting, grimacing and gesturing. Dharma's mother did not remain seated, either, and so the clamour and tumult began. With the onset of such screams of abuse all the crows in the dosad colony took flight.

'I'll not let my daughter marry your son! She could have had two children by now if she had been married!'

'You won't allow it! I'll not give my son to your daughter! I spit ten times on this relationship! Ten times let me kick it!'

Whenever anyone got married there would be an outbreak of war between Kushi's mother and Dharma's mother, while those over whom the epic battle was being fought would sit on neighbouring verandas, suppressing their laughter.

23

On any other day the dosad colony would be deserted and utterly silent from daybreak until evening, hardly resembling a human habitation, but today it was full of life with people enjoying the unexpected holiday. Even those who were independent, or the weak and elderly who did little work, did not go out looking for food. As the day wore on, charpoys were set out in open spaces and groups of men and women sat and chatted together. Some again sang songs. Throughout the colony there was a mood of carefree idleness.

Suddenly there came from the distance the sound of many voices shouting, although it was not clear what the people were saying. The dosads all stopped their conversations and songs and pricked up their ears. In a little while it felt as though the shouting was coming in their direction, and the voices became clear.

'Vote for – '

'Sukhan Ravidas!'

'Give your vote to – '

'Sukhan Ravidas! Sukhan Ravidas!'

'Make your mark on – '

'The sign of the camel! The sign of the camel!'

Everyone in the dosad colony had come out onto the stony field just as a group of about a hundred shouting people were coming down from the highway. At the front of them all was Sukhan Ravidas.

Everyone, especially the untouchables, in all the villages and marketplaces within fifty or sixty miles – and not only in Garudiya and Bijuri taluks – knew Sukhan. Not only did they know him but they revered the name of this spirited son of a tanner. He had no fear of anyone, not brahmans nor kayasthas nor Rajputs, not government officers nor police superintendents nor magistrates – he talked to them all on the same level. He was a truly stout-hearted young man. In this locality Sukhan knew as many people even as knew him, and he was a familiar acquaintance of at least ten or twenty men, including Ganeri, Budheri, Tiumal and Madholal.

Raising his hand to stop his cohorts, Sukhan went straight to Ganeri. Smiling, he asked, 'How are you, Uncle?'

It was evident from Ganeri's face that he was glad to see Sukhan, who was loved by so many in this region. With great warmth Ganeri replied, 'I'm well. How are you?'

'I'm well.'

Sukhan then went around to everyone in the colony listening to details of their news before coming back to Ganeri. 'Uncle,' he said, 'I've come to you on important business.'

Ganeri could well guess the nature of Sukhan's business, but nevertheless he asked, 'Tell me, what is it?'

'You must have heard that I am standing in this election.'

'I have.'

'So now you can guess why I have come to you, then?'

Ganeri looked somewhat embarrassed. Seemingly distracted he slowly nodded.

Looking straight into his eyes, Sukhan said, 'I've come to seek the votes of all of you in the election. I've come with high hopes. I need the vote of every single one of you. No one else must get votes from here.'

Ganeri remained silent.

Sukhan went on. 'My symbol is the camel. Put your mark on the sign of the camel. I know you are the sole authority among the dosads. If you give the word, they will all vote for me. Will I explain to everyone why it is necessary for me to win this election, Uncle?'

Again Ganeri did not answer.

Sukhan moved back a little to stand on a small mound. Then, raising his voice, he said, 'Brothers and sisters, you are untouchable dosads. Moreover, you are bonded labourers. Since the time of your grandfathers or great-grandfathers your people have spent their whole lives doing unpaid labour on the land of someone else. I too am an untouchable, the son of a tanner. At the mention of my name high-caste people will spit ten times. They will go ten miles away to prevent our shadows falling on them.'

The residents of the dosad colony listened to Sukhan with bated breath and their eyelids did not flicker. Sukhan went on, 'We have in our country currently the rule of the brahmans, the kayasthas and other high castes, and for as long as the sun and the moon have risen, all of us – tanners, washermen, dosads, dhangars – have been under their feet. They treat us like animals, they make us work like animals. But this cannot go on. It cannot go on. For the good of untouchables like you and me, it is essential that I win. If you bring me victory in the election, we can all try to live like human beings. At least if I am in the Legislative Assembly in Patna, I can let the world know of the conditions under which we untouchables live, how you bonded labourers waste your lives working on the land of others. Remember my symbol, the camel. Put your stamp on the sign of the camel.'

Immediately Sukhan's companions burst out with, 'Give your vote to – '

'Sukhan Ravidas!'

'Put your stamp on – '

'The sign of the camel! The sign of the camel!'

'For untouchables' welfare – '

'Sukhan must win! Sukhan must win!'

'Vote for change – '

'Give victory to Sukhan!'

Sukhan, signalling to his companions to stop, came down from the mound and went again to Ganeri. With one hand over his heart he said, 'I'm depending on you, Uncle.'

Ganeri looked greatly perturbed. He said, 'But – '

'No buts. I won't hear another word. I need the votes of all of you. I need, need, need them.'

'But – '

'Again but!'

'I want to say something first. Now listen.'

Sukhan considered for a moment. Creasing his brow he said, 'All right. Go on.'

Ganeri then went on to tell him that they had been bonded to the great master Raghunath Singh over generations since the time of their grandfathers or even earlier. That same great master was now standing in the election, and now Sukhan Ravidas also was contesting. Sukhan was one of them, and in their hearts they fondly wished to give him their votes and for him to win. But that would be bad for Raghunath Singh. They were his bondsmen, they drank water from the wells he had dug for them, and they were able to set up homes on his land for all of their lives, so would Raghunath Singh allow them to keep their heads on their shoulders if they were to put their stamps beside the camel instead of his elephant? He would set his strong-arm men on them to set fire to their huts, put an end to them and make their corpses disappear.

Sukhan said, 'Don't worry, Uncle. What sort of a state would we be in if we all took fright at the mention of the great master? Must we continue to be trodden under foot by the upper castes? Must we work ourselves to death on their land? This cannot be, Uncle Ganeri. You have to show some moral strength.' Having said this, Sukhan took Ganeri by the shoulders, perhaps to try to instil a little courage in him.

Meekly Ganeri said, 'I'll think about what you have said.'

Letting his hands drop from Ganeri's shoulders, Sukhan said, 'All right, Uncle. I'll go now, but I'll be back.' He raised his hand to the other dosads and said, 'Goodbye, brothers and sisters!' and then set off with his company across the stony field towards the distant highway.

They had gone only a little way when Naorangi came out from the midst of the crowd. Hearing all the shouting for Sukhan, she too had come out of her shanty, but no one had given a thought to her. Contriving various postures and gestures with her hands and feet, Naorangi said, 'That son of a pig has grown wings to bring about hisown end. He'll die. The bastard'll certainly die. That'll be the absolute end of him.'

Having seen her gestures and posturing and heard the abuse of Sukhan that came from her mouth, everyone kept quiet, dumb with fear.

Naorangi spoke up again. 'What a hide the dog's got, coming to solicit votes from the great master's own people! The bastard's grown ten heads, but they'll all be knocked off.'

Standing among the crowd listening to Naorangi, Dharma was reminded of Ramlachhman's words. That day when he saw Sukhan at the Chaharh market, St Satan had got angry in the same way. All of Raghunath Singh's lapdogs would get angry at any of the people standing against the great master in the election.

Naorangi waited there no longer, but after a few more words of abuse at Sukhan she strode back into the dosad colony.

The others all started to go back too. However, only a little later they were all amazed to see Naorangi leaving, all dressed up and adorned. On other days it would be long after sunset in the thick of night when the bullock cart came to take her to Himgiri, but today it was not even evening yet, with the red sun still fixed in the western sky. The dosads could easily guess the reason for Naorangi's hurrying off impatiently, alone and on foot. They just sat there, listening to the beating of their own timid hearts. Someone whispered to Ganeri, 'What's going to happen, dada? That slut will surely let Himgiri-ji know about Sukhan.'

'That's true,' said Ganeri, slowly nodding his head.

'And Himgiri-ji will certainly let the great master know.'

'That also is true.'

'Then?'

'Wait and see. But if someone comes to us, how can we tell him to go away?'

***

It was not very late – indeed, it was just starting to get dark after the setting of the sun – when Ramlachhman appeared, his long legs striding into the dosad colony. His eyes darted around looking here and there as he said, 'What possessed you all? This'll really finish you, you spawn of owls.'

Fearfully, the dosads asked, 'What's the matter, sir?'

'What's the matter?' Ramlachhman went on. 'Come with me. Then you'll see. All the men folk here, get up.'

'Where to, sir?'

'You'll see where. Come on!' In no time at all Ramlachhman's shouting had alarmed the entire neighbourhood.

A little later all the men of the dosad colony could be seen following St Satan towards the highway. They had no clear idea of where he was taking them, but there was an unmistakable hint of significance in his coming to them after Naorangi's rushing off in that direction. However, they would have to wait and see.

At last Ramlachhman delivered them at the mansion of the great master, where Raghunath Singh was lounging in a vast, cushioned easy chair on the marble-paved veranda, surrounded by his constant companions – the doctor, the lawyer, the headmaster, and the like – along with his campaign staff. On either side clusters of electric lights were burning, and everywhere it was as bright as day.

Ramlachhman said to Raghunath Singh, 'I've got them all.'

Raghunath Singh slowly inclined his head and gestured with a hand to Ramlachhman to go. It was now clear to the dosads that the great master had summoned them. They waited with bated breath. However, from Raghunath Singh's face it hardly seemed that he was angry, but rather his look reflected a profound affection and a degree of indulgence. Very gently he said, 'Well, now. Why are you all standing? Sit down.'

Ganeri and the others sat huddled together on the grassy ground. The thumping of their hearts would not stop as long as they did not know the reason why the great master had sent for them.

Raghunath Singh said, 'Has Tiumal's son's betrothal been fixed, then?'

Tiumal, in a trembling voice, said that by the grace of the great master the betrothal had been fixed.

Raghunath Singh inquired little by little about who had come from the girl's house, what was said, what Tiumal and his family had served to their new kinsfolk, whether all the formalities had been completed satisfactorily or not, and so on. Then he said quite suddenly, 'I hear that Sukhan Ravidas came to you seeking votes. He also delivered a long lecture.'

Raghunath Singh had spoken so sincerely about the business of Tiumal's son's betrothal that most of the dosads' apprehensions had been allayed. Now, suddenly, everyone became tense again and their faces were marked by worry. Only Ganeri, with irrepressible courage, got up and, with hands pressed together, said, 'Yes, master, he did come. He also said a few words.'

'Soliciting votes?'

'Yes, sir.' As he spoke, Ganeri's breathing quickened. Then with renewed effort, he went on, 'How can we drive away whoever comes to us? We are very poor people. You are our father and mother – '

Raghunath Singh said, 'No, no. Anyone who stands in a democratic election has the right to canvass votes. Today Sukhan came to you, tomorrow Pratibha Sahay will come, the day after Abu Malek will come, the day after that Sharma-ji will come. But you must all remember just one thing.'

'What, sir?' Ganeri asked.

'No matter who seeks your vote, you must all put your marks beside the symbol of the elephant. Remember, if you make your mark beside the sign of the elephant, I will get your vote. I am your own man. For your good I must win the election. Do you understand?'

Ganeri's feverish perspiration subsided and the throbbing in his breast ceased. Raghunath Singh, then, was not angry with them. Ganeri said, 'We understand, sir.' But then he remembered something. 'May I say something, master?'

'Yes, yes. Speak freely.'

'The other day Abodh-ji came to our colony.'

'Who is Abodh-ji?'

'The big businessman in the Bijuri market.'

'Oh, I know. Abodh Pande. He's working for Pratibha Sahay in the election.'

'He had come seeking votes for Pratibha-ji,' Ganeri said.

Magnanimously, Raghunath Singh replied, 'In a democracy – the rule of the people – it is no offence to seek votes.'

Encouraged, Ganeri went on, 'There is something else, great master.'

'What?'

'In seven or eight days Pratibha-ji's election mitin will be held beside the Garudiya market.'

'Why should she not have an election meeting? Of course there will be a meeting. So what?'

'Abodh-ji has told us to go to that mitin. He will take us there.'

'How? In bullock carts?'

'In motor vehicles, master.'

The headmaster Badrinathbishal Chaube spoke up. 'I see the

election has brought you all good fortune. How lucky you are! Untouchables being driven to an election rally in a motor vehicle! This is truly the apotheosis of the dark age.'

Raghunath Singh raised his hand to stop him. 'Please don't talk like this, Chaube-ji. In a democracy everyone has the right to be driven in a motor vehicle.' Turning back to Ganeri, he said, 'You should go. Of course you must go in a motor vehicle to Pratibha Sahay's meeting.'

This encouraged Ganeri and he went on, 'Sir, Abodh-ji also said that if we go to Pratibha-ji's mitin we will each get three rupees. Should we take the money?'

'If they want to give money and you don't accept it, then you are all fools!! In a democracy it is not right to take money. However – '

'What, master?' Ganeri stood there with questioning eyes.

'You may go to the election rally in a motor vehicle, you may accept the money, but I want your vote, even if you die! Don't forget to put your mark beside the sign of the elephant.'

'No, sir.'

From the right, where the tarpaulin provided a temporary camp for the campaign staff, there came a cry –

'For your own good – '

'Vote for Raghunath Singh! Vote for Raghunath Singh!'

'Make your mark on – '

'The sign of the elephant! The sign of the elephant!'

Raghunath Singh stopped the shouting and said to Ganeri and the others, 'Go home now. It has become very late.'

And so the dosads went home.

Now one of Raghunath Singh's chief lapdogs, the lawyer, spoke up. 'The factory owner, Pratibha, has made a lot of money to scatter about in the election.'

'There are poor people everywhere,' Chaube said. 'They would all give their votes for money.'

Up to now Raghunath Singh had been very happy, but now his face looked terribly sombre. He had not yet made any comment about Pratibha Sahay.

The Bengali doctor, Shyamdulal Sen, said, 'There is something else, Raghunath-ji.' Raghunath Singh rolled his vast body over on to its right side to look at Shyamdulal, who said, 'The nature of this election is rather unusual.'

'In what way?'

'Altogether five people are fighting this election – Pratibha Sahay, Nekiram Sharma, the tanner Sukhan, Abu Malek, and you.'

Raghunath Singh said, 'In other places too there are various candidates standing for election. Somewhere there are seven, somewhere there are ten, fifteen. What is so unusual about this?'

Shyamdulal raised his hand to stop Raghunath Singh, then went on to point out politely and briefly the more surprising things about the election campaign in Garudiya and Bijuri. Of the five candidates, the first was Raghunath Singh. Raghunath Singh was a landowner, a son of the soil and, for generations, his family had been sons of the soil. Then there was Pratibha Sahay. Although her father-in-law's home was in Bijuri, she was not a village girl but a city woman, an industrialist, a factory owner with no roots in the earth of the country. The third was Sukhan Ravidas, the representative of the untouchables. Number four was Abu Malek, representing the minority community. The fifth was Nekiram Sharma standing on behalf of the brahmans and other high castes. Thus it could be seen that the candidates – a landowner, an industrialist, an untouchable, a Muslim and a high-caste Hindu – represented the five classes of the region.

Raghunath Singh paid careful attention to what Shyamdulal said, but did not place great store on it. He said light-heartedly, 'So far there is nothing unusual or new. We know all this. Enough has already been said about it.'

Becoming impatient, Shyamdulal said, 'That is so. But I have more to say.'

'What?'

'With representatives of five classes of society standing in the election, the vote will, of course, be split virtually equally five ways. That is, indeed, a matter of some concern.'

Raghunath Singh was sitting back, supporting himself on his hand. He said, 'Is it, indeed? Explain this a little.'

Shyamdulal went on to say that some thirty percent of the people of Garudiya and Bijuri were untouchables. Sukhan Ravidas would draw almost all of their votes. Across the two taluks upper-caste Hindus made up thirty-five to forty percent. If Bijuri taluk's Mishirlal-ji were to be believed, Nekiram's casteist campaign would claim a good many of the brahmans' votes. The minority Muslims made up fifteen to seventeen percent here, and Abu Malek would get almost all of their votes. And the factory-owner, Pratibha, throwing money around with ten hands, would buy many votes. Consequently, no one would get many more votes than anyone else; whoever won would win by just a very small margin.

Raghunath Singh frowned. Shyamdulal's words had made a profound impression on him. With a sombre look he said, 'We'd not considered the election from that angle. We should have.'

Apart from Shyamdulal, Raghunath Singh's other lapdogs sat restlessly. If Raghunath were to treat Shyamdulal's words with so much seriousness, so too should they. They were a group of yes men, and they all said together, 'Indeed, we should have.'

'This has become quite perplexing,' said Raghunath Singh.

'Yes, yes – ' they all agreed.

An uncomfortable few moments passed in silence before Badrinathbishal spoke up. 'It's enough that Pratibha Sahay should be running factories. Why should the woman want to stick her nose into this election?'

Shyamdulal snorted and said, 'Class interest, Chaube-ji, simple class interest.'

'And Sukhan the tanner, Abu Malek and Nekiram Sharma – what are their interests?'

'Communal interests, quite clearly. Haven't you ever thought of how a group's strength increases with political power?'

Raghunath Singh now looked deeply worried. He said, 'What do you all think? That I'll lose the election?'

Even if the election were to be analysed in minute detail and the result predicted precisely, Badrinathbishal and the others could not dream of Raghunath Singh's defeat. Like a pack of hyenas they bayed together, 'No, no! No, never!'

'This is the first time I am standing in an election. If I lose, I'll not be able to look anyone in the eye again. For me it is a matter of honour.'

'Your dishonour would be the dishonour of every one in all of Garudiya and Bijuri. As long as there is a drop of blood in our bodies, we cannot allow it,' said one of them.

There was a pause for a moment, and then, after a deep breath, another said with renewed earnest, 'If you lose, the sun will rise in the west.'

Raghunath Singh's anxiety was somewhat dispelled by such strong vocal support from his constant companions. He said, 'My family have been living in Garudiya for twenty or thirty generations. I have never been separated from the village. I am a genuine son of the soil. The right to their votes is mine alone.'

'Of course. The munshi's words are a thousand times true – if you win the election the rule of God will come down to Garudiya and Bijuri. Real happiness will come to the people of this region.'

Hearing this, Raghunath made a sound that suggested he was gratified.

A short time passed in silence, after which Badrinathbishal Chaube coughed and cleared his throat. Then he began, 'But there is one thing, Raghunath-ji – '

Turning to Chaube, Raghunath asked, 'What?'

'It is necessary to be absolutely sure of your victory.'

'You have some doubt in the matter, do you?'

Chaube stifled something like a hiccup as he cried, 'No, no! But we have to take precautions.'

The frown that had left Raghunath's forehead now returned to it. With his eyes fixed on Chaube, he said, 'I don't quite understand you.'

'I said that it could be a problem if the vote were divided more or less equally five ways.'

'But what can you do about the distribution of the vote? You said a short while ago that the candidates will draw good support. That is the big problem. What must be done, then?'

'Some arrangement must be made,' Chaube replied. 'If one or two of the five candidates were not standing, the vote would not be distributed in such a way.'

Raghunath Singh, although a man of keen intelligence, was now confused. He said, 'Would they withdraw from the fray?'

'Anyone can easily be removed. There are ways.'

'Are you thinking of abducting and hiding them? But Chaube-ji, the old ways of my father's and grandfather's times no longer apply. Democracy runs the country now. How can you think of laying a hand on any candidate?'

Badrinathbishal Chaube put his hands to his ears, bit his tongue and shuddered as though he had heard talk of some monstrous sin, and in that pose he said, 'Oh, my goodness! What are you saying, Raghunath-ji! Do I not fear damnation? However, can someone not be removed in a way other than abduction?'

'How?'

Badrinathbishal winked and, rubbing his thumb and forefinger together, gestured the taking of money.

Raghunath Singh did not appear to be as enthusiastic. With a disinterested look he asked, 'Can everyone be bought with money? Apart from that – '

'What?'

'Sukhan the tanner is so proud that no amount of money will make him stoop. He wouldn't retreat from the election battle if his life depended on it. Pratibha Sahay is a millionaire, so there is no question of buying her. That leaves Nekiram Sharma and Abu Malek. Nekiram is a usurer, so he has a love of money, but Abu Malek has a very strong backbone, which cannot be bent.'

Raghunath Singh had missed nothing in this analysis of the characters of his rivals. His lapdogs looked very concerned.

More time passed in silence, and then Raghunath Singh spoke again. 'This is a real predicament.'

Suddenly the lawyer Girdharlal said to Raghunath Singh, 'Will you permit me to say one thing?'

'Of course. But why one thing? Say a hundred.'

'Looking at it from all points of view, I can see that Sukhan and Pratibha will not be put aside. But there might be a way to move Abu Malek and Nekiram Sharma.'

'What way?'

'It will probably require money, and it will be necessary to speak with them.'

'About what?'

'Nekiram will have to be persuaded that you will attend to the interests of the brahmans. Abu Malek will have to be persuaded that other than you, no one can look after the welfare of the Muslim minority.'

Raghunath Singh creased his brow and thought for a few moments. Then he said appreciatively, 'Well said. I'd not thought of it like that. However – '

'However?'

'If they see benefit enough in talk of the interests of brahmans and the Muslim minority to move aside, will that benefit us?'

'It will, Raghunath-ji.'

'How? If they withdraw from the election struggle, is there any guarantee that their votes will go to me?'

'Not really.'

'Then?'

'Arrangements will have to be made for their voters to make their marks beside the sign of the elephant.'

'How?'

'Nekiram and Abu Malek will have to stand up in support of your campaign. They will explain to the brahmans and to the Muslim minority that if they vote for you their interests will be fully protected. What benefit they would get from Nekiram or Abu Malek's winning the election would be doubled if they voted for you.'

Raghunath Singh moved about in his seat. From his face it was clear that he was happy. If Nekiram and Abu Malek joined his election campaign, the vast number of brahman and Muslim votes he would get would remove any scrap of doubt concerning the certainty of his election victory. Raghunath said, 'In that case someone must be sent to Nekiram and Abu Malek with our proposal.'

Badrinathbishal Chaube said, 'Indeed, someone must be sent.'

'Who will I send?'

In the temporary campaign camp that had been set up along one side of the vast compound, the contractor Ayodhyaprasad had been sitting up straight listening to Raghunath Singh's words. He now called out, 'Sir, please direct me to go.'

After about an hour of deep consultation, it was decided that the contractor Ayodhyaprasad and Badrinathbishal would go under cover of night to Nekiram; Girdharlal and Shyamdulal would go to Abu Malek.

24

After the midday meal Dharma and the others went back to labouring in the fields with their bullocks and ploughs. Up until the planting of the paddy they all did the same work, ceaselessly driving their ploughs through the rock hard earth to make it fit for cultivation.

Today Dharma was ploughing land to the south, while the tribal seasonal labourers were driving their ploughs in the field directly opposite him. Under the boundless sky, as far as one could see throughout the estate of Raghunath Singh, there came from everywhere in a variety of voices the incessant cries of 'Urra urra – move boy, move – ' made by the bonded labourers, the Oraons and the Mundas as they drove their bullocks. And just as on other days, the tractor with its sound of 'putt-putt-putt-putt' ploughed the fields on the other side of the dried up Koel.

Some days back, wisps of cloud had been seen in the west, but now there was no sign of them. The blazing rays of the summer sun were beating straight down, and the scorching wind gusted over the fields. Without any rain, the picture throughout the fields on either side of the highway had been the same since the month of Chaitra, and there was still no change in it.

As usual Kushi was running behind Dharma busily picking out the roots from the soil. Suddenly she stopped in her tracks. A little excited, she called in a suppressed voice, 'Dharma – hey, Dharma – '

Holding a firm hand on the head of the plough, Dharma stopped the pair of Patna bulls and turned around. 'What?' he asked.

'Look, look – there.' Kushi pointed to the field beside them.

Flicking the sweat from his brow with the back of his hand, Dharma looked to the right. Two men, wearing long trousers and expensive shirts and shoes, were talking with a middle-aged peasant. Dharma recognised him, having first seen him at the Chaharh market. Since then he could not tell how many times he had seen him from day to day. Most of the seasonal tribal peasants who had come to work on Raghunath Singh's land were Mundas, and this middle-aged man was their leader.

The faces of the well-dressed men also were familiar. Dharma looked at them for a few moments and recalled that he had seen them both when he went with Ramlachhman to the Chaharh market to fetch the seasonal labourers. They had seemed to talk a lot in whispers with the tribal workers. Then, when Dharma was taking the Mundas and Oraons along the highway back to Garudiya, the two men had run after them and asked about such things as whose land they were going to work on and where they were going to stay. It seemed likely then that one day they would come here in search of these seasonal workers.

Not all that the two men were saying to the Munda leader could be heard, but from the bits and pieces that did reach the ears it could be understood that they wanted to take the tribals to such places as Agartala and Assam, where they would get work the whole year round, be fed well, and make a lot of money.

None of this was new to Dharma. At the Chaharh market the two recruiters had already sought to entice the Oraons and Mundas with this kind of talk.

The middle-aged leader said, 'We need to think.'

'Yes, yes,' the two recruiters said at once. 'Of course, give it some thought. But you have to make up your minds quickly. Do you understand?'

The leader nodded his head.

One of the recruiters said, 'You'll do well to go to Assam or Agartala. There'll be no hunger or hardship, you won't want for anything – ' and they went on to paint a dream picture in bright colours before the eyes of the near-naked, middle-aged tribal man.

The Munda leader was about to say something when suddenly from the northern field an all too familiar, rough voice came drifting on the sharp, hot wind. 'Ram and Sita went to the forest hermitage –'

It was, of course, the hypocrite Ramlachhman going about superintending the work in the fields. Dharma turned around abruptly and caught a glimpse of him; quickly he twisted the tails of his bullocks and cried, 'Urra! Hat, hat, hat!' and the blade of the plough again began to cut into the soil.

Meanwhile, in the neighbouring field, the two recruiters waited not a moment longer. At the Chaharh market they had guessed that Ramlachhman was the landowner's man. If it got out that they had come onto the owner's land to lure away his peasants, they would be done for. The owner's men would flay them and bury their corpses.

As he drove his plough, Dharma wondered where and how far away Assam and Agartala were. To the north was Manpatthal taluk, to the west was the Bijuri railway station, to the east was Hanthiaganj, and to the south was Naosheraganj – these were the boundaries of the world as he knew it. Outside of this, where and how far away were Assam and Agartala he did not know. With all his powers of imagination the illiterate Dharma could not conceive of that distance.

***

Just before evening, as the sun was sinking towards the horizon, the bonded labourers and the tribal peasants came up onto the highway with their ploughs and bullocks. Then, in single file, they moved off towards Raghunath Singh's farm compound, raising the red dust on their way.

As they went, they suddenly caught sight of the two recruiters from the middle of the day wandering around the low-lying wasteland beside the highway where some tribals had set up camp a few days back. These Oraons, Mundas and Santals had come from the scorched earth of the east in search of food.

What were the two recruiters up to? Did they want to lure these tribals too, like the seasonal peasants, to Assam or Agartala?

Dharma suddenly wondered what it would be like to go to Assam with these long-trousered men. They had given assurances to the tribals that they would be well fed, well paid, and get work for the whole year. If they would take the Oraons and Mundas, would they also take him and Kushi and their parents? Surely they would. He would escape from driving the plough as a bondsman on Raghunath Singh's land. The great master would certainly not be able to send his thugs as far as Assam or Agartala to catch them and bring them back. Dharma would discuss this with Uncle Ganeri and see. And so, thinking of a wonderful life of freedom, Dharma and the others passed the tribals' quarter.

A few moments later, just as they were going down from the highway towards the farm compound, there came the shouts of a great number of people from the other side of the Koel. Dharma and the others stopped in their tracks and, turning around, they caught sight of two hundred, maybe two hundred and fifty people raising the red dust as they came running towards them.

As they came closer it was evident that they were the group of weak and feeble elderly people from the dosad colony who had been rejected for work on Raghunath Singh's land. With them were a few of the Mundas and Oraons who had come from the north. All of them, as soon as they got up each morning, would go in search of food in the jungle beside the river bed.

They were shouting continuously. The leader of the dosads,

Ganeri, moved towards them and cried out, 'What's the matter? Why all this commotion?'

They all answered, shouting together at the tops of their voices, so that nothing could be understood.

Giving them a gentle rebuke, Ganeri hushed them all. 'Now be quiet!' he said. 'Completely quiet. Only one person is to speak – '

Beating his breast, the old Bajrangi said, 'It'll be the death of us, Ganeri, the absolute death – '

At once all the others burst into wailing, saying, 'The death of us! We're all going to die!'

Ganeri raised his hand to stop them again. He said, 'Not all at once! Just one at a time!'

In a voice mixed with fear, excitement and anxiety Bajrangi, almost choking, explained that today, as usual, they had gone to the jungle on the other side of the river bed to fetch mahua, but when they got there they were astonished. When they had left yesterday evening, there was fruit on countless mahua trees, but today they saw that some people had already stripped about half of the trees.

Despite the assurances of the great master Raghunath Singh, Bajrangi and the others had had their doubts for some days, for each morning they saw that there was less fruit than there had been the evening before. For a few days they had thought that their eyes had mistaken them, but today they were convinced that before they went to the jungle at daybreak, or at night after they had left, someone or other had secretly picked the mahua fruit and taken it away. If this were to continue, everyone would starve to death in this hot season.

Hearing all this, Ganeri became very grave. Slowly he said, 'This is extremely serious.' He thought for a moment, then said, 'All of you sit down here. We'll be back after putting away the ploughs and bullocks.'

Bajrangi and the others sat down on the stony field beside the unpaved road.

A little later Ganeri and the bonded dosads came back from the farm compound. When they saw Ganeri returning, many among the crowd started asking questions one after the other.

'What do we do now, Ganeri?'

'What will become of us?'

'Should we go to the great master?'

Waving his hands to stop them all, Ganeri said, 'We should not go to the great master now.'

'When should we go?' they all asked.

Ganeri was a cool-headed, experienced man. He told them that first they should see who was stealing the mahua fruit. They should catch the thieves and then take them straight to the great master's residence.

'So then we must sit in hiding?'

'Yes, you must.'

There was silence for a little while, and then Ganeri started to speak again. 'Do you know what I think?'

'What?' They all wanted to know.

'No one is coming at daybreak to steal the mahua fruit.'

'When do they come?'

'At night, after you have left the jungle.'

'Then we have to sit in watch all through the night?'

'Yes,' Ganeri replied. 'Now go home. Once it is dark, hurry to the jungle and, after keeping watch for a night, see if people are coming to steal.' He turned to the Oraons and Mundas, 'And you too must go with them.'

Everyone was satisfied with the arrangement. One group followed Ganeri back to the dosad colony, and the Oraons and Mundas went towards the highway.

25

IT WAS NOW VERY LATE. THE DOSADS AND A FEW OF THE ORAONS AND Mundas were sitting under cover of the numerous trees and bushes in the jungle beside the Koel. No one had brought a lantern or, indeed, any kind of light, for seeing it from the distance the thieves would be cautioned not to come any closer, and Ganeri wanted to catch them red-handed. It was his guess that this had been the work of goatherds. Because of Raghunath Singh's warning, they did not come here in the daytime to strip the mahua trees but came under the cover of night.

None of the bonded labourers or landless Oraons and Mundas could remember which lunar day it was. Only part of the waning moon could be seen in the glimmering blue sky, its dim beams falling between the gaps among the mahua leaves. Everywhere in the thickets millions of fireflies darted about, glowing and dimming out, seeming to stitch the darkness like needles of green light, while swarms of jungle insects and mosquitoes incessantly stung and shed their poison on the skin of the dosads and tribals.

Natthu's uncle, Ramkhilaon, haphazardly slapping at mosquitoes, said, 'Well, then, Ganeri, what do you intend?'

'What do I intend?' asked Ganeri.

'Have you brought us here to feed us to the mosquitoes?'

'Be patient just a little longer.'

'I am patient. How much more patient must I be? My eyelids are heavy with sleep.'

'Is the heaviness of your eyelids greater than the hunger in your belly?' Ganeri said as something of a rebuff. Not another sound came from Ramkhilaon after this.

However, the elderly Bajrangi asked, 'Do you think these devils of thieves will come to the jungle?'

'They'll certainly come,' Ganeri said emphatically. 'If they don't come tonight, then they'll come tomorrow. If not tomorrow, then the day after. Or the day after that.'

Many voices then asked together, 'Does that mean we have to come and keep watch in the dark of the jungle night after night?'

'Yes,' replied Ganeri. 'Just for your stomachs. If you don't want to die of hunger, you have to come.'

Before anyone could say another word, they suddenly caught a faint glimpse of a few flaming torches swinging in the darkness and coming towards them over the river bed. The brown sand was gleaming in the torchlight.

Ganeri suddenly became terribly anxious, and in an intense voice he warned them all firmly, 'Keep absolutely quiet.'

Everyone sat up straight. Their breath was bated in apprehension and their eyes were unblinking.

In a few moments the torches came into the jungle, and as they came closer, their light revealed thirty or forty rough and tough looking men carrying gnarled bamboo lathis and gunny sacks, evidently to hold all the mahua fruit they intended to pick.

The men were not unfamiliar. They were the goatherds of many of the region's wealthy men and big and small landowners. There were even herders of Raghunath Singh's goats and buffalo too. They did not wait even a moment, but as soon as they planted their flaming torches into the ground and started to climb the mahua trees, Ganeri leapt out from his cover followed by a couple of hundred untouchable bondsmen, Oraons and Mundas.

Ganeri cried out at the top of his voice, 'Oh, no, you don't!'

The herders were startled. They could not have anticipated all these people sitting in the jungle in the middle of the night.

Crying out as before, Ganeri said, 'We won't let you take the mahua fruit!'

His companions all joined in with him. 'No, we won't! No! Never!'

At first the herdsmen were nonplussed, but they quickly got over that as one of them said, menacingly, 'Clear off, you pack of swine!'

'No, we won't,' said Ganeri. 'The mahua fruit is ours.'

'Yes, it's ours!' everyone cried out.

'Oh, yes, it's your paternal inheritance! Now clear off, you sons of dogs!' The herders threatened aggressively.

Ganeri too became aggressive. 'You lot clear off! The great master has given this fruit to us.'

'He gave it to you sons of whores? Get away, dogs, clear off!' So saying, one of the herders hit Ganeri over the head with an iron-studded lathi, and he cried out as he reeled and fell. Straightaway his forehead started bleeding.

Having worked without wages for generations, the bonded labourers suffered under an innate timidity. Stepping back a few paces, they whispered fearfully, 'They've killed Uncle Ganeri.'

The Oraons and Mundas, however, did not retreat but held firm where they were. Some of them ran and lifted up Ganeri, moving him to one side; one of them tore a strip from his own tattered loincloth and bandaged Ganeri's bleeding forehead. As for the herdsmen, now that the necessary work of felling Ganeri had been done, they again started climbing the mahua trees without any further ado.

Ganeri was not quite unconscious. He said to them in a weak and lifeless voice, 'No – no – the mahua fruit is ours – '

In support of his words, the free but landless tribals roared, 'Stop that!'

Showering abuse on their parents and fourteen generations of their ancestors, the herdsmen then ran at the Oraons and Mundas. However, the tribals had no fear in their blood. Most of them were carrying on their shoulders axes or bows and arrows, which they brandished as they held their ground.

The landowners' men ceaselessly rained lathi blows on the tribals, while the sharp blades of the tribals' axes flashed in the light of the torches and flights of arrows were shot from their bamboo bows. Ten or twelve men on both sides fell heavily to the ground. Some of them had their heads or foreheads split, some had gaping wounds in their chests left by arrowheads. The ground was awash with blood and all that could be heard was the swish of lathis and arrows and the sounds of moaning. The tranquil mahua jungle by the southern Koel, in the middle of a summer's night, was now like some ancient battlefield.

Like frightened animals the bonded labourers had gone well back into the jungle and were crying out constantly in terror. After centuries of driving the plough on the land of others, they seemed to be suffused with the spirit of feeble and faint-hearted slaves. They had never learned how to use a weapon to save themselves, and they had no skills in any kind of conflict.

No one was aware of how long this great war in the mahua jungle had been going on when suddenly a robust horse was seen running over the broad sands of the Koel. Behind it came many men, some holding long lathis with gas lamps tied to the ends, others carrying flaming torches.

In the dim moonlight and the light of the gas lamps the rider of the horse could be made out – it was no other than Raghunath Singh; following him was his force of strong-arm men. He held the reins in one hand and a rifle in the other. From time to time he raised the rifle and fired into the air. Accompanying him was his electoral agent, the contractor Ayodhyaprasad. The men continually shouted out warnings, 'Clear off! If you don't, you'll be shot!'

How Raghunath Singh had found out about this fight to the

death in the mahua jungle, he alone knew. Maybe he had been told by some people on their way along the highway to Garudiya who had heard the noise and commotion. But as soon as the magnificent horse with its splendid mane was seen – as well as the rifle, the strong-arm men and the great master himself – the fighting stopped and the combatants stood stock-still.

Raghunath Singh leaped down from his horse with his rifle. He took a quick look around at those who were badly wounded or lying in blood on the ground; he was not exactly unaccustomed to death, injury and bloodshed. In a deep and frightening voice he asked, 'What is all this?'

Not a sound could come from anyone.

Raghunath Singh roared, 'Well then? Why are you silent? Tell me – what has happened?'

They were all stunned, from the dosad bondsmen to the Oraons and Mundas. The Raghunath Singh in front of them was not the vote-seeking, kindly, compassionate Raghunath Singh, the master who in great affection had distributed with his own hands to untouchables like them *laddus* made of the finest ghee. This was the Raghunath Singh known ever by the dosads as armed, ferocious and fearsome.

Ganeri was lying on one side. Dragging himself along on his chest he approached Raghunath Singh and said, 'With your permission, master, may I say something?'

'Yes, yes, speak,' said Raghunath Singh.

Ganeri began in a weak, trembling voice, 'Master, this is a matter of our survival – '

'Don't prattle. Get to the point,' Raghunath interrupted impatiently.

So Ganeri told him how he, the great master, had himself ordered that this year, when the terrible heat had scorched village after village and there was nowhere a grain to be eaten, provision should be made, by the manifold grace of the great master, mother and father of the poor, for the destitute like them to take all the mahua fruit from the jungle. And he had also ordered that the herdsmen should keep away from the jungle, but they did not heed their lord's order and had come in the middle of the night and taken away the mahua fruit. And then the dosads and the tribals had come here to keep watch and then the herders had come and fought with them, especially with the Oraons and Mundas. Ganeri gave a detailed account of it all.

Raghunath Singh remained silent for quite a while. He noticed the herders out of the corner of his eye, among whom were some of his own men. In fact, Raghunath had had a clever plot. Keeping an eye on the election, he had shown great compassion in letting the rejected bonded people and the Oraons and Mundas take the mahua fruit, while in front of everyone he had also warned the herders that this year they must not go to the mahua jungle – but in secret he had made it known that they might go and pick the mahua fruit at night when the dosads were asleep. By such a stratagem the snake would die without the rod being broken. The vote bank of bonded labourers would be happy, and mahua fruit would be available for his own herders and those of other landowners. It was a scheme to please all, but now it was clear that it had fallen through. The untouchable sons of hell had probably not suspected him, even though it was obvious that the mahua fruit had diminished.

Ganeri spoke again. 'Master, tell us now whether animals should live or people should live!'

Most magnanimously Raghunath Singh proclaimed, 'People!' He was right. There was not long to the election. He knew well what to do once the election was safely out of the way, as he was also familiar with the truism concerning the prudence of making some small sacrifice in the present for a greater, future good. He turned to the herdsmen and said, 'Never come here again, you sons of dogs. If I hear that you do, I'll bury you in the sands of the Koel.'

As it had been at Raghunath Singh's secret indication that the herders might come to the jungle at night, this uncalled for abuse was most inappropriate, but no one had the nerve to say so. They just nodded their heads like puppets and said, 'Yes, sir.'

Raghunath Singh then ordered his personal army, his private thugs, 'Take the wounded to the hospital at Bhakilganj.'

'Yes, sir.' The strong-arm men took up onto their shoulders the bleeding and injured of both sides. Even the middle-aged Ganeri had the rare experience of being taken up onto the shoulders of some immense fellow.

Looking at the dosads and tribals all around him, Raghunath said, 'Of course, the parents or wives of the wounded may come tomorrow to the munshi Ajibchand and get ten rupees each.'

Raghunath Singh was indeed clever. What was the harm in giving a mere ten rupees a head as expenses if it made them happy? And it would do ample good for his election chances.

The hungry and ragged people were thoroughly gratified. Overcome, they said, 'Oh, my lord, you are our father and our mother – '

Waiting no longer, Raghunath Singh put his foot in the stirrup and mounted his horse. He nudged its flanks with his heels and the superb beast set off at a gallop. The contractor Ayodhyaprasad followed him. In a few moments horses and riders crossed the sands of the Koel and went on out of sight towards the highway. The strong-arm men then set off on the seven miles to the hospital at Bhakilganj, the wounded men on their shoulders, while the remaining Oraons, Mundas and dosads went back to their shanties.

No one knew how late it had become, but the dim fragment of a moon was sinking in the western sky.

26

FOR SOME DAYS THE BONDED LABOURERS WERE AT THE SAME TIME agitated over the fight with the herdsmen and overwhelmed by the immense compassion of Raghunath Singh.

During this time Ganeri came home from the Bhakilganj hospital. His body had become very frail from the profuse bleeding, and Raghunath Singh had been so kind and considerate as to send word to Himgiri to excuse Ganeri from work. As long as he was not completely well, he was not to go to the fields. But apart from all this, life in the dosad colony went on as usual, while election fever was steadily growing.

In the meantime Nekiram Sharma and Abu Malek held election rallies, one after the other, in the gaslight by the Garudiya market, and large numbers of people came to hear what they had to say.

As usual, when the day's work in the fields had finished and the bullocks and ploughs had been returned, Dharma and Kushi set off for the *sabui* grass beside the bed of the southern Koel. From there they took the trapped birds to the contractors. After they had sold the birds and the schoolmaster had counted their money, they came across an election rally as they walked through the Garudiya market. They stood there among the crowd.

This first rally was Nekiram Sharma's. The gaunt and wizened Nekiram's back was bent like a bow, his eyes were as sharp as a jackal's, and he had bushy ears and nostrils. He had the mark of the trident painted on his forehead. He had seated his very attractive sister-in-law on the stage as an added attraction, for wherever a charming young woman might go, a crowd will gather, buzzing around like flies.

He stood before the microphone and, in a voice as sharp as a hawk's, shouted out his speech. 'The dark age! The dreaded Kalyug! No one honours the Vedas and the brahmans these days. Therefore the country is in its present state. Have you ever known such severe droughts? Or such floods? What has brought all this about? Dire abomination! The practices of depravity! Who are the brahmans? Why are they supreme in terms of caste? It is because that pleases God. Brahma and Vishnu themselves sent the brahmans to the world as the supreme caste. But in this Kalyug they are not revered. Study the *Ramayana* and the *Mahabharata*. Everyone – from Lord Ram to Yudhisthir, Bhim, Arjun – all paid reverence to brahmans. The rule of brahmans is the finest rule. If the government were in their hands, there would be genuine well-being for all. There would be peace, and there would be an end to drought and pestilence. That would be the will of God. Therefore I say, in this election give your vote to me. Put your mark beside the sign of the buffalo.'

No sooner had the speech of Nekiram, the renowned usurer of the district, ended, than Phaguram, the Garudiya Nightingale, emerged from the crowd. He was wearing the clothes he had been wearing to election meetings recently – a coloured turban, a yellow dhoti, a red shirt and raw leather slippers.

Like a flash of lightning his fingers ran over the keys of the harmonium, he skipped about in a comic dance, and his magical voice took up a song:

Though Sharmaji wears big slippers,
and marks of piety his brow adorn,
he dispenses iniquity to all mankind.
Brothers, beat the drums!
Sharma fights the election,

but his cohorts have abandoned him.
Only his sister-in-law,
slithering like a snake
and flitting like a butterfly,
keeps his campaign running.
Brothers, beware of them both.
Brothers, beware.

Phaguram stopped singing, raised a hand to the heavens and cried out:

Break the legs of the buffalo
and blow Nekiram away!

No sooner had Phaguram finished his song than the meeting burst into a flood of laughter, while Nekiram's angry campaign workers delivered abuse. Some of them rushed towards Phaguram, and the election rally dissolved into a hubbub of shouting and laughter. Altogether it was a riot.

Dharma waited no longer but took Kushi by the hand and ran past the liquor shop and down into the distant fields.

***

The next day it was Abu Malek's election rally. Once the schoolmaster had, as usual, counted their money, Dharma and Kushi again went and stood among the crowd.

The middle-aged Abu Malek was large, both tall and broad. His skin was bright, and he had a slightly greying triangular beard. He was wearing freshly laundered tight white pajamas and a finely embroidered kurta. On his head was an embroidered silk fez.

Clutching the microphone in his vast palm, Abu Malek started his speech in a grave and solemn voice. 'In this country, no one gives a thought for the minority community. However, this will not do. The minority must be considered. They must not be neglected. Places must be reserved for them in government offices, colleges and universities. They must have guarantees of employment.

'Who now are the minority? Only Muslims? No, no. There are also all the Hindu untouchables, the Christians – all treated like animals by the high-caste Hindus. In their interests it is necessary that you vote for me. Remember, my symbol is the deer. Put your mark beside the symbol of the deer in the interests of the minority.'

As soon as the speech was finished, Phaguram emerged from the crowd with his harmonium, just as he had done on the previous day, and burst into a song, the words of which were as sharp as a knife. Dancing about as he sang, Phaguram sang of Abu Malek as being a thief, a cheat, a swindler.

After the song he cried out:

There is uproar in the back streets
as the cry goes out -
'Abu Malek is a thief!'
Give your vote to Raghunathji
and blow Abu Malek away!

And so the days passed.

27

AFTER THEIR MIDDAY MEAL, DHARMA AND THE OTHERS WERE TAKING a rest in the meagre shade of a tree when Tirke suddenly appeared from the highway. He sat down beside Dharma and, wiping the sweat from his brow, said, 'Well then, what about the cheetah cubs?'

Dharma looked a little embarrassed as he said, 'I've not been able to go to the jungle, dada. Within a couple of days I'll definitely go.'

'Don't leave it too long.'

'No, no.'

'The American's coming back to Ranchi in about three weeks. If he doesn't get the cubs, he'll kick up a real fuss. Understand?'

'Don't worry, dada,' Dharma said. 'He'll definitely get his cubs.'

Tirke had come all this way from Ranchi to remind Dharma, and after a few more minutes of making his position clear about the cheetah cubs, he went back to the highway. Dharma then rested a little longer.

As the sun was starting to move towards the west, the bonded labourers and the tribal seasonal workers were just about to go back to the field when some shouting came from the main road.

'Vote for – '

'Pratibha Sahay! Pratibha Sahay!'

'Make your mark on – '

'The sign of the horse! The sign of the horse!'

As the election day drew closer, the come-and-go of campaign vehicles along the highway increased. Sometimes there would be jeeps carrying the campaign workers of Raghunath Singh or Pratibha Sahay, sometimes there would be horse-drawn carriages for the supporters of Nekiram Sharma or Abu Malek. The followers of Sukhan Ravidas, however, went on foot, as they could not afford any kind of vehicle.

Watching the campaign vehicles of Pratibha Sahay with placid indifference, Dharma and the others were suddenly surprised to see them pull up on the side of the road. Abodhnarayan Pande, Pratibha Sahay's campaign manager, had got out of one of the jeeps, crossed over the gutter and was coming towards them.

Ganeri was sitting under a tree a little way away from Dharma and the others. He still had three thick layers of bandages on his head. By order of the great master, and by his magnanimity, he was not yet allowed to drive the plough, but he still came to the fields every morning with the others and sat under a tree the whole day. When the sun went down he went back with the others to the dosad colony.

Ganeri slowly got up and, with one hand shielding his eyes from the sun, he looked towards the highway. 'Abodh-ji is coming, isn't he?' he said.

'Yes,' answered everyone around him.

In a few moments Abodhnarayan approached them. He singled out Ganeri as the leader of the dosads and asked, 'Well then, do you remember what I told you the other day?'

Ganeri remembered. Abodhnarayan had turned up at the dosad colony that night with a very tempting proposal, although Ganeri had not been so very enthusiastic about it. 'I remember,' he said, indifferently.

'Pratibha-ji's election mitin will be tomorrow beside the Garudiya market. All of you go straight home after work. I will pick you up and take you. Every voter will definitely get three rupees each, and I will also give three rupees to everyone not having voting rights. I have come to confirm this.' Abodhnarayan paused for a moment, then he said, 'You will have cash in hand before getting into the vehicle tomorrow.'

Ganeri recalled what Raghunath Singh had said about being driven to Pratibha Sahay's election rally and taking three rupees for it, but he still felt somewhat uncomfortable about the whole business. Looking disinterested, he said blandly, 'All right, sahib.'

'I just came to remind you all. We'll meet again tomorrow.'

The next day Dharma and Kushi were unable to go to the *sabui* grove, though they would each get three rupees in cash, and for destitute people such as they that was no trifle. Just as the sun was setting, they returned the plough and bullocks to the farm compound and went back with all the others to the dosad colony where they sat in their shanties and looked eagerly towards the highway, waiting anxiously for Abodhnarayan to come.

Some time after evening had fallen some twenty-five or thirty gleaming luxury buses, raising the dust from the road, pulled up one behind the other. Abodhnarayan got out of one of the buses and went straight into the dosad colony. He hurried everyone along, shouting, 'Come on, all of you! Come on now! I have brought your transport. Hurry up and get aboard.'

The dosads came out of their houses and ran towards the luxury coaches. However, actually boarding such a vehicle was unimaginable to them, something they had never experienced in their lives. When they got close to the buses, they all stopped. They were very shabby looking: their skin was flaky and dirty and their clothes may not have been washed for a couple of months. They could not gather up the nerve to board such luxury buses with their dirty bodies and unwashed clothes.

From behind, Abodhnarayan urged them on gently. 'What's the matter now? In you get. Get in now.'

There were two men standing at the door of each coach. One of them held a steel tray with a pile of rupee coins on it. After continual urging, the dosads at last started to board the buses, and the second man at the entrance took three rupees from the tray and handed it to each one, including the children

There was probably not a soul left at home. The whole dosad colony was emptied of everyone from the toddlers to the aged. As Dharma sat down circumspectly on his comfortable, padded seat, he could not help thinking that none of his forebears could ever have known such good fortune. Why could there not be an election three or four times a year?

Meanwhile, Abodhnarayan was taking care of things outside. When he was just about to board the front bus and give the driver the order to start, there suddenly came a shout from inside the colony, 'Wait! Wait!'

Abodhnarayan looked out of the window and saw Dhanpat coming with his decrepit, one-hundred-year old father, Gairunath, on his shoulders. Behind them came Gairunath's daughter-in-law and his grandchildren. Thanks to the election, the dropsy old man, whose death everyone in the family longed for, was being carried on his son's shoulders one last time before mounting his funeral pyre. Getting three rupees in cash was no trivial matter!

No matter how old he was, how lame, or how much of his skin was flaking away, Gairunath was not a person as far as the election was concerned – he was a genuine vote, and as long as there were still twelve days to polling, he was not to be neglected. Abodhnarayan quickly got down from the bus and said very respectfully, 'Come, come,' and saw to the distribution of three rupees to each of Gairunath's family members; he also made sure that they were seated comfortably on one of the buses.

And then the luxury coaches set off, raising the dust from the road.

When they arrived at the big field at Garudiya market, Dharma's eyes almost stood out. The place was unrecognisable. Wherever one looked and as far as one could see there were just lights and more lights. Pratibha Sahay's campaign workers had brought about twelve or fourteen big, strong generators and the whole place was flooded with light. A 'putt-putt-putt' sound came continually from them.

At the far end of the field was a huge, decorated stage, in front of which were masses of people. Throughout the crowd stood bamboo posts to which big loudspeakers were attached. On the side of the road to the right were rows of trucks, luxury coaches and new and gleaming private cars. Evidently these vehicles had brought everyone from thirty or forty villages of the taluks of Bijuri and Garudiya.

Already the election rallies of Nekiram Sharma, Abu Malek and even Raghunath Singh had been held at this field of the Garudiya market. Raghunath had brought in a huge crowd from the surrounding villages on countless bullock and buffalo carts, but that rally could in no way compare with Pratibha Sahay's.

With his limited experience and even more meagre intelligence Dharma could guess that Pratibha Sahay's campaign workers could not have acquired such a vast crowd without the lure of three rupees in cash and a ride in a luxury coach. And the money went not only to the parents but to the children as well. 'Fathers and brothers are good, but money is even better'; this is a truth that cannot be denied.

Rows of tables and chairs were set out on the stage, and in the middle, among the most notable people of Bijuri and Garudiya, sat Pratibha Sahay. Raghunath Singh had had the lawyer, the doctor and the headmaster around him. Here there were also other doctors, lawyers, schoolmasters and learned men from the two taluks, all assembled around Pratibha Sahay. Of course, the hungry and ragged bonded labourers were hardly to understand that people will crowd around the smell of money and political power as flies will swarm around treacle.

Pratibha Sahay's campaign manager, Abodhnarayan, had brought the dosads to the rally and, before anyone knew it, had quickly heaved his vast body up onto the stage where he stood in front of the microphone and took charge of the meeting. The man had great organisational skills. A renowned lawyer of Bijuri was very smoothly appointed chairman of the meeting; a little girl garlanded him and all the other distinguished persons on the stage with fresh roses. These formalities were completed amid great applause, and then, at a gesture from Abodhnarayan, Pratibha Sahay's campaign workers threw their arms in the air and started to shout:

'Long live – '

'Pratibha Sahay! Pratibha Sahay!'

'Give your vote to – '

'Pratibha Sahay! Pratibha Sahay!'

'Make your mark on – '

'The sign of the horse! The sign of the horse!'

The slogan shouting aroused the rally, and then, one after the other, Pratibha Sahay's patrons and supporters delivered speeches at the tops of their voices, almost shattering the microphone. What they all had to say was much the same: brothers and sisters, give your votes to Pratibha-ji, for if she wins, the kingdom of God will come to rule here. There will no longer be any sorrow, hardship, want or poverty and the canals will flow with milk and honey. Everyone will have a brick house, no one will be hungry or have nothing to wear – and so on and so on.

One of them said, 'Brothers and sisters, has it occurred to you that of those contesting the election in this region, one has as a symbol the camel, one has the elephant, one has the deer, and one has the buffalo. The elephant is a very expensive animal. Put simply, an elephant is worth hundreds of thousands of rupees even if dead. But what good is such a huge beast? None at all. It is hard to see any value in a creature which just sits and eats. You must reject the elephant. Nor is the camel of any use to us here. The deer is an exceptionally fine animal, but it doesn't do any work, either. The buffalo works, of course, but it is a very slow beast, and this age is a progressive age, so whatever is slow also must be rejected. You know that thousands of years ago there were animals bigger even than elephants. They were the dinosaurs. But they all died out. We want speed, purpose, movement. What is to be done must be done quickly. That is why Pratibha-ji's symbol is the horse. Just make her win, and you will see her pave the roads of Garudiya and Bijuri with gold and silver.'

The scantly clad, hungry and illiterate people of the thirty or so villages of Garudiya and Bijuri taluks just sat and gaped. Perhaps ten percent of the impassioned language of the speeches went into their heads, the rest went over them. But the one thing they did understand was, as all the speakers had said, they had to make their marks on Pratibha Sahay's election symbol, which was the horse.

After all the speeches had finished, Pratibha Sahay got up to speak. 'No one in my family has ever gone into politics, never stood for election, so why should I suddenly get involved? In answer to that, I would say that Bijuri is my father-in-law's home. You know that for a woman, her father-in-law's house is her house.

'We live in a big city. We hardly ever come to our village home, except maybe once in three or four years. But I have seen how the condition of the villages has deteriorated. The poor have become poorer, the ragged have become even more ragged. Coming back and seeing all this brought tears to my eyes, and I thought that I would have to do something. If the villages don't survive, the nation will not survive. The village people have to be looked after. And, as my father-in-law's home is in Bijuri, my duty lies here.

'Brothers and sisters, you know that I have no needs of my own. The money from my husband's and father-in-law's factories and coal-mines is enough to keep my next twenty generations in comfort. However, I am a human being. Like you I have red blood in my veins. Here I see thousands of people trapped by debt. There is gross injustice in wages practices, in bonded labour, in the caste system. I will not let this go on. Poverty, bonded labour with only food for work, and untouchability are consigning India to hell. They cannot be allowed to continue. But if I don't have political power in my hands, how can I put a stop to these outrageous practices? Therefore I am now standing for election. Now everything is in your hands and dependent on your grace. If by your votes you bring me victory, I will devote my life to your service. Remember my election symbol – the horse.'

When Pratibha Sahay had finished speaking, her campaign workers were just about to rouse the meeting with slogans as before, when something happened. No one had been aware that Phaguram the Trouper, with his harmonium, had been sitting in anticipation somewhere in the crowd. Suddenly he sprang to his feet, his fingers ran with the speed of a storm over the keys of his harmonium, and he danced and skipped and leaped about as he broke into his song of fun.

The jewel of the kayasthas
is Pratibha Sahay,
soliciting votes in the huts
of destitutes like us.
She has cunning and wile
and a coquettish style;
she begs for our votes
and she weeps, we may note,
for us, like a crocodile.

A commotion broke out, just as it had at the election rallies of Nekiram Sharma and Abu Malek. Hearing his funny song, the people in the crowd all fell about laughing. And seeing the reactions of his audience, the enthusiasm of Phaguram the Garudiya Nightingale increased tenfold, as did the energy in his dancing and skipping and leaping about. Raising his voice, he went on with renewed earnest,

The jewel of the kayasthas
is Pratibha Sahay,
soliciting votes –

Phaguram could not finish singing, for suddenly a few rough and ready looking fellows with iron-studded lathis appeared out of nowhere.

'You devil! You son of a dog!' Delivering unspeakable abuse the men set upon Phaguram raining lathi blows indiscriminately on his head, back, neck and shoulders. In one blow his new harmonium was smashed. Phaguram tried to shield his face and his head with his hands, all the while crying out, 'Save me! Save me!' Three or four of his teeth were knocked out, and blood oozed from all over his head and face. The blood-smeared Phaguram wallowed on the ground, crying fit to burst his lungs.

'The bastard of a Garudiya Nightingale's got what he deserves! Now let's break his neck – ' And they kept on sending down blows with their lathis.

The people at the rally, especially the dosad bonded labourers, were utterly terrified. No one had any idea of what to do. Then suddenly Ganeri started to run like a man possessed. Just as a mother bird tries to protect her fledglings with her wings, so Ganeri spread out his arms to protect Phaguram from the blows, all the while crying out, 'Don't hit him! Don't hit him!'

In the meantime chaos and commotion had spread throughout the whole field as frightened people ran here and there. Some people seemed to be continually talking over the microphone on the stage. There was utter confusion everywhere.

Then for some reason the thugs stopped wielding their lathis. Maybe they thought that they had done enough for the time being.

Phaguram had got more or less what he had deserved for his outrageous song, and so they left him lying there and in a flash disappeared among the crowd.

At first Phaguram's cries might have burst his lungs, but gradually his voice lost all its strength. A whimpering sound came intermittently from his throat, until he completely lost consciousness.

A little way away the dosads were just standing like stone statues. Ganeri turned to them and called out reproachfully, 'You fools, come here quickly! We have to get Phagu to hospital straightaway.'

Dharma ran to him first, followed by Madholal, Shiumal, Natuwa, Dhano, and a number of the others. Dharma lifted Phaguram's unconscious, bloodied body straight up onto his shoulders. Ganeri told Dharma, Natuwa, Shiumal, Dhano and four of the younger men to stay, and then he sent the rest back to the dosad colony. There was no need for so many to go to the hospital; they would be more of a hindrance than a help.

A little later Ganeri and his men were walking past the liquor shop at the northern end of the Garudiya market, leaving the scene of the rally behind them and setting off over the vast and empty fields, which they crossed diagonally to the highway.

Bhakilganj was the nearest town, and even that was about six miles away. Such a distance would have been impossible for many people to trudge with an unconscious man on their shoulders, and so Ganeri had taken the four younger men, who would all take it in turns to carry Phaguram.

They crossed the dark fields in silence. No one could see anyone's face. Suddenly Dharma called, 'Uncle Ganeri!'

'What?'

'That was a terrible business.'

Ganeri's voice came from the darkness like some ethereal voice of sorrow. 'I knew it would happen. I knew it.'

Dharma remembered how Ganeri had so often warned all of the dosads of the severe consequences that might occur.

After they had come up onto the highway, Ganeri said abruptly, 'Not right, we'll go left.'

Dharma and the others were surprised. If they did not take the highway to the right, they would not get to Bhakilganj. Ganeri allayed their confusion. 'Before going to the hospital,' he said, 'we should go to the great master's house. We should tell him about Phagu. He should see what a state he is in.'

No one asked any questions. They took the highway to the left.

28

IT WAS NOW ALMOST MIDNIGHT AND A CAMPAIGN CONFERENCE WAS still going on the vast marble veranda of Raghunath Singh's mansion.

It was not a public session. On those days when they had no election rally anywhere, Raghunath sat in secret discussion at night with a few of his faithful and reliable friends, advisors and sycophants. The current Hindi cinema word for 'sycophant' was *chamcha*, and it was much used in these parts. Nevertheless, the English term, 'inner circle', could be used to describe these meetings where strategies and tactics in the election battle were decided.

So tonight, too, the inner circle was in session. Raghunath Singh sat surrounded by his faithful lapdogs – the headmaster, the doctor and the lawyer. Along with them were two new faces – Nekiram Sharma and Abu Malek. Raghunath Singh had sent his trusty agents under cover of night in order to win them over. They did not go empty-handed, and it had cost Raghunath dearly. The settlement had still not been made public, but it had been decided that Nekiram and Abu Malek would withdraw from the coming election and work for Raghunath Singh's campaign. They would assert that the interests of the high-caste Hindus and those of the minority community would best be safeguarded by one man – Raghunath Singh. It was hoped that this would reap rewards. Raghunath would get Nekiram and Abu Malek's share of the votes, and in a couple of days the public of Garudiya-Bijuri would see Abu Malek and

Nekiram Sharma sitting beside him on a magnificent platform at an election rally.

'The election battle,' Raghunath Singh proclaimed, 'has come down to a three-way contest – Pratibha Sahay, Sukhan the Tanner, and myself.'

Everyone nodded. The doctor, Shyamdulal, said in English, 'A triangular fight.'

'What do you think – can I come through this battle?'

'Certainly,' they all answered as one.

Nekiram Sharma said, 'Along with the votes you would have got, you can add Malek Sahib's and mine. Definitely you will win.'

But Raghunath Singh's underlying doubts would not go away. He said, 'Pratibha Sahay is throwing money around with ten hands. I think that woman will attract a substantial share of the vote. As for Sukhan Ravidas – ' They all looked at Raghunath with great eagerness and anticipation. He went on, 'That tanner's son also will get votes. Apart from my own dosad peasants, all the untouchables of Garudiya-Bijuri will vote for him.'

They all said, 'No, not at all, never.'

Emphatically Raghunath said, 'They will indeed.'

They were all somewhat put back. After a brief silence one of them asked, 'How do you know?'

Raghunath gave them a detailed description of his experiences in going about the villages and markets of Garudiya and Bijuri in quest of votes. He said, 'Whenever I spoke with untouchables about their votes, the dogs just kept quiet, as though they were completely dumb. But I could read in their faces who they would vote for.'

They all had great admiration for Raghunath Singh's powers of observation, yet could see no solution to the problem. The question was playing on everyone's mind: how to get a substantial part of the vote of the region's untouchables. The advisory council of the inner circle was suddenly so silent that a leaf might have been heard falling from a tree.

Then Raghunath spoke up. 'I have a plan. Let's see what you think.'

'What plan?' They all looked at Raghunath with immense curiosity.

In a low voice Raghunath Singh elucidated his new strategy. First of all, under cover of night, some six or seven untouchable villages would be set on fire. Then he, as the champion of the untouchables, would distribute generously tin, thatch, bamboo and cash for the building of new houses. Naturally, the untouchable communities would be grateful to him, and the result would be shown in the ballot box.

Everyone was overwhelmed by the ingeniousness of the scheme. No one could have thought of a better or more valuable move in the tactical battle of this election.

'Do you approve, then?' Raghunath Singh asked.

'Of course. But the job must be done very carefully.'

Arrangements were finalised for setting fire to the untouchables' villages. The contractor Ayodhyaprasad suddenly appeared while the detailed discussion was proceeding about which villages would be burnt and how it all would be done. Seeing Ayodhya, Raghunath suddenly remembered that he had sent him earlier that day to the Garudiya market to make a report on Pratibha Sahay's election rally. 'How did it go?' he asked.

Ayodhyaprasad was sitting on the floor. He said, 'It was a very big meeting, Raghunath-ji.'

'How many were there?'

'There would have been about a hundred thousand. Three times I've seen elections here, but I've never seen a rally as big as this one.'

Raghunath Singh's face became very grave, and Ayodhyaprasad's heart began to thump when he noticed it. Hastily he added, 'And why not? The woman tossed about hundreds of thousands of rupees. Yearning for money, the hungry destitutes came running. Throw a piece of meat on the ground and won't twenty hungry dogs run for it? Just because they went to the meeting, does that mean they will vote for the woman? Not at all.'

This seemed reasonable to Raghunath Singh. He remembered that he himself had told his own bonded labourers to go to Pratibha Sahay's rally so that the poor people might get a few rupees.

Raghunath thought for a moment, and then asked, 'What did they say?'

'All the same old things,' Ayodhyaprasad replied. 'I will do this and I will do that. I will bring heaven down from the sky and establish it in Garudiya-Bijuri.' And with remarkable skill he went on to present the essence of what Pratibha Sahay's speakers had said, but then he suddenly stopped.

'What's the matter? Why have you gone quiet?'

'There's something bad to report, Raghunath-ji.'

'What?' Raghunath Singh frowned.

'There was an uproar at the mitin over Phaguram.'

Raghunath Singh sat up straight and asked, 'What sort of uproar?'

Just as Ayodhyaprasad was about to answer, a voice was heard from outside the main gate. 'My lord – '

Raghunath Singh and his lapdogs turned to see Ganeri Dosad standing there, and behind him in the darkness a few more could vaguely be made out.

Raghunath Singh did not want his bonded labourers here at this moment. At any other time he would have had the servants send them away, but with polling day fast approaching, he should not do anything indiscreet now. Although he was irritated inside, he smiled automatically and said, 'What is it at this late hour?'

The dosads did not have the nerve to enter the great master's compound without his call. On the few occasions they had come here before, it had been at Raghunath Singh's summons. Apprehensively Ganeri said, 'If my lord should command, we will come in.'

'Come.'

When the dosads came in and Raghunath Singh saw the blood-smeared, unconscious body of Phaguram on Dharma's shoulders, he was quite taken aback. 'What happened to Phaguram?'

Ganeri gave a detailed account of how Phaguram had been set upon at Pratibha Sahay's election rally, and with a melancholy look said, 'They beat him, master. Pratibha-ji's thugs finished him off. We came to let you see him before taking him to the hospital.'

So far Dharma had been silent, but suddenly something snapped inside him to make him burst out, 'My lord, he went to sing election songs for you. Now Uncle Phagu is dying.'

That some bonded labourer, more insignificant than a worm, should speak like this was beyond Raghunath Singh's comprehension, and he was amazed at Dharma's audacity. His face took on a fearsome look, his jaw becoming set like a stone. As he was wondering whether to flay the dosad's face with a shoe or a whip, he remembered how close the election was. Controlling himself, he said through clenched teeth, 'We'll see about this sterile bitch of a factory owner. To come to Garudiya and assault my man is an insult to me. I am no son of a Rajput kshatriya if I do not avenge this.' There was still a remnant of the feudal tyrant inside him that seemed to come out with those words, but the dosads, of course, would not get much consolation from Raghunath Singh's vengeance.

Ganeri said, with a trembling voice, 'If it is your command, my lord, we will go to the hospital – '

'No,' said Raghunath. 'Phagua is in this state because of singing songs for me. I will send him to the hospital.' Shouting out orders, he had the campaign jeep brought out right then and gave instructions for taking Phaguram to the hospital. Thanks to Raghunath Singh's generosity, Ganeri and the others would go with him.

In a few moments the jeep was running along the highway towards the Bhakilganj hospital. The five dosads sat numb, holding Phaguram's wounded body. When they were walking from the election rally to Raghunath Singh's mansion, Phaguram was making a whimpering sound, but now he was making no sound at all.

When they reached the hospital, the doctor felt Phaguram's pulse and declared that he had been dead for about an hour. The experienced, middle-aged Ganeri covered his face with his hands and sobbed, saying in a shaky voice, 'I knew this would happen. I knew it.'

The untouchable trouper, Phaguram Dosad, was the first one in these parts to give his for democracy.

29

RAGHUNATH SINGH HAD DECLARED BEFORE HIS ADVISERS, HIS sycophants and Ganeri and the other dosads that he would indeed avenge Phaguram. He would not let Pratibha Sahay off. But three or four days had passed since the death of Phaguram and Raghunath had shown no signs of taking any action. Perhaps he thought that, with the election coming, being involved in such strife would jeopardise his polling chances. Anyhow, the life of some insignificant dosad was not so valuable in Garudiya and Bijuri that a man like Raghunath Singh should be wasting his time and energy over it.

The great master was now constantly beset with anxiety about the election. Throughout the day his jeep raised the dust from village to village throughout Garudiya and Bijuri. He had regular rallies in the markets, and recently, Nekiram Sharma and Abu Malek had been seen with him at all of them. Having withdrawn from the election, they set out to persuade the high-caste Hindus along with the minorities to vote for Raghunath Singh, explaining that should he win, their interests would be taken care of and their security would be guaranteed. Pratibha Sahay and Sukhan Ravidas did not rest, either, for they too went about all the villages holding election rallies.

Notwithstanding all of that, Phaguram's senseless death kept Ganeri and all the other dosads in sadness for a few days.

***

One morning, after collecting their ploughs and bullocks from the farm compound and setting off for the fields, Dharma and the others were surprised to see rows of bullock and buffalo carts beside the settlement of makeshift straw and bamboo huts set up only a few days earlier by the tribals. The two men who had been persuading them at the Chaharh market to go to Assam or Agartala were also there, shouting at the Oraons and Mundas to hurry up and get aboard the carts.

Suddenly it occurred to Dharma to stop and ask the young Munda near him, 'Where are you all going?'

'Assam,' the Munda replied.

Dharma was breathing quickly. The two recruiters had said that if they went to Assam or Agartala they would be fed well, they would be clothed, and they would get money. These tribals would be looked after, but bonded labourers like him would have to drive the plough on the great master's land for the rest of their lives.

Behind him Budheri said, 'Come on now, Dharma. Are you going to the fields or will you stay here on the road?'

Dharma did not answer. Glumly he started on his way again.

From the time they got to the fields until noon no one had the chance to look anywhere. When at noon the sun had risen directly overhead, Dharma and Kushi wiped their faces and sat down with everyone else to eat their meal. It was just then that they saw Tirke coming from the highway. Dharma had no difficulty guessing why he should be coming in this scorching summer noontime, with the dry wind blowing fire all about. As Tirke approached them, Dharma said, 'I'm going into the jungle in three or four days, Tirke-da. I've taken your advance payment, and I'll get the cheetah cubs. Don't you worry.'

'That's all right,' said Tirke. 'But I'll need the cubs very soon. The American's coming back next week. He'll stay for seven days. In that time you'll have to do everything you can to come up with them.'

'That's all right. But – '

'But what?'

Dharma remained silent for a few moments, then he said, 'Dada, you'll have to give me another two hundred rupees.'

Tirke flared up at first, but then he said, looking him straight in the eye, 'I finalised the price with you the other day. And now you want more?'

'You must give it to me, otherwise take back your advance,' Dharma said. Actually, he had learned from the schoolmaster, having counted his money, that a further two hundred rupees was required to settle the debt to the great master.

'You're talking really tough,' said Tirke.

Looking embarrassed, Dharma said, 'You give me the money now. Later I'll get you some other animal for nothing.'

Tirke's profit would be reduced, but there could be no turning back now as he had taken a considerable advance from the American. Suspiciously he said, 'You're not going to put the price up again, then?'

'No, no, I swear to God — '

'All right, then. I'll give you the two hundred. But you go to the jungle in the next couple of days.'

'Yes. Definitely.'

Tirke did not sit any longer, but left with a rather long face. To have to part with another two hundred rupees could hardly make him leap for joy.

***

When the sun was starting to sink in the western sky, the bonded labourers took their ploughs and bullocks back to the compound just as they did on every other day, and as they went along the highway, Dharma saw that the low-lying land was now completely deserted. Not one of the Mundas and Oraons was to be seen anywhere, nor any scrap of straw or bamboo from their huts. They had gone away leaving not a trace of their temporary settlement.

After returning the plough and bullocks, Dharma and Kushi, according to their daily custom, went to the *sabui* grove. From there they went to the contractors, and from there to the schoolmaster to have their money counted. It was very late when they passed the liquor shop and came down onto the empty summer fields, where suddenly they heard in the distance the shouts of many people. They stopped still and looked this way and that to see where all the noise was coming from.

Her voice suppressed in fear, Kushi said, 'Fire.' The entire sky behind the southern end of the Garudiya market was red.

Dharma thought exactly the same thing. There was a fire blazing somewhere over there. He nodded slowly. 'Yes.'

'There are two gunjus' villages over there.'

'Yes, and a tanners' village.'

They both knew that on the southern side of the market there were a few untouchables' villages all very close together. Dharma said, 'Who knows whose villages have been set on fire?'

Kushi said nothing.

Neither was aware of how long they had been standing there looking at the blood-red sky when suddenly they were alerted to the sound of footsteps. They saw seven or eight rough looking fellows running towards them and, as they ran past, Dharma recognised them, even in the darkness – they were Raghunath Singh's domestic strong-arm men, carrying lathis and kerosene tins. Had they, then, set fire to the untouchables' villages? The thought made Dharma and Kushi's blood run cold.

The men ran past a little way, then turned back. They looked at Dharma and Kushi fiercely and demanded, 'What are you doing, standing here at this time of night?'

Dharma gulped in fear. 'We've been with the schoolmaster. We're on our way home.'

'Don't tell anyone you've seen us. If you do, you'll get your throats cut.'

Dharma's throat and mouth dried up completely, but somehow he managed to croak out, 'No, no.'

'Watch your step!' And having delivered their warning, the men went on their way.

Late at night, when Dharma and Kushi returned to the dosad colony, they woke up Ganeri and told him in whispers about the burning of the untouchables' villages by Raghunath Singh's thugs. Ganeri sat there for quite some time, stunned. Then he said, 'Never breathe even a word. Be careful.'

The next morning, when they got to the farm compound, Dharma and the others were taken aback to see Raghunath Singh himself there, sitting in a huge chair. Before him Himgiri stood at attention, waiting obsequiously at his beck and call. A little way away, their hands folded in supplication, sat a thousand or more dhobis, gunjus and tanners, whose villages had been reduced to ashes the previous night. They were weeping incessantly, saying, 'It will be the death of us, my lord, we will die now – '

Dharma and the other dosads did not know that before daybreak Raghunath Singh had sent for the tanners, gunjus and dhobis. With immense tenderness, he said, 'Why will you die? Am I not here? I am your own man, you are mine. I will build you a new village.' He turned to Himgiri and said, 'Give them whatever they need – bamboo, straw, new tin – everything. Oh, yes, and give them ten days' rations of wheat, millet, maize, salt and kerosene.'

The untouchables were overwhelmed. Moved with gratitude, they could only say with choked voices, 'My lord, you are our mother and our father.'

'We are saved by your grace.'

'My lord, you are God.'

As though he were embarrassed, Raghunath Singh said, 'Don't say all these things. Just remember that I am your own man – and you are only mine.'

30

For the last few days, Dharma would finish his work in the fields and then, with a battleaxe slung over his shoulder, go off into the distant jungle. He would send Kushi to the *sabui* grass in the hope that she might get three or four *bageri* birds to sell to the contractors for maybe one and a half rupees. Dharma had taken an advance from Tirke, and if he did not get the remainder of the money, they would not get their freedom from a life of bonded labour. He simply had to catch the cubs.

Kushi was not at all amenable to Dharma's going alone into this jungle full of cheetahs, wolves, tusked boars and all sorts of other fierce beasts. She said, 'There are dangerous animals in that jungle. Don't go there, don't go – '

Dharma had gone a few times already, paying no heed to Kushi's words, and he was now going again. He explained to her that once he had got the pair of cheetah cubs he would not go back, but Kushi was very upset and very worried. Fearfully she said, 'Then take me with you.'

Dharma tried to convince her not to be frightened, asserting that, as long as he had his battleaxe in his hand, no beast would be able to so much as scratch him. However, there would be trouble if he had Kushi with him. If a beast should suddenly spring at them, should he save himself or her?

So each day at sunset, having returned his plough and bullocks to the farm compound, Dharma would hurry over the mounds of sand on the river bed, with Kushi following him. And so it was every day: a young bondsman and his young bondswoman, running breathless across the vast expanse of sand under the boundless sky in quest of the price of their freedom.

They went together only as far as the *sabui* grass, where Dharma said, 'Check the traps for *bageri* birds. I'll keep going.'

Kushi stopped and, looking sad, said slowly, 'Please don't be late. Come back soon.'

Dharma did not delay, as he needed to go into the jungle while there was still some daylight. When night fell and the jungle got dark, one was virtually blind. 'Yes, I will,' he called as he ran.

Kushi, however, did not go straight to the *sabui* grass to check the traps, but went on watching Dharma as long as she could see him on the dry sands of the Koel. The blade of his axe, slung across his broad shoulders, glinted in the last light of day. As she watched she felt that he certainly could bring back a pair of cheetah cubs from under their mother's nose, but then the next minute she saw the jungle as a truly dreadful place with dangerous and ferocious animals, and her mind kept swinging between hope and fear.

Dharma had gone out of sight around the distant bend in the river bed as Kushi went on muttering, 'Oh, Lord Ram, oh, God, be merciful, be merciful,' praying to Lord Ram that no kind of harm should come to Dharma, and with his safety on her mind she went in among the *sabui* grass.

Evening was starting to fall when Dharma had gone into that labyrinth of trees beside a crystal clear stream. On tiptoes he went on into the depths of the jungle, his ears pricked up like a rabbit's, keeping a watchful eye all around. Some three days had passed like this, and in that time he had seen only a wolf, two tusked boars and many deer and rabbits, but not the smallest spot of a cheetah's body had caught his eye. He had seen one or two other animals, but only in the distance. Once he had come face to face with a snake, and with one stroke of his axe he had sent its head flying.

When he started to stagger with exhaustion after wandering around for so long looking for cheetahs, Dharma left the jungle and went back along the bed of the Koel. Each day he would cross over the river's sands and pass the *sabui* grove, and then, after a little way, he would catch sight of Kushi standing on a high mound of sand near the highway. Each day his girl waited for him there. The night was absolutely still. The vast fields stretching to the horizon and the hazy sky were all empty. The dim light of the moon, low in the boundless sky, made Kushi look like a fairy in a dream standing there, and suddenly Dharma, the permanent bonded labourer, went running to her as though possessed by some wonderful fantasy.

31

THERE WERE ONLY FOUR DAYS LEFT TO THE ELECTION. THE thirty or so villages in Garudiya and Bijuri taluks were adorned with festoons and posters of the three election candidates, and red cloths adorned with the symbols of Sukhan Ravidas, Pratibha Sahay and Raghunath Singh hung everywhere. Even the trees along the highway could not escape, as posters had been pasted to their trunks. The election campaign was now in its final phase.

***

Day had still not broken, though there was a faint tinge of light in the sky. The dosads were awake, however, and right now, having eaten some simple breakfast, they were hurrying to the farm compound and the fields.

Suddenly Ganeri, looking ahead, called out in amazement, 'Oh, Lord Ram, what's this, now? What's happening? Am I seeing things?'

'What is it, eh? What is it?' some people asked.

'Look there.' Ganeri pointed towards the road.

For some moments nobody could articulate a sound. No one would have been as surprised had the sun and moon come down from the sky. The great master, Raghunath Singh himself, was coming on foot to this neighbourhood of untouchable dosads! This was the second time that he had come here, although never before in his fifty-five years had he set foot in this locality. Now, within fifteen days of the election, he had come here twice. He was accompanied by his campaign workers as well as by such faithful lapdogs as Himgiri, Ajibchand and Ramlachhman.

Was the sun rising in the west these days? Even the experienced Ganeri could never have imagined that, no sooner had night ended, the great master would come to the neighbourhood of his untouchable bonded labourers.

After few moments of amazement the entire dosad colony, almost together, started calling out, 'The great master is coming!' and those who were still inside came running out. But then no one knew how to treat Raghunath Singh or where to seat him. They could even offer their chests to the great master on which he might rest his feet. But although his distributing *laddus* to them by his own hand had been a magnanimous precedent, the master would incur sin should he come in contact with untouchables so early in the morning, so they could hardly offer their chests to his feet. However, Gidhni had had the nerve to bring an old chair out of her hut and offer it. None of them had any personal possession more valuable than this.

Although Raghunath Singh had on a few occasions declared himself to be their own man, they all nevertheless stood back apprehensively, their hands pressed together. They all felt that the great master would not touch Gidhni's chair with his big toe, so they were all immensely surprised to see him actually sit down on it. Smiling, he said, 'For some time I have been thinking that I must come and visit you, have a chat. While I am indeed your own man, a few problems have kept me from coming.'

Had Dharma and the others heard right? None of them said anything. They just stood there, their hands together as before.

Raghunath Singh then started calling each of them one by one and asked how they were and what difficulties they were having. After hearing from everyone, he said, 'I've now got some good news for you.' After a pause he continued, 'You will not have to go to work for three days from today. Just eat, drink and rest. My men will give you rice, wheat, ghee, chillies, potatoes – all these. You have worked my fields for a long time, so now have a complete rest, and only rest, for these three days.'

What was Raghunath Singh saying? Did he understand his own words? Or were they hearing things?

Now Raghunath Singh's number one lapdog, Ajibchand, suddenly seemed to go into a frenzy, crying, 'Oh, oh, oh! Who has ever heard the like! Lord Ram himself has come to us! Oh! Oh! Oh!'

Gesturing Ajibchand to stop, Raghunath Singh said, 'For three nights from tomorrow, there will be a *nautanki* performance in front of my home. Each one will run for the whole night. You must all come, then.'

There would be no work for three days and good food would be brought from the great master's granary – and not only that, they would see *nautanki* performances for three nights! Never in their lives had the dosads of Garudiya known anything like this.

Ajibchand again started crying out, 'Oh! Oh! Oh! The kingdom of God is indeed coming here! It is certainly coming!'

Raghunath Singh sat there no longer. As he got up, he said, 'So then, we'll be going now. But you must come to the *nautanki*.'

His campaign workers who were with him then shouted out, 'Long live – '

'Raghunath Singh!'

'Long live – '

'Raghunath Singh!'

'Vote for – '

'Raghunath Singh!'

'Vote for – '

'Raghunath Singh!'

As the shouting stopped, Raghunath Singh said to Dharma and those with him, 'You all know I am standing in the election.'

They all inclined their heads. 'Yes, great master. That's why we all ate *laddus* that day.'

'I am your man, your own man. On the voting paper, put your mark on the sign of the elephant. Then I will get your vote. Remember, the elephant.'

'Yes, master – ' and again they all inclined their heads.

Ajibchand was going around crying out, 'Oh! Oh! Oh! The kingdom of God is coming! *Ram raj* is coming! Listen, all of you! Take heed! For your own benefit, you must all vote for the great master – '

Many of them all said together, 'We certainly will. Of course we will.'

Smiling, Raghunath Singh said, 'Let us go, then. We have to go from village to village inviting everyone to come to the *nautanki*.'

After Raghunath Singh and his party had left, Dharma suddenly remembered that he was, fortunately, free from work in the fields for the next three days, so if he spent the whole time in the jungle, he would be able to come up with the pair of cheetah cubs. It was unlikely he would ever in his life get a better opportunity than this. Raghunath Singh had given him total freedom for three days; now it was all up to him.

About three hours after Raghunath Singh had left, two or three of his men came from his granary with a cart piled high with rice, dal, wheat and maize and even ghee. The untouchable bonded labourers' locality now overflowed with joy. The dosads had never known such happiness, nor had they ever heard of any of their ancestors knowing it, either. What Ajibchand had said about *Ram raj* coming to Garudiya taluk was turning out to be true.

Throughout the whole locality now there was a mood of carefree lethargy. The women got about the business of cooking while the men sat around on charpoys, making *khainis* and talking over and over again about Raghunath Singh and wondering, in amazement, what had suddenly come over him to offer them such bounty. It could only be due to the grace of God, Lord Ram.

In the meantime a few of them had drunk some *mahua* wine and were sitting about drunk or babbling in confusion.

***

Just around noon, when the sun had risen directly overhead, Dharma finished his meal, tucked his long, curved knife into his waistband, slung his battleaxe over his shoulder, and set off, accompanied by Kushi. The blade of the axe gleamed in the blazing midday sun.

They took the highway to the river bed. As far as one could see to the left of the main road, stretching as far as the horizon, Raghunath Singh's fields were now completely deserted; nowhere at all was anybody to be seen. For a full three days it would not be necessary to drive the plough on Raghunath Singh's land. No one would come to the fields, not even the Munda and Oraon seasonal workers, for Raghunath Singh had given them all three days' holiday. However, on the other side of the highway, the 'mishin' plough ran as usual over Mishirlal's land, making its 'putt-putt' sound throughout the vast fields.

As usual Dharma and Kushi left the highway and came down to the dry river bed. They went together as far as the *sabui* grass, where Kushi stopped and Dharma strode on across the mounds of sand towards the jungle. Earlier they had decided that they would go together as far as the *sabui* grove. Kushi would set the traps for the birds and Dharma would go on to the jungle beside the crystal clear stream.

Kushi called out after him, 'Don't be long. I get very worried.'

'I'll be back soon,' Dharma called back over his shoulder. 'What's there to worry about?' Indicating the sharp blade of the battleaxe slung over his shoulder, he added, 'I've got this. No matter how fierce the beast, it won't be able to scratch me.' He had said the same thing a number of times before, but it had done nothing to allay Kushi's fears and worries.

She called out again, 'Will you go to the *nautanki* at the great master's house tonight?'

'You go to it. Don't wait for me.'

'No, no. I won't go until you come.'

'You mustn't wait here on your own, Kushi. There are many men going along the highway, and many of them are dangerous animals. Someone might come with evil intentions. You're a lone woman, keep clear of them.'

Kushi stood there with her head down. She had no wish to obey Dharma and leave.

Dharma called again, 'Once you've gathered up the *bageri* birds and sold them to the contractors, you go to see the *nautanki*. I'll come straight there.' And Dharma went on his way.

As on every other day Kushi watched Dharma for as long as he and the glinting blade of his battleaxe could be seen going around the large bend in the river, and then she went into the *sabui* grass.

***

Dharma reached the jungle early in the afternoon. He looked all around very carefully as he went gradually deeper inside. Again today, as he looked for cheetah cubs, he noticed countless deer leaping about. He also saw three wildcats, a porcupine and, in the distance, a tusked boar, grunting as it headed towards a thicket. Dharma had no interest at all in the likes of wildcats, deer or tusked boars. He had a deadly aim with his knife, and if he wanted to he could throw it from a distance and get any animal, but he had no inclination to waste his energy or his time in this. His one concern was the cheetah cubs.

As he wandered about, the sun started to set and the jungle shadows soon became heavy. Staying here now would be very dangerous, for in the dark a fierce beast could leap at his neck from behind or from the branch of a tree overhead. So now Dharma came out of the jungle. One day of his holiday had passed, but still his work was not complete, and he felt particularly bad about it. There were, of course, still two full days left. Tomorrow he would come to the jungle even earlier.

Today Kushi had not waited for Dharma at the *sabui* grass or on the high mound of sand beside the highway, and Dharma returned alone to the dosad colony.

It had become quite late. There were still a few days left in the fortnight of the new moon, which would not rise until close to midnight. At the moment it was quite insipid, and whatever little light came from it hardly reached Garudiya taluk, and so the fields of the region, the sandbanks of the Koel, and the villages and markets were all sunk in darkness.

The dosads' neighbourhood was completely empty. There was no one in any of the shanties, for everyone had gone to enjoy the *nautanki*. Dharma went into his shanty, hung his knife and battleaxe on the wall, groped around for the lantern and lit it. He then took off his sweat-soaked shirt and shorts, put on a red kurta and pair of striped pajamas, and set off for the home of Raghunath Singh.

***

It was just like festival time in front of the great master's house. There could not have been anyone in any of the homes of any of the villages of Garudiya and Bijuri taluks, as everyone seemed to have gathered here.

Dharma had not been here since the night he brought Phaguram's unconscious body in on his shoulders. He had no idea of when, in the meantime, the huge marquee had been set up for the *nautanki*. Under the marquee there were just people and more people, and the performers were sitting on a high stage in the middle. Extremely strong lights lit up the entire auditorium. After some searching,

Dharma spotted Kushi in the middle of the crowd, and he forced his way through the tightly packed audience and sat down beside her.

Kushi was wearing a short yellow sari and a red blouse that she had washed that day with cheap soap. Her hair was tied up and highlighted with a wild flower, and a green beetle wing adorned the middle of her forehead.

'When did you get back?' she asked.

'Just now,' Dharma replied. 'I took the axe home and came straight here.'

'Did you get the cubs?'

'No. They've all fled the land. I searched so hard and didn't even catch sight of one. I'll go back to the jungle as soon as I wake up tomorrow.'

By now a harmonium, tabla and flute were being played together. Then came the song of a woman with a high, sweet voice. Raghunath Singh's men had arranged for a microphone, so that the people right at the back were able to hear.

Dharma and Kushi quickly turned around and watched the performers. This girl of the musical troupe was so like a fairy in her dress and adornment and her dazzling style, as well as in the ornamentation of her song. And how lovely was her face! The entire audience watched, enchanted.

My love does not come back,
and I am getting old
while my joys turn into sorrows.
In the town the drums beat out a warning –
'Don't be beguiled by love!'
Through the window of the upper room
Laila's cry is heard,
'O Majnu, do not beat me!'
Smoke rises up from the riverbank.

Again I hear Laila's plea, 'O Majnu,
do not scold me!'

'It's a beautiful song,' said Dharma.

Kushi was absorbed in the song. 'Yes,' she said, 'The troupe is from Farbeshganj.'

'They're very famous. The Farbeshganj troupe is known throughout the world.'

Raghunath Singh had arranged for musical troupes to come from not only Farbeshganj, but from such distant places as Arariya Ghat, Purnia and Mirzapur, to perform on successive nights.

Having sat through the performance throughout the night, Dharma and Kushi were soon asleep when they returned home at dawn.

***

The effect of listening to music all night was that in the morning Dharma was unable to go to the jungle in search of cheetah cubs. He had gone to bed and went straight to sleep as soon as he got back from Raghunath Singh's house, and it was already midday when he woke up.

Dharma got up in a flurry and saw that the whole dosad colony was still sound asleep, including his mother and father, who were quite dead to the world and would not respond to his repeated calls. He washed hurriedly at the well and ate some leftovers from the night before. He tucked his knife into his waistband, slung his battleaxe over his shoulder, and hurried off to the jungle.

Although the whole colony was asleep, needless to say Kushi was awake and waiting to follow him as he went on his way to the jungle. And, as usual, she stopped at the *sabui* grass while Dharma hurried on under the blazing sky towards the jungle.

Today too Dharma roamed about for a long time, but could not spot any cheetah cubs. He came out again as the sun was going down and the jungle shadows were getting heavy. He returned to an empty neighbourhood, as he had the day before, put away his knife and axe, changed his clothes, and set off for the mansion of the great master to see the *nautanki*. Amongst the swarming crowd under the marquee he again found Kushi and went and sat beside her. Then, for the rest of the night, he listened enchanted to the songs of a very famous and expensive troupe from Ara district.

Everyone likes my lovely face –
mother-in-law, father-in-law –
but not my stupid husband.
Everyone likes my lovely face –
both my husband's elder brother and his wife –
but not my mean young brother-in-law.

When they all got home at dawn, their eyes were heavy with sleep. And so two successive days had been wasted. Still, one whole day remained.

32

IT WAS THE LAST DAY OF THE THREE-DAY HOLIDAY. FROM TOMORROW the dosads would have to go to the fields of their master and drive their ploughs again. For Dharma, what had to be done had to be done today, for tomorrow, because of his work with the plough, he would not have so much time. After a full day in the fields, no sooner would he get to the jungle than night would fall, and in the dense growth there would be a great danger of wild animals. Suddenly taking off half a day from his work in the fields in order to go to the jungle was out of the question, as cultivation had to be completely finished before the rains. Now, on account of the election, the great master and his men were being very amiable, but the election would not last the whole year. And then what? If Dharma had to spend the whole night in the jungle this time, he would. The simple fact was that he had to ransack this jungle by the Koel and get two cheetah cubs.

As on the previous two days, again Dharma did not wake up until midday, and his parents were still sleeping. Without waking them he washed, took up his knife and battleaxe and went out, and Kushi, like his shadow, followed behind. Just as they were leaving the highway and going down to the river bed, they noticed the huge car of Raghunath Singh, its roof open, coming from the direction of Bijuri taluk, raising the dust as it went. Dharma and Kushi stopped, overcome by curiosity.

When the car came close to them, they saw the master of Bijuri taluk, Mishirlal, sitting beside Raghunath Singh, with a few of their faithful and favourite friends. Dharma and Kushi guessed that Raghunath Singh had gone to Bijuri to pick up Mishirlal, but they did not guess that there was any more to it than that.

Raghunath Singh's constituency covered the thirty or so villages throughout the two taluks of Garudiya and Bijuri. Raghunath was more or less confident of getting the votes of the villagers in Garudiya, but he could not be sure about the votes of Bijuri. However, if Mishirlal so much as lifted his finger, everyone there, like a flock of sheep, would come and stamp Raghunath Singh's symbol on their ballot papers. It was in Raghunath Singh's interest to keep Mishirlal happy and entertained.

Despite his near sixty years, Mishirlal was a man of very fine appearance. His greying hair was parted on the right and combed to the left. His well-fed body was dressed with a fine cotton kurta and finely spun dhoti. There were at least eight rings on his fingers, including one set with a diamond, one with a pearl, one with a ruby and one with an emerald. Even the buttons of his kurta were set with diamonds, and he wore gold rings in his ears. On his feet were hand-crafted Lucknow slippers. A devout brahman, he had a mark of sandal paste on his forehead and on each ear lobe, with his sacred thread visible through his finely woven kurta.

The Touch-my-Feet Zamindar, Mishirlal was also famous for other reasons. Throughout the twenty or so neighbouring taluks everyone knew him as a notorious womaniser. Every night some young woman or another had to be provided for him. In the matter of women Mishirlal maintained no prejudice. He was happy to take any young woman, tribals and untouchables included, so all the young women of Bijuri taluk were constantly apprehensive, for none of them knew when Mishirlal's men would pounce. Of course, he always paid the girl a fair price.

The huge open car of the great master came close and went by. As he watched, Dharma said suspiciously, 'Why is that lecherous old wolf coming here? I'm worried. You be careful, Kushi.'

'Yes. Yes, I will,' said Kushi. 'Don't you worry. Now let's go.'

The two of them started to walk again, and after a little while Dharma went on to the jungle, his axe over his shoulders, and Kushi went into the *sabui* grove. She saw that seven or eight birds had been caught, which she took from the traps, bound them around the feet with a cord, and laid them on the sand. Then she set the traps anew, picked up the birds and set off to the contractors.

These days, as Dharma was not with her, Kushi did not dig up the their box from the sand and take it to the schoolmaster for counting. As there was no want of low-down scoundrels in the world, anyone could confront a single girl and steal the box. So Kushi took the money she had been getting recently from the contractors and hid it at home. She would give the money to Dharma when he came back from the jungle with the cheetah cubs. Today two and a half rupees came from the sale of *bageri* birds. Kushi kept the money tied in her sari and tucked in at her waist.

By the time she got back to her own neighbourhood, the afternoon had passed, and by now, especially among the women, the business of getting dressed up had started. Once evening had come, they would go to the *nautanki*.

In the homes of the poorest of the poor, the untouchable bonded labourers, there were very few items to aid in dressing and make up. Hair would be washed with fuller's earth, clothes would be scrubbed in alkaline water, and there was home-made *kajal* for the eyes and wild flowers for the hair. Throughout the afternoon they had been busy with hand-mirrors and combs and with the washing of clothes.

As Kushi arrived, Gidhni called to her from her veranda, 'Hurry up and get ready. The sun is setting.'

'There's still much of the day left,' Kushi said. 'The *nautanki* won't start until after dark.'

Kushi went inside, took the two and a half rupees from the knot in her sari, and stowed it inside her pillowcase. She then went out onto the veranda and sat down against one of the posts. Since noon she had walked mile after mile under the blazing sun, going to the *sabui* grove, then to the contractors, then home. If she did not take a little rest now, she would not be able to walk another step.

The young dosad women went in a group each day to the *nautanki*. They worried about getting there late and not getting a place near the performers. Long before sunset crowds of people would come from this village and that in order to lay claim to the best places. And so they needed to leave early.

From here and there all the other girls were urging, 'Hey, Kushi! Get up, now! Come on, hurry! If we're late we'll have to sit outside.' In fact, none of them wanted to go without Kushi.

'I'm getting up. Just let me rest a little longer,' Kushi said.

The other girls all started talking again, but just then the sound of bells could be heard. Kushi and the others noticed two carriages coming across the neighbouring stony field. The jingling sound came from the bells tied around the necks of the horses. Even from a distance the girls could recognise them as Raghunath Singh's. But why were they coming here? The great master's carriages never came this way. The girls all watched, stunned, as the two carriages drew near and pulled up. Then, out of the front one, stepped St Satan.

The dosads were dumbfounded as, in a flash, his long stork-like strides had taken him into their midst. As soon as they saw him, everyone got up. Baring his big, crooked teeth, Ramlachhman said, 'Everybody listen. Today is the last day of your holidays. The great master has happily sent his carriages to take you to the *nautanki*. For all the men the great master is giving dhotis and kurtas, and for the women saris and blouses.'

What had St Satan said! So much had happened in just a few days that their fortunes had seemed to change just overnight. From among the crowd, Budheri – somewhat apprehensive and a little incredulous – asked, 'Is this true, sahib?'

'Why wouldn't it be? Look – ' and he rushed to the front carriage and took out from it four very attractive coloured saris. He came back and said, 'I've brought these to convince you. D'you hear me?'

They all looked in amazement at the saris and blouses. No one could think of anything to say.

Then Ramlachhman did the unbelievable – he tossed a sari to each of Gidhni, Kushi, Sombari and Tisi, saying, 'Hurry and put this on. The carriages can't take too many people. I'll take you first to the great master's house, then I'll come back and take the others in turn.'

The young dosad women were utterly beside themselves with joy at getting these expensive saris and blouses. The poor and innocent young women were completely overwhelmed. Without a second thought they hurried inside with their new saris and blouses. When they came out again a little later, they were hardly recognisable.

St Satan looked at them for a little while, his eyes widening. Lustfully he said, 'What do we see here but fairies from heaven? What beauty!' And he hurried them along, 'Come, come, now. Hurry and get into the carriage.'

Gidhni, Kushi, Sombari and Tisi ran and got into the carriages.

Ramlachhman turned to the remaining dosads and said, 'Don't you go anywhere. I'll come back with the carriages.' He leaped up onto the front carriage beside the coachman and gave the order to drive off quickly.

All the while the experienced Ganeri said nothing, but watched Ramlachhman's doings with keen eyes. Suddenly, as though something had just occurred to him, he rushed towards the carriages calling, 'Brahman-ji!'

The carriages were just starting off. Ramlachhman turned around and said, 'What?'

'Take me with the girls – '

'You'll go next time.'

'But – '

'Don't worry. The great master has called, what is there to worry about? The great master is the mother and father of all of you.'

Ganeri was about to say something else, but by then the carriages, with the speed of a storm, virtually flew up onto the highway, and from such a distance there was no way Ramlachhman could have heard him even if he had called at the top of his voice.

What was there about the four girls being taken away like this? Ganeri could not think that it was all right, and a feeling of uneasiness plagued his mind.

A long time passed after the two carriages had taken the girls. All the bonded labourers kept anxiously watching the road. When would Ramlachhman come? When would the horse-drawn carriages come and take them to the *nautanki*? However, Ganeri's worries were not about the *nautanki*. He sat on his veranda, his cheek in his hand, constantly wondering why Ramlachhman had taken the girls in this way.

Soon evening came, and then night gradually fell around them. But Ramlachhman was not to be seen, nor were the two carriages.

Having waited such a long time, at last everyone set off for the *nautanki*.

***

The people of the dosad colony found themselves places and sat down amid the pressing throng under the vast marquee at Raghunath Singh's mansion. Later they would press Ramlachhman for the clothes, but for the time being they would listen to the singing. Ganeri, however, could not stop worrying. He went about looking everywhere, but neither Ramlachhman nor any of the girls were to be seen. He felt as though his blood were thickening with fear and worry. They were dosad girls, and the dosads looked to him as their leader. Ganeri had a moral responsibility. But where had they gone?

Suddenly Ganeri caught sight of Raghunath Singh and Mishirlal sitting side by side on velvet-cushioned, throne-like chairs right in front of the performers. Just to look at Mishirlal was enough to stop Ganeri's breath. What was that womanising Touch-my-Feet Zamindar doing here? Was there some connection between Mishirlal's coming to the *nautanki* and the girls' being taken away in carriages?

The show began. Tonight Raghunath Singh had brought the finest music troupes from Mirzapur and Azamgarh in Uttar Pradesh. The Mirzapur troupe had started singing:

I cannot go on churning,
for Krishna comes in haste.
The sky is atremble,
the wind is gusty
and the whole creation teeters.
King Sheshnag in his nether realm
shakes his head,
the other snakes tremble too.
Hark! The sound of the tabla, the drums
and the harmonium!
Hear the sound of Lord Krishna's flute
and the tinkle of Radha's anklet bells!
Oh, how can I go on churning?

But Ganeri's mind was not on that. Moving along one side of the marquee, he kept his eye on Mishirlal. Then, when the song had built up to a crescendo, Raghunath Singh and Mishirlal suddenly got up, and everyone cleared the way for their exit.

Ganeri was standing some way away, on the opposite side of the marquee. A flash of panic shot through him like a bolt of lightning. With bated breath he rushed out of the marquee and looked around for Raghunath Singh and Mishirlal, but it was too late – just in front of him they were being whisked away in the old model car with its open roof.

33

In the late afternoon when Ramlachhman had come with the carriages to the bonded labourers' quarter, Dharma was still wandering around in the jungle with his knife and battleaxe. He had gone into the jungle just before midday and since then he had been continually roaming.

As he wandered about, the colour of the sunlight through the tops of the dense jungle started to change to yellow, and it was then that he caught sight of three cheetah cubs. A thin, shallow stream ran from the southern Koel, with the branches of many trees hanging over it. Of course, the jungle here was not very dense but rather open. The three cheetah cubs were playing beside the water under a pipal tree.

Dharma's eyes lit up immediately, for he had roamed around here for a whole three days, and before that he had come here a few times and wandered around after completing his day's work in the fields, but he had not seen a hint of a cheetah. He could never have dreamed that he might find the cubs unprotected like that, without a parent. Taking his time, he carefully approached the pipal tree, but just as he got close to the cubs, the whole jungle seemed to reverberate with an enormous roar.

Dharma flashed a look to his left. A female cheetah was crawling out from a thick copse, her eyes blazing and her sharp teeth bared as she approached step by step, growling ferociously.

The question of picking up and taking the cheetah cubs was now not as simple as he may have thought. Dharma took his battleaxe from his shoulder and stood cautiously poised. No sooner might he blink his eye than the cheetah would fly at him. He moved slightly, then with all the strength of his body he brought down the axe on the cheetah's neck.

The beast fell heavily to the ground, bleeding, just ten feet away, where she sprawled on the ground and roared. She lay on the ground for only a few moments, however, then got up and sprang at Dharma once again, fierce after the blow from the axe.

Again Dharma readied himself for attack and brought the axe down on the cheetah's face, which immediately became awash with blood; Dharma himself was not completely unscathed as the cheetah's paw had ripped some flesh from his shoulder. Perhaps she was somewhat subdued after this second blow; she wallowed restively on the ground for a few moments, then ran off into the thick of the jungle.

Dharma waited for some time, but no sound came from the cheetah.

It was quite likely that, having taken two successive violent blows, the beast had fled. Meanwhile, above the canopy of the forest the sunlight was becoming dimmer and the jungle shadows were thickening. Dharma would have to be out of there before nightfall. There were so many ferocious beasts in the jungle besides this female cheetah, and in a tight corner Dharma would not be able to escape them. He did not hesitate, but took up the three cubs and strode off.

However, after he had gone some way a growl started to come from his right. He turned momentarily and saw the cheetah behind a tree. The beast had not fled, but was following him.

Dharma stopped in his tracks, and saw in the distance the cheetah stop too. She would not let Dharma out of this jungle with her three cubs. Dharma decided then not to go where the jungle was thicker; he would be in less danger where the growth was sparse, for among the dense foliage he would have no hope of seeing the wounded cheetah. He headed quickly towards a relatively open space, while he could see the animal, still keeping her distance, moving between the trees. Then the jungle trembled with her violent roar.

After he had crossed a wide, open space the jungle became thick again, and Dharma kept a cautious eye out as he went. Suddenly he heard a roar from above him. He put down the cubs and held his axe ready as the cheetah leaped at him from a high branch of a tree. This time the beast's paw tore some flesh from Dharma's chest, and his whole body became smeared with blood. By now he had taken the knife from his waistband and thrust it to the hilt inside the cheetah's stomach. The animal screamed in pain and again started to run.

Dharma did not wait. He took up the cubs and started to walk off hurriedly, as running was impossible in this dense part of the jungle. But even after the attack with the knife the cheetah still had not left him. From all around as well as above, the sound of her growling persisted.

Meanwhile, the light of the end of the day was becoming more and more meagre and the jungle became dimmer as evening fell.

Dharma left the jungle very cautiously and came to the mounds of sand on the river bed, where it was not so dark. Suddenly he saw in the distance the cheetah slowly coming towards him. The beast just would not leave him.

Dharma had lost a lot of blood and he was feeling dizzy. He had no desire to fight any more with the cheetah. He must somehow evade the beast and get up onto the highway where, with the traffic and so many people, she would not dare to go. He now began to weave and dodge. He did not keep to the river bed but sometimes went a little to the right, sometimes a little to the left, although it was quite likely that the cheetah was able to discern his intentions as she moved along with him, keeping a distance between them.

When he had come close to the *sabui* grass the cheetah suddenly surprised him. She was no longer keeping her distance but had now come very close to him. Perhaps the beast realised that she could no longer delay, and that if he could go any further, Dharma would get away with her cubs. However, it would be impossible for him to take the cubs without fighting with their mother. For a moment he thought of giving them back to her, but then he remembered that his and Kushi's independence – and their parents' – depended on these cubs. The cubs were the price of the freedom of six people. And so he decided to fight. He put the cubs down on the sand and stood with his axe raised. The cheetah stood ready, too.

In a moment the dried up bed of the river Koel looked like some primordial battleground, and it was only after about three hours that the cheetah at last lay dead on the sand. The blood-smeared Dharma, like a corpse himself, lay with his head bowed, his breath shallow and rapid. He stayed like this for quite some time, and then sat up. Beside him the cheetah cubs were blithely sleeping. Dharma picked them up and, still panting, went up to the highway.

The ghostly midnight now hung over the boundless fields. As Dharma stood on the highway, he thought that he would return to the dosad colony, but then he remembered that there would be no one there as they all would have gone to the *nautanki*. He decided to go straight to Ranchi. The long-distance bus from Patna to Ranchi was still running at this hour. Dharma had taken it to Ranchi once or twice before with deer horn or tiger skin. He would deliver the cubs to Tirke, get his payment, come home on the dawn bus and go to work in the fields.

He always kept three or four rupees in his pocket, but actually he was not so much concerned with the fare as with his own wounded appearance. The cheetah's scratches and bites, together with his torn clothes, made him look appalling, but what could he do about that now?

He did not have to wait long, as the Ranchi bus came very soon and picked him up.

It was well into the night when Dharma woke Tirke at the hotel in Ranchi. Tirke was alarmed at the sight of him. Quickly he woke the hotel's medical officer, who bandaged Dharma's arms, legs and chest, then Tirke took him to the American. The gentleman inspected the goods and was delighted to get three cubs instead of two. He gave Dharma a two-hundred rupee tip, and Tirke gave him the amount previously agreed to.

34

IT WAS STILL DARK WHEN DHARMA, NOW HAVING BEEN PAID, boarded the return bus. At Garudiya he got down and ran towards the dosad colony. Today he would buy the freedom of six people. In all his life he had never known such intense joy. From today he would no longer be someone else's bondsman, but a dignified, independent man. He had earned the price of that independence by fighting with a cheetah for almost half the night.

As Dharma reached the dosad colony, the sun was coming up over the horizon like a vast golden plate. But as soon as he set foot in the quarter, he stopped. The whole neighbourhood had gathered in front of the huts of Kushi, Gidhni, Sombari and Tisi. Their parents were continually weeping and wailing and slapping their foreheads. Everyone else stood there, looking overwhelmed with grief. A little way away their leader, the middle-aged Ganeri, was sitting with his head in his hands.

Dharma's pulse suddenly quickened. He had not been here for one night. Had someone died in that time? Slowly he went and stood by Ganeri. 'What happened, Uncle?' he asked.

'We are ruined,' he said, and in a broken voice went on to tell Dharma how the day before Ramlachhman had beguiled four of the neighbourhood girls away. He had delivered them into the hands of Mishirlal, and they had been kept confined the whole night; only a short time back had they been brought home by the household thugs of the great master.

As he heard all this Dharma started to lose control of his legs and he could stand up no longer. Reeling, he sat down.

***

Towards midday that day Dharma met with the munshi, Ajibchand. After the atrocity that had just occurred, he would not stay another day in Garudiya. He would settle the debt of his forebears and leave with Kushi and their parents.

'Well, then, what news?' Ajibchand asked. 'How did you get into that state?'

Without answering him Dharma said, 'Show me my debt paper. I will pay what is owing and leave this place.'

Ajibchand sat up straight. Looking at Dharma over the top of his glasses he said, 'You will pay what is owing! How did you get the money? By theft, or highway robbery?'

'I have it. Now you can take it.'

'Do you know how much is needed?'

'I do. Kushi and her parents and I and mine comes to two thousand,' Dharma said. He then took out the entire sum. Before coming here he had taken it to the schoolmaster to be counted.

Taking some sort of a paper from a cupboard, Ajibchand said, 'Who told you two thousand? The total is five thousand.'

A terrible noise inside Dharma's head threatened to split it. With a trembling voice he said, 'Whenever I inquired before you said two thousand. Now you are saying five thousand!'

'Utter lie! I never told you two thousand. Now go on, get out of here. I've got important work to do.'

In his rage Dharma's blood started to boil. Had he had his battleaxe over his shoulder he might have delivered a blow with it to Ajibchand's neck. And Ajibchand would never know just how much he had stirred up the heart of a bonded labourer.

Dharma staggered out.

35

AND SO, LIKE HIS FATHER AND GRANDFATHER AND THEIR FATHERS and grandfathers before them, Dharma went with his bullocks and plough to the fields of the great master Raghunath Singh. He went on driving the plough through the rock-hard earth, and Kushi ran along behind him, sorting out the weeds.

In the meantime the election had been held in Garudiya and Bijuri taluks. Everyone in the dosads' neighbourhood – except for Ganeri and the members of the four families – had stood in line to mark their ballot papers. That those few did not vote was neither here nor there. Eventually Raghunath Singh won over Sukhan Ravidas and Pratibha Sahay.

After the victory, *gulal*, though well out of season, was thrown about in celebration and the air of Garudiya seemed for a time to have turned red. The great master, Raghunath Singh, his neck adorned with garlands and his hands folded reverentially, went about in a jeep from village to village making known his gratitude to all who had voted for him, while his campaign workers rent the skies with their shouts of 'Long live Raghunath Singh'. And the lapdogs almost burst their blood vessels crying, 'Oh! The kingdom of God has come!'

At the end of his rounds Raghunath Singh finally came to the bonded labourers' quarter. After the posting of the election result, he had given them all a day off from driving the plough. Standing in his jeep, Raghunath Singh said, 'I was able to win because of you. How can I thank you enough? What more can I give? For indeed, I am one of you – your man. Your own – '

Dharma was standing among the crowd watching and listening to everything. Before Raghunath Singh had finished speaking he cried out, 'Lies! Lies! Lies! You are not our man! You are not our man! You are not our man!'

A thunderbolt would not have been more startling. In an instant the whole quarter was stunned, and in that time Dharma's voice, like an explosion, echoed throughout the boundless fields of Garudiya and Bijuri, 'You are not our man! You are not our man!'

It had taken generations and a few hundred years for one man to come out with these words.